Praise for B

2020 Fantasy Book of the Year Winner
-INDIES Awards

Top Ten Best Debut Speculative Fiction Novels of 2020
-Booklist

2020 Bronze Medal for Fantasy
-IPPY Awards

"A haunting and beautifully written gothic tale."
-Natalie Jenner, internationally bestselling author
of *The Jane Austen Society*

"Sure to win over fantasy readers."
-Publishers Weekly (starred review)

"Brilliant."
-Booklist (starred review)

"An engaging fantasy with an original world
and timeless themes... [that] speaks to the heart
of the reader on a deeply personal level."
-Den of Geek

"Utterly charming and engrossing."
-Novel Notions

"Asperfell manages to bring in politics,
supernatural terror, magic lessons, murder mystery,
romance... This is the first time in a long time
that I have not wanted a book to end."
-Quail Ridge Books

Explore the world of Asperfell:
ThatJamieThomas.com

For more great science fiction and fantasy novels:
UproarBooks.com

THE SECOND BOOK OF THE ASPERFELL TRILOGY

The Forest Kingdom

JAMIE THOMAS

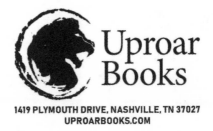

Uproar
Books

1419 PLYMOUTH DRIVE, NASHVILLE, TN 37027
UPROARBOOKS.COM

THE FOREST KINGDOM

Published by Uproar Books, LLC.

Edited by Rick Lewis.

Cover illustration by Khristian M. Collins.

ISBN 978-1-949671-28-5

First paperback edition.

FSC
www.fsc.org

MIX
Paper from
responsible sources
FSC® C005010

This book was written on the traditional lands of the Wenatchi and Yakama peoples

1

Long ago, when I was far less of a child than I ought to have been to
think it a good idea, I decided to run away and live in the Morwood.

Upon the day in question, I'd been caught scaling the outer wall
on the second floor in an effort to sneak into a storage room my
Aunt Eudora kept locked.

Saren's boy claimed that, hidden amongst the broken furniture
and dusty rugs within, was the shriveled heart of my second great
uncle, who was a playwright of some renown during his lifetime
and, therefore, an utter disgrace to the House of Tenebrae. From
what little I was able to glean from the annals in the library, his plays
poked quite a bit of fun at the nobility, scandalizing his own class
and endearing him to the common folk, who claimed that underneath all his fine silks and velvet, his spirit was fashioned from the
same mettle as their own. I thought it exceedingly wonderful then,
a nobleman gleefully mocking his own kind, until my tutor pointed
out some years later that hardly anyone amongst the common folk
could even afford to see his plays due to the extravagant cost of a
seat at the theater and that, despite having ample means to do so,
my second great-uncle did nothing at all to ease their burden other
than declare himself their champion on the page. To make his

wealthy nemeses hot under their jeweled collars was his delight, and yet the common folk dearly loved him for it.

Never have I loved so well, or been so loved, as by the people of my heart, and thus, it is theirs, he wrote in a letter to his wife, who, upon his death, took the sentiment quite literally.

His heart was removed, embalmed, and displayed in a glass case for many years in the library before my Aunt Eudora's mother deemed it unseemly and relegated it to the aforementioned storage room, apparently believing that disposing of it might bring down the spirit of the deceased playwright upon her.

Naturally, I *had* to see it.

And display it in my room where, with luck, my maid Mora would see it and suffer a dramatic fainting fit.

It was not that I disliked Mora. It was that Mora had discovered the painting I'd done of my Aunt Eudora with fangs and a barbed tail and tossed it in the fire, and I was keen that she should feel the full, righteous anger of a thirteen-year-old girl most cruelly wronged.

I'd been discovered halfway between the window at the end of the corridor I'd crawled out of and the window of the storage room I hoped to enter, fistfuls of ivy clutched in both hands and my skirt torn in several places from the spires meant to deter birds. Of course it would be my sister, Livia, practicing the harp in the music room, who heard the unfortunate disagreement between my boot and the window casing. She immediately summoned my aunt despite my pleas for sisterly camaraderie, which, to be fair, we'd never had in the first place.

Aunt Eudora forbade me from the library for a month as well as from dessert, which stung only slightly less than the loss of my beloved books, and in a fit of furious tears, I told her that I'd rather live amongst the toadstools and trees of the Morwood than suffer one moment more under her roof. She simply stared back at me in that infuriatingly placid way that told me she did not believe me one bit, which angered me all the more.

I packed my sketchbook and my sturdiest clothes in a satchel, stole bread and cheese from the larder, and dashed into the wood through one of the tunnels behind the storage room.

Tiralaen's most ancient forest stand, the Morwood, had over the centuries become quite mythical in its depiction, particularly in the Shining City and the lands in the south, whose citizens thought us northern folk as wild as they believed it to be. Haunted by the messengers of the Old Gods and teeming with all manner of eldritch creatures, they said. All of it was true, of course, but they really needn't have worried themselves over it. I'd spent many days roaming about the Morwood since I'd arrived at Orwynd and, to my very great disappointment, I'd yet to see *any* messengers of the Old Gods, or eldritch creature besides, no matter how many offerings I left in the hollows of trees. There were moments when I held myself still, no mean feat for I was never easy with myself for long, and in such moments I thought, perhaps, I felt their eyes upon me, but even if 'twas so, when I looked, nothing was there.

Reclusive though they might've been, I'd never felt uneasy in their presence, and so I thought they would not mind terribly if I invited myself into their bowers and groves. It was with a stout and determined heart that I forged ahead into my new home.

The effort of covering ground enough that I would not be found right away made me frightfully hungry, and I polished off my meager meal after the first hour and sipped the frigid water of the little stream nearby. Another hour passed during which my pace slowed significantly, then another, and by nightfall, I lay curled into the thick root of a tree, deeply regretting my decision.

Everything I'd learned regarding living out of doors came from novels, and I was beginning to suspect the information was rather inaccurate. For one thing, I'd yet to encounter a single bush of wild berries or nest of eggs, which meant I would have to hunt and cook my own supper, and for another, I'd brought nothing with me with which to do this. I attempted to build a fire to keep myself warm but could not work out how to light my paltry pile of sticks, and after my teeth began to chatter from the cold, I finally gave up and slunk back home to Orwynd in defeat.

Aunt Eudora was waiting for me in the parlor, sitting quite unbothered before a cheerful fire with a cup of tea, as though I had not been missing in the forest for the better part of the day. I stood inside the threshold and stared at her sullenly.

"Good evening, Briony," she said, setting down her cup. "Have you tired so soon of dwelling amongst the fairies?"

"My preparations were not quite thorough enough," I admitted grudgingly. "But you'll see—the next time I decide to run away, you'll not see me again."

"Yes, I will. Because you are a lady, and ladies do not live in the forest."

"I am no lady!" I exclaimed. "And if I wish to live in the forest, I will do so!"

"No, you won't," she answered quite calmly. "For there are no books in the forest, nor dessert. Now go wash the dirt off your face. I'll have Layn send a tray up to your room."

In the end, my aunt was proven quite wrong indeed.

For many weeks now, ever since I'd fled the Mage prison of Asperfell with the rightful heir to the throne of Tiralaen and our three companions, I'd dwelled within a forest, proving beyond doubt that I was no lady.

Though she was, unfortunately, right about the books and dessert.

What I wouldn't have given in that moment to be sitting before the hearth in Orwynd's kitchen, devouring a warm apple tart with cinnamon custard or one of Layn's blackberry cakes! Instead, I was crouched uncomfortably behind a bush in several inches of snow, watching my supper across a glen.

As for my companion on the hunt, Arlo Bryn was notorious amongst the prisoners of Asperfell as a drunkard, gambler, philanderer, and precisely the sort of man whose company alone might inspire my poor Aunt Eudora to banish me to the Morwood in earnest. I myself found him neither so scandalous nor so charming as his reputation, although perhaps that was to be expected after so many days and miles together in a seemingly endless wilderness. We'd been tracking our quarry since the early afternoon, and I'd long since grown weary of the chase as the shadows of the trees lengthened with the fading of the day.

Any moment, lights would appear in the distance; lights that flickered and fluttered and darted here and there amongst the glistening white that blanketed the gnarled remains of fallen trees, setting aglow the sleeping world. If we drew too near, they whirled about in earnest before vanishing entirely, appearing once more only when we were well enough away. As such, we had no idea what they truly were but could only imagine that, in this world beyond our own, their beauty concealed horror within.

Once the lights appeared, we had perhaps two hours before the darkness gathered and the nameless creatures of the glades and groves of this forest stirred and slunk forward into the world in search of prey. Most were of little consequence; our magic easily deterred them. They circled our campsites at night, keeping to the

shadows and watching us balefully with gleaming eyes, afraid of
our Magefire, and of Thaniel's weapons.

Others required far more persuasion to leave us in peace.

Nightfall was a perilous thing in these woods, this much we had
learned. It would not do to linger.

Beside me, Arlo blew into his hands and then rubbed them
together with a grimace. "If I wasn't so bloody hungry, I'd say we
should pack it in," he said grimly. "The wind here is murder when
the sun sets."

Indeed, the wan sunlight was hovering over the tree line, and
the warming spell I'd put on my cloak only hours before had begun
to fade against the onslaught of wind, bitterly cold, that had begun
to gnaw mercilessly at my nose and cheeks. My hands, chafed and
raw, were having difficulty recasting it and it was with a sigh of
defeat that I allowed Arlo to perform the service for me, the painful
ache in my limbs easing somewhat as the spell took hold.

"We can't return with nothing," I told him. "We've not had
meat in several days."

"And I'll be damned if I eat another parsnip."

My brow furrowed. "You will if you're starving."

"I'll eat the lot of you before I eat another parsnip."

"Quiet!" I hissed.

The creature had heard us, or sensed us perhaps, because it
lifted its impossibly long neck and stared at the clump of bushes
where we hid. Its long ears twitched, and we held our breath until,
satisfied it was in no danger, the creature lowered its head once
more to the fallen log and resumed tearing long strips of bark with
its wedged teeth. It was the size of a fawn, with legs as graceful as
its neck, and though its meat was sparse, it was rich and gamy,
particularly about the ribs. Thaniel had killed one during the first

week of our journey and we'd been hoping to find one again. They were a skittish sort, easy to startle; we had but one chance once we made our presence known.

Arlo rested his palm on the frozen ground at our feet. "Are you ready?"

I nodded. My hands had begun to shake again, but not because of the cold. I was about to take a life, and though I'd performed the gruesome task with startling frequency since we'd begun our journey through the forest beyond Asperfell, it had grown no easier despite Thaniel's assurances that it would.

"All right," Arlo whispered. "Now!"

At the creature's feet, roots burst from the ground, scattering dirt and snow into the air. They coiled around the animal's feet with ruthless speed, dragging it down even as it threw its head back and screamed, a primal, guttural scream of rage and fear that echoed in the empty glade around us.

I stepped out from behind the bush, knife in hand, and approached the creature with cautious footsteps as it twitched and groaned in futile struggle. I knew Arlo's magic to be more than capable of holding such a beast, even in the depth of winter when the world was frozen, but I was wary; the horns upon its head were thick and sharp. Kneeling beside the creature, I tried to fix my gaze only on its exposed throat and not its eyes, wide and moving with frantic fear. The pungent smell of the creature's fur filled my nostrils, and I braced myself against the wave of nausea that rose within me at the stench, and the task at hand.

"Hurry it up, will you?" Arlo shouted from behind the bush.

Gods, I hated this part. Pressing the edge of the blade against the animal's throat, I closed my eyes. "Forgive me," I whispered, and then I struck.

The animal's blood bubbled up from the gash I'd opened in its neck and flowed in lurid rivulets down its tawny fur as it jerked and struggled against the roots that held it fast to the forest floor. Despite my visceral desire to drop my knife and retch into a nearby bush, I stayed beside the dying animal until its movements grew feeble and it lay still at last. Then, and only then, did the roots go slack and retreat back into the earth from whence they'd been summoned. The knife tumbled from my fingers into the snow and I bent to retrieve it, wiping the creature's blood from the blade with shaking hands.

"Excellent," Arlo said, and a moment later he crouched down beside me. "This fellow will make quite a tasty meal, I expect."

"That's all very well, but first we have to get it back to camp," I pointed out as I tucked the knife back into the sheath at my waist.

Arlo Bryn made no secret of the fact that he was a Mage of mediocre skill, preferring a great many other more leisurely activities to the study of magic, which, I believed, was what Elyan found most abhorrent about him despite the plethora of other attributes he might choose from. To a consummate scholar like the prince, the idea of wasted potential was an unforgivable affront. But Arlo was still far more skilled than I, and so I watched with fascination as he laid his hands upon the fallen tree trunk the creature had been feasting upon and shaped it into a litter of sorts. Together, we lifted the creature onto it with magic, and Arlo lashed it down securely with branches from a nearby bush.

"That's it, then," he said, rubbing his hands together. "Let's get back before my balls freeze and fall off."

Twilight had settled over the forest by the time we returned to camp with our burden, and Phyra was waiting for us. Crouched in front of an enormous Magefire ringed in stone, the raven-haired Necromancer stirred something in a large-bellied caldron that I strongly suspected was parsnip; Arlo's protestations would be sublime.

"Phyra!" Arlo greeted her, dropping the litter with a flourish on the ground beside the fire and spreading his arms wide. "We come bearing gifts. Now, where is that protector of yours? This thing wants butchering, and if I ask Briony to help me, she'll faint dead away at my feet. Of course, women do that to me all the time..."

I scowled. "I would do no such thing."

Phyra looked up at him with her dark, fathomless eyes and pointed to the domed shelter that Arlo had fashioned for us from the roots of an enormous tree earlier that afternoon. Then she turned her gaze to me as the Naturalist stomped off, bellowing for Thaniel.

"Are you all right?" she asked, her voice a soothing counterpoint to the uncivilized cursing coming from inside the shelter.

I mustered a smile. "I'm fine. But, unfortunately, I believe Thaniel might've been wrong about me and hunting." Sinking into a crouch beside the Magefire, I let the warmth of the flames wash over me, the glorious heat blooming on my face until my cheeks tingled and burned. "Oh my, that is wonderful."

"There is no shame in finding killing abhorrent," Phyra said, and there was such knowing in her gaze that I felt quite exposed despite my coarse-spun cloak.

"Do you react so? When it is your turn?"

"No," she answered quietly. "But often I wish I did."

Necromancers passed through their lives with one foot in the land of the living and one in Death, where they bargained with his envoys. They were at all times keenly aware of the hairsbreadth that separated the two, and how perilously we all walked, tilting one way, then the next, from moment to moment. Perhaps that made it easier to take life.

Thaniel emerged from our shelter, a murderous scowl on his face and the cause of it on his heels, chattering away either in ignorance of Thaniel's disapproval or, more likely, because of it. The two men's disdain for one another began long before their mutual imprisonment at Asperfell, stretching back into another world and, it seemed at times, another life.

An Alchemist by aptitude and a swordsmaster by trade, Thaniel had forged the blade at my side five days after we'd escaped Asperfell and begun our journey north. We'd discovered a cave near the river by which we'd set our course, and after feeling an irresistible pull to its depths, Thaniel discovered rich veins of ore running through the ancient stone. Despite Thaniel's uncanny skill, the metal was foreign to him and difficult to bend to his will. In the end, and only after Elyan siphoned a considerable amount of his own magic into Thaniel, he was able to extract the ore and, amid flame and water, shape it to his design.

The knife had proven most useful, particularly in the service of keeping our bellies full and, thus, our strength at the ready.

I unsheathed the blade and handed it to Arlo as he passed, and the two men began the grim task of skinning the creature I'd killed. They used what magic they could, but their hands still grew bloody, their faces taut, and they looked quite barbaric, which I'd found shocking the first time I'd seen it. I'd spent my childhood in the splendor of the Shining City and come of age in Orwynd, the crumbling estate of my noble family; I was not accustomed to seeing my supper butchered. Darkness was nearly upon us by the time they completed their gruesome work, and the final member of our company had yet to show his face.

"Where is Elyan?" I asked Phyra.

"By the river."

"Fool," I scoffed. "Even if he is so very mighty."

"You disapprove his seeking solitude?"

"Entirely. He puts himself at risk. Arrogant man."

"You should tell him that."

"I intend to."

"Do you want me to go with you?"

"No," I answered quickly; too quickly. Phyra's brow rose, and the corner of her mouth tilted upward. I look away guiltily. "I'll be all right. Stay and keep warm."

We had precious few moments alone, Elyan and I; despite the bitter cold and the dangers that dwelled in the gathering shadows, I would not squander this chance to be near him without the prying eyes of our companions, though it came at great risk, for I was a Mage of little skill and the night was hungry.

Once I'd left the bower, bright with Magefire, I was enfolded in shadow, my only retinue the moonlight upon the snow and my own meager handful of flame. Within the silence, deep in the darkness, I felt eyes upon me and quickened my pace, cursing Elyan with every step.

I found him on the bank of the river, a solitary figure, impossibly tall, shrouded in dusk. At my approach, he turned his head, his black curls blowing gently across his forehead.

"It's dark," I called. "You ought to come back to camp."

He raised one eyebrow at me. "I am perfectly capable of defending myself, but your concern is duly noted."

"Is it?" Minding the ice, I stepped gingerly down onto the bank. "If that were the case, I don't expect you would venture out alone at all. You know how it vexes me."

"Does it now?"

I tucked my arm within his and pressed close to him, grateful for the warmth his body provided. The top of my head only just reached his chest. "Our magic may not work the same beyond Asperfell."

"Noted," he answered, and I heard rather than saw the frown on his face. "Again."

And yet, he stubbornly persisted. He'd so often sought these quiet places since we left Asperfell. At first, I thought it might've just been Arlo and Thaniel's bickering, but in the weeks since, I'd suspected otherwise.

When first I'd noticed it, I'd asked Phyra if perhaps remnants might be left within Elyan from his time in Death's realm at the hand of Master Viscario. But knowing so little of her own power and having only returned three souls to life, and only twice on purpose, she could tell me little other than that she believed Elyan was, in fact, in mourning.

"For Asperfell?" I'd asked.

"Perhaps. And for himself."

"How so?"

"He is a king without a throne, and without a people."

Before the night he'd been deceived into killing his father, Elyan had been the crown prince of Tiralaen by virtue of his bloodline. In truth, it was Master Viscario who had orchestrated the murder of the king, along with the exile of the kingdom's rightful heir to the otherworldly prison of Asperfell. And thus, the young Prince Keric, nothing more than a frightened child at the time, had taken the throne as Viscario's unknowing puppet.

In the years that followed his father's murder by dark magic, Keric's fear and hatred of all Mages had become a twisted obsession, and it spread throughout Tiralaen like an infected wound, until all magic born were nothing more than prisoners or slaves to the crown. Elyan blamed himself for all of it—noble, stupid, egotistical man that he was. one of it had ever happened—the murder, the banishment, the slaughter and oppression of magic born across Tiralaen—Elyan's reign was always destined to be far more tempestuous than his forebears by virtue of his magic. It was not that a Mage had never sat on the throne before; indeed, many had. It was that Elyan possessed one of the rarest and most dangerous aptitudes known to our world, that of a Siphon. Had he been more like his brother in temperament—charming, vigorous, and oft-laughing—he might have won the adoration of his people in spite of his arcane powers, but Elyan was a tall, serious man with a sharp tongue and a head for books rather than hunting and sport. And though he governed his immense power with restraint and gave every indication of leading as his father had before him, with fairness and compassion, he had been respected, but not loved.

Whatever fate had awaited him as king of Tiralaen, it had been stolen from him long ago, and long had our people suffered for it. If only we could return to our own world, we had cause to hope that Tiralaen would rally to its rightful king and cast down his brother. And thus, we'd escaped Asperfell together, trudging a slow path through the unexplored and unpeople north of this world, where spirits of the dead had whispered to us that a Gate back to our own kingdom might be found in a cave far away.

We knew not how far we need travel to find it, nor what signs to seek to guide our way, and Elyan felt heavily the weight of each day lost to journeying. Another day with his brother on the throne. Another day of suffering and death for his people.

"How fared the hunt?" Elyan asked when the silence began to stretch too thin between us.

"Successful. We caught one of the horned creatures."

He pulled back just enough to look down at me, his brow raised in pleasant surprise. "Truly? Haven't you become quite the hunter."

"Not by choice, I assure you," I said, shuddering. "The river is restless tonight."

"And has grown more so the farther north we've traveled," he agreed. "At first, I thought I might've imagined it but look there—the ice is nearly melted."

"Spring come early?"

"Perhaps, though it would be exceedingly strange."

"And, therefore, not entirely outside the realm of possibility," I reminded him, for we were very far from everything familiar.

"Indeed." His deep voice rumbled beneath my ear, which was pressed to his chest. "And do you still believe this mad scheme of yours will work?"

Against the warmth of him, I angled my face so that I might meet his gaze. "I told you, it is not within me to yield."

He leaned down, a considerable effort given how dreadfully short my stature, and captured my lips with his own, a chaste kiss over all too soon.

"I do worry for the state of your back, you know," I teased as he drew back, brushing his lips upon my forehead. "Perhaps you shall no longer wish to kiss me when you can no longer stand properly."

I felt his lips curve into a smile. How changed was he since the night I first came to Asperfell; how bitter he'd been, how hopeless, contemptuous of my untried fervor, and quick to deride me for it. And yet, I feared this mourning of his, were it mourning as Phyra suspected and not simply arrogance and pride. He slept poorly; his tongue had sharpened; there was something hollow growing behind his extraordinary eyes.

We stood so long together staring out at the ice and snow and swiftly moving water that I thought perhaps I would have to go back without him when I felt him sigh beneath my ear, heavy, resigned. He took my hand, helping me up onto the embankment, and then, Magefire in our hands, we plunged into the gathering darkness.

The smell of roasting meat greeted us as we stepped into the clearing, and my mouth began to water in a quite unladylike fashion. I'd not thought to miss the simple fare of Asperfell, especially after I had been quite thoroughly spoiled by Layn at Orwynd, but after little more than parsnips, oats, and a few handfuls of bitter greens the last several days, I desperately missed bread and butter.

Thaniel and Arlo had stripped the animal of its skin, removed its offal, and skewered it over the Magefire, where the fat dripped down into the flames, sizzling and popping merrily.

"Tonight, we eat like kings," Arlo declared, rubbing his hands together. "No offense, your highness."

Elyan lowered himself down beside me in front of the fire. "Now, Bryn, don't say things you don't mean."

"I never mean any of the things I say," came Arlo's blithe reply.

Thaniel scowled at him. "Then perhaps you could try saying nothing at all."

"He could not," Phyra said softly, wrapped in her cloak so tightly I could see only the shadows of her face. "He is quite incapable."

Arlo gave a shout of laughter at that, and I could not help but grin, though with Phyra one never could tell whether she was in jest or entirely serious.

Once the beast was well and truly roasted, we tore at its flesh with as much decorum as we could muster after days of eating lackluster fare, its juices and fat dripping down our chins and running in rivulets over our fingers. Our conversation turned, as it so often did these days, toward our memories of Asperfell, for even then, we dared not speak of a life beyond this world, so tenuous was our hope.

Even I, who'd only dwelled within its walls the last two seasons, had found a measure of happiness, however strange. I missed Yralis and the Healer's Garden. I missed Willow in the kitchen. I missed the library and its scholars, the courtyard with the terrifying and beautiful black oak tree, and I missed the little desk that stood before the window in my chamber where I'd so often sat and watched Nollie and Perkin shuffle about the graveyard, the former laying souls to rest and the latter accidentally raising their various extremities.

We often wondered aloud to one another about the people we'd left and what would become of them should Master Viscario ever return. We'd told Mistress Philomena the truth about him before we'd fled. Did this make her vulnerable? Had she told others?

"She is one of the most formidable people I have ever met," Thaniel said as he looked around at our somber faces. "She has a better chance than most."

When at last Phyra began to nod off inside her cloak and Arlo let out a truly impressive yawn, we decided it best to retreat into our shelter of tightly woven roots. Within minutes of wrapping herself inside the folds of her cloak, Phyra was fast asleep. My head pillowed by my hands, I listened to the distant gurgling of the river as Thaniel set a small Magefire at the center of our shelter to keep us warm through the night.

Elyan lay on his back, his hands folded at his chest, his eyes fixed on the roots above. I did not know how long he stayed awake staring into the darkness, for I fell asleep watching the light of the Magefire play about the sharp angles of his face, and as my eyelids grew heavy, the flames formed a crown upon his black hair.

2

We'd begun our journey from Asperfell to the rumored cave in the north nearly five weeks ago and discovered straight away that surviving in the wilderness of a world not our own would require all our skill, and full as much determination.

We had ferocity aplenty between the five of us—even delicate, ethereal Phyra with her strange, terrible aptitude—and more than a modicum of cleverness and familiarity with hard work. Thaniel and Arlo had come from humble beginnings; Phyra even more so. And I'd grown up a trifle wild myself, despite my ancient family name and the once illustrious position of my father at court. Even Elyan, who had lived as a prince in a palace until the age of sixteen, had survived far more horrific things than sleeping on the ground and skinning animals for his supper during his twelve years incarcerated in Asperfell.

And, of course, we had our magic.

Or some version of our magic.

That magic was put to the test two nights after we feasted upon the horned creature, as we prepared to pass the night in a wide clearing surrounded by tall, thin trees that grew in such numbers and in such close proximity that they more resembled several large trunks than hundreds of smaller ones. Elyan insisted I extinguish the Magefire that evening so that I might develop better control, and so I was kneeling before the blaze, coaxing it further and further into submission, when I looked up and saw something in the darkness beyond the trees that made my scalp prickle with alarm.

An enormous pair of glowing, bulbous eyes.

Phaelor were well known to the prisoners of Asperfell. Decidedly feline in appearance, but nearly the size of a horse, they often prowled the moors and terrorized the Renovas. Whether it was skin or a sleek black fur that covered their gaunt frames, I could not say, but their tails were impossibly long and their eyes—oh, their eyes! Huge and bulging and luminous.

My breath coming in short, shallow gasps, I stumbled back from the fire.

Taking my retreat to mean I'd completed my task, Elyan shook his head in disappointment at my meager progress. "Briony, did you mean to leave half of it behind?"

"Phaelor!" I choked out, pointing a trembling finger into the black, where the pair of eyes had drawn closer.

Elyan tensed and uttered a muffled epithet.

"I think we may have a problem," called Thaniel from across the clearing, and to my surprise, he was looking the opposite direction, and not at the Phaelor at all.

Or, at least, not at the same Phaelor. Another pair of glowing eyes emerged from behind us to join the first.

"Stay your magic," Elyan warned, his shrewd gaze glancing back and forth between the two Phaelor who now surrounded us. "They may not wish to court death, and we should not hope for it."

Even so, I lifted my hand and felt the familiar warmth of my magic rush to the center of my palm, where I would call Magefire should the need arise. With any luck, it would not simultaneously cause the entire clearing to erupt in flame and my companions to perish in agony. With my magic, one could never be sure.

I drew breath slowly and watched the first creature's eyes draw closer. Thaniel's hand hovered at Maelstrom's hilt; Arlo slowly crouched down, his palm inches from the frozen ground, wherein his weapons lay waiting.

The Phaelor lunged into the clearing.

I conjured a sorry excuse for a shield and threw myself to the ground as it flew over my head, landing gracefully where I had been tending to the Magefire only moments ago. Emboldened, the second reared up and roared, a terrible sound that both rumbled and screeched, and I clapped both hands over my ears in an effort to stifle it.

"Your highness?" Arlo murmured under his breath. "They do not appear to agree with your earlier assessment."

"Indeed, they do not," Elyan conceded.

The first Phaelor still had its eyes fixed upon me, drawn by my fear. As my shield began to falter and my hopes with it, Thaniel leapt in front of me, his blade drawn. Magic glimmered down its length as he swung Maelstrom at the creature, and it howled in agony as the blade sliced across its chest, opening a grisly red gash that rapidly began to seethe and grow as the spells took hold. I watched in horror as it spread, blackening the bones of its exposed rib cage and singing the flesh and fur around it.

Roaring in pain and anger, the beast swiped its massive paw at Thaniel, and he was thrown backwards like a rag doll. Maelstrom flew from his hands and skittered across the dirt and leaves.

"Thaniel!" I screamed.

Phyra was at his side at once, Magefire gathered in her hands as she stood ready to defend him. Even though it was bleeding profusely and its wounds grew increasingly necrotic, the Phaelor strode forward, ready to strike, and I braced myself to witness a terrible battle of flame and claw that would surely leave one or both of them dead.

But that battle never came.

I watched in fascination as the creature stood perfectly still, save its labored breathing, watching the young Necromancer with wary eyes. Then, beneath its midnight fur, the Phaelor's taut muscles rippled and relaxed as Phyra lowered her hands, the flames there disappearing—and with them, the fervor in her dark eyes.

I could hear no sound, and yet, in the strange stillness that lay between them, I knew a guarded sort of connection had been forged. I could not decide whether it was magic or something else, the peculiar way in which living creatures, be they man or beast, sometimes understood one another. In either case, I let out a shaking breath when the creature bowed its great head in deference to Phyra, thankful, I imagined, for its life, ruined as it was by Thaniel's blade. The poor thing would likely find some snowy bower beneath which to hide itself and perish sometime before the dawn.

I found myself unexpectedly melancholy at the thought.

The Phaelor took one step back, then another, and disappeared into the black of the brush beyond the trees.

"What should I do with this one?" Arlo panted, gesturing at the second creature, its sullen eyes barely visible within the roots that held it fast upon the ground at his feet.

"Let it go," Phyra told him.

"I'm sorry, what?"

"Let it go," she repeated. "They are hungry, just as we are."

"One of them nearly killed Thaniel!"

I snorted. "And that is of great concern to you because…"

"Well, of course it's not, but it's the principle of the thing!" Arlo grunted in disgust and kicked at a clump of dirt and snow at his feet, but he did not argue further. He released his magic, and the roots that held the creature slithered back beneath the frozen ground. Around me, I thought I heard the trees groan.

As the Phaelor darted off, perhaps in search of its injured companion, I scrambled across the clearing and knelt beside Thaniel. Blood spread rapidly from a long, terrible gash in his arm and pooled on the dirt below. Together, Phyra and I helped him shrug off his coat, and he gasped in pain as the fabric brushed the wound. Then I examined the damage that had been done to his flesh.

"It's not as bad as I'd feared," I announced with relief. "First, we stop the bleeding, and then we'll need to clean it." Looking up at Elyan, I added, "A bit of magic wouldn't hurt, either."

Arlo grumbled heartily but nevertheless set a pot of water to boil over a hastily conjured Magefire, and I tore several strips of cloth from one of our blankets. Phyra would not hear of Elyan using any other magic than hers, and so he took her hand in his and—fingertips hovering with the utmost care above Thaniel's wound—let her magic flow through him.

As a Siphon, Elyan could perform wonders of magic far beyond the rest of us, but only at a cost to another. Just as an Alchemist could draw metal from ore and craft it into a sword, or a Naturalist could summon and shape the flora in the world around him, Elyan's aptitude allowed him to pull raw magic from another Mage and bend it to his own purpose. As I watched in amazement, tendrils of light coiled around the raw, red edges of the deep gash on Thaniel's arm and stole within; his breath hissed between his teeth, and despite his best efforts to appear stoic, he could not suppress a grunt of pain.

"Here." Arlo thrust the bottle of Laetha into his hands. "If you break it, I'll do more than cut your arm."

White-faced and scowling, Thaniel took a long swallow, dragged the back of his hand across his mouth, and thrust the bottle back, the liquor sloshing about within.

The cuts were far too deep to be fully healed by any magic but a Healer's, but the magic Elyan siphoned into Thaniel's blood helped somewhat.

My abominable sewing was a well known fact amongst our company, and Thaniel would not allow Arlo anywhere near him with a sharp object, so it was Phyra's graceful fingers that passed a bone needle through Thaniel's skin and drew the flesh together while I held Magefire aloft and murmured what reassurances I could, though I suspect the Laetha was of far greater assistance.

"That doesn't happen to be your sword arm, does it?" Arlo asked once we'd finished.

Thaniel grimaced as Phyra used another long strip of cloth to fashion a sling, knotting it firmly at his opposite shoulder. "No, thank the Gods."

"Indeed," Arlo answered gloomily. "Thank the Gods."

I sat back on my heels and took in Thaniel's sweaty brow. "I hope the magic will stave off any putrefaction. I don't know a single plant in this forest, so I'm afraid I'll be of no help."

"I'll be all right," he croaked. "Water. I need water."

"Do not use this arm until it has been properly healed," Phyra reminded him sternly while I rummaged about for one of our waterskins. "No matter how much danger we are in."

"An impossible thing, that," Elyan said softly, and indeed, he had been so silent during our ministrations that I had nearly forgotten he was with us. "Though we may try to hold him back,

Thaniel will always charge headfirst into danger in defense of others."

I looked up at him, for his voice was strange and reproachful, but also distant as if he were talking to himself. And by the rich, golden light of the flames in my hands, I saw loathing in his eyes, such terrible loathing. Then he turned and strode away.

Shoving the water skin at Thaniel, I hurried after him.

"What is it?" I asked, grasping his sleeve to stay his flight. "Thaniel will heal, if that's where your worry lies. There'll be a scar, no doubt, and a rather nasty one at that, but I dare say he'll be proud of it—"

"Proud!" he spat. "Yes, of course, he'll be proud. 'Tis such a noble thing to earn scars in service of your king, is it not?"

Though I knew he would never harm me, I recoiled at the raw, unbridled anger he barely managed to hold in check; he fairly trembled with it. "Has he then earned your contempt for his loyalty?" I whispered.

"Don't be daft, Briony. Thaniel is the best of men. It's the king in whom I place my doubts. He wouldn't have to heal at all if I weren't so bloody useless."

"You are far from useless," I told him. "Your spellwork is still better than mine will ever be, even without your aptitude."

"If you imagine simple spellwork will be enough to see us through this forest alive, you are not nearly as intelligent as I thought you were."

"Well, it is a relief you thought me intelligent at all," I said. "Is this your solution, then? Feeling that you have nothing of practical value to offer our company, do you propose to make up for it by contributing insults instead? I am, at the very least, intelligent enough to know that being rude to your friends will accomplish nothing to improve your situation, or your temperament. You sleep poorly, you frequently seek solitude—"

"There is no harm in wishing to be free from mind-numbing chatter and pointless arguing."

"You are making excuses."

"And you are quite determined to overstep your boundaries."

I'd grown used to his moods, to the way his tongue sharpened when he sought to punish himself for what he believed were his shortcomings. Still, this talk of borders between us was especially cruel.

"You will simply have to make do without your aptitude. As much as it may vex you, there is no recourse for it, so you'd better get used to it."

His expression was so indignant at that moment that I might've laughed were I not so terribly exasperated at him. "It is fortunate that I hold you in such high esteem," he gritted out. "Were you anyone else—"

"Do you not think I regret my own uselessness?" I demanded, ignoring entirely whatever ridiculously intimidation he was on the verge of issuing. "My aptitude requires a source of magic beyond myself, just as yours does, and I haven't even the mastery of common spellcraft to contribute to our survival. I am least endowed of all to help our company reach the northern cave, and yet my desire is every bit acute as yours."

"It is not even remotely the same between us! I *must* return. If I do not, my people will continue to suffer and die at the hands of Viscario and my puppet of a brother." He sighed and scrubbed a hand across his face, his long fingers resting upon his temple. "How am I to do so when I cannot even keep you all safe?"

"We are not without means to do so ourselves," I pointed out, even as he fixed me with a withering expression. "Yes, all right, I acknowledge my shortcomings in this particular area, but I am not alone, nor are you."

"I know that."

"If you do, then trust us!" I reached out and took both his hands within mine. "We may not be Mages of rare talent or destined to sit upon the throne, but we are more than capable of fighting for you!"

"But at what cost?"

We stared at one another in terrible silence, our hands clasped tightly between us, and though I could feel the warmth of him, feel the pulsing of his heart through his skin, he felt so very far away.

"I cannot lose you," he said at last, and his voice was so low I could scarcely hear him. "But I cannot protect you. I cannot protect any of you."

He gently drew his hands from mine, and I watched helplessly as he disappeared into the dark of the forest.

3

The air grew unseasonably warm as we continued our journey north, and soon the ice and snow began to melt in earnest, leaving us to slog through mud whilst thoroughly drenched with rain, an experience so unpleasant that we grew sullen and baleful and snapped at one another unnecessarily.

Arlo was particularly loathsome. I'd grown used to his humor even if it was a bit scandalous from time to time, but now his whining grated on my nerves and I was in such an ill-humor I could only abide him in very small measures. He'd taken to singing to distract himself, and though he had a pleasant voice, his timbre rich and clear, one could only tolerate so many drinking songs, for that seemed to be all he knew. To prevent Thaniel from strangling him, I taught him "Wand'ring Rose" and the Estelland Carol, and soon he quite eclipsed me, though even songs so beloved to my ears grew tiresome after so many iterations.

It was most strange; winter had only just begun when we'd left Asperfell, and I'd not expected it to loosen its icy grasp on the land for months to come. The malevolent presences amidst the trees, whose eyes we felt upon us at all times, especially at night, had seemed languid and sullen when white covered the world. Now, those same eyes were awake and eager, and although I was glad of the respite from the bitter cold, there were many days in which I wished the world asleep once more and feared why it did not.

"Which is it, then?" Arlo asked that night, as we drowsed before the Magefire. "Do the seasons here change after only weeks, or is the forest warming as we draw closer to something?"

"It cannot be the first," I answered, my eyes fixed on the patch of sky speckled with stars above, framed by the grasping, black fingers of the branches. "Else the seasons would've passed the same at Asperfell, and they did not."

"The second, then," Arlo said, and took a long swallow of Laetha from Walfrey's enchanted bottle. I wished often that I'd been at Asperfell when she'd discovered its liberation, for her face turned an extraordinary shade of red when she was angry; I would've dearly loved to see it.

Thaniel stretched his hand out, and Arlo reluctantly passed him the bottle. "If that is so, what could be at the center?"

"And will we have to pass through it to reach the cave, or go around it?" I added.

I'd thought it the perfect riddle for Elyan to devote his shrewd mind to, but he'd slid further into reclusive silence since our harsh words and offered no opinion.

The next day, the rain let up and the ground began to dry. We were grateful, for it made our steps swifter, and the sight of so much green and so many growing things lifted my spirits considerably. I was only sorry that we did not have time to stop so that I might gather the peculiar leaves and flowers and press them carefully within the pages of a book to show to Layn when we returned to Tiralaen. If we returned to Tiralaen.

The world grew warmer, the air sweeter, and I gloried at the sun's rays upon my face as we journeyed, dappled by riotous bursts of green leaves above.

The lights that heralded the coming of the twilight appeared now by the gnarled stumps of fallen trees where the slender branches of new saplings grew from the rot within and vivid red toadstools dotted the ground below, no larger than the tip of a finger.

Near evening, we chose a suitable glen of ancient trees whose roots were sure to provide ample shelter. Our path had taken us somewhat away from the river, but I could still hear the rushing of the water; a comfort, that.

We were to have fish that evening, for they'd become plentiful. After several disastrous attempts at levitation, I succeeded only in smacking Thaniel about the face with my silvery prey, but Phyra at last managed to snatch one from the air and hold it fast. Arlo gave a shout of jubilant laughter, and though her reaction was quite a bit more sedate, Phyra looked rather proud as she clutched her wriggling prize. A second fish followed the first, and triumphantly we bore them back to where a Magefire awaited.

As I helped Thaniel pass a sharpened stick through the gaping mouths and mount them above the flames, I wondered what my Aunt Eudora would say if she could see me now. Scandalized beyond all imagining, no doubt; Layn would've been proud of me, though, cooking for myself after all the years she spent trying and failing to teach me not to spoil even the simplest of dishes.

Suddenly, Elyan's voice cut across the clearing, sharp and low: "Stop."

"What is it, mate?" Thaniel asked, reaching for the sword at his side.

"Something is nearby," Elyan answered, his narrowed eyes surveying the forest beyond the safety of our glen.

Arlo groaned. "Oh Gods, we're all going to die, aren't we."

"Quiet," Elyan snapped.

In the silence that descended, I realized that the usual sorts of forest sounds I'd come to know had vanished completely, save the river. The birdsong, the rustling of the underbrush, the faraway calls of creatures; gone, all of it.

The unnatural silence stretched on as we held our breath and watched the forest around us for the slightest movement.

Then they appeared.

Like the shedding of skin, they peeled themselves from the trees that surrounded us with a peculiar sort of grace, their movements delicate and yet disjointed and halting.

They were men and women, certainly, but they were oddly shaped, with long, spindly limbs covered not with skin but with bark, roughened and cracked and brown, with lichens and mosses growing here and there in blotches of pale green. Leaves and twigs were woven into the braids and strands of their hair, and their eyes were large and beetle black.

In their hands, they held what I first thought to be sticks of varying size and shape, but upon further inspection were weapons: bows and arrows, spears and knives of sharpened rock, and staves. They held them at the ready as they crept toward us on their strange limbs so much like the branches of the trees from whence they came, and then, quite abruptly, they stopped.

They stared at us with wide, fearful eyes, taking in our superior height and our no doubt strange attire and tools, but they did not approach, and if they had speech, they used it not.

"What are they waiting for?" Thaniel murmured.

His question was answered not a moment later when a ripple passed through the strange folk and they began to part, a river of bark and moss, to admit a figure slightly taller than the rest, a man by the looks of it, with a very long beard made up of twigs stripped into fiber and sinew. Woven into his garments were lovely smooth stones; a symbol of his status, perhaps, or his age.

Most unfortunately, I was still on my knees beside the Magefire, and thus at a disadvantage when the man moved toward me. In the perfect stillness, I could hear my heart hammering wildly in my chest at his approach, and I held perfectly still as he leaned down so close that our noses nearly touched.

He smelled ancient, musty even, yet there was a hint of the verdant about him, the scent of stalks and the unfurling of leaves. He spoke to me then, in a language that sounded less like words and more like the snapping of twigs and the rustle of dry leaves. He tilted his head, waiting, it seemed, for my reply.

"I'm sorry," I answered. "I don't understand you."

The man slowly turned back to those gathered behind him and spoke quickly in his native tongue.

"Briony," Elyan said quietly. "Perhaps they have magic. Try speaking to them that way."

I reached out with my own magic, seeking its like within the man, within his companions, but found nothing that I could attempt to communicate with. I tried anyway: "My name is Briony," I said, wrapping my magic about my voice, using it to shape and guide my words. "We are merely travelers and mean you no harm."

The man's black eyes narrowed. Then, before I could fully comprehend how he'd done it, a long, ragged knife appeared in his hand and its edge was at my throat. He bore me down until my back was pressed against the roots of the tree and began speaking quickly in a harsh, guttural tone, and even though I could not begin to comprehend his words, I understood well enough the feral gleam in his eyes and the fury in his coiled frame. I'd made a grievous mistake in believing him infirm; I'd mistaken his beard for age. With a strangled cry, I tried to shove him off of me, but for his slight size he was surprisingly strong, and I felt a sharp pain in my neck as his blade pierced my flesh.

Elyan reached me in two strides and, gripping the man's arm, wrenched him away from me, sending him sprawling back on the forest floor.

The uproar that followed was utter madness.

The men and women of the trees hissed and gnashed their teeth and screamed at us in their strange language as they brandished their blades. The underbrush rustled, and dozens more of their kind emerged behind them, all bearing weapons of wood and stone.

"That's done it," said Thaniel, as he drew Maelstrom with his uninjured arm.

Phyra dipped her fingers into the Magefire she'd conjured, extracting a handful of flame. Arlo's palms rested on the earth, and I saw movement below the surface of a nearby tree.

"Don't hurt them!" I cried. Though their weapons were fierce, I feared that our magic would devastate them, made of the woods and brittle as they were.

"We may have no choice," Elyan said.

"*Fal haer!*"

A voice, powerful and commanding, filled the glen, and whatever the words meant, they must've been important to the folk of the trees, for they froze the moment they heard them.

We turned as one.

Wreathed in the golden light of the fading afternoon, a spindly, hunchbacked creature with three legs staggered through a large gap between the trees.

But no... What approached was no creature of the forest. She was human—as human as we!—though she was the most ancient person I had ever seen, and she leaned heavily upon a gnarled staff as she hobbled toward us.

Her simple robes were of pale linen, her white hair was woven in a single plait that hung over one frail shoulder, and her luminous green eyes were set deeply in her wrinkled face. She barked at the man who had attacked me, speaking in their guttural tongue, and the way her voice rose on the last word, I thought perhaps she asked him a question.

The man regarded her sullenly and answered in kind, sweeping his hand out behind him to indicate the trees surrounding us.

"Bah," said the old woman, and spat upon the ground. Then, she looked to where I lay sprawled upon the forest floor, Elyan at my side, and gestured with her staff. "Who are you?"

Her accent was strange, but the words were, unmistakably, our words; the common tongue spoken in Tiralaen and beyond. "You speak our language," I breathed. "How?"

"My question first," she answered. "Who are you?"

Elyan rose slowly to his feet, and the old woman took a cautious step back, and then another, holding her staff in front of her with both hands as the full height and measure of him was revealed. "We mean no harm to you, or to them," he said. "We are travelers passing through these lands, nothing more."

At this, the man who'd drawn my blood began to speak, and the old woman listened intently before turning back to Elyan. "Riet says they've been tracking you through the Heimslind for several days."

"What is the Heimslind?" I asked.

The woman's gaze flicked from Elyan's face to mine. "A place of winter, and of dead things."

"That sounds about right," Arlo muttered, and I glared swiftly at him.

Elyan ignored Arlo entirely. "We hail from beyond your Heimslind. From the prison on the moor, and the Gate beyond."

The old woman smiled. "From Asperfell."

"How is it that you know that name?"

The old woman craned her neck so far to look up at him that I feared for her no doubt brittle bones, but the gaze she fixed him with was far from fragile. "I know many things," she said. "After all, I have lived a long, long time."

She turned to the men and women of the trees then, and as she began to speak again, they howled in protest at her words, pointing at us furiously and brandishing their weapons, their voices a cacophony of skittering and rasping. When at last they fell silent, the old woman turned to Arlo, of all people.

"They say you desecrated their trees."

Arlo snorted. "I didn't desecrate anything. I moved some roots about to shelter us at night, but I always returned them to their proper place afterward."

"He is a Naturalist," I explained. "That is, he can manipulate trees and plants."

The old woman nodded. "I know what he is. But they do not. To them, what he did was the deepest blasphemy."

"Blasphemy!" Arlo laughed. "I've done a great many things more worthy of blasphemy than shaping a few tree roots."

Thaniel glanced sidelong at him. "That is *not* something to be proud of, mate."

"Please," I begged her. "Please explain it to them. Assure them we mean no harm to them or their trees."

She regarded me for a long time before turning and, presumably, delivering my message to the tree folk. I was not met favorably, it seemed, for their black eyes narrowed and they began to grumble and point and hiss.

But the old woman seemed to grow tired of all their protestations, for she bellowed an order and pointed her staff deep into the forest.

They complained heartily at first, and some shook their weapons at her, but it became obvious that the old woman, whomever she was, held sway over them. Eventually, they slunk back into the forest, muttering amongst themselves. The old woman watched them go. Then, satisfied that they meant to stay gone, she turned and took in our strange, bedraggled company.

"Well," she said at last, hitching her staff to her shoulder. "Who are you, then?"

"We do indeed come from Asperfell," said Elyan. "And from the world beyond it: the kingdom of Tiralaen."

"And yet, you are here, far beyond your men of stone," the woman answered. "How?"

Elyan narrowed his eyes. "How came you to know of our men of stone?"

I'd been in her place many times before, on the receiving end of Elyan's scrutiny and distrust. But, unlike me, the old woman chortled rather than threw insults and indignation back into his face as I used to. Well, still did, when the occasion called for it.

"My goodness, you are a demanding sort, aren't you?"

"Forgive me, but as I was told none of our kind had ever escaped, I am quite taken aback by your very existence. Are you from Asperfell?"

"Not me, not me," the old woman grunted in amusement. "But you are not the first to escape. Others came before, although it was quite a while ago. I imagine it's faded into history."

"I assure you I am the keenest of historians."

Oh, for pity's sake. "It matters not," I said. "We are most eager to hear your story."

"I'll say no more here, for by the time the story is told, nightfall will be upon us and far more treacherous things than the Bra'ata prowl these woods. My name is Garundel, and you are welcome to my supper, such that it is, and may rest your feet at my door this night. But I will require your assurances that you will not use your extraordinary gifts to murder me in my bed."

Elyan snorted. "I am not given to murdering defenseless old women, let alone while they sleep. You have my word we mean you no harm."

"The word of a criminal."

"The word of a prince."

The old woman's face wrinkled in a wide grin. "Is that so? Well, then, I think you'd better come with me."

"Hold on," Thaniel said. "How do we know you won't murder *us* in our beds?"

"You don't," the old woman cackled. "But if I wanted you dead, I wouldn't have sent the Bra'ata away. Besides, that arm looks as though it needs tending, and though I am no healer, I do have a garden in which I grow a few useful herbs."

"How did you send the Bra'ata away?" I asked.

"They swore a blood oath long ago to one of my ancestors," the woman answered. "Another story far too long to be told here."

"We'll go with you," Elyan agreed reluctantly. "But only for tonight. We seek a place far to the north and are in haste."

The old woman raised one white eyebrow. "To the north? If that be the case, then coming with me is in your best interest, as there is much you do not know... and much you should."

She would tell us no more until we followed her, and so, as Arlo returned the roots of our intended shelter to their sleep beneath the ground, we gathered our supplies. The going was arduous, but Garundel refused any assistance, preferring to walk by herself, however slowly, leaning against her knobby staff. I wondered that she had cause to be so very far into the forest that day, and so I asked her as we traveled.

"Collecting volcri eggs," she told me. "They pickle exquisitely."

"You've no basket," I pointed out.

A smile played about her wizened lips. "Have I not? Dear me, I must've forgotten it."

4

Garundel dwelled in a dome of uneven gray stones. A great tree rose from her moss-covered roof, its roots snaking down the gently sloping walls of the house to bury themselves in the ground below. Long ago, someone had trained the roots to grow around the home's small windows and crooked door, and they held the stones of the humble structure tightly in their embrace. On either side of the tree, smoke curled invitingly upward from twin chimneys.

Standing alone in a meadow of tall grass, the small stone home was surrounded by groves of silver-barked trees whose red leaves hung from their branches like drops of blood against pale flesh. A gentle breeze rippled through the grass, a sea of gold in the fading light of the day, and set the leaves shivering and dancing upon their fragile branches, a fluttering sound not unlike sheaves of ancient parchment being shuffled. In the distance, reeds bordered a pond with a rickety dock stretching, half-sunk, into the water. A small boat was moored there, and a collection of wooden fishing rods stood in a roughly woven basket beside them.

It was a strange and lovely place the likes of which I had not expected to see after the darkness of the forest from whence we'd come.

"Come on, then," Garundel called from the steps to her home. "We've much to say to one another, and stories like these are best told in front of a fire, don't you think?"

I'd wondered when first I saw the dome of stones how all six of us were going to fit inside; indeed, I thought Elyan might have to bend himself in half to accomplish it! Now as I stepped inside the door, I realized with surprise and delight that what we'd seen from outside was but a fraction of what was within.

A wide set of stairs led down into an enormous circular space with walls made of the same stone as without, bolstered by beams of dark, gleaming wood and lined with shelves. Some were filled with books, others scrolls, and still others held treasures of a life well lived. Or rather, as I suspected given the state of the tree growing out of the roof, the lives of many generations.

To the right and left of the room stood two enormous hearths, one that served as the kitchen and one as a place of comfort and leisure. That hearth was flanked by a sumptuously cushioned bench on one end and two matching chairs on the other. A small stack of books rested upon a small round table beside one of the chairs, and a basket filled with brightly colored skeins of yarn lay beneath.

Before the other hearth stood a handsomely carved table of no mean size, flanked by several chairs, and with a clay jug of colorful flowers at its center. Over the fire hung a big-bellied caldron, and to either side, the familiar comforts of a well tended kitchen. I could see no beds, but given how remarkably well the outside of Garundel's home had fooled me, I could well imagine that one bedroom or many were tucked away somewhere.

"Cursed stairs," Garundel grumbled as she gripped the wooden railings on either side and began a slow, laborious descent. "One day I won't be able to go up and down them anymore."

At the tip of my tongue was the question of what would become of her when she could no longer do so, when a small figure appeared at the bottom of the staircase: a child. The boy was perhaps seven or eight, with the same large, candescent green eyes as Garundel and a mop of unruly chestnut hair. He stared at us with open-mouthed surprise as we moved down the stairs, and we were no less shocked to see him as he was to see us.

"My late brother's grandson," grunted Garundel. "Tarseth."

"Who are they?" the boy asked, his eyes darting between the lot of us.

"Escaped convicts."

"Oh," the boy said. Then, "What's a convict?"

Garundel let out a bark of laughter.

I waved and smiled at the boy as we passed, and he offered me a lopsided grin in response.

While we set down our packs and removed our cloaks, Garundel took up a basket and handed it to Tarseth. "We need more vegetables for the stew," she told him. "Out with you."

The boy scampered up the steps, clutching the basket, and turned halfway to look back at us. "Don't say anything interesting while I'm out," he implored, then dashed away through the front door.

"Where are Tarseth's parents?" Elyan asked.

"Gone. Now, help me with this."

This turned out to be putting more wood on each of the two fires, which seemed unnecessarily arduous and wasteful to Elyan, who offered to light a Magefire in each grate instead. Garundel refused.

"You'll not be here forever, will you?" she chuckled. "And what if something were to go awry? Oh no. I'll not risk my home for such a flight of fancy."

"Your home is marvelous," I told her.

"I've known no other, so I shall have to take your word for it."

Tarseth returned with his basket overflowing with vegetables I did not recognize: yellow gourds striped with deep green, long white roots, and bunches of greens that might have been herbs. He turned the basket over onto the long table and Garundel picked them over before she nodded in approval.

"You, with the fancy sword," she called to Thaniel. "Help me with these, if you want a full belly tonight. My stew isn't meant to feed seven such as it is. You're lucky—I caught a brace of Celer this morning in one of my traps, so at least there is meat."

Thaniel made a congenial show of bowing and scraping. "I am at your service."

Garundel poured more water into the pot and added several pinches of spice from a shallow dish on the hearth above, while Thaniel and Phyra chopped the roots and gourds into pieces according to Garundel's instructions. They were so natural together, Thaniel and Phyra, and such lovely counterpoint to one another with his golden hair and noble features, roughened by the close-cropped beard at his jaw, and her dark, ethereal beauty. Although there had been no clergy at Asperfell to perform the customary rituals, many of the inhabitants nevertheless said vows to one another and pronounced themselves to be married in the eyes of the Gods. And yet, when I'd asked Elyan if they considered themselves man and wife, he'd stared at me so very strangely that I'd not the courage to ask him to elaborate further. I reminded myself to revisit the topic with him when next we had a chance to speak together alone, although I doubted I would remember; other things always seemed more pressing in those rare and precious moments.

If Garundel wondered about them, she said nothing at all. Instead, she began rummaging around in one of her cabinets; I heard the soft clinking of glass and her low mutterings, and then she emerged clutching several small, dusty bottles.

"Now, then," she said, as she set them gingerly upon the table. "If you're done with the vegetables, let's take a look at that arm."

Thaniel set down his knife, lowered himself into one of the chairs, and then carefully extracted his arm from the makeshift sling. With a sharp intake of breath, he unrolled the bandage. The wound was still raw and red and angry, but Elyan's magic had, at least, staved off an infection.

"You'll have a scar, and a nasty one at that," Garundel told him as she poked and prodded the skin around the wound. "But I've got some senomile for the swelling, and a bit of toffange for the pain."

"Thank you," I told her, as I committed the strange herbs to memory. *Senomile for swelling, toffange for pain.* "And thank you for sheltering us."

Garundel shrugged her bony shoulders, then set to work mixing various powders and dried leaves with a brackish liquid that caused the lot of it to steam and hiss. I watched her with rapt interest and asked about each and everything she used and where I might find it in the forest should the need arise. The resulting ointment Garundel smeared liberally on Thaniel's wound. Then, she wrapped the arm with clean, white bandages and replaced it within the sling.

At last, the stew was ready, and not a moment too soon; we were ravenous. It had been far too long since we'd had a proper meal around a table, not eaten with our hands. Somehow, we resisted the urge to behave like complete heathens until Garundel had bowed her head and muttered something unintelligible, a prayer of some sort to no god familiar to us, and then we fell upon the food with enthusiasm.

The stew was wonderful: thick and rich and deliciously seasoned. As I looked around the table at my companions devouring the simple fare gratefully, I felt a lightness within me that I'd not felt in a very long time. Engrossed as we were in the food, we did not speak for a long while, until Garundel prodded us to share our story. Then, we painted for her as true a portrait as we could of what really was quite an extraordinary series of events that began one day when a prince was exiled through a Gate to a strange world for the murder of his father and a wild young woman with flaming red hair and no idea of the magic that resided in her blood followed twelve years later, charged with retrieving him in order to save a kingdom from ruin. It was Elyan who told her somberly of the foundation of bone hidden beneath the black oak of Asperfell and Master Viscario's twisted plan to live forever off the magic of those imprisoned there, and Thaniel who crowed triumphantly about our battle with the Sentinels and our escape into the forest, and Arlo who caterwauled quite dramatically concerning our long trek across the snow-covered Heimslind.

"And there is, of course, the matter of the rapid shift from winter to spring," Elyan said. "It has certainly made our journey most interesting."

Garundel leaned forward thoughtfully. "Yes, well, I may know something about that, but it can certainly wait until we've finished our meal."

We fairly choked on our stew so eager were we to hear tell of it; she laughed at us, and there was merriment in her eyes. How long had it been since she'd had visitors or cause to speak of the remarkable things she knew? I looked at Tarseth at the other end of the table and wondered if he, too, knew of Asperfell.

Only when every bowl of stew was emptied, the bread devoured, the dishes scrubbed clean and left to dry, the fire stoked, and a heavy woolen shawl settled around her shoulders, would Garundel begin the tale. At last, she folded her paper-thin hands in front of her and looked around at us, her eyes bright.

"Now, then," she said. "Where to begin?"

Unable to contain myself, I fairly exploded out of my chair, my eyes wild, every bit the whirlwind my father had once described me. "Who else has escaped from Asperfell? Did you meet them? I searched every scrap of parchment in the library and never found any record of anyone making it past the Sentinels—how did they do it? And who built this house?"

Garundel chuckled at my outburst, and out of the corner of my eye, I saw Elyan stifle a smile.

"Well, to start, I never met anyone who escaped Asperfell before today," Garundel said. "It's been two hundred years since my ancestors escaped that cursed place, and I imagine they were none too keen to return and write their story down."

"Nor would Master Viscario have wanted anyone to know that escape was possible," Elyan said.

I, for one, would have dearly loved to see the look on his wretched face as they thwarted him, but I supposed I would have to make do with the satisfaction that his rage must've been apocalyptic indeed.

"How did they escape?" asked Thaniel.

Garundel shrugged. "That part of the tale has not survived the passage of time. I only know they fled past the guardians of stone, then journeyed through the Heimslind just as you have, and farther on to the kingdom at the heart of the forest."

Beside me, Elyan went perfectly still. "What did you say?"

Garundel looked at him. "The Forest Kingdom. Syr'Aliem, it is called. They made their home there, marrying into the local families, and passing the magic in their blood down through the generations. I've a dash of magic myself, though I've had little training in the use of it, as you see." She gestured to the fire crackling merrily in the hearth, of wood and not magic. "But I see things, from time to time."

A Scrivener!

"How extraordinary!" I breathed.

"This kingdom," said Elyan. "Do its people have magic of their own?"

Garundel tilted her head thoughtfully. "Of a sort, but it does not reside in the blood, as yours does—as *ours* does. It comes from a different place altogether."

"What sort of place?" I asked.

Garundel's eyes gleamed. "I've never seen it. But I feel it. In him." She glanced over at Tarseth, so small, nestled as he was in the chair. "He may not wish to pass his life as a hermit in this place as I have, though if he does not, I will be the last of my family to dwell here."

"How came you to be here, if your ancestors stayed in the kingdom?" Thaniel asked, a frown creasing his forehead. "Why leave?"

Garundel grunted. "Having never been to Syr'Aliem, I cannot speak to its charms. But evidently some of my ancestors did not find it charming enough to stay. And others still come this way from time to time, seeking what they could not find in the kingdom."

"And Tarseth?" Phyra asked softly. "He is of Syr'Aliem?"

Garundel glanced over at the boy with fondness. "I suppose someday he will wish to leave me, leave this place. My brother did. He spent most of his life in Syr'Aliem and returned only after his wife had passed, and with his children in tow. He died shortly thereafter, and one by one, his children returned to the Forest Kingdom."

"But one came back, yes?" Thaniel said.

"My father," Tarseth told him. "His name was Harald."

Garundel nodded. "He wanted Tarseth to be raised far away from Syr'Aliem."

"Why?" I asked.

"He never said. I do not believe he cared for life in the Forest Kingdom overmuch."

"And who is master of Syr'Aliem?" Elyan asked.

"A king," Garundel answered. "Though I do not know his name. He has ruled only five years, so I imagine he is a young man. His father ruled before him, and his father and grandfather before."

"Such is the way of kingdoms," Elyan huffed impatiently.

"Is it?"

Garundel seemed genuinely curious, but Elyan ignored the question. "Does he have magic?"

"Yes, of course," she answered. "How else would the magic flow unto the people?"

Elyan only stared at her, so I asked the question for him: "What do you mean? Is the king the source of their magic?"

Garundel cackled loudly. "What? No, that's nonsense, of course. But..." Here, she eyed Elyan strangely, as if he were an animal of a sort she'd not seen before. "I'm forgetting how different your magic is. Yours is in the blood."

"Like yours," Elyan said.

"Yes, like mine, like mine," Garundel sighed. "It's not so odd to think that magic could originate from a person, I suppose, if you're accustomed to magic lying in the blood. But it is not so in Syr'Aliem.

Their magic comes from the land. It flows freely through the king to the people, and back again."

"How marvelous," I whispered. "Magic that comes from the land."

"And are there any in Syr'Aliem with our kind of magic?" Elyan asked.

Garundel nodded. "Of course. The blood of your people is mingled with theirs. But they're like me—they have no one to train them, so they cannot wield it quite so well as you do, I imagine."

"If we should seek their help to find our cave," Elyan mused, "do you believe that we can trust them?"

"I can think of no reason to the contrary."

Though we spoke for hours more as the fires burned low, she had little else to say of Syr'Aliem, for she knew little. Even less did she know of Tiralaen; and so, she and Tarseth listened with wide, hungry eyes as we spoke of the Shining City, of the countryside and villages, of the Gods and of the people; of home. The telling of it was at once a great joy and a great sorrow, and it was with full and heavy hearts that we unburdened ourselves, for if we never reached the cave in the north, or if Kasam had been mistaken and the veil between our worlds could not be pierced there, this was all we would ever have of our home: memories, and nothing more.

5

I woke to hard stone and the lingering scent of woodsmoke, and for a moment, however fleeting, I imagined I was back at Orwynd, where occasionally I'd fallen asleep in front of the fire in the parlor, reading late into the night.

We'd spent the night near the fire, for Garundel's dwelling had but one proper bedroom, with a small alcove beyond where Tarseth slept.

My limbs protesting spectacularly, I rolled over and looked about at my companions in the bleak light of the morning, ever watchful that they were all still with me. I could scarce see Phyra's face beside me for the tangle of her black hair above the heavy blanket she'd burrowed under, but she was there, as surely as she had been when we'd fallen asleep some hours before.

Beyond her I could see Thaniel's golden hair and, as far removed from the rest as possible, a lump that I supposed was Arlo.

A fissure of alarm ran through me when I saw that Elyan's blankets were empty.

The fire had been stoked, and Garundel sat in her chair before the hearth, wrapped in a thick blanket and staring into the flames as though she could see so many things written there in the unbearable brightness and heat. Perhaps she could. Opposite her, stretched out on the bench with his eyes closed and an open book laying upon his chest, was the heir to the throne of Tiralaen. I smiled at the sight of him; ever the scholar, Elyan must've waited until we'd all fallen asleep before helping himself to the books on Garundel's shelves.

I wrapped my blanket around my shoulders and, wincing at the cold against my bare feet, I padded over to where Garundel sat and tucked myself into the empty chair beside her.

"He's a handsome one," she said, and looked over at Elyan with a smile.

"He is that," I agreed. With his dark hair mussed by sleep and his face relaxed, he looked far younger than his nearly thirty years, as if the weight of his cares had been lifted from him in repose.

"It is a heavy burden he carries."

"Yes."

"And you carry, in helping him."

"There are many lives dependent on our success," I answered, wincing as I rotated my sore shoulders. "And so, I must carry it. Though I cannot deny I am not particularly keen to carry it so early in the morning."

Garundel shifted in her chair, reaching toward a clay pot, and I watched her pour the contents into a chipped cup, which she offered me.

I lifted it to my nose and inhaled its rich, spiced aroma. "What is it?"

"Steeped bark from the red elger trees behind the house. They've a natural spice that is quite bracing."

Well, that was certainly an understatement; I'd taken an enormous swallow and was now attempting to smother my violent coughing lest I wake Elyan; he mumbled something and shifted in his sleep, but his eyes stayed mercifully closed.

"It's good," I wheezed.

We talked a little of her life growing up in this place, and mine at the Citadel and later at Orwynd, until our laughter roused Elyan and he stirred, the book on his chest sliding to the floor with a thud.

"Briony?" Elyan scrubbed his hands over his eyes, his voice hoarse and rough with sleep. "Gods, what time is it?"

He was most displeased that he'd overslept, even more so that I'd been awake for some time and let him alone, for he'd hoped to leave at first light. I endured the lashing of his tongue for I was secretly glad I'd done no such thing; he desperately needed the rest. Phyra had been up for some time, listening quietly to Garundel and me with a soft smile upon her face, and Thaniel was easily roused with the brush of her hand against the stubble of his jaw. She attempted the same with Arlo, but when he'd merely snorted and rolled over, pulling his blanket firmly over his head, Thaniel took great pleasure in kicking him roundly in the back.

While Garundel smeared something that looked very much like jam on warm slices of bread and arranged slivers of an orange-skinned fruit with pale purple flesh on a platter, Tarseth wrapped a second loaf of bread in a cloth and placed it in Phyra's pack along with a round of cheese that I very much doubted they could afford to part with, despite how grateful I was to have it, and a pile of fruit and vegetables from the garden.

"I find nests in the hollows of trees sometimes," Tarseth told Phyra. "There should be eggs, though they're not very large."

Phyra smiled at him. "I'll be sure to look."

I plopped down onto one of the chairs at the long table and seized a slice of bread from the platter, tucking into it with gusto.

The jam was a trifle too tart, but I polished it off in three bites and reached for another.

"Are you ready, Briony?" Phyra asked me. She bit delicately into a piece of fruit and brushed the juice from her lips with her fingers.

"Yes," I answered with great reluctance and wiped the crumbs from the skirt of my gown. "I hope so."

Arlo appeared behind Phyra and reached over her shoulder to grab a slice of bread off of the platter. "Come on, you two," he said. "His highness and his knightliness are beginning to fray my nerves."

Thaniel and Elyan were, indeed, deep in conversation at the base of the staircase. Garundel had found in a stack of scrolls a map, and though it was old and practically falling to pieces in her hands, it showed the forest surrounding the meadow, and the road that led to our destination: Syr'Aliem, the Forest Kingdom.

"I guess we'd better get to it, then," I said gloomily, as I slid the folded map carefully into my satchel. And it was with a heavy heart that I dragged myself up the stairs and into the open air of the bright morning.

"Here we go again," Arlo bemoaned, looking balefully at the path ahead of us into the woods, an admittedly friendlier one than those we'd thus far traveled, but loathsome after too short a modicum of peace.

Garundel shuffled out the door behind us, leaning heavily upon her staff. "You all go on ahead," she said to Elyan. "I would have a word with Briony, as I've knowledge to impart regarding particular plants and roots she might seek out for their healing properties."

Elyan narrowed his eyes and looked very much as though he would like to protest, but thinking better of it, he nodded curtly. I watched Tarseth lead my companions across the meadow until we could no longer hear their voices, and only then did she take my hand in hers and lead me to a nearby bench much older than she.

"I may not remember all that you tell me," I said. "Should I write it all down?"

She waved her hand. "Oh, never mind that. That's not why I asked you to stay behind. I simply did not want to arouse suspicion in your companions, though I fear his highness will not be so easily fooled."

"What do you wish to speak of, then?"

"Do you know, it occurred to me to send Tarseth with you. I'm too old for the journey and only getting older, and the day will come when he insists on returning to his people. I would not have him travel so far alone," she told me. "But no, the path you're treading is much too perilous for a child. You do not know your danger. I've seen things."

My eyes went wide. "You mean, you've seen—"

"Yes," she whispered, and her hands folded about mine, holding them fast in her lap. "Yes. Do you wish to know?"

My pulse leapt beneath my skin, beneath her brittle fingers, and the world stilled as I held my breath, waiting. I'd known but one Scrivener in my life, and it had been her prophecy that set me on the path to freedom from Asperfell, though it had been no easy thing untangling the woeful mess of her mind and words.

"If you tell me, will it still come to pass?" I asked, chewing on my lower lip as I considered.

"I never know if the things I see come to pass," Garundel said. "I've never left this place. And you may not wish to know what I have seen. But, if you do, I will tell you."

Torn between the desire to know what would become of us and fear of the same, I could only sit in dumbstruck silence as a merry war ensued between the rational part of my mind and the side that, unfortunately, tended to win out—the ever-curious side of me that even now urged me to accept without reservation the chance to know what might befall us, for better or for ill.

"And if I do not like what you tell me, what then? Is there anything to be done about it?"

"You mean, are my visions etched in stone, unchanging and unchangeable?" Garundel's eyes fell to her lap. "A fair question, but not one that I know the answer to, regretfully. It may be that a word of warning from me is all you need to change your fate, or it may be that my words will set you down the very path you seek to avoid. Or perhaps the gods will not allow you to deviate from the path they've chosen for you, whether you walk it with eyes open or closed."

"If I cannot change it, perhaps it is better not to know."

Garundel's bony shoulders lifted in a shrug. "As I've said, I know not. Perhaps one day you will return and enlighten me. But for now, all I can do is tell you what I've seen, or not. What happens afterwards is entirely up to you."

Garundel and Tarseth saw us to the edge of the meadow a short time later. By her reckoning, we were a week away from the kingdom of Syr'Aliem, perhaps less, and the weather would continue to warm as we approached, making the journey far easier than it had been at the start.

"The colors of the royal house are green and gold, and they bear a symbol that looks like this," Garundel told us, drawing crudely with a stick in the dirt at our feet. It appeared to be a circle bound from above by hanging vines that dangled from a chair or a throne.

"You will likely encounter guards in the woods when you get close. Do not give them reason to distrust you; remember, no one has come from Asperfell in hundreds of years."

She could tell us nothing more, despite Thaniel's barrage of questions regarding defenses and weaponry. Instead, she embraced us one by one, though she held me the longest, and I found tears had sprung to my eyes as I felt her bony fingers press into my back. I'd hardly known her, and yet I would miss her; I would miss this place.

Then, one foot before the other, I walked away.

We walked for hours, hours that I did not know had passed until I ran right into Phyra's back, not realizing that she, along with the rest of my companions, had stopped abruptly. Thaniel had evidently declared the clearing ahead suitable to pass the night. My protesting feet and turbulent mind agreed wholeheartedly.

Phyra watched me, suspicion in her eyes, as I stumbled past her absently, but she said nothing. Elyan, however, did me no such courtesy. I had no sooner tossed my pack down on a rock when I felt his hand on my elbow and knew a reckoning was at hand.

"Briony and I will ascertain our surroundings," he announced loudly. No doubt the others imagined us sneaking away to whisper endearments to one another or steal kisses.

I only wished it were that.

Instead, when we'd reached what Elyan determined to be a reasonably safe distance from prying eyes and ears, he spun me about until we faced one another and demanded: "Out with it."

"I cannot imagine what you mean," I answered.

He fixed me with a face of flint. "I know Garundel offered you foresight. You've a great many talents, Briony, but deception has never been one of them. What did she tell you?"

I hesitated but a moment, but it was long enough for him to ascertain that whatever I'd learned, it did not bode well for our journey. My eyes prickled with the hot sting of tears, and sorrow took hold of my throat and held it fast; I gasped, and a stifled cry escaped me.

How could I tell him when we'd come so far?

For thirteen long years, he'd listened to news of his brother's increasing madness and boundless hatred for magic born, and he could do nothing for them but wither away his youth in exile, the Raven King of Asperfell, as they'd called him. By the time I made his acquaintance, he was a bitter, broken thing and would have nothing to do with my impossible quest. I'd thought him hateful then; cruel and derisive and arrogant. It was only after I'd learned of the great pains he had once taken to escape Asperfell and return to his people, and the cost of his failure, and the years after spent giving of himself to make it right, that I understood: he'd endured so much, and lost so much, that the thought of hope again was not to be borne. But I'd not allowed him a choice. He'd risen from ashes long grown cold by *my* hand, my bidding, and become a king once more.

Elyan closed his eyes. "We fail, then. There is no path for us home."

"There is a path," I whispered. "For some of us."

Elyan looked up, and his eyes were not distant, nor cold. He reached out his hand, brushing his fingertips against my cheek as he pushed a lock of hair away from my face and tucked it behind my ear.

"You must tell them," he said softly. "They deserve to know, and to make their own choice."

"But not you?"

His lips turned up in a bitter smile, and I longed to take his face in my hands and smooth the edges of his mouth with my thumbs and kiss his stubbornness away. "My choice was made long ago," he said.

"So was mine."

I trudged miserably back to camp with Elyan behind me, wondering how I could possibly make Garundel's words sound any less than completely and utterly awful, and found that I could not.

Arlo was just beginning to summon the roots of a cluster of trees that had long ago entwined themselves together, and Thaniel and Phyra were unpacking the food that Garundel had gifted us. Upon seeing my face, they all stopped abruptly and stared at me with wide eyes.

"Oh Gods, what is it?" Arlo's hands dropped to his sides, and the wriggling roots retreated back into the ground. "What's happened?"

"Nothing," I began hesitantly. "Yet, that is."

"Wait!" Arlo shouted, then darted to his pack, where he withdrew the bottle of Laetha, pulled out the cork with a flourish, and took several long swallows. "All right, there," he said. "Now tell us."

Thaniel shook his head in disgust. "Idiot."

I looked to each of my companions in turn, knowing none would choose to turn back, but that only made it all the harder to force myself to speak. "Before we left, Garundel spoke to me. She told me she'd had a vision. About us."

Complete silence filled the clearing.

"A vision about us," Thaniel repeated at last.

I nodded.

"Well, if it was a good one, you wouldn't look as though someone had just died," Arlo said, then he blanched. "Oh Gods," he croaked, and drank again from the bottle, long and deep.

"Death, then," said Phyra softly.

"Not..." My throat was dry, and I had to swallow before I could get the words out. "Not for all of us."

"For who?" demanded Arlo.

"She did not know."

Phyra stood and walked to me, lifted her hands, and put the tips of her fingers on my two cheeks. She meant to comfort me, I am sure of it, but her fingers were so cold. "What were her exact words?" she asked.

"You all know a Scrivener's visions do not always come to pass," I began. "And even if they do, perhaps knowing of it will help us avoid it. That is, unless it cannot be changed, which sounds utterly ridiculous to me—"

"Briony," Thaniel interrupted.

"Yes?"

"Get on with it, will you?"

"Right."

Well, there was nothing for it.

"These were her words," I said, and my voice had shrunk to little more than a whisper. "'*I have seen footsteps leading between this world and your own, but too few. Not all of you will tread that path.*'"

The bottle of Laetha hit the forest floor with a soft thump, and Arlo's head dropped into his hands. Thaniel's brows narrowed in furious thought; already he sought a way to circumvent it, a way he could save us. But Phyra's dark eyes, her unsettling, unfathomable eyes, bore into mine and I could not bear it.

I wanted to tell her that I was sorry. I wanted to tell her that I was so very sorry.

"Well, that's wonderful," Arlo said at last, looking up from his hands. All mirth had gone from his face, a strange sight indeed. "I came with you lot to *escape* certain doom."

"Then it would serve you perfectly right to die in pursuit of your own selfish gains," Thaniel snapped. "Have you really so little honor?"

Arlo snorted. "I don't give a damn about honor."

"Or anything else, for that matter."

"Peace," said Phyra softly, and both men fell silent, though they still continued to glower most sullenly at one another.

"I wish I'd never heard it," I lamented. "And perhaps you wish I'd not told you, but it hardly felt right to keep such a terrible secret."

Elyan put his hand upon my shoulder. "You did right. I do not think that ignorance can ever be an advantage, no matter what the circumstances."

"I, for one, do not prefer to wander around in the dark, even if I do not like what the light reveals," said Thaniel. "And besides, I cannot bring myself to believe that I am nothing more than a pawn being moved here and there by the hands of fate, regardless of my own will. If a prophecy cannot be broken, then life is nothing more than a cruel joke."

"Hear, hear!" said Arlo.

"You actually agree with Thaniel?" I asked.

"Indeed! Life is a cruel joke and nothing more. That's exactly what I've been trying to tell his knightliness all along."

Thaniel let out an exasperated groan. "Can anyone who is currently drunk please keep themselves out of the conversation?"

"Anyone who's not drunk by now isn't paying attention to the conversation," said Arlo, pounding the bottle of Laetha on the ground, making a small geyser pop out of the top.

Thaniel sprang forward, grasping Arlo's tunic in both hands and yanking him to his feet. "Turn back if you want, coward! I stand with Briony," he shouted. Then he shoved Arlo backwards, sending the drunken fool sprawling in the dirt.

"Enough," snarled Elyan, but the fight was already over. Arlo was too drunk to stand back up, and angry as he was, Thaniel was not the type of man to kick an opponent when he was down.

There was no point in trying to carry on the discussion any further that night. We went about the simple task of setting up our camp in silence.

We ate little and spoke even less.

Arlo drank Laetha as though the enchantment might wear off the bottle at any moment, and Elyan and I snapped at one another as we had early in our acquaintance. None of us slept well.

6

For three days we traveled, subdued and wary, through woods steaming and sweltering with the summer. Rich and riotous were the flora and fauna around us, and when I remembered to lift my head and look around me and not huddle within the mire of my thoughts, I often found my breath stolen from me by the beauty of our surroundings. Insects with jewel-bright wings darted to and fro in search of prey, and the underbrush rustled with the citizens of this strange and lovely place, their eyes watching us with curiosity and wariness. The very worst sort of trespassers were we: our blades sharp, the magic in our veins quite deadly; our intentions unknown. Indeed, our bedraggled company by now looked as dangerous as the native creatures no doubt thought us to be, with our travel-roughened clothes and wild, unkempt hair; our drawn, haggard faces and our hollow eyes. Little by little, this land had set its seal upon us.

At our lead, Elyan stopped and thrust his hand sharply into the air. We froze instantly, and in the silence that descended, we heard it: the distant sound of voices shouting, and a roar of pain, a roar that belonged to a creature we knew all too well.

"We're near Syr'Aliem, if the old woman is to be believed,"

Thaniel said to Elyan in a hushed voice. "It may be people of the Forest Kingdom."

"Whoever they are, they stumbled upon a Phaelor," I said.

"An angry one," agreed Thaniel.

"Better them than us," Arlo said. "Let's go around."

"We should help them," I urged Elyan.

"Have you gone mad?" he answered flatly. "Or have you forgotten Garundel's words so soon?"

"Of course I've not forgotten, but listen to them—"

A mighty bellow went up, rousing the birds in the canopy above us into the air, followed by the frantic, frightened shouting of men.

I turned to race toward the noise, and the vice of his hand clamped down on my arm. "Get back here, you little fool, before you endanger us all."

"Let go of me!" I hissed, but when his grip only tightened further, I bared my teeth like the wild thing the forest had made of me and sank them into the flesh of his wrist. He swore quite emphatically, but his fingers slackened—and I darted through the underbrush toward the commotion.

He followed; of course he followed, cursing my recklessness. As the shouting grew louder, the roars of the Phaelor became bellows of pain and rage. And then we were upon them: six valiant knights in gleaming steel armor with billowing green cloaks and filigreed blades at the ready.

Tall and proud and beautiful, they reminded me so much of the guardians of the Citadel that my heart seized at once with an unbearable longing. Elyan, Thaniel, and Arlo stopped abruptly behind me, mouths quite agog as they took in the strange and wonderful sight. But a small, dark figure streaked past us all, and before I could dislodge the scream within my throat, Phyra charged into the clearing, not for the knights but straight at their beleaguered prey.

I had not spared a glance for the Phaelor until then.

It was—impossibly, but without a doubt—the same beast we had encountered six days before.

Maelstrom had left a gaping wound in its chest that had festered with the enchantment placed upon the blade, and its hide was pierced at its shoulders and rib cage in shallow succession. Thaniel had been responsible for these wounds. But beyond this, the shafts of two arrows protruded from its chest, rivulets of blood black as night pooling on the ground below, and, most horribly, a sword had sliced clean across one side of its face and through its eye, grown cloudy now with blindness, but no less fierce.

"Stop!" Phyra shouted, and threw herself upon the huddled body of the bloodied beast.

The soldiers turned to one another in confusion, but then one stepped forward. "Be gone, witch, if you wish to live," he announced in a voice clear and strong. "We have no quarrel with you this day, but the beast is an abomination and must be destroyed."

"Who are you to decide what is an abomination?" asked Phyra.

The soldier raised his sword to point not at the beast, but at her. "Does this creature belong to you, then? Was it you who gave it that unnatural wound?"

"No, that would be me, mate," said Thaniel, stepping forward into the clearing with Maelstrom drawn. "With this."

The soldiers showed no hesitation this time. This was no woodland witch, but a man with a sword—a threat they were well trained for—and they immediately spread into formation around their new enemy.

Turning their backs on the wounded Phaelor, however, was a

grave mistake. One enormous paw connected with the nearest soldier with a sickening crunch of bone, and he was tossed to the ground, limp and head lolling.

His comrades were quick to avenge him. Bellowing, they rushed the beast from both flanks, skewering it with thrust after thrust of their swords. With a shriek of agony, the beast thundered to the ground.

Phyra's retribution was swift. Magefire barreled through the air, and one of the knights was flung aside into a tangle of bushes. The left half of his armor was scotched black, and his long cape was ablaze with bright flames.

"Oh Gods, Phyra!" Thaniel groaned, flinging himself between the Necromancer and the four knights who were still standing.

This was the moment Elyan decided to make his presence known. I know not how he did it, but he brought his hands together in a clap and the sound was like thunder. The leaves of the trees shook, and the birds scattered from their branches. And at once, all eyes were upon him.

"We are not your enemies," he announced. "Lower your weapons and go tend to your men."

He gestured at the two fallen soldiers, and I was relieved to see them both alive. The first was sitting on the ground, helmet off and struggling to unfasten the straps of his battered breastplate, while the other was still trying to disentangle himself from the thorny bushes.

A tall man with craggy features stepped in front of Elyan and held his blade in a dueling stance, though Elyan was not armed with a sword. "Not our enemy," he repeated. "That would be joyful news indeed. Is the Atriyen at last ready to acknowledge the king of Syr'Aliem, then?"

"I know nothing of the Atriyen or your conflict with them,"

Elyan answered. "We are strangers and travelers in this land, passing through on our way north."

A look of utter confusion fell upon the knight's face. "Strangers. Passing through." He seemed to study the gleaming edge of his blade as he considered the words, then he lowered the point to the ground. "Truly?"

Elyan nodded.

"Then you're under arrest."

At this, I jumped forward, revealing myself to the knights. "Arrest! On what charges?"

The knight showed no surprise at my sudden appearance, and I realized he must have noticed me some time ago, and probably the still-cowering Arlo as well. He glanced quickly to my hands and belt, presumably looking for weapons, then answered calmly: "Assaulting a knight in the king's service."

"Oh."

It was, I had to admit, hard to deny our guilt.

Far off in the distance, I heard a cry, a series of whoops and trilling shrieks that made my skin prickle.

"Did everyone else hear that?" asked Thaniel.

It was an unnecessary question, for every single knight within the clearing reacted with immediate fear. Even the two injured men brandished their swords and joined their comrades in a circular formation, eyes darting about the trees in anticipation of something none of us could see.

Elyan inched closer to where Thaniel and Phyra were standing, and I followed him cautiously, listening for another series of whoops and cries. Even Arlo finally jumped up from the underbrush to join us, seeking safety in numbers.

"The Atriyen, I presume," Elyan whispered.

"If an enemy is hunting Syr'Aliem's soldiers, perhaps we ought to help?" I said.

"Can't hurt for the king to owe us a favor," agreed Thaniel.

"We should wait and offer our help to whichever side will win," said Arlo. "Best way to make sure we don't end up on the wrong end of a sword."

A shout went up from the forest. A battle cry.

A dozen men and women—women!—raced from the trees with swords and axes held high. They wore no armor but leather, and their unpolished weapons did not gleam in the sunlight. No smooth and finely crafted blades, these were savage, brutal tools for the killing of men and beasts.

If Syr'Aliem's knights reminded me of home, these warriors were like the Bra'ata. Not soldiers, but a force of nature.

"And this would be our cue to exit," Arlo said. "Immediately."

"We have to help them."

Arlo exploded: "Which *them?*"

Ignoring the protestations of the men on either side of me, Elyan wishing me not to risk my neck and Arlo demanding me not to risk his, I threw myself into the midst of the clashing steel.

I knew nothing of battle save what I had read in stories, and the fine script upon the manuscripts in my aunt's library spoke of chivalry and honor, bloodless thrusts and parries, white flags of surrender billowing upon the breeze of a field in which victory was measured by color: how many wearing one remained standing, and how many of the other would never rise again. I was entirely unprepared for the savagery before me, the raw grunts and screams that rent the air and the dull grating of metal.

These were not new enemies; they hacked and swung and parried one another like old friends engaged in familiar merry dances. The knights were well trained and flawless in form, but they were at once outmatched by the ragged band. I could not say with any certainty why this was, but there was something about these fierce warriors that exuded power. They moved with a fluidity like water, and a swiftness like the wind. And yet, when they took a blow from the knights, they endured it, standing strong and never giving ground.

I watched in horror as they quickly overwhelmed Syr'Aliem's knights.

"Garundel told us to seek Syr'Aliem!" I shouted to Elyan above the horrid din. "We should trust her!"

He nodded once and called to Thaniel: "Aid Syr'Aliem!"

The Alchemist needed no further encouragement before lifting Maelstrom in both hands and charging into the writhing body of the battle. Phyra stared after him a long moment and I thought surely she meant to follow, but she turned abruptly, and dashed to where the Phaelor lay.

I called after her, but she either could not hear me or did not heed me, and when I turned back to the fray, a man was rushing toward me, twin daggers in his hands.

If an umbra had been about, I could've bid it protect me or attack in my name, but I had nothing of the sort. Instead, I conjured what I fervently hoped was a decent shield and darted forward.

My spell for banishment had resulted in disaster back at Asperfell, but I hoped my overenthusiastic efforts might prove somewhat useful here. I sliced my hand sharply through the air, hoping to disperse my enemy and fling him away like dust from my bedroom floor. This did not happen. Rather, my magic reached out to the dirt and leaves and stones at our feet, and a spray of muck flew up between us, pelting the man in the face. It was nothing of consequence, but it did momentarily blind and bewilder him so that his charge faltered. I still rushed forward, crashing into him with my shield before me, knocking him clear off his feet so that he fell mightily, smacking the back of his head upon the hard ground.

My triumph by way of spell gone wrong would no doubt have caused Elyan mortification, so hard had he tried to teach me the proper ways of magic. For myself, I would much rather chuck armfuls of dirt and debris in error than fail to act for fear that my technique would be found wanting.

As for the man himself, there was no magic about for him to siphon, and so he used his own, drawing from the deep well within him and casting it out in great waves that threw the men in his path back into the trees with such force that they did not rise again.

Within moments, the enemies of Syr'Aliem fell back in terror of our brutal magic. They left their dead but gathered the injured as they fled back into the forest, scattering in all directions.

"Spread out!" shouted the man with the craggy features, who seemed to be the captain. "I want one of them alive!"

I did not care overmuch whether they were successful, simply that my companions were unscathed. Blood dripped from Maelstrom into the dirt, and the way Thaniel cradled his injured arm suggested Garundel's careful ministrations might've been ruined, but he seemed otherwise himself.

Elyan sagged down onto one knee, the use of so much of his own magic having left him utterly spent, but he waved me away irritably when I dashed to his side, the loathsome man. "I'm fine, I'm fine. Where is Phyra?"

I stared at him in confusion. "Phyra? I don't know, she—"

And then I remembered: she'd gone to the Phaelor once the melee had begun. I found her kneeling beside the massive carcass, one hand splayed against the lustrous black of its fur, and when she looked up at me, there was little of the woman I knew in her eyes.

"They killed him," she said, and her fingers tightened within the beast's fur. In the golden light of the evening fast approaching, I gasped in amazement at the myriad of colors amidst the black: glimmering violet and gold and lush, rich greens.

And then my eyes fell upon the gaping wound in its chest, at the exposed bone and blackened skin, rotted and bleeding. We'd done this to him, in defense of our own lives. And after he'd fled, he'd found only more frightened men and sharp blades.

"He did not deserve this end," Phyra whispered.

At this, the air in the clearing became very thick and heavy, and I struggled even to open and close my eyes as if my lashes clung to something viscous I could not see. The captain of the knights seemed to slow before my very eyes, his limbs moving through the air as though it were made of honey. Time in the clearing had not stopped; Phyra did not have such power, but as she descended into Death to greet his envoy, the awareness of all living things was heightened, as if our very souls opened themselves fully to this tenuous world, desperate for every sensation and every moment of time.

It was with great difficulty that I turned my head to see the young Necromancer kneeling beside the Phaelor, her eyes closed and her chin raised. Phyra had once told me she saw the realm of Death as shallow water wreathed in fog, stretching as far as the eye could see. I wondered if she were there now.

After what seemed like hours, a tremor passed beneath the skin of the creature, and then, slowly, its chest began to rise and fall as life returned to its body.

Phyra let out a deep shuddering breath, and when her eyes

snapped open, her irises were as completely, utterly black as her pupils. Then she blinked, and they were as they'd been before.

I'd not seen her raise Elyan; I'd been quite occupied with Master Viscario and could not say if the passage of time had stilled or if her eyes had changed so terribly. I wished I'd not seen it now. With what must've been considerable effort given the extent of its injuries, the Phaelor let out a deep groan that shook the very ground on which we stood, and staggered to its feet, rising behind Phyra like an avenging phantom, her unforgiving gaze fixed upon Syr'Aliem's soldiers.

As I watched in horror and fascination, the beast raised its great head and nudged Phyra gently. Weak as she was from the use of so much magic, she stumbled on unsteady legs and reached out to steady herself against the bulk of the massive, ruined creature.

Panicked whispers broke out amongst the soldiers, and the captain pushed through his men with his sword brandished, his eyes full of fear. I scrambled to my feet, ready to defend her however I might, but it was Thaniel who stepped between the captain and Phyra, Maelstrom lifted in warning.

"Go no farther."

At the sight of the mercurial blade churning with magic, the man stopped in his tracks, but he did not take his eyes from Phyra and the Phaelor.

"It is unnatural," he stammered. "Blasphemous!"

"Again, that word," Arlo sighed. "Honestly, I don't think any of you actually knows what it means."

"The beast was dead, and now it lives. 'Tis not possible!"

"It is possible, and it is not blasphemous," Elyan answered evenly. "Lower your weapons, and I will explain."

Unfortunately, the captain did not take Elyan at his word. "To me!" he shouted, and at once, his men fell in behind him, weapons raised.

Elyan sighed at the display. "We come from the Mage prison of Asperfell beyond the Heimslind. I am told you have encountered our kind before, that you know of our magic."

"Not for hundreds of years." The commander gestured at Phyra with his sword, and it did not escape my notice that his hand shook. "And what she did is not magic—it is abhorrent, an anathema to the Incuna."

"Without the aid of our magic, you and your men would be dead," said Elyan. "A little gratitude is in order, I think, but if that is too much to ask, then I suggest you take us before your king so we may discuss all such matters with him. We are under arrest, are we not?"

The captain considered Elyan's request in silence for a moment before nodding curtly. "I serve His Most High above all, and I believe he would be most keen to make your acquaintance."

His Most High? I very dearly hoped Elyan never expected me to call him that, because I absolutely would not.

"Excellent," Elyan said.

"Wait," I interjected. Though I had no fear of these six soldiers against the might of our magic, placing ourselves at the mercy of their king in his own castle was another thing entirely. Given the way these soldiers looked upon Phyra, there was every possibility the king would order her execution on the spot. "Perhaps we should discuss this amongst ourselves—"

Elyan did not spare me a glance. "We accept," he told the captain, "and wait upon your lead."

"Elyan—"

"Enough!"

Everything about him was sharp in that moment, from his tongue to the way his eyes narrowed, every inch the king these men had no idea he was. He spoke to me in that moment not as a woman for whom he held considerable affection, nor as an exasperating pupil, nor even as a vexing thorn in his side, but as his subject. And in mortification, my lips snapped shut and my cheeks burned.

With reluctance, Arlo lifted his palms from the ground, where he'd been holding at the ready the branches of a rather large tree above the soldiers' heads. The tree groaned slowly back upright, then shook its branches with a delicate shiver. He stood, brushing the dirt and forest ephemera from his hands.

The captain of the knights removed his helmet, revealing short-cropped gray hair to match his craggy face. "I am Commander Nidaan," he told us. "This is Rimuel, my second."

He gestured to a lanky young man behind him with a long face and hair the color of hay.

"I am Elyan of House Acheron from the land beyond the Gate," Elyan answered. "And these are my companions: Thaniel, Arlo, Briony..." He paused. "And Phyra."

She still stood beside the Phaelor, and despite a few cautious glances toward us, the eyes of Syr'Aliem's soldiers had not left her, as though they expected her to use what they clearly saw was the darkest of magic against them. Unfortunately, Phyra offered little in the way of reassurance, staring back at them with a face of stone, unyielding and unforgiving. I may have imagined it—the dappled light of the late afternoon cast us all in peculiar shadows—but her eyes seemed different somehow, as if some small part of the black they'd been after the rising had remained within the natural brown of her irises.

The commander's eyes slid from Elyan to Phyra and his men

shifted uneasily as he studied her, the mountains and plains of his weathered face the field upon which instinct battled with reason and duty.

"We depart at once, but... the creature must remain."

Phyra wanted to argue; her eyes widened and her hands dug deeper within the iridescent fur of the Phaelor. But Thaniel spoke to her gently: "It is a wild thing, Phyra. Let him return to his life. After all, he has you to thank for it."

She pressed her lips in a flat line, and for one horrifying moment, I feared she meant to refuse. Her fingers tightened in the Phaelor's fur, and then, after a long moment in which every soul in the clearing seem to be teetering on the edge of something untoward, Phyra relaxed and took a single step forward; her hand fell to her side.

Between the wounds our magic had inflicted and those caused by Syr'Aliem's weapons, the sorry creature was utterly ravaged in its second life, and I had the uneasy feeling that wounds such as these would never heal. The scorched, peeling edges of its ghastly red flesh marred the once lustrous, oily fur, and the sight of its ribs, raw and gleaming white with sinew, filled me with revulsion. We had caused these wounds, we and Syr'Aliem's soldiers, and now we would abandon it to its fate, reborn at a cost we knew not; Phyra had never spoken of the bargain she'd made with Death's envoy when she'd returned Elyan to life, and little had been written about Necromantic magic in Asperfell's library. Even Elyan himself with his royal education had learned disappointingly little throughout his studies. Evidently Necromancers guarded their secrets carefully.

Commander Nidaan and his men watched the Phaelor with utmost weariness as we gathered our supplies, fallen in disarray behind the nearby bushes. Before long, we were ready to be on our way to Syr'Aliem.

Well, most of us were ready.

It was with great reluctance that Phyra finally stepped away from the ruined creature, taking her pack and cloak from Thaniel with arms of lead and a dour face. Casting one last, longing look behind her, she began to walk away.

The Phaelor followed.

A great shout went up amongst the men of Syr'Aliem, and a half-dozen swords slid free of their scabbards with a metallic slither, our reluctant truce ended in a single moment. Phyra whirled around, her palms raised high into the air in supplication.

"No, stop!" she cried, and I did not know whether she addressed man or beast, for she was caught between the two and Thaniel's hand was full of flame.

"Hold your swords, for Coleum's sake," he shouted in desperation to the soldiers. "You are in no danger!"

And Elyan and Arlo were shouting, too, and I was shrill above them all, begging them not to hurt my friend, that the Phaelor did not mean to harm them, as if they knew what the word meant.

As the creature watched, she pointed sharply at the ground at its feet, the myriad of emotions upon her face testament enough to what she desired of it, and what it cost her. It was a sort of speech, I supposed, and the Phaelor appeared to understand it. Lifting one enormous paw and then the other, it retreated from Phyra's shaking hand, head hunched low, and no one present could possibly fail to see the agony in its eyes. Once in their gleaming they'd filled us with terror; now they were as the winter sky, a terrible, bleak expanse of white clouds tainted with blooming gray.

The Phaelor lowered its body to the ground and watched in perfect stillness as Phyra wrapped her cloak tightly about herself and walked away.

Commander Nidaan sent two of his soldiers ahead to inform their king and his court of our impending arrival. The palace walls were but an hour's walk, we were told, and as we marched, I shed my cloak and wantonly turned my face to the dappled sunlight. All around me, soft birdcalls and the rustling of leaves mingled with the sound of armor and heavy footfalls.

The knights' armor really was quite beautiful, gold and whisper thin, with delicate etchings of vines and leaves. At the center of their breastplates and shields was a curious design: a sphere held fast by thick, curling branches that grew into a throne as they rose. Garundel had drawn it for us crudely in the dirt, but here it was etched in exquisite detail.

I asked the soldier nearest me: "The symbol on your shield, what is it?"

"The Incuna and the throne of Syr'Aliem."

"And what is the Incuna?"

My question was met with determined silence, and I pulled a face at his back.

As we drew nearer the palace, the air around us grew not merely warmer but heavier somehow, and I found myself stretching my hand languidly in front of me to slide my fingers through it like the silken gowns of my childhood.

Everything felt lovely and heavy and full, and I could not seem to stop the smile that spread across my face.

"Do you feel that?" I asked no one in particular, and my voice sounded far away and dreamy. Beneath my skin, my magic began to stir quite unbidden, and I pressed my hands to my cheeks, finding them unaccountably warm. "I feel strange."

Beside me, Arlo grinned, and I smelled green in the air. "So do I. It's rather wonderful, isn't it?"

It was indeed wonderful—a golden happiness that made me slow and languorous. My steps felt lighter; indeed, I quite felt like dancing. How odd! I laughed suddenly, then pressed the back of my hand to my mouth to stifle the sound and I tasted my magic.

"I have no idea what you two are on about," Thaniel grumbled. "I feel wretched."

"As do I." Phyra's voice was little more than a whisper.

Elyan turned swiftly to the soldier behind him. "The change in the air," he demanded. "What is causing it?"

"What change?"

"Damn it, man, the air!" Thaniel barked. I turned to see Phyra slumped against him, her face shockingly pale and pinched in pain. "Something's wrong with it!"

Ahead, Commander Nidaan glanced back at us. "We're nearing the palace and the heart of the Incuna."

"But why should that make her ill?"

"I told you, her magic is unnatural," he grunted, not bothering to hide his disgust. "Perhaps the Incuna does not favor her."

I pointed my finger at him, swaying slightly. "Well, that is most impolite of it." Goodness, when had I become intoxicated?

"Have other visitors to your kingdom ever felt thus?" Elyan asked.

The commander shrugged. "We are a kingdom under siege by those savages in the forest. Few visitors ever reach us from the north. And from the south, well... you are the first in my lifetime," he answered. "No one has crossed the Heimslind since your lot first came here, all those years ago."

I tugged on Elyan's sleeve. "The magic here flows from the land to the king," I whispered. "Perhaps it favors growing things."

"Well, that would certainly explain a lot."

Arlo held his hands in front of him, and the silvery light of his magic churned beneath the surface of his skin. The verdant smell of him fairly filled my nostrils, and everything about him seemed wilder: his hair, his eyes, his very skin. When first I'd met him, presiding over a game of Flisket at the Melancholy Revels, I'd imagined that, crowned with laurel, he would've made a fine fresco on the faded white walls of an ancient manor on Iluviel's coast, with his laughing hazel eyes and wide, smiling mouth. Now, he could've been one of Sator's tricksters, robbing men of their favors and women of their virtue.

Thaniel gaped. "Coleum's balls, what's happening to you?"

"I have no idea," Arlo answered. "What do I look like? Do I look sharp? I feel sharp."

"You look like a dryalis."

I failed to see how this was an insult, for everything I'd ever read about dryalises in the library at Orwynd made them sound positively lovely, if somewhat vicious, but evidently Arlo did not agree, for his face grew murderous.

"I can think of quite a few words to describe how you look right now, but every single one of them means shite," he said. "Give Phyra to me. I feel as strong as an ox, and you look as though one good round would do you in."

Indeed, the Incuna did not seem to approve of Thaniel, and it was no wonder, for his magic no doubt bore the stench of metal and smoke.

Arlo swung Phyra into his arms as though she weighed no more than a child's poppet, and although she endured it with as much decorum as she could, the discomfiture on her face was plain. Her dark hair clung to the pale, damp skin of her face and neck, and

I began to fear there would be no need for the king of Syr'Aliem to order her execution, for the very air of his kingdom might accomplish the task first.

"You seem cheerful enough," Thaniel said as he glanced balefully at me. "I suppose speaking magic is more natural than Alchemy."

If that were the case, the Incuna had not taken into account exactly what sort of magic I usually spoke with.

We walked on, we citizens of Tiralaen, and the magic within our blood churned in response to whatever it was in the air that set it aflame, called to it, made it sing. I felt keenly for Phyra and Thaniel, the former of whom was positively overcome, much to the latter's dismay. As such, I attempted to conceal as best I could how positively lovely I felt, but oh, how strange it was, and not entirely unwelcome.

The peculiarity of the Incuna and its effect on our magic did not, unfortunately, cease as we drew near Syr'Aliem's borders, but neither did it intensify; a small mercy, that, for I did not believe Phyra could bear much more. Perhaps we'd become accustomed to it; perhaps its effects were only so potent. None could say except those whom we'd journeyed to see. As lush and teeming with life as the forest that surrounded their kingdom was, someone in Syr'Aliem was bound to know herb lore and, with luck, a cure, for I very much doubted Phyra would wish to be carried to and fro like a sack of grain for the duration of our journey.

I'd no inkling of what he was saying, for his voice was pitched low, his cadence easy and free, but Arlo had been talking to Phyra for some time now, to lighten her mood, I suspected, or distract her from her pain. Every once and a while, I heard her soft voice followed by Arlo's laughter, and when I glanced back, I was pleased to see a modicum of color had returned to her cheeks, though I worried still at the crease between her brows.

The path before us began to widen and soon met with a well traveled road of cobblestones. The crossroad was flanked by four men bearing Syr'Aliem's peculiar sigil upon their shields, and they stared at our bedraggled company with unabashed curiosity. While Commander Nidaan exchanged a few hushed words with them, Elyan drew close to me once more.

"I thought by now we understood each other fairly well," he said, his voice pitched low so that our escort would not hear us. "But you appear determined to believe I care nothing for Phyra's safety, and you are wrong."

"One or more of us is walking toward our death," I hissed. "You know that! And you see how the knights of Syr'Aliem hate her. Can you really believe she will be safe amongst them?"

"You were the one who wanted to rush to their aid."

"That was before I saw how they reacted to Phyra's magic. Look at her, Elyan. Look at her face. I am afraid for her, and I want to flee with her, as far and as fast as we can, away from this place and its people."

"We need them, Briony. The only path forward is through Syr'Aliem."

"Why? We can find the cave on our own."

"No, we cannot."

At this, I finally looked up at him. It was the first time he'd spoken thus, and it gave me pause. "Why do you say so?"

"Garundel's maps."

"What did you find?" I asked.

"This forest is vast," he whispered, bending down so that his lips very nearly brushed my ear. "'Tis as large as any ocean in our world.

We cannot hope to find the cave by chance alone. We could wander our entire lives without coming within a hundred miles of it. We do not even know what signs to seek."

"And you believe they have such knowledge in Syr'Aliem?"

He shook his head almost imperceptibly. "That I cannot say. But a kingdom that outfits its soldiers so extravagantly is likely in possession of a library that may hold the answers we seek."

"Am I permitted to disagree?" I asked. "Or have you grown so mighty now that I may no longer offer my opinion without fearing you shall grow a set of fearsome teeth and relieve me of my head?"

"Certainly you can," he snapped. "But not in public, or in front of men who would be led by your example. How am I ever to be seen as a king if my companions so easily contradict my decisions? We are not in Asperfell anymore, Briony. You must understand that."

"Then I am most unfortunate, for according to my Aunt Eudora contradiction comes as naturally to me as breathing."

He groaned. "For Coleum's sake, Briony. Do you plan to throw yourself at the feet of the king of Syr'Aliem as a beggar and escaped convict? Or would you rather that I entreat with him as the king of Tiralaen in exile?"

I was, I had to admit, stunned into silence, for I had not considered what we would say to the king, save the plain and straightforward truth.

"We may not look it, but we are, from this moment on, a delegation from the kingdom of Tiralaen, here to negotiate with a foreign power and establish a friendship between our peoples."

I might have laughed in Elyan's face had he not been so incredibly earnest. Instead, I raised a skeptical eyebrow and gestured toward our companions, only one of whom was capable of walking steadily on his own feet, and that one being a gambler and lout.

"Us?"

"Indeed."

"I am not known for being diplomatic."

"Fortunately, I am long and well trained in the art." He touched his long fingers beneath my chin and lifted my face toward his. "Briony, I will want and need your counsel in the coming days, but even more so, I need your trust. Promise me that you stay your contrary tongue whilst in the company of the king of Syr'Aliem and do nothing to interfere with our business here."

"Have you considered that I am not, in fact, contrary, but that everyone else is simply wrong?"

"You will be the death of me," he answered through teeth clinched tight.

I smothered the grin that threatened to bloom upon my lips and conceded: "Fine. I shall try."

"Promise me."

Affecting an exaggerated tone that I hoped properly conveyed my exasperation, I sighed: "*I promise.*"

We walked on in companionable silence; indeed, I found it quite impossible to maintain an ill mood while breathing in the giddy magic in the air. And when I felt his eyes upon me inquiringly, I offered him a small smile, and he returned it in kind. He truly was a most beautiful man when he smiled.

We followed Commander Nidaan and his men for a mile more until our path emerged abruptly from the forest upon the most enormous wall I had ever seen. Not even the gleaming white stone that surrounded the Citadel at the heart of the Shining City could compare; indeed, I could scarce glimpse the top for its superior height, rising proudly above the canopy of the trees.

The masonry was fine; too fine to not have been fortified by some

manner of magic, but even more extraordinary than that, even more
extraordinary than the wall's towering height, was the riot of golden
leaves and coiling vines that climbed the stones, burrowing into
cracks and fissures, grim gifts of age, only to emerge again, and again,
and again, a shimmering web holding fast Syr'Aliem's battlements.
Remembering the commander's words about the lack of visitors to
this land and considering the lack of any other settlements nearby,
I wondered why such extraordinary fortifications were necessary.
Surely the men and women of the forest, for all their peculiar grace,
were not so very dangerous? Their weapons had seemed positively
benighted by comparison.

Set into the wall, and flanked by five heavily armed soldiers on
each side, was a large wooden door bearing the same symbol as that
on the knights' shields. Commander Nidaan spoke to them, and they
could not help but cast curious glances at us as we passed beyond the
door into a tunnel through the wall, which was as thick as a farmer's
cottage. We emerged into the sunlight once more, and here the road
beneath our feet was of polished stone, gleaming and painstakingly
tended. It led into an expanse of greensward, also meticulously kept
and dotted with trees and statues, fountains and topiaries. Again, the
Citadel of the Shining City was put to shame by its beauty.

At the end of our path, walls of white stone rose, gleaming with
the rich, golden light of the swiftly fading afternoon: the palace of
Syr'Aliem. I felt swift disappointment that we were to be brought
in through what appeared to be a service tunnel, for it was guarded
by no one, traveled by no one; but we were, after all, criminals and
could hardly expect fanfare and ovations.

Commander Nidaan led us beneath a portico and through a set
of sturdy doors, and at last we entered the palace of the Forest
Kingdom.

7

When Garundel had called this place the Forest Kingdom, I'd
expected a place as ancient and decrepit as Asperfell, claimed by
trees and carpeted by moss and toadstools. I'd expected saplings
taking root between uneven stones, curling lovingly about
crumbling archways hung with curtains of vines and glowing with
the same pinpricks of whirling light we'd grown accustomed to on
our travels through this strange land. I'd expected loam and rot and
decay beneath my feet, and shadows upon my skin.

Rather, the palace's gleaming walls were tessellated with gilt
and filigree finer than anything I'd seen since my childhood within
the walls of the Citadel, and I gasped in delight.

Alcoves of Magefire did not light the halls we traveled; in their
place, sconces dripping with crystals were filled with orbs of gold,
their hearts aglow, and even though Commander Nidaan shouted
at me and Elyan's face dropped into his hand with a groan, I could
not help darting forward to inspect one, close enough to ascertain
that they provided heat as well as light, though not close enough to
burn my fingers, for what magic was contained within them
repelled my touch.

We climbed a set of spiraling stairs, and then another, until we reached a wide hall with such magnificent vaulting that a gasp was wrenched even from Elyan, who had lived for years within such splendor. To our right, windows of stained glass from floor to ceiling depicted stories and figures unknown to me; to our left, a large pair of handsomely carved wooden doors were set into a marble wall; and beneath our feet, intricate tile mosaics stretched on and on.

Above our heads hung enormous gold and crystal chandeliers lit by hundreds of the same gold orbs we'd passed in the lower corridors, saturating every corner with light such that no shadow dared creep near.

Behind me, Arlo whistled low.

Commander Nidaan led us not to the grand doors but through a small archway at the far end of the hall, and we passed into a sitting room with walls of deepest green. To one side, the entire breadth of the room was covered by a tapestry depicting a comely youth playing a stringed instrument for a woman at his feet, as animals unknown to me crept forth from the forest to rest their heads upon her lap, as entranced by the music as she.

Across from the tapestry, an enormous fireplace with panels of intricately carved stone held not flames but an enormous sphere of green and gold, warmth and light radiating from it, the same marvelous magic that had lit the hallways below. Before it stood two couches richly appointed in ivory brocade and a low round table of dark wood between them. Arlo lay Phyra there at once, keeping hold of her arm as she sank down, her face pinched with pain and exhaustion.

"Rimuel has, by now, informed the king of your arrival, but he will wish to hear from me directly," Commander Nidaan informed us. "Please, make yourselves comfortable."

He bowed stiffly and left us blessedly alone.

"How do you feel?" Thaniel asked Phyra as he brushed her cheek with the knuckles of his hand.

"I'll be all right," she sighed. "It is the magic of this place. It does not suit me, but I believe I am becoming used to the effects."

"If I could but trade places with you, my dear, I most certainly would," said Arlo, who had spied a looking glass upon the wall and was quite absorbed in his appearance, turning his head this way and that, frowning at the subtle change in his features. "Gods, why has it affected me so?"

Elyan shrugged. "I could not say with certainty. But as Phyra's magic lies with death and yours with life, or some form thereof, it appears that whatever magic permeates this place, it prefers the later. Whatever the case, we must hope it does not affect our magic overmuch. We cannot know what wonders they may perform with theirs."

"Right," Thaniel said, as Arlo abandoned the mirror and slumped onto the opposite bench. "Well, if we are to be brought before this sovereign of theirs, we need some sort of a plan. No doubt that Rimuel fellow already informed the king of what transpired in the forest, and Commander Nidaan is corroborating his tale."

"They know we're criminals," Arlo pointed out. "Between that and the Phaelor, they may already be preparing their cells. If not their gallows."

I looked up at Elyan, leaning against the carved stone of the hearth, and remembered our conversation in the forest, how very badly he believed we needed Syr'Aliem's aid if we were to ever find the cave.

"We protest our innocence, Elyan and Phyra and I, and then we vouch for the content of your character," I declared.

"Earlier today, his highness threatened to punch me in the face."

"I still might."

It was at that most unfortunate moment that the door opened and we five turned at once. Commander Nidaan had returned, and he had brought another man with him.

He was portly, of middling years, and wore sumptuous garments of celadon shot through with gold brocade. Gems glittered on his fingers and ears, and his moustache was curled and tipped with what appeared to be gold paint. I'd not seen a person so lavishly adorned since my childhood in the Shining City, and even then, his ornamented person quite eclipsed any of them.

"My name is Fellior," he told us with an air of superiority I found not at all surprising given the audacity of gold upon his person. "I am the Steward of Syr'Aliem, and I have been charged with bringing you before King Anwar, the Dowager Queen, his mother, the Princess Evolet, his sister, and the Court Eternal.

The king of Syr'Aliem intended to make a spectacle of us, it seemed.

"Could not a private audience be arranged with his highness?" Elyan asked. "As you can see, we are in no fit state to stand before such illustrious company."

"No," the Steward answered peevishly. "The king and his court desire your company *now*. He is most excited to make your acquaintance."

My heart fluttered within my chest as Fellior led us from the sitting room, the magic in my blood all alight with the memory of the last time I was brought before a king, before a court. The bones in my face had nearly been ground to dust upon the floor, and I'd been sent through the gate to Asperfell for my trouble. We knew nothing of this king other than his appetite for extravagance; in my experience, however limited, this was rarely a sign of a ruler that favored those less fortunate.

The gallery that led to the throne room was even grander than the one before, but I could little see its beauty for the mounting fear within. My eyes were fixed upon the enormous doors wrought from pure gold at its end, and as we drew nearer, I could hear the sound of voices, the strains of music, and tinkling of glass. We had, it seemed, interrupted a most splendid party. Fellior nodded to the two men who stood at attention there, and together, they pulled the doors open.

The voices of the Court Eternal trailed off and fell silent as they became aware of our presence, and as the lovely strains of stringed instruments sputtered, hundreds of pairs of eyes turned in our direction.

They were astonishingly beautiful, every one of them, and I could not help but stare. I'd never seen such splendid company, and yet my cheeks flamed as I beheld them, for too much of their skin was bared to the candlelight, and what remained was covered by the most shockingly sheer fabric, in a variegated riot of color. Their skin shone like the richest metals, from shades of palest silver to deepest bronze and darker still, and about their eyes and down their graceful necks were painted cunning designs to flatter the eye.

They all wore jewelry, even the men, and I imagined the sum of what decorated their persons could fund an entire kingdom for generations. I nearly laughed at my absurdity for thinking Fellior was well adorned. Gems and precious metals dripped from necks and ears and wrists and were woven into the elaborate coiffures of the ladies in all manner of diadems and headdresses, and I wondered that their shoulders did not stoop with the weight of such wealth.

Although it did not seem possible, the room in which they gathered was even more striking than its company.

Its domed ceiling revealed a night awash with stars through glass panes held together with achingly delicate gold filigree. They shone upon a floor of polished white stone shot through with glimmering veins of gold, bearing intricate patterns no mere mason could have conjured; no, there had been magic in the making of this place, I was certain of it.

Columns lined the circular space, and beyond them, small vestibules draped with hanging vines and twinkling lights where men and women lounged on cushions and sipped from crystal flutes with impossibly long and beautifully wrought stems. The same brilliant orbs of gold I'd seen before lit their indiscretions, playing upon sly faces that were in the same breath curious and condescending.

Beyond them all, at the head of the breathtaking room, was an enormous throne carved from rich, dark wood, its back rising in a twisted coil of branches. Beautiful and wild, it was an arresting counterpoint to the opulence of the room it presided over, almost savage in its imposing stature, and I found that I quite preferred it to everything else I'd seen thus far of this strange place, though I could not rid myself of the feeling that there was something iniquitous about it; that it did not belong in such a place as this.

Upon this savage throne sat the King of Syr'Aliem.

He was a handsome man indeed, of an age with Elyan, or perhaps slightly older. His skin and hair were of richest amber, and his mouth, wide and sensual, seemed oft used to smiling.

He was flanked by two smaller thrones made of white stone, and though lesser in size, these seemed much more in keeping with the opulent grandeur of the palace than the king's seat. Upon them sat two women: one young and one old.

The older must've been the Dowager Queen, King Anwar's

mother, and she could only be described as handsome so strong were her features. Her tall, silver crown, set perfectly atop hair the same shade as her son's, had faded and become soft with time, but her eyes were shrewd and sharp. Standing just behind her throne was a fascinating reed of a man, tall and slender and hollow-eyed, holding a velvet cushion upon which sat what appeared to be a doll, quite large and incredibly lifelike. The leonine figure was a man in the prime of his life with a mane of tawny hair and golden eyes, and he was dressed in clothing as fine as any member of the Court. A crown similar to the one upon the head of the king sat upon its brow.

'Twas the strangest thing I had ever seen, and I'd spent many an afternoon in Asperfell's cemetery with Perkin.

With difficulty, I tore my gaze from the doll and looked at the younger woman, who was undoubtedly Princess Evolet, and I thought that perhaps she favored her father rather than her mother, for milk and honey was the princess of Syr'Aliem. Among a sea of beautiful gowns, hers was by far the most exquisite: shades of purple gauze that darkened as the gown descended to her feet, and with a delicate girdle of gold flowers and vines. More gold flowers adorned her hair, wrought into a towering crown that sat perfectly atop an elaborate coiffure of hair nearly the same shade. She gave us a dazzling smile, and the tiny scattering of gems that surrounded her brown eyes sparkled in the candlelight.

The eyes of the Court Eternal feasted upon us as we began the journey across the marbled floor to stand before their sovereigns, and although we wore the simplest of traveling garments and no doubt appeared as filthy and road weary as we felt, they stared at us with as much interest as we did them, eyes wide and rapt, whispering excitedly to one another.

To my very great surprise, my magic began to stir within my

veins, and the nearer we drew to the throne, the more insistent I felt its thrum. And as I looked around at the striking company around me, I realized that there were Mages among them.

"Do you feel that?" I whispered excitedly to Elyan.

He inclined his head, the briefest of acknowledgement, and then we were standing before the king of Syr'Aliem.

He smiled at us, his teeth white and gleaming. "Welcome, prisoners of Asperfell."

Elyan bowed, not the bow of a subject to a king, but that of deferential respect to an equal, and I sunk into what I hoped was not too horrid a curtsey.

"Your highness," Elyan said. "We thank you."

"I am King Anwar of Syr'Aliem," he said. "This is my mother, the Dowager Queen Urenna, and my sister, the Princess Evolet."

King Anwar looked to us then, and in the breathless hush that followed, Elyan stepped forward. His clothing was plain, his traveling cloak well-worn despite its intricate spellwork; he was far too tall, too sharp, too devastating to ever be called merely handsome. He was every inch a king, equal to the man who rose above us, sprawled upon his wild throne. Unfortunately, no one but we who traveled with him knew it. Elyan, possessed of pride and arrogance despite his many years of exile, must've felt heavily the humiliation at having appeared less than his exalted position demanded.

"I am Elyan of House Acheron, the rightful King of Tiralaen."

King Anwar leaned forward, a playful curiosity in his smile. "So, a prince, then."

Elyan tilted his head, his expression unchanging, though I knew it cost him dearly. "If you like."

"I am told a bit of your extraordinary tale, but I am eager to hear more. Indeed, I believe we all are. Are you truly from Asperfell?"

"We are."

The room around us erupted in delighted gasps and a flurry of chatter. "I must confess, I did not quite believe Rimuel when first he told me," said the king. "The long years have rendered Asperfell little more than a bedtime story told to children to frighten them away from the southern woods. How long has it been—two hundred years? Three?" He looked to Fellior with raised eyebrows.

The steward cleared his throat. "Two hundred and fifty-seven, your highness."

"You are, as you see, the stuff of legend. You must be Mages of extraordinary skill indeed to have escaped when so few have ever done so. Asperfell is still a prison, is it not? Come now—tell us first what you have done to warrant your imprisonment."

Elyan's jaw clenched. He disliked speaking of such matters even with me; I could little imagine him keen to discuss his brother's betrayal in a roomful of strangers, however fine their jewels and silks. "I was falsely accused of taking my father's life," he said at last, his words sharp and clipped. "When, in fact, it was my younger brother who coveted my birthright."

Scintillated gasps and shrieks broke out around us, and though they feigned some modicum of scandalized horror, they were smiling, whispering to one another with little effort to conceal it. I'd learned quite unpleasantly during my time at Asperfell that even the highest born could scarce resist the shocking and macabre, particularly when there was no possibility of it affecting them whatsoever.

King Anwar's eyes glittered. "A tempting prize, to be sure. I must consider myself fortunate, then, that I have but a sister."

If Princess Evolet objected to his careless disparagement, she gave no indication as the Court Eternal broke out in uproarious laughter.

"And the rest of your companions?"

"Their stories are most unfortunately woven within the tapestry of mine, your highness," Elyan said. "Two are innocent entirely, and the other two are guilty only of resisting my brother's tyrannical reign. None amongst our company mean you or your court the slightest harm. On this, I give you my word."

The word of a criminal, Garundel had said.

The word of a prince.

And he was both.

Elyan then recounted our story in brief, leaving out the matter of Master Viscario entirely. Arlo and Thaniel's shared history made Anwar's court sigh and gasp even as the two men stood glaring at one another during the telling of it; Phyra's made them uneasy. Mine, they found positively riveting, and I shifted uncomfortably under the weight of their penetrating eyes as Elyan's deep, measured voice laid bare how I'd come to learn I was a Mage only hours before being thrust through the Gate into his world.

"And this magic of yours..." King Anwar leaned forward on his throne of tangled wood. "It comes from within you, is that so?"

"It does, your highness."

"In your blood."

The Court Eternal waited upon our answer with hands clutched tightly around the stems of crystal glasses, their faces rapt and desperate.

"Yes."

"The stories are true, then," the king said, with the smile of a man well satisfied. "We have among us descendants of your kind, though they do not well understand their own gifts, nor are they properly trained in them. Our attempts to awaken their talents have been entirely unsatisfactory. It is sad, I think, to let such potential lie dormant and wasted. I am sure you have much to teach us. For instance, the stories say Mages like yourself each have a particular gift within them. A special talent, if you will." He cocked a playful eyebrow. "Is this true?"

A murmur rippled through the crowd, and there was no mistaking that the eyes of the Court Eternal were turned now upon Phyra.

Elyan allowed the silence to lengthen before he answered: "It is."

"Well, we certainly do not need to raise the dead," the king laughed, and his court answered in kind. "But the rest of you, well..." He paused. "It would be a great honor indeed to see your magic this night."

I exchanged a swift, dismayed look with Elyan. Did they truly expect us to perform tricks for their amusement?

I had thought it much more likely that the king would view us as vagabonds and escaped criminals rather than a visiting delegation of dignitaries as Elyan seemed to hope. That we might be invited before the court for their entertainment, as if we were nothing more than a traveling band of minstrels and mummers, was the furthest thought from my mind.

Quite apart from the indignity and impropriety of the request, it was entirely impractical. Neither my aptitude nor Elyan's could be demonstrated without a person or creature imbued with magic, and Thaniel required materials most specific to demonstrate his.

Arlo's aptitude, at least, could be easily proven by what surrounded us, and he was ever the most eager of us to enjoy the praise of an audience.

"Your highness, some of us possess magic that cannot easily be shown," Elyan said. "However, we have among our company a Mage whose skill lies in the flora of the natural world. He would be pleased to demonstrate his aptitude for your court."

To my surprise, Arlo did not immediately step forward. "I don't like this," he hissed. "Everything green here is smothered."

At this, I looked around at the room anew. Indeed, the walls were so decorated with gilt and glass and all manner of finery that I had difficulty believing his aptitude might thrive here at all.

"Just do it, Bryn!" Thaniel muttered.

Arlo swore heartily under his breath and approached the three thrones.

"Your name?" the Dowager Queen asked. It was the first I'd heard her speak, and her voice was deep and resonant.

"Arlo Bryn, your highness," he answered and, the fiend, he winked! "I am a Naturalist. My power lies in growing things."

Sweeping his traveling cloak behind him, Arlo dropped to his knees and placed both hands upon the fine floor, and for a very long moment, I feared nothing would happen. But all Arlo needed was time; time to find the growing things beneath the weight of gold and stone. At last, something stirred at the edge of my vision.

The dark, glossy leaves in the ornate pots that flanked the sumptuous room began to rush and slither, tumbling over each other as their vines grew with astonishing speed and spilled out of their confinement in a torrent.

The glittering women shrieked in delight and lifted their skirts as the vines snaked past their ankles and coiled about the columns, stretching and grasping. As the excitement of the crowd rose to a fever pitch, I could not only smell the green of his power, I could taste it.

King Anwar rose from his throne, his face alight. "Remarkable!" he breathed. "Truly remarkable!"

Applause broke out among the Court Eternal, and I expected Arlo to bask in such lavish attentions. Instead, I was surprised to find him quite subdued, as though he were uncomfortable, and I could not account for it at all.

"And what of the rest of you?" King Anwar asked eagerly. "Come, now—do not be shy!"

Thaniel stepped forward, determined, it seemed, to keep the king's focus well enough away from the Necromancer at his side. "I am an Alchemist, your highness. I manipulate metals and other elements," he explained, drawing Maelstrom from its scabbard and holding the churning, mercurial blade up that the assembled company might see the many splendid colors that swirled and rippled across its surface. "I am particularly talented with weapons."

"Most impressive," the king murmured. "And what can this sword do other than appear formidable?"

Thaniel smiled indulgently. "Your Highness, Maelstrom can pierce any metal known to you, and its blade holds spells of poison, if I will it, or of sleep, or madness."

"Truly?"

"Truly."

The king's hungry gaze fell upon me then, and his smile widened.

"And what of your gifts?" he asked. "Surely they must reside within the flames, what with the... unusual color of your hair."

It had not escaped my notice that not a single man or woman among the dazzling crowd possessed a riot of hair the color of my own, nor a face full of freckles.

I lifted my chin. "They do not," I answered. "Indeed, I should hate for something as inconsequential as my appearance to have any bearing upon my skill."

"No? Then your stature has little bearing upon your magic?"

I found it most strange indeed that I could scarcely move

beneath his gaze; I could only stare back at his handsome face, my cheeks aflame.

"No," I said at last. "A Battlemage may be small, an Animalis enormous, it is of little consequence. Our magic cares not, and we have no choice in our aptitude. Thus, we must embrace it whatever it may be."

"And if you should dislike your aptitude? Can it not be changed?"

I'd asked this same question before of a man I once considered a great friend, and been disappointed both in his answer and, later, in him.

"No," said I. "But of all our aptitudes, there is not a single one that any of us should be sorry for."

"And yours?"

"Never."

His smile grew. "Indeed! Come, now, and tell me."

"I am an Orare, your highness," I replied. "I speak to the magic in our world, and as there is none here at present, all I have to offer are parlor tricks, and poor ones at that."

He regarded me thoughtfully. "What is your name, *Orare*?"

"Briony Tenebrae, Your Highness."

"I do not mind parlor tricks, Briony Tenebrae," he told me softly, and his leisurely smile had suddenly become quite sharp. "In fact, I would rather like to see one now."

Before I could answer him, Elyan abruptly cut in: "Mistress Briony is new to her magic. What she refers to as parlor tricks might better be described as small explosions."

The court tittered with laughter at his slight, and I flushed in indignant mortification.

"Perhaps we might discuss my magic instead," he added.

King Anwar's gaze lingered on my flushed face overlong before he lifted his eyes to Elyan and smiled in agreement. "You claim kingship in your own land. Your magic must be very great indeed."

"I do not claim kingship, your highness," Elyan answered, and his carefully measured tone barely concealed fury. "I am a king in my own land by virtue of my birthright."

"And your father—did he have magic? And his father before him?"

"No," Elyan answered. "Magic does always follow the blood as the crown does. It is exceedingly rare."

"And your magic?"

"Rarer still. I am a Siphon. I draw magic into my person."

"And what do you do with this magic once you possess it?"

Elyan's eyes narrowed. "A great many things, your highness."

"Show me."

"Regrettably, I lack a source."

For the first time since we had been brought before the Court Eternal, the Princess of Syr'Aliem spoke: "Did you not tell us that your magic resides within your blood?" She cocked her head with a smile. "Why, then, any of you could be considered a source, could you not?"

It was to avoid this precise predicament, I suspected, that Elyan had been so reticent regarding his abilities.

"Indeed!" King Anwar exclaimed. "I should very much like to see this siphoning of yours." Here, he paused, and his gaze slid from Elyan to my flushed face. "Perhaps Briony would be willing to serve as a source, as her own gifts have been denied us."

For a moment of excruciating tension, I thought Elyan might refuse the king his entertainment, and whatever unpleasantness that followed would be entirely my fault. And so, despite my reluctance to endure a siphoning, for I'd experienced its unpleasantness once before, I stepped forward and laid my hand upon his arm.

"It will be all right," I told him.

It was quite clear from his expression that he did not believe me. Nevertheless, though quite reluctantly, he rested the back of his hand against my cheek, and I felt my magic rise at his unspoken call.

He'd siphoned magic from me once, when we'd knelt together in the snow and together healed the rifts his disastrous attempt at escape had caused in the walls of Asperfell, but I'd been a more willing participant then. Now, my fear rendered my magic far less willing to be parted from me, and rather than a pleasant warmth beneath my skin, I felt a peculiar burning as it resisted.

Unable to support my weight any longer, my shaking legs gave out and I fell to my knees, the veins of gold upon the white stone floor swimming before my eyes, and then, mercifully, the siphoning ended.

His pale skin shining with the gift of my magic, Elyan's dark brows were drawn together in fierce concentration as he brought his palms together until his long fingers steepled. Then, with a deep, shuddering breath, he flung his hands apart. I felt in the very marrow of my bones the promise of so much magic as it barreled toward the glass ceiling in a howling rush.

The glass shattered in spectacular fashion, disintegrating into little more than dust that fell like new snow from the lofty heights of the splendid room, and a great cry went up from the assembly— a horrified, delighted cry.

Then, before the remains of their brilliant glass ceiling could fall upon them, Elyan brought his hands up slowly, so very slowly, above his head, as though he were holding up the night sky itself, and the shimmering dust stood perfectly still as if held aloft by the bated breath of the Court Eternal.

Then the dust began to rise, reforming into slivers and then shards, until they built once more the magnificent ceiling, held fast within delicate golden tendrils as though not even the wind had dared touch it that night.

Elyan opened his eyes, and the cacophony that arose was deafening.

He looked to me at once, and knelt down amidst their wild applause, searching for my hands with his. He helped me gently to my feet, and I swayed and settled against him, exhausted and thoroughly spent.

The man for whose entertainment my magic had been so painfully given leaned forward upon his throne, and it was concern I saw in his amber eyes. "Are you all right, Mistress Briony?"

Elyan's arms tensed about me. "She will be well enough."

I would've scowled at his impudence at having replied for me were it not for the exhaustion settling into my bones.

"Your magic truly is extraordinary," the king was saying. "I've never seen its like. I hope that we may see more of it by and by, in gratitude for our hospitality and assistance. For it is aid you seek, is it not?"

Elyan answered: "Yes, your highness. We made our escape from Asperfell not because we wished freedom for ourselves, but for our people in Tiralaen. We still have a long journey ahead of us, and much work to do when we arrive."

The King of Syr'Aliem studied most carefully our bedraggled company, and his amber eyes lingered upon me longest of all.

"You are welcome here as guests of the Court of Eternal," he said at last. "After all, we've not had occasion to host prisoners from

Asperfell in a very, very long time, and I think it likely we have much to teach each other."

Elyan bowed low, a gesture, this time, of gratitude, and the rest of us followed suit; or, at least, I managed as best I could.

"Fellior," King Anwar said, never taking his eyes from us.

"Yes, Your Most High?"

"Call forth the Tacé and see that the needs of our guests are well and truly met. They are no doubt exhausted from their journey. We will speak further on the morrow."

Fellior turned and gestured sharply, and from the shadows of a nearby column, a cluster of women emerged, all dressed identically in simple gowns of green and brown with no ornamentation save the pleasing patterns woven into their garments that resembled the veins of leaves, an unexpected contrast to the glittering spectacle of the Court Eternal. Upon each of their heads was a veil of white held fast by a woodland circlet of slender green branches woven together, reaching high in uneven spires. Like the throne of their king, there was something jarring about the sight of such natural splendor, both beautiful and unsettling in its savagery, surrounded by pristine elegance.

"Come along, now," Fellior told us primly. "The Tacé have prepared chambers for you."

The Court Eternal began to whisper as we were borne from the throne room through a handsomely carved door, and no sooner had we passed than their voices rose to a clamor that stopped quite abruptly when the door closed.

To my dismay, we were not to be housed together. Once we had passed through corridor after corridor until I could no longer remember the way back to the throne room, Fellior informed us that, due to the large number of guests in the palace that night, there was, unfortunately, a shortage of available chambers, and thus our accommodations lay separate from one another.

Promised a hot bath and supper, Arlo was all too happy to see the backs of the rest of us and gamely followed one of the Tacé down a corridor, chattering away. The Tacé bore his company in perfect silence; in fact, none of them had yet spoken, as if their thin white veils muted their voices entirely.

When Phyra was led away by one of the silent women, however, her face was far less keen, and Thaniel insisted on following her at least to her door.

"Sleep well," Elyan told me, once we were left with the last two Tacé.

I wondered at his formal farewell, until he bent low and, under the guise of tucking an errant lock of hair behind my ear, whispered to me: "I should hate to see us evicted from the kingdom on our very first night, so I'll ask you to remember your promise."

I stared after him in annoyance as he walked away. Remember my promise indeed. The intoxicating effects of the Incuna, whatever it may be, had by now faded to almost nothing. How much trouble could I possibly cause in one night?

The Tacé who waited on me was, perhaps, ten years older than myself and had the most startling silver eyes. She was rather pretty, with nut brown hair and a heart-shaped face. She bid me follow her with nothing more than a curt nod, and she walked quite primly several steps ahead of me, never pausing to look back to make sure I had not gotten lost along the way.

At last, we came to an unassuming door quite far from where we'd left my companions. She produced a delicate golden key, and I followed her inside.

If the Citadel of the Shining City held chambers so fine, they were not something an impudent eight-year-old girl might ever have cause to visit, and so my accommodations were opulent beyond anything I'd ever seen. The sitting room was richly appointed in palest lavender and gold, the same gilt that seemed to adorn each and every surface of the palace, and through glass doors framed with sheer ivory draping was a high balcony, and beyond that was a well manicured garden that I dearly hoped to explore tomorrow in the daylight.

Above my head was an enormous chandelier dripping with crystals, set alight with hundreds of the same gold spheres that lit the rest of the palace, but the most joyous sight to my eyes was the copper tub set before the fireplace. No doubt my silent companion thought me ridiculous as I gasped with joy at the sight of steam curling from the surface of the water, but it had been so very long since I had felt well and truly clean that I did not care a whit.

"Oh, this is marvelous," I breathed as I dipped my fingers into the water and found it pleasantly scalding. "Is there—"

As if she'd already known what questions clamored about in my mind, the Tacé gestured to a chair beside the fireplace, where clean linen and several stoppered bottles that must've been soap were neatly arranged.

Then, she gave me a curt nod and left me alone at last.

I shed my gown in haste and, relishing the sharp jabs of fire in my cold feet, slid into the water with a contented sigh. No doubt my skin would be as red as my hair before long, but I cared so little that I submerged myself ever farther. Oh, how glorious such a simple thing could be after so long without it!

I had just begun to rub the contents of the bottle into my hair when my chamber door opened, and I sat up with a gasp, sloshing water all over the floor. The Tacé had returned, her lips pursed in disapproval at my clumsiness, and she bore a covered tray that she set upon the table. Over her arm, she carried a bundle of fabric, and I watched as she laid a gown of apricot upon the bed, layers and layers of gossamer fabric. Surely I was not to sleep in something so extravagant?

I pronounced myself clean at long last, and the Tacé helped me step carefully out of the now-murky water and into a wonderfully soft length of cloth that she wrapped around me.

She carefully combed the snarls from my hair while I devoured most ravenously the entire contents of the tray: a very small bird stuffed with fruit and nuts, surrounded by a crimson sauce flecked with spices, and a cup of what I supposed passed for tea in this strange place; it was hot and sweet and yet the herbs were entirely unfamiliar to my tongue. As lovely as I found the meal, my stomach was still woefully empty once I'd finished it and I found myself wishing there were more.

As the Tacé continued her ministrations, I attempted to converse with her, asking her questions about the palace and the royal family, but she spoke not a word, and gradually we fell into uneasy silence. When at last I'd swept the last of the sauce from the plate with the last bit of bread, she bid me stand and, despite my protestations, pulled the cloth from my body. I gasped as my naked skin, rubbed raw and red from my bath, was exposed to the air.

"I am quite capable of dressing myself, thank you!" I protested, but she ignored me entirely and turned me around with deft hands so that she might slip the apricot gown over my head.

The sleeves were little more than dainty caps trimmed in copper gilt that left my arms bare, and the bodice was so low that I tried to tug it higher and earned a stern glare for my efforts.

"Surely I'm not to sleep in this," I said to her in dismay. "It's far too fine."

"You are not meant to sleep in it," said a voice from the doorway.

The Dowager Queen had been so silent upon entering my chamber that I had not even realized she was there. She appraised me quite thoroughly, her hawkish eyes taking me in from head to toe. "You're woefully unadorned, but I suppose you'll have to do," she said at last. "Come along, now. He's waiting for you."

8

I stared at the Dowager Queen in confusion. "Who?"

"His Most High, of course," she answered flatly. "My son."

She swept from the room and I stood gaping after her until the Tacé nudged me none too gently in the small of my back. I followed the king's mother into the corridor. She had not come to collect me alone. At her side, just as he had been in the throne room, was the tall man, the velvet pillow with its odd occupant in his hands. When the Dowager Queen began to walk swiftly away, he followed.

"Wait!" I called to her. "Should we not collect my companions?"

The Dowager Queen did not slow, nor did she look over her shoulder at me as she replied, "His highness has sent for you and you alone."

"No, I cannot!"

At that, she stopped, as did her companion, and turned to face me very slowly, one eyebrow arched. "No?"

My mind scrambled for the purchase of some excuse, any excuse, I could give. "That is, I cannot possibly see his highness alone without a chaperone."

"You've no need of a chaperone," she informed me tartly, resuming her brisk steps. "Guards and servants will be in attendance."

This did nothing to alleviate my worry, but I could think of no further excuse to give, save my own exhaustion, which the Dowager Queen did not seem likely to accept. Thus, I followed her apprehensively as she led me down the corridor and up a short staircase, where two guards opened the massive doors for us, and I stepped across the threshold into the chamber beyond.

It truly was a lovely room. A grove of white trees was painted upon its pale green walls, their leaves the purest silver, and when the light from the glowing orb within the large stone hearth struck them, they seemed to undulate, rippling as with a gentle wind.

Two high-backed chairs faced one another on either side of the hearth, and King Anwar rose from the larger at my entrance. He bowed low, a sly smile playing about his lips, and I sunk into a curtsey.

"Greetings, Briony." He resumed his seat and beckoned to one of the liveried servants. "I beg your pardon for delaying you from your bed, but I could not sleep and desired conversation. As you were so... free with yours earlier this evening, I thought perhaps you would join me."

Had I been? I'd considered myself positive demure, having earned less than a half-dozen reproachful looks from Elyan, but perhaps even that was too many in such company.

"Me?" I said.

"You."

"Regrettably, I cannot."

He had not expected me to refuse, for the self-satisfied smile he wore slipped ever so slightly. Doubtless he was rarely refused, especially by women; perhaps he never had been.

"May I inquire as to why?"

"In Tiralaen, where I come from, it is considered indecent for

an unmarried woman such as myself to be alone with a man
without a chaperone present."

"Even if the man is a king?"

"Especially if the man is a king."

"Why, perchance?"

"Kings are quite used to taking whatever they like and getting
away with it."

His smile faltered again. "I've no desire to take anything from
you," he answered me gently. "I desire only your company and
conversation."

A goblet made of crystal so delicate I feared the stem would
shatter to pieces was pressed suddenly into my hand by a nearby
servant, and within, the liquid was pale green. I looked at it warily.

"It's merely Calique," the king offered. "A spirit we distill from
the nectar of the calahanthas fruit. You've nothing to fear from it
unless you are easily given to intoxication."

I brought the goblet to my lips and took the smallest sip; spring
spilled across my tongue, clear and verdant and fresh.

"Oh, it's delicious!"

"And is it enough to secure your company this evening, or must
I call for musicians as well?"

My eyes narrowed at the mischief in his eyes. "No," I answered
slowly. "This will do."

"Excellent." King Anwar gestured to the chair opposite him.
Mindful of the voluminous skirts of my gown, I sat and took another
small sip of Calique. He took a long swallow from his own glass, then
twirled the stem between his fingers, watching the light from the
green and gold sphere within the hearth reflecting off the cut crystal.

"What is it?" I gestured to the blazing sphere. "Magic, I
presume?"

He nodded. "It is called a Lumen. They provide light as well as heat."

"And they come from the Incuna?"

He raised his eyebrows. "And what do you know of the Incuna?"

"Frustratingly little," I admitted. "Our escort was hardly forthcoming."

"They are an extension of it, yes," he answered, and there was amusement in his voice. "A bit like your Magefire, though not as... destructive. As I understand it, one of your kind could cause quite a bit of harm with a handful of flame."

He was a different man altogether when he was not upon his throne: his posture was relaxed, languid even; his smiles were softer and reached his eyes, gleaming with barely suppressed mirth.

I ducked my head that I might hide the flush I felt creeping up my neck. "Is that why you brought me here tonight? To learn about Magefire?"

He shrugged. "No, though your magic does fascinate me so."

"Then what is it you wish to know?"

"How you managed it, of course."

I shook my head slightly. "I am afraid I do not take your meaning."

"Your miraculous escape! It's been two hundred and fifty-seven years since anyone has last managed it. Come, now, I'm sure it is a wonderful tale indeed!"

"We used our magic to best the men of stone who guard the prison," I answered. "And escaped into the forest beyond."

"A pretty answer of little substance. Come, now, and tell me."

"I might ask the same of you," I countered. "No records exist in Asperfell of anyone having escaped before, and yet my kind live among you to this day, is that not so? How did *they* manage it?"

"Regrettably, there are no stories of their ancestors' remarkable flight to be found in our library."

I surged forward in my chair. "You have a library?"

He tilted his head, the amusement on his face indicating that if I were to hear more, I would do well to answer his question first.

Charming though he was, I'd learned well enough that even a friend could prove otherwise, and he did appear altogether too keen to help us. How strange my life had become that I would look upon charity so suspiciously and keep company with men of dubious morals.

"Well, if you must know, we had help," I said at last.

"That must've been some help. And why are they not with you now?"

"They are dead, your highness."

His face fell. "Oh, Briony, I am so sorry."

"Oh no, no!" I rushed to say, hating to see his merry face suddenly distraught. "There is nothing to be sorry over—they were quite dead to begin with."

Granted, it was not the most perfectly reassuring thing I might have said in that moment, but even so, the king laughed. "Is that so! Well, now you *must* tell me, for I heard stories as a boy of prisoners who sprouted wings and flew to their freedom, and this sounds far more fascinating to be sure. In fact, I think you'd best start at the beginning."

He was, in truth, a most excellent listener, his eyes never leaving mine, his smile encouraging, his questions intelligent and thoughtful. He put me at ease most thoroughly, and before I knew it, I'd told him my story—and Elyan's, for they were inextricably bound together—and of the task I'd been set to the day I'd escaped death upon a scaffold and been thrust through the Gate to Asperfell.

"And who was it that set you upon this dangerous path with no guarantee of safe return?"

"My father," I answered, then paused. That was not correct; how could it be? I'd not seen my father since I was ten years old. He could not have possibly bid me rescue Elyan and return him to Tiralaen. I shook my head free of shadows that threatened to cling there.

Anwar was most keen to hear about Asperfell itself: the peculiar magic that permeated the ancient walls of the prison, the strange and varied characters who lived out their exile within, and the rules that governed the way we lived according to our former stations.

The Melancholy Revels utterly fascinated him, as did the lower levels of the prison. My recounting of the antics of Nollie and Perkin, the Necromancers who tended the graveyard, had him in uproarious laughter and, remembering vividly the latter's sagging backside jiggling merrily in the frigid winter air when he'd danced away from me holding the hem of his sack in his hands, I could not help the mirth that bubbled from my chest.

'Twas strange—I could not remember laughing so much or so freely since Yralis and I had giggled like girls on Serus morning.

Of particular interest to him was my life in Tiralaen: my family, my childhood at court, even my wild upbringing in the north, though I could not imagine why. I took great pains to explain that my family was of little consequence, particularly now that my father's head was no doubt nestled upon a spike outside the Tower Maer, but he would hear none of it. Syr'Aliem, he stated, was absolutely nothing like the land from whence I came, and thus he found even the mundane existence of a minor nobleman's daughter particularly exciting.

He drew it from me with his smiling mouth and encouraging

eyes, the story of Tiberius who was Viscario, and what he'd done to Kasam and the builders of Asperfell, how I'd stumbled upon it by virtue of my newly acquired aptitude, and what they'd done to aid our fight against the Sentinels.

"And so, you crossed the Heimslind and found yourselves here," he said. "In my kingdom."

"Yes, and we are most grateful for your hospitality, your highness, truly."

"'Twas was not by accident," he continued as though I'd not spoken, "else you would not have risked your own lives aiding my men in the forest. So, why have you come here, Briony Tenebrae? What is it you want from Syr'Aliem?"

A fool was I, indeed, to have imagined this mere company and conversation.

"I believe it best for Elyan to speak upon such matters," I answered at last, proud that under his probing gaze my refusal remained perfectly civil.

He was not so easily deterred. "Perhaps, but I would rather speak with you."

Had I any inkling I'd find myself alone in the company of a king that night, I'd have asked Elyan exactly how much he wished for Syr'Aliem to know of what we sought, and what I should say when pressed. But I'd no such notion, and I suspected that was exactly why Anwar had sent for me. I'd proven myself impulsive in the throne room; here were the consequences. I briefly contemplated throwing the contents of my glass into his face and sprinting from the room.

In the forest, Elyan had lamented my inability to conceal my emotions, and he was not the first. Someone long ago had told me the same, and that this quality would make me an utterly wretched spy. Now, those words were proven true, but in that moment, I could not remember who had spoken them. How odd... Had it been a man or woman? I tried to recall their voice, but could not; and when I tried to picture their face, I saw only a dense, thick shadow.

My head began to ache, and I pressed the heel of my hand to my forehead. In my pain and distraction, the fingers of my other hand slackened upon the stem of my glass. It plummeted to the floor at my feet and shattered, the sound causing the servants to flinch.

I looked down at the glittering shards in dismay, and before I'd given any particular thought to where I was or in whose company I sat, I bid my magic rise and, stretching out my hand over the ruined glass, brought it whole again. Were it an object of larger size, had it broken into more than just a few pieces, I would've likely spent all evening attempting to rectify my mistake, so inexperienced was I, but within the time it took me to draw a deep breath, my fingers clutched the stem of a delicate, crystal flute once more.

"Briony?" The king's voice seemed to come from very far away, muffled by the thick shadow lingering within my mind. "That was extraordinary!"

I looked up. He was watching me with such admiration in his eyes that it quite unsettled me. Compared to the exhibition of Elyan's magic only hours before, I was surprised he found my trifling spells to be of any note at all, but then, I remembered all too well how astonishing it was to see magic for the first time, or even the second or third. Indeed, though I had been surrounded by it for many, many months now, the wonder of it still rendered me hopelessly transfixed.

"I am well," I told him, desperate that he should stop staring at me so. "I apologize for the glass."

He laughed. "Please do not. What your prince seems to think are parlor tricks are rather wonderful in my opinion."

The shadow had receded, leaving in its place a dull, persistent throbbing, and I wished to stay no longer. Placing my glass carefully upon the table at my side, I asked: "Save what we seek, for truly I must defer to Elyan upon the matter, is there anything else you require of me this evening?"

The gleam in his amber eyes softened somewhat. "I have exhausted you. 'Twas not my intention. I will speak with your prince upon the morrow."

"He will ask to be admitted to your library," I offered. "Of this much I am certain, and I do not think he would mind the telling of it."

The king seemed puzzled, but his kind smile remained. "I shall certainly think upon the request."

"His highness would be most grateful."

"What is he to you, this would-be king?" he asked, as the light from the Lumen grew low and shadows gathered in the corners.

I was taken quite aback at his question, and at the boldness in his eyes.

"My sovereign," I answered coolly. "And my companion."

"Your friend?"

"Certainly."

"Your lover?"

I flushed in outrage. "No!"

"But you wish he were."

I stood and set my glass on the table beside my chair, my shaking hands nearly upsetting its contents. "Forgive me, your highness, my long journey has made me overtired—"

"Wait." The king rose from his chair and took my elbow gently in his hand, halting my flight. "Wait, please. I merely noticed his concern for you earlier and was curious. Please, stay."

My temper was likely to get the better of me if I did, whatever his intentions, but his face was open and guileless, his guilt palpable. Although his words had wounded me, I found I could not remain angry at him. Rather, I fought the most peculiar urge to push back the curl of bronze hair that had fallen into his eyes. Fisting my hands firmly in my skirts, I lowered myself reluctantly into my chair.

He leaned back in his chair and held his empty glass out into the air; a servant appeared, and more Calique was poured into it. "I do not suppose it matters," he said at last. "For regardless of how you came to be here, you are here, and that pleases me greatly."

"May I ask you a question, your highness?"

"Of course!" he said with a laugh. "After all, I've spent the better part of the evening interrogating you. 'Tis only fair."

"The woman who has been attending me—the Tacé. Forgive me, I do not know her name. Why does she not speak? Is it that she cannot, or that she will not?"

"Isri. Her name is Isri. And to answer your question... will not," he said. "And cannot. It is most complicated. The Tacé take an oath of silence when they enter service."

"But why?" I asked, aghast, for I could not imagine a worse fate, nor a cause for which I would be willing to endure it.

He shrugged. "Why indeed? It has been a mark of their conviction for centuries."

I stiffened. "Just because it has been done for centuries does not mean it should continue."

"And are not traditions important, Mistress Briony?" he asked. "Do you not have them in your own land?"

"Yes, but—"

"And do you agree with each and every one?"

"I most certainly do not."

"And yet they endure."

I lifted my chin. "Any tradition can be changed."

He leaned back in his chair and folded his hands before him, a damnable smile playing about the corners of his lips. "Indeed. And do you believe I should change this one?"

"All should be permitted to speak."

"And if I told you their silence is in service of their goddess, what then? Would you still wish me to demand them to speak?"

His words gave me pause, and I felt my face growing hot with embarrassment.

"Forgive me," he said. "I did not mean to torment you."

"You did not." I shook my head. "I assumed. Wrongfully, as it were."

"We have a great deal to learn about one another, I suppose," he said, and lifted his glass to me.

"Their goddess," I ventured. "Who is she?"

"She is very ancient and worshiped only by the Tacé now." He waved his hand and, in that gesture, dismissed her away as though she were nothing at all. "And do you have a goddess in Tiralaen?"

I nodded. "Several, in fact. There is Sator, our Mother Goddess, and her daughter, Thala, who gifted us with magic."

"Indeed!"

"Indeed. And Coleum, who is the father of all."

"The father of all," he mused, dragging the tip of his finger around the rim of his glass. "Yet it was a woman who gave your people magic."

"A goddess," I answered, "is no mere woman."

"I do not suppose she is."

We spoke a half-hour more before I attempted another retreat to my chamber. He was quite reluctant to part with me, despite the late hour, but smiled good-naturedly and bid me goodnight nonetheless. To my very great surprise given how long her son had kept me in his company, the Dowager Queen was waiting for me just outside the door, her companion and the doll by her side. As I emerged, she took my hand and placed it in the crook of her arm.

"I do hope you acquitted yourself with the utmost decorum in the presence of my son," she said as she led me back down the corridor, presumably to my chamber; I was so exhausted that I feared I might not make it to the bed and collapse upon the floor the moment I set foot inside. "Next time, I do hope he informs me in advance so that I might inspect your appearance and counsel you properly on how you must behave in the presence of His Most High."

It was such an odd thing to say that I thought her in jest. "And do you often inspect the women your son entertains?"

"Every single one."

Evidently, she was not.

"I enjoyed his company most thoroughly," I said. "Though as to whether or not I acquitted myself with decorum, I suppose you shall have to inquire it of him yourself."

"Oh, I will. We've no secrets between us, nor have I with my husband."

My brow rose at this. "I was told he passed."

"In body, 'tis true, but he is still with me." At this, she reached over and took the doll's hand, gazing fondly at its frozen face.

Again, I thought it a jest, a harmless, if tremendously unsettling, prank pulled on visitors to the kingdom, but then she lifted her finger and caressed its cheek.

Casting about for something to say that we might speak no further of her husband's effigy, my eyes landed at her throat where an enormous wreath of smokey gray gems glittered. "That is a beautiful necklace. What sort of stones are those?"

Her fingers brushed them reverently. "Crystals made of my husband's ashes."

I resolved to keep my mouth firmly closed after that.

She delivered me then to the care of two guards who saw me the rest of the way to my chamber. Once I was safely within, they closed the door behind me, and I was dismayed to hear the scrape of a key in the lock. So I was to be a prisoner again. I did not entirely blame the king for that. He did think us criminals, after all, and in truth, some of us most unfortunately were.

A white nightdress lay upon the bed, and the copper tub that I'd used to clean myself only hours before had vanished without a trace. The Lumen in the hearth suffused the chamber with warmth, and the coverlet upon the bed had been turned down for me.

I removed the lovely gown and placed it carefully across the back of the chair, then slipped the nightdress over my head and crawled into the sumptuous bed, softer than any I'd ever known, even in Tiralaen.

The Lumen in the grate began to fade, bespelled, I supposed, to do so as my eyelids grew heavy and the weight of so many weeks spent traveling the decidedly hostile forest pulled me under.

The dream began with a whisper, the rustling of dry leaves in the darkness behind my eyelids, words I did not understand.

I heard whispers often in my dreams, remnants of my magic, but these words, if they were words at all, were in no tongue I'd ever heard before. Woven throughout them were sighs, quiet sobs, and weeping that settled over my skin and sunk deep into my bones, and beneath the insubstantial fabric of my nightdress, my flesh began to prickle.

I opened my eyes. The forest glade beneath my feet was moss and bone; I walked upon death, held fast by life.

Hollows of endless, devouring black stared up at me, skulls, with jaws yawning wide as delicate tendrils wove between their teeth and the pitiful caverns of their noses. Long, thin ribs poked up in rows, like brittle fingers, and I saw finger bones as well, and spines, and all of them woven together with creeping green strands covered in tiny white blooms. With a crackling like broken glass, they gave way beneath my soles, crumbling and ancient.

Before me was a specter, and helplessly drawn was I to follow her. There were the aspects of the familiar about her: a cascade of luminous white veils, covering not just her face but her entire form, and a crown of grasping branches, and yet this was no Tacé.

"Who are you?" I called, and my voice felt small and strange within the confines of my mouth.

The figure stopped, and though it only inclined its head, it was no human silhouette beneath its endless veils. I recoiled, and my foot sank into a ribcage covered in creeping flowers.

She continued on, and despite my hesitancy, despite my fear, I followed, our path littered with the remains of those whose stories I did not know; I minded them carefully. It might've been mere moments; it might've been hours, but the forest around us began to blur and shift into stone, an ancient, suffocating tunnel at the end of which lay a simple wooden door with a handle of braided wood.

It opened before the veiled creature, and for the first time since I'd laid eyes upon her, I was afraid, for I could see nothing on the other side save darkness. She passed the threshold, turned, and beckoned to me.

Enthralled was I in that terrible moment, helpless to resist her pull; my feet moved of their own accord. *No, no, no, no* I begged, my lips moving, no sound escaping, tears streaming down my cheeks until, at last, I stood before her.

She extended her hand to me, her impossibly long fingers of wood wrapping around my soft, delicate ones, and I tasted salt on my lips as they formed the word, *please.*

The world around us stilled. We shared a breath, a second, and then she struck. Her fingers coiled around mine, curling down and digging into my flesh so hard I cried out in pain, and she pulled me through the door.

I stood in a field of dead grass beneath a gray sky and a bloodied sun, and before me was death.

The corpses of blackened trees loomed over dwellings reduced to moldering piles of stone, and scattered amongst them, wretched, skeletal creatures clad in rags pulled their brittle hair in agony, their mouths open in silent screams full of rotting teeth. Spread out before them on the ground were dead animals, carrion insects crawling about in their rotten flesh, and shriveled vines bearing putrid fruit. The creatures—no, these were people!—crawled toward their dreadful feast with grasping fingers, tearing and biting and swallowing until it became a frenzy, for there was little and they were many. I could bear no more; I looked away, and she was beside me, the apparition covered in veils.

She grasped my wrist once more, and I lurched violently awake.

The Lumen in the hearth had disappeared entirely, and in the darkness of my borrowed bedchamber, I began to shiver as images flooded my mind, vestiges of my nightmare, of the apparition in white. Surely my imagination must've conjured her, and yet she'd seemed so real; felt so real. I lifted my arm, the one she'd seized, and finding it sore, I lifted the sleeve of my nightdress.

There, around my wrist like a shackle, were the imprints of her brittle fingers upon my pale skin.

9

For long hours, I could not sleep, for each time my eyelids grew heavy and dropped, I saw her—saw *them*—and I was wide awake once more. 'Twas near dawn when I did sleep at last, and too few hours later when I woke, disoriented and irritable, roused by the opening and closing of my chamber door, tenaciously and unforgivably loud.

Sitting up, I dug the heels of my hands into my bleary eyes and tried to tame my curls, gone feral from tossing and turning. The light forcing its way through the gaps in the brocade curtains was buttery yellow, and I knew from the sun upon my west-facing windows that it was already early afternoon. Yet, I wished for nothing more but to bury myself under the coverlet and slide back into oblivion.

Isri, however, had no such idea. She stalked across my chamber and pulled open the curtains, her grim smile growing with each and every one of my winces and scowls. Then, she knelt before the hearth, her hands moving in the air before her, molding and shaping magic I could not see, drawing it from some secret place until a flickering of light appeared.

She made it grow with loving ministrations, coaxing it from little more than a spark into a radiance that banished whatever shadows still remained within the room and filled it with warmth. It was beautiful magic, a privilege to behold, and yet when Isri rose and turned to see me smiling foolishly, she scowled and busied herself most thoroughly with my attire for that day.

"Where are my companions?" I asked as I climbed out of bed, helplessly drawn by the tantalizing aroma of the meal she'd brought. I'd never been able to resist a good breakfast. "I wish to see them."

She shook her head firmly in response and gestured for me to sit. Clearly, I was to receive no help from her until I had seen to my morning ablutions which, unfortunately, included tending to my hair. I endured her wretched pulling and combing as best I could while I devoured that which she had brought: some sort of sweet bread with butter and a deep purple jam, along with a cup of a heady, sweet beverage, redolent of flowers, which I sipped slowly.

After Isri finished torturing my poor, smarting scalp, she produced a gown of layer upon layer of ivory fabric, gossamer-thin, and a bodice—well, I was not entirely sure it could even be called a bodice when it was made up entirely of leaves in gold brocade and nothing else at all.

I looked at her in dismay. "Why can I not wear one of my own gowns? Or at least the gown I wore last night? Surely there is no need for anything new."

Or anything so positively indecent.

Alas, it appeared as though the apricot gown I'd worn the night before had disappeared while I slept, as had the gown I'd been wearing when I first arrived. As Isri did not appear willing to allow me to leave my chamber in my nightdress, I allowed her to help me into the golden leaves that covered not even half the freckles upon my person.

Once the last delicate clasp was fastened, Isri led me to a magnificent looking glass, and the woman who stared back at me was a stranger.

It had been months since I'd seen my own reflection; the change was far beyond anything I'd ever imagined. My Aunt Eudora had once called me elfin (which she feared would repel most men of noble stock who favored more traditional ideals of beauty, the sort my sister Livia had possessed in abundance), and my freckled face was still quite sylphlike, my brown eyes too large and my chin too pointed; but where there had once been the roundness of youth, there were angles and hollows, and I looked a woman now, and not a girl.

Isri had arranged my unruly curls atop my head and bound them there with a band of gold studded with tiny diamond sunbursts. And although I blushed furiously at the expanse of pale skin of my chest and arms so exposed by the scattered arrangement of golden leaves, I experienced the most peculiar sense of pleasure at what I saw.

Oh, but *that* would not do. Abruptly, I turned away.

Isri produced a pair of green velvet slippers and I winced as my toes were squeezed tightly into the tips. My heels burning, I stumbled over the additional inch or two I was suddenly afforded.

"These are pointless," I told her, wriggling my toes with a grimace. "I cannot walk properly!"

She pinched my ankle, and I scowled down at the top of her veiled head.

Once I'd demonstrated that I could walk the length of my chamber and back without pitching forward onto my face, Isri proclaimed me suitable with a satisfied nod and led me from my chamber down the corridor to our right, the opposite direction from where I'd met the king the night before. After a time, we descended a wide staircase into a grand colonnade bordered by a peristyle, an enormous fountain at its center.

Everywhere, members of the Court Eternal gathered in the indolent warmth of the midday sun, some reclining on benches covered in mosses, others perched about the fountain, their lovely shoes tossed aside, scattered upon the grass like the glittering carapaces of insects so that they might submerge their feet in the water.

They nibbled daintily on slices of fresh fruit, passed on trays of gleaming silver by silent servants, and drank Calique from tiny crystal glasses while a pair of musicians played a flute and harp. Their laughter drifted lazily across the courtyard.

They marked my passage through the colonnade with appraising eyes and sly smiles, whispering their opinions to one another freely rather than concealing them behind their hands as would've been done in Tiralaen. Yet, they may as well have spoken their objections aloud to my very face for all that I cared, the silly things, though my face grew warm when more than a few male gazes lingered far too long where they most certainly should not have.

Once she had seen me safely delivered to an enormous door flanked by stone-faced guards, she disappeared without a backwards glance, no doubt to madden some other poor, hapless victim with her severe silence and vicious pointing. I was not the least bit sorry to see her go. The guards took hold of the ornate golden handles, and I was admitted to an overly large drawing room.

Elyan looked up from where he leaned against the mantle of the fireplace at the far end of the room, and relief mingled with joy in my chest, stealing my breath away.

Upon the tip of my tongue was my strange, terrible dream and the evidence left upon my pale skin, but as I rushed toward him, my usually insatiable urge to speak faltered and I stopped, for he was staring at me with the most peculiar expression upon his face.

I remembered then my reflection in the mirror, and a rush of heat suffused my skin.

"My own clothing seems to have mysteriously gone missing," I explained, and my fingers nervously smoothed the skirt of my borrowed finery. "Evidently what passes for a gown in Syr'Aliem is, in fact, half a gown and—"

I found suddenly I could no longer speak, could scarcely breathe, as I watched him walk toward me, his eyes drinking in the sight of me as though I were Thala herself and him come to worship at her altar. I imagined him, suddenly, upon his knees before me, and that turned out to be a grave mistake indeed, for suddenly I could think of little else.

I lifted my eyes and we studied one another in a silence achingly heavy.

"I want to kiss you," he said at last, and his voice was very low.

Fool that I was, all I could think to whisper was: "Where?"

His hands rested upon my neck, thumbs moving slowly upon my too-hot skin, then they slid upward and brushed gently along my jaw, below my ear.

"Here," he murmured.

My lips parted; I nodded, and he lowered his head as I held still, my heart thundering so forcefully that I felt certain he could hear it through my chest.

The doors opened then, and Elyan turned and groaned against my hair.

"There you two are!" Arlo's cheerful voice was a torment. I turned in Elyan's embrace and saw, to my dismay, that he was

grinning widely as he strode into the room. "Have I interrupted
something?"

"Would you care if you had?"

"Not really." His grin widened at the sight of my attire. "Now
that is some dress."

"Thank you."

"Where's the rest of it?"

The Tacé had dressed Arlo and Elyan as elegantly as they had
dressed me, in fine silk shirts and richly embroidered tunics, and
though Elyan had eschewed the jewels and finery that adorned the
men of the Court Eternal, Arlo had no such qualms. Earrings of
gold and deep green gemstones climbed his ears in a pleasing pattern
of vines and leaves, and shot through his brown curls were gleaming
strands of gold, as though someone had plunged their hands into a
jar of paint and run their fingers through it with abandon.

"Where are Thaniel and Phyra?" I asked.

Arlo flung himself onto one of the benches before the fire and
leaned forward to inspect the tray of delicacies that had been
placed on a low table. "I haven't the faintest. I figured they'd be
here with you lot."

I looked to Elyan in alarm. "You don't suppose they met with
some danger, do you?"

I could not help but remember the soldiers' response to Phyra
in the forest the day before, the terror in their eyes. I'd learned all
too well the monsters fear made of men.

At that moment, the doors opened again, revealing Thaniel in a
truly bewildering silver morning coat with voluminous, puffy
sleeves. And it was with the utmost relief that, behind him, I beheld
Phyra's lithe form, walking steadily and calmly under her own
power. She was dressed in an exquisite gown of pale pink trimmed

in copper. Her long, black hair—which I'd only ever seen in a wild tangle, even at Asperfell—was now deftly braided into a coronet with a circlet of filigreed copper across her brow.

She was resplendent. She could have been one of them.

I rushed forward, despite my wretched shoes, and gripped her hands tightly. "Are you all right? Did they treat you well?"

"I was kept as a prisoner," she answered flatly. "I asked the Tacé if I might see you, and I was refused."

"Me as well," Thaniel added. "I tried to find you lot after the silent woman left, but there were bloody guards at my door. Was it the same for you?"

"Just so," said Elyan.

From the bench, Arlo called: "I couldn't say. I never asked about any of you."

Elyan ignored him. "Were you similarly detained?" he asked me.

Their eyes fell upon me, and I remembered the apricot gown and the lingering taste of Calique on my tongue, and knew I must tell them.

"I asked for you," I began tentatively, "but was refused. And, yes, my door was locked last night, but I had a visitor."

I bade them sit, and Arlo moved aside with an exaggerated sigh to allow room on the chaise beside him. His eyes widened when they fell upon Phyra. I expected him to quip inappropriately as he'd done with me, but instead he quickly averted his gaze and rubbed the back of his neck. Thaniel dropped himself down between the two of them.

Elyan refused to sit, preferring to lean against the mantle once more, watching me with eyes that held none of the warmth of before, when our lips had almost met. Oh, why must everything always be in the way?

"Well?" Thaniel urged. "What is it, then?"

I folded my hands anxiously in my ivory skirts. "Last night, after we left the Court Eternal, I was summoned by the king."

Elyan's eyes dropped to his shoes, and his grip upon the superbly carved stone mantle was so tight that his knuckles turned positively white.

It was Arlo who spoke first, damn it all. "Well, then! I trust you did everything you could to earn his good favor, eh?"

When he waggled his eyebrows to ensure I understood his crudity, it was all I could do not to punch him in the nose. "Oh, for Coleum's sake," I sighed. "There was nothing untoward about it. Honestly!"

Elyan asked, very softly: "What did he want?"

"Conversation. Stories of Tiralaen, and of Asperfell."

"Did you tell him about the cave?"

I bristled. "No!"

"But he did ask."

"He asked what favor we intend to ask of him and his court, yes. And I told him to address all enquiries to you. He knows we are no mere travelers seeking shelter until we are rested enough to continue on our journey."

Elyan's eyes sharpened. "And what cause has he to suspect such a thing?"

"Because, despite what I am certain you believe of him, he is no fool," I answered. "In fact, he is rather cunning."

"I assume you speak of my brother."

I'd not heard the doors open; indeed, I'd heard nothing at all. But suddenly, Princess Evolet was standing within the chamber, smiling pleasantly as though she'd not overheard us arguing over the intellectual merits of her kin. She was as arresting as I remembered, her alabaster skin shimmering and without flaw.

My cheeks flushed. "Your highness, I did not—"

She laughed, the sound high and clear. "It's quite all right. I have many a time begrudgingly admitted the same of him. Unfortunately, he is much occupied with matters of court, and so I'm afraid you are burdened with me instead."

It was quite clear by the expression on Arlo's face that her presence would be no burden.

"As we hope you will remain our guests for at least a little while, my brother and I thought you would like a tour of the palace," the princess continued. "Is there anything in particular you should like to see?"

Elyan answered at once: "The library"

As Thaniel declared: "The armory."

And I said: "The stillroom."

"Well, that is not at all what I expected to hear. But if it would amuse you, I would be happy to show you these things." Princess Evolet paused and smiled apologetically at Elyan. "With the exception of the library."

His brow rose. "Why the exception?"

"Only the royal scholar and my brother are permitted in the library," she answered. "But I would be pleased to show you to our stillroom, Mistress Briony, and we can visit the armory afterward."

We dutifully followed Princess Evolet through the palace until we descended a set of stairs and passed beneath an arch of white stone into a large room flooded with light.

It was quite unlike any stillroom I'd ever seen, for there were only three beds, all unoccupied, their linens crisp and unlined. The rest of the space held a great many potted trees in golden urns, which lent a rather peaceful air to the room, and upon the far wall was a long work counter with several shelves above. These shelves held all manner of neatly labeled jars filled with dried herbs and flowers and powders, phials of liquids in all colors and consistencies, and several pots bearing living plants I was quite shocked to find I recognized.

"Oh, I know some of these!" I exclaimed.

"As well you would," a pleasant voice spoke from behind me, and I turned and beheld a tall figure silhouetted in the doorway. "I understand they grow all about the Heimslind moor."

He had the darkest skin I had ever seen, a rich, luminous ebony, and his smile was warm and friendly, the sort of smile I could not help returning. He wore a high-collared tunic of pristine white, and unlike nearly everyone else I'd seen thus far in this strange place, it was quite simple, bearing only silver scrollwork.

"And beyond it," I said in return.

"You have magic!" He stepped down into the stillroom eagerly. "I can feel it—you see, I'm descended from your sort."

Just like Garundel! Indeed, when I reached out tentatively with my own magic, I felt the familiar thrum in his veins, and yet it was not entirely like mine. There was something else there, something akin to the heaviness in the air that left me so giddy upon our approach to the palace. I told him so.

"The Incuna," he explained. "With which I also share a connection. I suppose you might consider me a man of both worlds."

"This is Kevren, our Healer," Princess Evolet informed us. "Kevren, may I present our guests from Asperfell."

Kevren bounded forward. "Well met, Thaniel! Wonderful to see you again. How is your arm this morning?"

We all looked to Thaniel in surprise, and a flush appeared on his cheeks. "Very well, thanks to you."

"Let's have a look, shall we?"

Thaniel obediently eased his arm from what I realized was a

fine new sling. (It had remained mostly hidden amidst the ruffles of his jacket sleeves, which I now realized was the purpose of its unruly waves of fabric). As Kevren gently began to unwind the bandages that covered his wound, Thaniel said: "Kevren was sent to me last evening to see to my wound."

The healer probed his skin with gentle fingers. "Does this hurt?"

"Not a bit. Whatever it was you put on it is quite extraordinary. I hardly feel a thing."

"I've been experimenting for some time now with herbs imbued with magic from the Incuna," Kevren said, and there was no mistaking the pride in his voice. "This combination is best to prevent scarring."

"May I look?" I asked hopefully.

"Briony has a particular interest in herbs and healing," Thaniel explained as Kevren stepped aside, allowing me to see the thin red line that had only the night before been an angry red gash.

"When they told me you were an Alchemist, I wondered if perhaps you had experience with remedies yourself?" Kevren asked Thaniel as I stood back and allowed him to place his arm carefully back into the sling.

"Unfortunately, no," Thaniel admitted. "I have a talent for... That is, my experience, for the most part, lies in... Well, in weaponry, though I have dabbled in minor concoctions when bespelling blades."

I expected him to unsheathe and display Maelstrom, but he did not. Only then did I realize the blade was not at his side, and I thought it most odd.

"What sort of spells?" asked Kevren.

Thaniel shrugged. "Rendering an opponent unconscious is quite helpful," he said.

Arlo snorted. "Unconscious? I've seen that blade poison a man such that his tongue turned black and he vomited up his own spleen."

"Indeed?" Kevren's eyes went wide.

"His spleen!" Arlo assured him.

"That was one time, you ass," Thaniel snarled. Then, to Kevren: "I would apologize for him, but he is beyond forgiveness."

"No, no, not at all," Kevren assured. "In fact, I am rather intrigued. If you are able to produce spells of such destruction, are you not also capable of healing? I feel certain you must be."

Color appeared high on the Alchemist's cheekbones. "I don't know," he answered. "I've never tried, but... I do have knowledge of some such spells."

"And do you think your spells might cling to my instruments the way they hold fast to your blades?"

"I don't suppose why not, though I would have to examine the materials your instruments are made of."

Kevren gestured around us to the empty room. "As you can see, I'm quite at my leisure at the moment. Would you be willing to examine them now?"

A broad smile spread across Thaniel's face and when Kevren responded in kind, I felt a prickling heat bloom upon the back of my neck, spreading to the tips of my ears for although it was only a smile, I felt that in witnessing it I had suddenly become an intruder.

"Of course."

And with that, Kevren and Thaniel vanished through a nearby archway draped in moss, without a *by your leave* to Princess Evolet or a farewell to the rest of us.

Looking once more upon the empty beds, I frowned at the princess. "I've never seen a stillroom so empty."

"We are not easily given to illness," Evolet replied. "Poor Kevren's talents are utterly wasted upon us. Come—let us next to the armory."

I glanced behind me at the archway. "Thaniel?" I called.

A hand pushed aside the curtain of moss, revealing Thaniel's face. "You go on without me," he said. "I've a mind to stay and see if I might be able to assist Kevren with his instruments."

"You're the one who wanted to see the armory!" I reminded him, but he'd already disappeared from sight.

Phyra's hand fell upon my arm. "Let him stay," she said softly, and we followed the princess up the stairs and back into the airy hall.

I'd no wish to see racks full of weapons, and so Princess Evolet instead guided us through a myriad of corridors that led to various chambers meant only for pleasure and entertainment. One was a gaming parlor with marble tables where members of the court were given to play games of chance with wheels and dice. Another was a cavernous concert hall with velvet seats, all of which were placed around tables for food and drinks rather than facing the stage.

Next, we visited the Culum Foyl, a room richly decorated in burgundy and with a throne made entirely of gold. Here, according to Princess Evolet, the king met with his favorite counselors to discuss matters of governance.

"The throne room is far too merry and boisterous a place for serious conversation, and so we chase the offenders away to this shabby little place when they insist on discussing policy with His Most High," she said with a laugh.

The princess had her own receiving room, as did her mother, though their thrones were much smaller, and they did no governing at all, preferring to lie about on chaises and pillows, eating and drinking and exchanging gossip about one another, the invitations to future gatherings dependent entirely on how excellent the quality of said gossip.

There were plenty of other chambers designated for these same activities, but after seeing three of them, I politely requested we explore the rest of the palace, and so Princess Evolet turned our attention to the dining halls.

There were no less than five, each with a different name and purpose, depending on the number of guests and the extravagance of the meal and whether or not there was to be dancing afterward, as well as how far inebriated folk may have to travel to their chambers. Princess Evolet took great pleasure in describing to me in excruciating detail the design of the dishware for each room, the number of pieces, whether the cutlery was silver or gold, and what patterns decorated each of their handles.

"And then there's the matter of the candelabras," she told me very seriously as we left the last dining hall. "The Lumens must be maintained quite regularly to ensure proper light depending on the occasion."

"And who creates and maintains them?" I asked, for who performed the magic was certainly of far greater interest to me than the room which it was meant to light.

She waved her hand vaguely. "Every servant within the palace walls harbors some connection to the Incuna."

As though that explained anything at all.

"I simply *must* show you the Thesa," she said suddenly. "I promise you've never seen its like, even in your Tiralaen!"

"What is the Thesa?" I asked, but she was already tugging me along with gleeful enthusiasm.

We found ourselves in a circular room made of glass in variegated

shades of green, held fast by vines and leaves wrought of gold. The
wan light of the afternoon cast patterns of emerald and teal upon
the floor at our feet. It reminded me somewhat of the orangery at
the townhome of my earliest youth, my favorite hiding place to flip
through books I'd pilfered from the library. Inevitably I would be
found out by the young Naturalist who managed the grounds of
our estate, a woman with close-cropped curls and the subject of
endless tittering gossip amongst the rest of the staff. She'd refused
to wear skirts, and I'd been sick with jealousy at her trousers and
the easy, self-possessed way she stalked the grounds in them,
moving not as a man but as herself, true and whole. My father had
chosen her personally from hundreds of eager men and women
with vastly more experience and decidedly less sarcasm because
she had done what none other could: coax his stubborn citrus trees
into blossom, and then into fruit.

There were no orange or lemon trees in this beautiful green
glass room, but there were flowers, pots of them, and plants and
trees of all manner, each achingly lovely in its own way. Bronze
bowls held other treasures: feathers, nuts, pinecones, stones, even
shells, their natural beauty a stark contrast against the true purpose
of this marvelous place: the crafting of the sumptuous costumes of
the Court Eternal.

Gowns and coats and tunics in various states of completion
adorned marble statues, and like the one upon my person at that
very moment, all were far more scandalous a fashion than could be
found in Tiralaen. At one statue, two men argued over the drape
of a sleeve, each insisting with a vehemence near violence whether
the fabric should fall this way or that, though I could tell no
difference between the two.

At the center of all, seated upon a tufted velvet cushion, must've been the head seamstress, for the stunning pink confection she wore could not be matched, it's multitude of ruffles artfully arranged to fall just so. She'd hair the same color, and the fine strands were teased and arranged so high upon her head that they resembled the spun sugar Livia and I had eaten at street fairs when we were very young.

She was poised above a pile of stones as large as cherries, picking over them with nimble fingers and pursed lips, flicking most aside and saving only those whose shapes were perfectly rounded and smooth.

One of the men who had been tsking at the sleeve peered over her shoulder. "Is that for Betina?"

"It's her diadem for the pleasure garden."

"She'll want more."

"Well, I don't have more," the woman huffed, and the flowers painted on her cheeks wrinkled along with her delicate nose. "Unless you wish to gather them from the river yourself, Aeric?"

The man brought his hand swiftly to his breast, his fingers splayed in alarm. "Me? Darling Friella, I haven't been outside in two years."

I watched as the woman with the towering pink hair began to move her soft, fine fingers in elegant patterns in the air above the three round stones, her face pinched in concentration. Tendrils of light began to shimmer in the air between her hands, enveloping the stones in magic, and as she plied her remarkable skill over and over again, gradually the white river stones began to shimmer and grow translucent. Facets began to form—flat plains and sharp angles, dozens of them, *hundreds* of them—until three dazzling crystals stood where stone had been.

The woman with the pink hair slumped upon the stool, her

hands going slack and shaking, and her assistant, a plump girl in garish shades of aubergine with a dainty, heart-shaped mouth painted the same shade, approached with a crystal goblet of water flavored with thin slices of some sort of fruit.

"She wants them set in silver," Friella said, after she'd drained the contents. "A rather mundane choice if you ask me."

"But she did not ask you," Aeric laughed as the stones were wrapped in a velvet cloth and borne away by the girl who had brought the water.

"No sharp lines!o" she called after her. "She prefers her filigree rounded!"

"That was extraordinary," I breathed, drawn helplessly forward to where the white river stones had been. "Did you truly change them?"

Friella drew back at the sight of me, her eyes traveling up and down my form, taking in the details of my gown.

"Ah," she huffed. "So you're the one we repurposed that gown for. I do hope you appreciate it—'twas no easy task to alter it at such short notice."

I looked down at my bodice of golden leaves, then to the many plants and trees that surrounded the room of green glass until I found... Yes, there it was: vines with rich, glossy leaves spilling riotously from the confines of their glazed prison; the very same as the tendrils and leaves upon my person.

"Who was it originally made for?"

Aeric looked down his nose at me, taking in every woeful inch of my less than illustrious stature. "Someone taller."

"Someone in a delicate condition," the other man added slyly.

"Hush," Friella hissed, her gaze sliding to the princess standing beside me.

"Well, I suppose we've heard quite enough for now," Evolet said, then reached out her hand for mine. "Come—you simply must see our jewels."

The room that held the royal jewels was larger than the third-largest dining hall, and each piece was a work of art: a diadem of jagged red crystals joined together with delicate threads of copper; a necklace of flowers, each petal a gem of a different color; rings bearing stones the size of quail eggs. It was a trove without equal in my world, and I truly wanted to appreciate its splendor—but as the princess chattered endlessly, my dazzled eyes could no more appreciate the artistry on display than a woman who is drowning in wine might pause to savor the terroir.

As I studied a large aquamarine gem hanging at the end of a delicate silver lariat, I asked: "What was this jewel once? A river stone like the others?"

"Does it matter?"

After a period of polite observation, we bid farewell to those who worked in the treasury and continued upon our tour. I could think of only one place left in the palace I wished to see. "Perhaps we might visit the Incuna?"

She stopped suddenly, and slowly turned to face us, her smile somewhat fixed in her lovely face. "The Incuna?"

"Indeed."

"Why, it is below us," she answered. "Far below us."

"I do not mind the distance."

Her laugh was high and false. "Nevertheless, I shall have to consult my brother."

"And do you always consult your brother when you've a decision to make?"

"Oh yes."

"Behave," Elyan murmured as the princess floated away down the corridor.

"Why should I?" I scowled. "She's ridiculous."

"She is," he agreed. "But do try not to insult hosts before we've had the chance to ask for their assistance."

"As though she even realizes she is being insulted."

He frowned, and his eyes trailed across the gilt and splendor around us. "All the same. I do not believe anything about this place is quite as it seems."

The memory of white veils and the vice of brittle fingers surfaced, yet even as I opened my mouth to tell Elyan of my peculiar dream, my words were swallowed up by the sudden arrival of a stout, glittering person, blustering as though he'd run the length of the palace, though the guards behind him seemed wholly unruffled.

"What ever could bring you here in such a hurry, Fellior?" Princess Evolet asked with a tilt of her head. "You look flushed."

"Princess," he wheezed in return, bowing so low it was a great wonder to me his lips did not scrape the marble floor. "I am most fortunate to have found you, for I come bearing an invitation."

"For me?"

"For *him*."

To our surprise, it was Elyan whom Fellior had come to seek, for King Anwar had granted him permission to visit the library. And though I felt keenly a rush of pleasure that my private audience with the king had yielded this fruit, I also felt a stab of indignation that he'd granted entry to Elyan, and only Elyan.

Although Elyan cast me an apologetic glance as he was led away, he did not protest; the promise of knowledge was, without doubt, of far more importance to him than my wounded feelings, or my boredom.

"I'm afraid I must depart as well," Phyra said softly. She looked positively wretched; I pressed the back of my hand to her brow and found her skin feverish.

"The magic of this place troubles you still."

"I need to lie down is all. I will be well by and by."

A pair of passing servants were tasked with escorting Phyra back to her chamber, and I was left alone with Arlo and the princess. They were speaking most enthusiastically of gaming parlors, and though I'd no desire to see them nor to partake in the goings-on within, I allowed myself to be led through yet another maze of elegant hallways to yet another collection of garish rooms.

As it happened, I did not need to endure them for long.

The moment our little party arrived at the foremost daytime gaming room, Arlo was borne away, disappearing into smiles and mirth and bottomless carafes of Calique, and Evolet followed, leaving me to linger in the doorway alone, and I seized my opportunity to escape.

The parlor was every bit as raucous and loud as I'd hoped. Men and women shuffled idly through brightly painted cards and piles of coin while they sipped punch in a dizzying array of colors from crystal chalices and laughed, luminous skin aglow by the light of hundreds of Lumens strung in arcs across the ceiling. A quartet of musicians played admirably, but the sound of their instruments was quite drowned out by the din and the occasional shriek. I could not have asked for a better distraction.

I slipped out of the room and took off at as fast a run as I could manage in my unfortunate shoes.

My path was haphazard and guided entirely by whim and instinct, ensuring that if the princess did indeed seek me, she would not be able to do so easily. When at last I came to an alcove framed by drapery, I hid within, pulled them around myself, and waited.

A quarter of an hour passed, and Evolet did not come, or anyone else calling my name. Now, I would be quite at my leisure to explore Syr'Aliem without a chaperone; 'twas as intoxicating as the Calique I had sampled the night before. Giddy at the thought, I fairly floated down the sun-dappled corridor.

Rounding the corner, I beheld a barefoot man in gold velvet breeches and a billowing white shirt unbuttoned to his navel, sitting upon a stool before an easel. He was of middling years, though no less handsome for it, with sandy curls that brushed his collarbones and a closely trimmed beard to match. His eyes were fixed upon the courtyard before him, a lovely haven with walls of ivy that surrounded a patch of lush, green grass, and at its center stood a towering fountain within whose crystalline waters a woman stood. She wore a translucent shift that had slipped off of her shoulders and, from her waist down, was soaking wet and clinging to the gooseflesh of her thighs.

Pots and bowls of pigment were strewn about the painter's feet, along with cups of brushes and discarded pallets stacked upon one another, smeared with rich color. Several half-finished sketches of a female form—*hers*, I imagined—looked as though they'd been crumpled, smoothed, then crumpled again once more.

He twirled a brush between his long fingers; another was tucked behind one ear, and he positively vibrated with restless energy, flexing his hands upon his thighs, rising to graze the bristles of his brush, reaching toward his unfinished work, falling again, knees jangling. He jumped up from his stool and began to pace impatiently; the hand that held the brush raked through his hair, discarding the other one; they both clattered to the floor. He ignored them.

"No, no, no, no," he muttered feverishly. "No, it's all wrong!"

The woman in the fountain pouted and sighed. "How long is this going to take, Yveme? My fingers are positively *wrinkled.*" She thrust them out in demonstration, and the straps of her gown slipped farther down her arms.

"Apologies, dear Cezann," the painter snapped, clearly not sorry at all. "You are simply too... *majestic* to capture with such rudimentary colors."

Cezann sighed again and sank back into the fountain, her fingers toying idly upon the surface of the water while Yveme fussed and fidgeted with his paints and brushes until his frenetic eyes fell upon the hem of my gown, then traveled upward. Our eyes met; his widened.

"You," he said.

"Me?"

"Yveme," the woman in the fountain grumbled. "My fingers..."

"The forest take your fingers," he replied.

She spluttered and spat and, shooting me an expression that could have frozen the fiercest Magefire, gathered her soaking skirts in her hands and extricated herself from the fountain.

"I'm sorry," I winced. "It was not my intention to ruin your painting."

He waved his brushes in the air chaotically. "She ruined it already. She was not enough."

"Enough?" I laughed. "But she is beautiful!"

"They are *all* beautiful," he mourned, raking his fingers through his already crazed hair; the brushes in his hands left streaks of paint in shades of emerald and moss. "I need more."

"More," I echoed, for I did not understand him.

"Yes, *more.*"

He gestured to his painting, and I stepped forward that I might look at it properly.

To call it ostentatious would've been a kindness.

It was as though someone had chewed up a chest of gold and jewels and spewed it forth upon canvas, then smeared it about for good measure. I could see little resemblance to the courtyard before me, nor the woman in the fountain, for he had altered it so irrevocably. The creamy white blooms that covered the archways were rendered hard and glittering, their petals and leaves made of gems and not of growing things; the fountain was three times its size, and of gold rather than stone, hundreds of streams of water arching into the air, forming dizzying patterns. And as for Cezann herself...

The artist was staring at me with wild, hungry eyes, hands planted firmly on his hips. "Well?" he demanded.

"It's certainly something!" I answered, my brightness so false even I found it grating.

He waved the hand holding the brush, sending droplets of paint flying. "Of course it is. But it's not enough. It needs *more*."

I winced. "Does it?"

Sinking back upon his stool, he surveyed his work with loathing. "I've painted this scene over and over and over again, and I know not what more I can do to make it speak, to make it sing, to make it clutch at the heart and squeeze! Nothing is never enough."

"How many times?" I ventured.

"This is attempt fifty-seven, I believe."

"And you've not thought to try something else? Something new?"

He stared down his long nose at me most witheringly. "Impossible," he sniffed. "For there is nothing left that is new within the palace. I have painted it all."

"Then why not go outside of the palace? Surely there are many wonderful things to paint in the village, or the forest beyond?"

His reaction was immediate and visceral. Surging forward, his long fingers closed around the knot of pearls at his throat as he fixed me with wide, wild eyes. "I can't," he insisted, voice strangled and desperate. "I can't!"

The strands broke beneath his grip, and pearls flew and scattered at my feet. I fell to my knees, gathering them in my palms as Yveme returned to his canvas, and it was then that my eyes fell upon something far more precious than pearls: a muslin skirt, worn and many times let out, its color faded.

It belonged to a harried young woman with a head full of golden ringlets, dark circles under her bright blue eyes and a tray in her hands, its contents covered by a golden dome. A servant! And one unaccompanied and unbeholden to anyone at the moment, save the person who was to receive her burden. Oh, but this was a most wondrous find indeed.

Servants knew intimately the secrets of those who employed them, and for the proper price and a promise of discretion were more than willing to divulge them. This was as true of a palace as it was of a country estate like Orwynd, although the gossip was considerably less exciting in the case of the latter, particularly when the family in question consisted of an aging spinster and her unruly great-niece who ran half-wild through the woods.

"Forgive me," I murmured to Yveme, but he no longer heeded me. He had ripped from his easel the fifty-seventh painting of Cezann and a blank canvas stood in its place, ready for his fifty-eighth attempt.

Leaving the pearls where they lay, I left him to his curses and his mutterings and followed the girl and her gold-covered tray until she came to a door no less ornate than my own, and I was forced to conceal myself behind a nearby pillar.

She rapped smartly upon the door; a muffled voice granted her entry, and I waited. A conversation was taking place within: a cheerful, pleasing tone against another, shrill and petulant.

There was a sudden shriek followed by the sound of breaking glass, and I flinched. A moment later, the servant reappeared, flustered and red-faced, an empty tray in her hands and tears gathering in her exhausted eyes. Keeping a careful distance between us, I followed her once more through passages and down several flights of winding stairs until I recognized the walls that surrounded me, for we had passed through them upon our arrival only the day before.

These were the servants' corridors. Nothing gleamed here. The stone was gray and undecorated, the Lumens set into simple alcoves, every surface rough and aged and long forgotten. When first we'd arrived, I'd thought it perfectly serviceable; I'd thought it the Forest Kingdom. Now that I had seen what lay above with all its gilt and crystal, I found it very sorry indeed.

At the end of a particularly long corridor, the girl passed beneath an archway and, as I approached, I caught my first glimpse of Syr'Aliem's kitchens.

They were enormous, and how could they not have been, for though I'd sampled only a little of the Forest Kingdom's rich fare, it far outrivaled any I'd had in Tiralaen, even that of the Citadel. Men and women in aprons and caps rushed about in a merry dance of knives and long-handled spoons and pots so complicated it was incredible they did not collide into one another.

Long tables were piled high with fruits and vegetables unfamiliar to me but no less breathtaking for the fact, and my delighted eyes roamed over them, and over the haunches of meat and whole fish on ice, ropes of aromatics and baskets of tubers. There was a rather cunning wooden tray that spanned the entire length of the table nearest me, with round indents made to hold eggs of various sizes from various beasts, and each was full. Some eggs were as small as my thumb and others larger than my clenched fist, and their shells were as many different colors as Yveme's pallets, some speckled, others smooth and pristine.

Upon no less than ten stoves, gleaming pots and pans bubbled and sizzled, and the aromas that permeated the air were so tantalizing that, starving as I was after eating so little that morning, my mouth began to water most unbecomingly.

The girl I'd followed approached a stout, matronly woman with copper hair streaked with white peeking from beneath her cap.

"She didn't like it?" the older woman asked as she eyed the empty tray.

"She wouldn't even try it. Threw it at my head."

"And what was her complaint this time?"

"Too thick."

The older woman turned and slammed the tray down upon the table behind her. "That is the third time in as many days I've made that dish."

"And she wants you to make it a fourth time."

A string of words I did not recognize erupted from her mouth, though the foulness of their meaning was evident from how the girl recoiled. "As if I did not have enough madness to contend with today!"

"Why, what else has happened?" The girl glanced around with a frown. "Where's Perol?"

In the discourse that followed, I learned much about this poor

Perol, who was given to fits of hysterics, especially when confronted by an entity known as "The Spectre," as he had been earlier that afternoon. After dissolving into tears and dropping a vat of soup, he'd rushed from the kitchen and had not returned.

The young woman appeared incensed to hear it. "I worked for hours on that soup. A pox on that menace!"

While they mourned the loss of the soup, I was far more interested in this Spectre, for though they had described it only in the fleeting way those already long familiar with it would, it sounded more than a bit like an umbra.

10

I was halfway through the archway, questions almost tumbling from my tongue, when my wrist was seized by a vice, and I was whirled around to face silver eyes shimmering with anger.

Well, this was most unfortunate.

Her fingers digging unforgivably into my flesh, Isri marched me back through the corridors of the servants' hall and into the dazzling white light of the palace.

"I would ask you where I am bound, but I know you cannot answer me," I gritted out, struggling to keep pace with her broad strides. "Please, take me to Prince Elyan."

Her steps only quickened, and I cursed the shoes she'd bound me in as I did her.

She did not take me to Elyan, nor to Princess Evolet. Instead, she dragged me through an archway to a secluded alcove hung with creeping vines with dark, glossy leaves. Standing alone, his hands laced before him and a smile tugging at the corner of his mouth, was King Anwar.

He bowed low, and Isri departed.

"Mistress Briony, I hoped you would take the air with me this afternoon. I've a mind to show you my favorite of our gardens."

"Oh," I answered, relief at not having been discovered mingling with confusion. "But what of my companions? Should not they see these splendid gardens too?"

"They will. Later."

Ah, so 'twas not a garden for which he had called me at all.

Livia would've known what to do, of that I was certain and, in that moment, I wished most fervently I'd listened to her on the dreary autumn afternoons when she and my Aunt Eudora would endlessly discuss the etiquette of courting whilst the rain lashed against the windows. Rather, I would take my leave of them and go in tromping about the puddles that formed in the pasture, frightening the horses. Although such pastimes were unlikely to be instructive regarding the predicament in which I now found myself, it was rather wonderful to see their faces when I appeared sometime later sopping wet.

I affected what I hoped was a perfectly charming smile but was, I feared, closer in resemblance to a feral grimace. "Then, on behalf of myself, I thank you, though I do wish you had not included Isri in the bargain."

He gave a shout of laughter. "She is rather ruthless, isn't she?"

I could not help but smile at that. "I believe she delights in tormenting me."

"And I believe you are more than capable of handling her." He stretched out his hand. "Shall we?"

Indeed, the garden was every bit as exquisite as he'd promised, and I drank in hungrily the sight of hundreds of plants and shrubs and flowers I'd never seen, their many scents mingling with the warmth of the sun, an intoxicating elixir that I breathed in slowly and

deeply as I wandered amongst the rows and paths, King Anwar
following close behind.

Every plant and flower was placed just so in orderly patterns to
delight the eye, punctuated by statues and fountains, the gurgling
of water and the trilling of birds the only sounds save our footsteps.
We traversed a staircase that spiraled up through a luscious canopy
of purple flowers, their heady perfume hanging low in the warm
air of the afternoon, and emerged upon a balcony that overlooked
the garden in its entirety.

"How lovely," I breathed, bracing my hands against the wrought
iron railing of the balcony.

The king lowered himself upon a bench behind me. "You
must've had gardens in Tiralaen."

"None like this, for I grew up in the north, your highness."

"And what were the gardens like in the north?"

"A great deal more disorderly."

He chuckled softly at this. "Come, Briony, and sit beside me. I
promise the view is still quite wonderful from here."

I could think of no reason to refuse him other than my own
dreadful manners, and so I sat, smoothing my skirts, quite
determined that I should acquit myself with all the decorum my
family had long ceased imagining I possessed.

"I, too, prefer a bit of the disorderly," he continued. "Only, this
garden belonged to my wife and was cultivated specifically to her
every wish."

"Oh!" I exclaimed. "I did not realize you were married."

"Many years ago."

I'd thought him of an age with Elyan, nearing thirty, but perhaps
I'd been mistaken for him to have been married, and then lived
many years without his wife.

"What sort of person was she?" I ventured.

"She was lovely. Sweet, good-humored, kind. Far, far too good for me. Indeed, I could scarce believe it when she accepted my hand."

"Was she from the court?"

"She was. Much should it tell you of the nature of men that I overlooked her as long as I did. For that, I am ashamed, for we might've had more time together, if not for..."

"Your Highness?"

He looked down at me then, and his smile grew sad. "She was happy, Briony, she truly was, but there were wistful days, melancholy days, and as time passed, they became so frequent that she would spend weeks at a time lost in the shadows of her mind where I could not reach her." Here, he drew a deep breath and looked out into the sea of light and color before us. "She woke early one morning with a mind to see the sun rise in the garden—the very same garden before you now. When she did not return, I sought her out, only to find she was not there."

I waited, poised exquisitely between wishing he would go on and hoping he did not, for I already knew how this story ended.

"She jumped from the highest parapet of the palace," he said at last, and his voice was rough and altogether unsteady.

"Oh Gods," I breathed. "I am so very sorry."

"I can only hope that she at last found the peace she so coveted."

"And have you?"

"It took a very long time, but yes, I have. Loved me though she might have, this life did not suit her. A burden is kingship, and so too for those with whom he is intimately connected."

I grimaced. "I do know a bit about that."

"I do not envy him," Anwar mused, and I knew he spoke of

Elyan. "Even if his innocence could be proven and the trust of his people restored despite his magic, he must still remove his brother from his throne, and your Master Viscario with him. Such a task will require resources far beyond what I can imagine."

"On our side of the gate, his magic is immensely powerful."

"Yes, of course, but he is one man, one Mage, and did you not say his brother has hundreds if not thousands in his employ? And what of his armies? I know very little of war, of course, Syr'Aliem being so isolated and with little strategic value, but I would imagine your Prince Elyan will need armies of his own."

"I suppose he will."

"And where is he to find them, pray?"

"I imagine there are many who'll be keen to follow him to victory, Mage or no, for Keric's madness has harmed Tiralaen irrevocably."

"Yes, but they also stand to lose everything should he fail."

The man sitting beside me knew nothing of my homeland but what I'd told him, and yet he seemed to more fully grasp the enormity of our task and the opposition we would likely face than I had. I realized then just how ignorant I was, how provincial I must've seemed, with a head full of fire and knowledge gleaned only from books, not from life.

Before I could soothe my bruised ego and troubled thoughts, King Anwar continued: "I imagine Keric has many allies outside of Tiralaen, neighboring kingdoms who are beholden to him."

"Indeed, though many have turned against him in the last several years."

"Elyan should seek them out first—the ones who have turned, that is, provided they have sufficient armies and funds," he said thoughtfully. "Do you know if their sovereigns have daughters not yet promised?"

I frowned. "Yes, but why should that matter?"

"Because it seems to me that the easiest way to form an alliance with a neighboring kingdom of means is marriage."

If I had looked down at my feet in that very moment and seen a gaping black maw where the floor should have been, it would have made perfect sense for I felt suddenly as though the ground upon which I stood had disappeared entirely, leaving me weightless and utterly bewildered.

"Marriage," I repeated.

"Of course. Prince Elyan has little to offer but his name, but should his campaign prove successful, his future wife would be queen, and his children kings after him—a boon for any kingdom, and well worth the risk, particularly if his power is as great as you say. His children may not be Mages, but his bloodline will, eventually, yield fruit."

"He could make alliances without the offer of his hand and crown," I said. "After all, many neighboring kingdoms have suffered under Keric, and they've Mages aplenty. It follows that they should wish to see him dethroned as much as we do."

King Anwar shrugged. "Perhaps, but they will expect compensation for their contribution, especially if their people may die in the attempt. Places in his court, perhaps, and upon his council, these he can promise them, but Elyan is young and unmarried. They will expect him to make an advantageous match. Indeed, I rather think they will insist upon it."

"And if this should be unfavorable to him?"

"Does your prince only do what is favorable to himself?"

"No," I agreed softly. "I do not suppose he would."

"I've upset you," King Anwar said, studying my face with worry upon his own. "It was not my intention."

"You've not upset me." I tried yet again to force a smile upon my face and found that I could not; good, for it hardly suited my mood.

"A pretty lie," he said softly.

"Indeed not."

"You need not conceal your thoughts from me. I know you care for him."

"You've no right to my thoughts, king or no," I snapped.

It was cruelty, and he'd been nothing but kind, even if his words were abhorrent to my ears. It was not his fault I'd given more thought to mysteries and scheming than I had to more practical matters, assuming that the degree of freedom I'd become accustomed to this side of the Gate would inexplicably follow me through.

"Forgive me, your highness," I said. "That was unforgivably rude."

"Only if you will forgive me first. I meant no disrespect."

I answered softly: "Nor did I."

"Come." He smiled and stood, offering his hand to me. "I think I've kept you from your companions long enough."

//

We met Evolet and Arlo as we descended from the balcony, come from the gaming halls flushed with drink and merriment, the latter bearing the spoils of his cunning in the form of several necklaces that he wore one over the other, gold and silver and encrusted with gems. The sum of such a prize in Tiralaen could have sustained a small village for a year.

"There you are," Arlo scolded. "Why did you run off? You missed a most marvelous afternoon."

I flushed, remembering my earlier deception. "I stepped out for a bit of air and must've gotten turned about."

"And how did you enjoy my brother's favorite garden, dear Briony?" Evolet asked, and though her tone was sweet and she fluttered her eyelashes most beguilingly, I did not for a moment believe that she had not been somewhat responsible for Anwar finding me the way he did; she'd allowed my flight from the game room too easily, and I'd been foolish not to realize it.

A low bell reverberated in the distance, a summoning; we were to dine shortly, a most splendid occasion, we were promised.

"You go on ahead," Princess Evolet said. "For I am not properly dressed and must first to my chamber."

I could not imagine what finer gown she planned to wear than the layers and layers of pale blue silk with bracelets of silver that curled up her arms from wrist to shoulder, but she bid us farewell nonetheless, as did her brother, who had some matters of state to attend to before he might join us for more pleasant things.

It was Fellior who appeared with two guards to escort us to the dining hall, and with him was Thaniel, looking cheerful after his work in the stillroom with Kevren.

"Granted, I'm no expert with tools meant to heal, but I think we may have cracked it," he told us with great enthusiasm as we walked. "In fact, I rather hope I'll have time to assist Kevren again tomorrow. He has a great many more ideas to improve the treatment of injuries among Syr'Aliem's soldiers."

Arlo snorted. "A little outside your area of expertise, wouldn't you say?"

"What exactly do you mean by that?"

"Well, this Kevren of yours heals, while you—how shall I put this?—maim."

"Can magic not do both?"

"Yours certainly has not."

I feared they meant to goad one another into blows over Kevren and the instruments in the stillroom, and so I said hurriedly, "Will you ask him about the particular mix of herbs he used to heal your wound? I should very much like to know in case we come upon them again in our travels."

It was with considerable difficulty that Thaniel tore his gaze from Arlo's mocking grin. "Of course," he answered. "I am sure Kevren would be happy to help us in such a way."

We were to use the smallest of the dining halls we'd seen that afternoon, and waiting at the door as we arrived were Elyan and

Phyra, the latter looking disappointingly unchanged since leaving our company earlier. I hoped a good meal and a night's rest might restore her spirits.

As Thaniel took her arm gently and inquired after her health, I bounded to Elyan and grasped one of his large hands with both of mine. "I am ever so envious of you! Tell me everything—what did it look like? How many books were there? Did you find anything useful?"

Elyan's eyes flickered over the top of my head to Fellior, and he frowned slightly. "Perhaps we will discuss it later, hm?"

I wished then that the Steward of Syr'Aliem might meet suddenly with some unfortunate ailment or another. Rather, he waved his arms about with a ridiculous flourish, and the liveried servants standing at attention upon either side of the door opened it to admit us beyond the threshold.

"The king and his family will be with you shortly," Fellior told us. "In the meantime, please do enjoy yourselves."

"By the Gods, this place is amazing," Arlo declared as delicate glasses full of pale green liquid were presented to us by more servants. "What is this?"

"Calique, sir."

"I have no idea what that is, but I'm going to drink it anyway."

I was far more interested in the trays of savory delicacies and sampled no less than three before they were whisked away; I keenly mourned their loss.

Glasses in hand, we were led to a magnificent table set for eight, covered in sumptuous fabric of the deepest green and set with a dizzying array of plates and gold flatware. Candelabras rose up between urns of flowers, and everywhere crystal glittered by the light of a hundred Lumens. The display was set before a magnificent hearth, above which hung a painting of a hunting party: the gentlemen were outfitted with bows and arrows, and the women reclined at their feet upon blankets, their gowns slipping below their shoulders and baring their breasts in such a way that would be inappropriate even to paint in Tiralaen, and yet, based on what I had thus far experienced, I had no difficulty believing was quite commonplace in Syr'Aliem.

Thaniel took a cautious sip from his goblet and glanced sidelong at Elyan. "Is this what your life was like all the time, mate? Crystal and servants and such?"

"Sometimes," Elyan admitted. "But I find it as ostentatious now as I did then."

Arlo, however, had no such qualms. "After the hovel I grew up in, I thought Asperfell was grand. I may never leave this place."

"I think that is a spectacular idea," Thaniel answered at once.

"Oh, I don't know," Arlo said with a wink. "I think Phyra would miss me too much."

Phyra usually took Arlo's teasing in stride, with a withering look or a flat comment that sent Arlo into a fit of laughter. But now, she pressed her lips together tightly and said nothing.

Elyan looked about, a slight frown upon his face. "In fact, this place rather reminds me of the Citadel in many ways. Strange, that."

Spoken aloud, I realized it was true. The Citadel was made of the purest white marble, and although the white stone that surrounded us did not glimmer with the same golden sheen, owed to threads woven in by the most skilled Alchemists when first the Citadel was constructed, these walls were still strikingly similar, as were the chandeliers and golden sconces dripping with crystal, the sumptuous fabric of the curtains and heavy brocade and tasseled ties. And King Gavreth's throne room had boasted a breathtakingly intricate mosaic floor similar to the one we'd stood upon the night we'd come to the Forest Kingdom, and there had also been windows from floor to ceiling that opened onto balconies, and hadn't I seen in paintings that the throne room had once been surrounded in marble columns as well?

Even the ceiling of this dining hall was painted in airy shades of blue with languid smears of white clouds and a dusting of stars, and I could've sworn I'd seen just such a ceiling in Queen Alenda's receiving room when my mother had been called to attend her and brought Livia and myself along.

"Well, having never been in the Citadel, I shall have to take your word for it," Arlo announced and, noticing his glass was empty, promptly beckoned a nearby servant.

"And you, Briony?" said Elyan, watching me closely. "What do you make of Syr'Aliem?"

"It is perfectly splendid," I answered. "I never realized how much I'd missed the Citadel until now. This place is extraordinary—I cannot fathom how they managed to create so much beauty in such a wild place, and everyone has been so generous and obliging."

Well, all save Isri, though I did not say as much.

"It is a pity Iluviel wasn't built around its own Incuna," I added. "Think of how much more wonderful it would be if 'twere so! Instead, all we have is the Gate."

Elyan did not smile at my jest. "Ah yes, what is a Gate between worlds compared to an ostentatious palace?"

I frowned. "Was the veil between the worlds already thin in that place before the Shining City was built around it, or did the concentration of so many Mages in the capital make it thus over time? I seem to remember Master Aeneas lecturing me about it many years ago, but I cannot remember."

"That is because no one knows for certain. I made a thorough study of it in my youth, only to find that for every one scholar who claimed the Gate existed centuries before the city, there was another who declared 'twas the city that begat the Gate. All of them claimed to have proof, which of course meant none of them did." He shrugged. "It is, unfortunately, a riddle I do not imagine will ever be solved."

Before I could inquire further, we were summoned to the table; the arrival of our hosts was imminent.

We sipped Calique as we waited, and within moments, King Anwar appeared, followed by Princess Evolet (who had, indeed, changed into a breathtaking gown of deepest red), the Dowager Queen, and her slender manservant, whose name I did not know but whom I had decided to call Bean Pole. He was, of course, carrying the likeness of the late king upon his customary velvet pillow.

The princess had, indeed, changed into a breathtaking gown of deepest red, and the crowns that she and her mother wore atop their flawless coiffeurs were encrusted with so many glittering jewels I was surprised their necks did not bend with the weight of them. I was chagrined to see the wreath of gray still about the queen's neck and wondered if she ever took it off. After she had taken her seat, her faithful servant positioned himself beside her and lowered the pillow so that the effigy was close enough that she could reach out and absentmindedly run her fingers over its hand and cheek and through its mane of hair.

Now that they'd been made aware of the morbid nature of the Dowager Queen's affectations, my companions averted their eyes and attempted the appearance of disinterest; Arlo failed spectacularly, smothering his laughter in his napkin until Phyra nudged him sharply in the side.

"Welcome, friends," King Anwar said, his bronze hair gleaming in the candlelight and his smile every bit as radiant. He took his place in the grand chair to my right, and servants brought forward our first course, a disappointingly small bowl of pale green soup swirled with cream. I busied myself with the tasting of it.

"I apologize for my absence this afternoon," the king continued as we ate. "I do hope that my sister was a suitable guide."

"She was indeed," said Arlo. "I must confess I found your gaming halls most diverting."

"They are splendid, are they not? And you, your highness? I take it you enjoyed our library, humble though it must be compared to your own in Tiralaen."

"Why was it that only Prince Elyan was allowed to see your library?" I asked before the man himself might respond. "I dearly longed to see it for myself."

King Anwar's fingers idly traced the rim of his goblet as he studied me. "Only the king and the royal scholar are permitted within the library. To allow another was a remarkable thing, and I would not but that he is a king himself. No woman has ever been permitted within."

"But that's ridiculous!"

A spoon fell at the far end of the table, clattering quite unfortunately upon a porcelain dish.

"Shit." Arlo scrabbled to snatch it up again. "Sorry, sorry."

Down the length of the table, the Dowager Queen's narrowed eyes bore into my own. "You are astonishingly free with your opinions of a kingdom in which you've been a guest all of one night."

It was King Anwar who swept in to rescue the conversation. "Tell me, Prince Elyan, is anyone other than the king and his scholars allowed in the royal library of Tiralaen?"

"Those at court are, yes," Elyan answered reticently.

"They were far more than allowed," I said. "Such pursuits were encouraged, for how else could they properly advise their king?"

King Anwar turned, regarding me with mild amusement. "How radical your kingdom!"

Across the table, Elyan fixed me with a look of admonition.

I ignored him. "Why should the education of those who guide the decisions of a kingdom be radical? Or anyone else, for that matter. My own family was a great contributor to the common libraries of Iluviel."

Elyan looked as though he would've happily murdered me in that moment.

"Libraries, did you say?" asked Anwar.

"Indeed. The royal library is by no means the only one. The university boasts a fine collection from all over the continent, and most of the temples have libraries in addition to their archives. Why, most noble houses have their own libraries. In fact, we had quite a large one in Orwynd where I spent my youth."

"Is that so?"

"Oh yes," I continued, my tongue quite run away with me such that I could not seem to stop talking, even as I wondered if I ought to. "My Aunt Eudora was a fearsome creature indeed, but she was most free with it. No book was ever denied me. Indeed, she even allowed the staff to borrow whatever they liked so long as they returned the books in pristine condition."

A stillness settled over King Anwar, though his smile did not falter. "The staff," he repeated. "You refer to the common folk."

"I do."

"And you agree with their education?"

"Of course! For how else are they to improve their minds and elevate their stations?"

"Elevate their stations," Anwar repeated slowly, rolling my words about his tongue, and I began to feel a flush creep up the back of my neck.

I'd not thought what I'd said terribly shocking; I'd certainly said far worse. But their expressions told me very well otherwise, and when I dared glance across the table at Elyan, I saw disappointment mingled with restrained fury in his pale eyes. Only one day had passed since he'd exacted a promise from me to show restraint, to acquit myself with decorum and modesty, *not* to speak. All afternoon, I'd endured the tedium of behaving the way a proper noblewoman should and, save the occasional unfortunate comment here and there (which I exceedingly doubted the princess understood), I'd succeeded tolerably well, only to stumble now—and before more significant company.

On the tip of my hapless tongue was an amendment to my statement which I most certainly did not believe, but before I could speak, Anwar's lips curled into a wild and indulgent smile. "My mother is right, Mistress Briony: you *are* free with your opinions. A testament to your unique upbringing, I think."

"I assure you, your highness, my opinion on this matter would've been the same had I come of age in a palace or a prison. Knowledge is power, and all should possess it."

Knowledge is power.

Someone had spoken those same words to me before, but I could not remember who. An ache began to grow between my temples, and I pressed the heel of my hand to my offending head.

"You have a handsome stillroom," Thaniel spoke up from farther down the table, mercifully diverting the conversation and freeing me from King Anwar's penetrating gaze, and from the pain blossoming behind my eyes. "And your healer is most adept."

"He is quite something, is he not?" the king answered. "And possessed of your magic as well as ours."

"Are there many such in Syr'Aliem?" Thaniel asked. "With our magic within their blood?"

"Not so very many. Tell me, is magical blood as rare in your own land as it has been in Syr'Aliem since your kind settled amongst us?"

"It is indeed," Elyan answered.

"How does it pass within families?"

"With difficulty. Before me, my great grandfather's sister was a Mage. And before her, there had been no other for at least two generations."

Phyra added softly: "Three for me."

"My mother was a Mage," Thaniel said, and his voice was terribly wistful. "A Naturalist."

A faint flush appeared on Arlo's cheekbones, and he downed the contents of his glass in one swift swallow.

"And what of your magic?" Elyan asked King Anwar. "We've demonstrated and discussed ours at length, but have yet to see yours."

"Oh, but you have, though it is far more subtle, less easy to show. The manipulation of light, the nurturing of crops, the healing of the body. The natural magic of the Incuna."

"What exactly is this Incuna?" I asked as our bowls were whisked away, replaced by equally small plates of what appeared to be large, brightly colored roots sliced paper-thin, arranged so beautifully as flowers that I was loathed to eat them, though the sauce drizzled artfully about them was so decadent that I had to make a concerted effort not to groan aloud when I tasted it.

My companions appeared as enamored of the rich fare as I was, though not, perhaps, as enthusiastic; all except for Phyra. She had taken no drink, eaten very little soup, and at that moment appeared lost in thought, staring down at her plate without seeing anything upon it. Quite unexpectedly, for it was not often that he showed consideration for anyone but himself, Arlo appeared to be trying to coax her to eat something, or perhaps drink a bit of water.

"If you don't," he warned, "I'll be forced to sing to you again, and absolutely all of the lyrics will be extremely, shockingly inappropriate."

I was heartened to see that, even as she afforded him a withering stare, she nibbled weakly upon the edge of a root.

"The Incuna was here long before we were, so we cannot know its history," the Dowager Queen said from the far end of the table. "Members of the Court may draw upon its magic, through its chosen king, my son. It is through him, and him alone, that we are blessed by the bounty which the Incuna provides."

"The king is chosen by the Incuna?" I said. Though Garundel had told us as much, I had not quite recognized all of the implications at the time. "Then who was king before you?"

"My father," he answered. "And his father before him, and his father before him."

"The Incuna has chosen our family to govern the Forest Kingdom for almost three hundred years," the Dowager Queen added, gazing fondly upon her husband's effigy. "We have been most fortunately blessed and, in turn, have blessed those within our care."

"Has Syr'Aliem never had a queen?"

"It has not."

"A pity, that."

"And your Tiralaen?" King Anwar inquired.

"Regrettably, no," I answered. "Titles, and thus nobility, are bequeathed only from father to son. I had thought perhaps your Incuna might be more like our magic and bestow its favor with more... equanimity."

"Do not disparage the will of the Incuna," the Dowager Queen fairly growled. It was a most unexpected and animalistic noise from her thin, painted lips.

"I'm sure she did no such thing, mother," said the king. "In fact, I must confess to find the idea of titles and nobility fascinating. You see, we have nothing like it here in Syr'Aliem."

Elyan frowned. "But what are the Court Eternal, then, if not nobility?"

King Anwar reclined in his chair as a servant silently stole forward and refilled his glass. "They are quite spectacular, I grant you, but they've no titles like your nobility have, for, you see, they have no land, no... what is the word?"

"Estates," I offered.

"Yes, that's right! Estates. They give the throne neither coin nor soldiers as yours do, for they have none of their own."

"Then what do they give the throne?" Elyan asked. "Counsel?"

"Occasionally, though they are not terribly good at it. No, the court's purpose is much like the magic of the Incuna itself: subtle and hard to demonstrate."

Arlo outright guffawed to hear a king talk so about his own court, and even Thaniel could not contain a hearty laugh. As for myself, I must confess an audible chuckle did escape my lips.

"Yes, you may laugh," said Anwar, "but the jape is nearer the truth than you realize. The Court is simply this: those people who are capable of wielding the magic that pours forth from the Incuna through me. Nothing more, nothing less."

So, it was magic that determined status in Syr'Aliem, not riches. There was no joy to be had in such a revelation, for magic appeared quite capriciously in our world, and little different did the Incuna seem to me: it was all an accident of birth, just as titles were. Just as thrones were. A world away from everything I'd ever known, and yet it was exactly the same, infuriatingly so.

"Why does it affect us, then?" Arlo asked. "We are not of Syr'Aliem, and yet the Incuna has seen fit to wreak havoc with our magic."

"From what we can tell, and mind you, much of what we know has been derived from what scholars wrote hundreds of years ago about your kind, the Incuna amplifies your magic," the king said.

"But why should that render some of us ill?"

The Dowager Queen turned her nose up. "Some of your magic is quite untoward."

"You refer to Phyra's magic?" Thaniel offered, and though he kept his tone perfectly civil, there was no mistaking the sharpness in his gaze.

King Anwar attempted to intercede with a shrug. "The Incuna is ancient, and quite unfathomable."

"Decidedly *not*," his mother stated. "Power like hers, to return whomever she chooses to life, is too important to be held by someone so common."

Thaniel stiffened while Elyan begged me with silent eyes not to climb onto the table, crawl across china and crystal and smash the Dowager Queen's face into her soup.

It was Arlo who broke the terrible silence: "Phyra being anything but common notwithstanding, her power doesn't work like that."

"Indeed?" King Anwar's eyes gleamed in sudden interest, and he leaned forward. "And how exactly does it work?"

"She must bargain for the souls she seeks to return. In the end, the choice is not hers if balance cannot be struck."

Phyra looked up from her plate, her dark eyes wide with surprise.

Arlo shrugged. "I do listen on occasion."

The Dowager Queen glowered at her son, then bent over the velvet cushion, whispering harshly into the ear of her dead husband's effigy.

The next course arrived, as woefully sparse as the last, and King Anwar shifted the conversation to Tiralaen. The meat was sliced into perfect medallions atop a bed of mushrooms, surrounded by pinpricks of thick, peppery syrup. Beside it was a narrow, delicate tower of pastry and mousse in alternating layers, and both were tragically meagre, all the more sorrowful for how delicious they were. I finished mine in moments.

The dizzying array of wines that accompanied them were far more liberally poured, and I found my head growing muddled.

It was becoming increasingly obvious that the only reason Princess Evolet maintained her delicate figure eating such decadent food was that she ate so little of it. As for myself, I'd have much rather eaten three or four more helpings of everything and happily accepted the consequences, for I felt dreadfully unsatisfied when a servant asked the king in murmured tones if we were ready for sweet wine.

When glasses of rosy liquid shimmering with tiny bubbles were before us all, Anwar lifted his own, studying the effervescence within momentarily before his gaze slid to Elyan. "Briony was kind enough to share with me the story of your rather remarkable escape from Asperfell," he began. "But she was reluctant to tell me how you came to be in my forest yesterday, or what it is you seek."

I opened my mouth, indignant words poised on the tip of my

tongue; under the table, Elyan kicked me swiftly in the shin and my mouth snapped shut. I busied my mouth instead with sipping the dessert wine, the bubbles tickling my nose, though not unpleasantly.

Elyan took a long, slow swallow from his own glass, then said: "At Asperfell, we learned of a place in the north, a cave where the veil between worlds is thin enough that we might, with some luck, pass from this world back to our own."

"And you require my help in finding it," King Anwar finished. "This is, of course, why you offered us aid in the forest, is it not?"

"It is," Elyan answered. "But now will you indulge me a question, as you have asked many of us?"

"Of course."

"Who was it that attacked you in the forest such that you were in need of our help at all?"

King Anwar gazed down the table to where his mother sat, her fingers curled tightly around the base of her goblet. "They are a primitive people who dwell deep within the forest," he said at last.

"They have magic," I said, remembering the way the forest folk had fought, the supple, fluid grace with which they'd handled their weapons—indeed, their own bodies, for they'd been grace itself, however vicious.

Anwar's eyes narrowed. "They draw from our Incuna. They are thieves."

Elyan frowned at this. "They are able to draw from the Incuna without being chosen by it, as you and your court are?"

King Anwar seemed even less inclined to answer this question than the first, and I wondered if we had not stumbled into a rather contentious subject. We were, after all, strangers to this land and had no knowledge of the shared history of its peoples, nor of the intricacies of their present relationship, which was, evidently, very poor indeed as they'd been hacking at one another with swords when we'd happened upon them.

"They were once of the court, it is said, but that was long before my family's reign. They took more from the Incuna than could be sustained. The flow of magic began to suffer, the *people* began to suffer. We had no choice but to cast them out."

"Yet they stubbornly persist," the Dowager Queen said flatly. "Fools."

Down the table, Princess Evolet took up her glass. "Well, that is quite enough about them," she declared, smiling about at us. "You've positively spoiled the mood, dear brother."

"My apologies," Anwar said with a nod to Elyan, and not his sister. "We were, I believe, speaking of your cave."

"We were, indeed," said Elyan.

King Anwar leaned back in his chair, his fingers steepled at his chin. "As it happens, I may know somewhat of what you seek."

I had quite a few more questions about the deserters poised upon the tip of my tongue, but his admission sent me bolt upright in my chair. "You know where it is?"

"Not precisely, but I remember reading about a series of caves in the mountains beyond the forest to our north," he answered, amusement at my outburst dancing in his eyes. "One is said to be possessed of a strange magic that quite baffled the scholars of old."

"That must be it!" I exclaimed.

"Briony." This, from Elyan, whose eyes were narrowed in skepticism most acute.

"*Elyan*," I said, mocking his tone. "Master Viscario returned to Tiralaen weeks ago. We must make ready to leave!"

"Peace, Mistress Briony!" Anwar laughed. "It will take time to seek out the proper records and chart the journey. And if I may, it has been centuries since Syr'Aliem has had occasion to host your kind. I should very much like you all to stay as my guests, even for a short while. So that we may know you better."

"Your highness is most generous," Elyan answered. "But we are in haste. Every moment we spend this side of the Gate exacts a heavy price."

"If you dare journey farther into the forest without our aid, you will not survive the deserters," King Anwar said, and though his tone was pleasant enough, there was no mistaking the shrewdness in his gaze. It was not advice he gave, but a warning. "You would do better to avail yourselves of our hospitality before beginning your journey anew. My scholar is most astute; like as not, he will find some mention of your cave in the ancient texts that will help you considerably."

"I, for one, think that is a spectacular idea," Arlo volunteered. "If we've got a long way still to go, perhaps a bit of rest would do us good. But I suppose his knightliness will want to leave immediately."

Thaniel looked slightly abashed. "Actually, I agree. What?"

"I said, 'bullocks,'" Arlo said.

"Regardless, I do agree. We're likely to journey faster once we're fully rested and recovered."

"We've recovered enough," Elyan declared, then turned to Anwar. "Though we thank you for the offer of your hospitality."

The king would not be deterred. "A fortnight, only. Time enough for my scholar to locate that which you seek, and for you to recover from your arduous journey thus far."

I knew full well Arlo was interested merely in immersing himself in as much opulence and gluttony as he could, but that

Thaniel should wish to delay our journey gave me pause. Before he had passed through the Gate to Asperfell, Thaniel had been a member of the resistance against Keric, fashioning explosives and other weapons for them with his unique abilities. I'd expected him to be irate at the prospect of delaying our return.

Two against leaving, and two for it. But there could be no doubt about Phyra's desire to flee, and quickly. For her sake, we must surely—

"A fortnight," Elyan agreed. "And then, map or no, we must depart."

King Anwar raised his glass in salute. "Wonderful," he said. "Now that's settled, shall we to tonight's entertainment?"

"Actually, your highness," I said, "if I may, there is one thing."

Elyan's gaze fell hard upon me, but King Anwar's face remained merry. "Name it," he said.

"I understand the inconvenience our arrival must've caused for you and your court, but my companions and I are housed quite far away from one another. If we are to be your guests for so many—" Here, I shot a harsh glance at Elyan— "*many* days, we should prefer to be housed together."

The king considered me for so long in silence that I feared I'd made a terrible miscalculation and quite overestimated the small measure of my influence over him. At last, he smiled. "You will forgive me, but you came to us as criminals possessed of powerful magic. Until I knew you could be trusted, I could hardly allow you the freedom to scheme together as you please."

"And do you now believe we can be trusted?"

"I am not yet decided on the matter," he answered, his smile slow and warm. "But I would certainly like to think so." He beckoned with a flick of his wrist to a nearby servant. "See that

Fellior prepares a suite of rooms for Mistress Briony and her companions."

My heart swelled. "Truly?"

"You will still be under guard, of course. And all of your movements reported upon as necessary."

"We understand," I answered in a giddy rush. "Oh, thank you, your highness!"

He regarded me with amusement. "You offer your thanks with much enthusiasm for so small a favor."

It was no small favor to me, nor to Phyra, but it was perhaps better that he not know that, and so I merely smiled and said nothing at all.

12

King Anwar was true to his word. After he, his mother, and sister bid us goodnight, we were given to the care of two Tacé who led us to a large suite of rooms, resplendent and gleaming with dark wood paneling and walls of deep forest green stamped with medallions of gold.

At the end of the common room, a large hearth with a white stone mantle held the largest Lumen I'd seen yet within the palace, and before it, chairs and divans surrounded a low table upon which sat a gameboard unfamiliar to me, its pieces made of glass, one side clear, the other black.

Candelabras full of smaller, flickering Lumen lined the room, and a decanter of Calique sat upon a small table, surrounded by gleaming crystal. Arlo made for it at once while Thaniel watched one of the Tacé lead Phyra away. She looked even more weary than she had at dinner.

"I must congratulate you," Arlo remarked as he swallowed deeply from his goblet. "I'd always assumed your gift extended only to umbras and that sort. Huzzah, and all that."

"What do you mean? I used no magic against the king."

Arlo smiled slyly. "Did you not?"

"No!"

"Indeed? Well, either way, his highness is in a right huff."

Elyan was, in fact, nowhere to be seen, having selected a room for himself and shut himself within it without a word to any of us. I'd caught his eye when we first entered the suite, hopeful that we might have a moment to speak alone so that I might discuss with him my veiled apparition, but he'd turned from me, his eyes cold beneath black hair grown too long.

"Well, that is utterly ridiculous."

"It is. It really is." Arlo handed me a glass of Calique, which my frayed nerves gratefully accepted. I took a rather unladylike swallow and welcomed the lightheadedness that followed. "But I cannot say I blame him. He does seem rather intrigued by you."

"Elyan?"

"Well, of course he is, but no, I meant the king."

"Nonsense."

"If you say so."

"He finds me irksome, most likely."

Arlo gave a shout of laughter. "Oh, yes. The way an itch is irksome, and yet so glorious to scratch."

My face flushed in mortified outrage. "You speak out of turn."

"I do, I really do."

"Sometimes I wish we had left you back at Asperfell," I told him, and his laughter followed me as I left him for the sanctity of my new chamber.

The moment I set foot within, I decided I would happily endure Arlo's ill-mannered teasing rather than what lay in wait for me.

Isri stepped forward and began to unfasten the hooks of my gown with deft fingers and, despite the no-doubt delicacy of the brocade, jerked it down the length of my body. "I'm sorry. I did not know you were waiting."

She knelt and slapped my leg none too delicately. Glaring at the top of her head, I stepped out of the circle of fabric and she bundled it up into her arms as though it were soiled bedlinen and swept from the room, leaving me to my own ministrations. I was glad to see her go, so tiresome did I find her, and after scrubbing my face far too vigorously and attacking my teeth as though they were Isri's face, I threw myself into bed with far more force than necessary.

It was a very, very long time until my stubborn eyelids remained closed and I felt myself begin to drift.

Into this fragile sleep stole a faint sound at the window behind me, a scratching such that branches might make when tossed in the wind, tapping and scraping and dragging their brittle fingers across the glass. It was so innocuous at first, so perfectly mundane a sound, that I drowsed further, little troubled until it grew bold, insistent. And into my ear, something began to whisper.

I came awake fully in a black room, my heart fluttering so quickly in my chest that I could scarcely breathe. Earlier I'd admired the lovely balcony outside the windows.

And I'd seen no trees.

Twisting under the heavy covers, I sat up and stared behind me into the night beyond the glass, waiting, poised upon the edge of a breath for whatever it was that had awakened me, that had whispered, for I was certain the two were connected somehow.

Moments passed, and the world outside the window was still.

I should have felt relief, for did such stillness not reveal that it had been my imagination and my exhaustion that had conjured such peculiar sounds? And yet I could not forget them, the unrelenting, brutal raking upon the glass nor the anguished whispers. It had felt so very real; deep within my marrow, I was still shivering.

Climbing hesitantly from the bed, I crept to the windows with a hand full of flame, but I could see nothing in the glass but my own face peering back at me, pale and unsettled, by the merry glow of my magic. Dark smudges marred my eyes and, had I more than passing care for my appearance, I might've been mortified that King Anwar had seen me thus; I looked as weary as I felt.

As I stared at my visage floating in the dark, the whispering began again, creeping forth from the shadows gathered in the corners of the room, stealing into the recesses of my mind: the same strange language, the same echoing sobs, soft as a breath, anguish and sorrow permeating me so thoroughly that I began to tremble.

Before me, something white rose within the midnight glass.

Fog, I thought perhaps, or smoke, but as I stood, quite unable to move as dread mingled with irrational anticipation, a shape emerged: veils, endless veils of white, and beneath them, a face. It was long, inhumanly long, with sunken eyes and a mouth that seemed to grow and stretch as the whispering in my head grew louder.

As I watched, horrified and yet transfixed such that I could not turn away even as my heart hammered painfully in my chest, the creature lifted one long, spindly hand and rested it against the glass, drawing the tips of its shockingly brittle fingers down slowly, and I recognized the sound, for it had been the same that had stolen into my dreams and roused me.

Beneath the veils, the mouth gaped, a terrible, dark hole, and she rushed toward me.

I stood again in the field of dry grass and at my feet, stretching on and on endlessly, were the dead, vacant and gone, and yet still they gasped through blackened mouths and stared through sightless eyes, their skeletal fingers reaching for me. Little more than bone beneath skin gone gray, the stench of them filled my nostrils and my throat until I gagged. Recoiling in horror, I stumbled backwards, and my heel collided with skin that slid against what lay beneath until it snapped and shattered; arm, shoulder, jaw, each step devastating them beneath my fear.

A scream caught in my throat and it was then I saw her: the apparition standing on a hill in the distance. Beneath the billowing white veils, her ghastly mouth opened, stretching further and further, and I could hear her dreadful voice as clearly as though she stood at my side and spoke in my ear:

What will come to pass.

I stumbled backwards, flinging my handful of flames as I fell, and the bedcurtains nearest me caught fire. My back struck the bed, and I collapsed into an undignified heap upon the floor. The fire was rapidly spreading up the post where it would no doubt set the whole bed alight.

It took me several attempts to quell the blaze, and by the time I'd extinguished it completely, the curtains were a smoldering, smoking mess and the chamber reeked with the foul scent.

My breath coming in rapid, uneven gasps, I approached the window once more and stared, wide-eyed, into the night. There was nothing at all but the darkness, and the stars glittering in the distant sky.

I was alone once more.

A quarter of an hour passed, and then another, and once I was satisfied that my midnight visitor meant not to return, I sprinted across my room and threw open the door.

I'd thought her a dream the night before, a figment of my

exhaustion on our first night in Syr'Aliem; I'd been wrong. She was truly, absolutely, terrifyingly real.

So, therefore, was what she'd shone me.

What will come to pass.

I'd not spoken to Elyan of his visit to the library; regrettable, for 'twas there I must go, and I certainly could not ask him to take me. Not only was I exceedingly certain he would not, but there was a very good chance he would lock me in my room until the loathsome Isri arrived to wrest me into yet another fine gown for yet another palace tour.

Alone, I was far from certain that I could find the library before being discovered, my spellwork as unreliable as it was. Therefore, it was most fortunate indeed that Arlo's door was unlocked.

"Arlo," I hissed. My foot collided with something solid as I crept into his chamber, and I winced at the sound of glass rolling across the floor, disappearing under the bed. A bottle, no doubt. I nudged the lump under the covers gingerly, then, when he responded only with a grunt, with greater force. "Arlo, wake up."

"Bellus fucking take you," he groaned as he shifted. "Who is it?"

"It's me," I whispered, clasping my hand firmly over his mouth. "Be quiet or you'll bring them all down upon us."

He blinked in the darkness and frowned when my face came into focus. "Briony?"

"As you see."

"Why?"

I sat back on my heels as he sat up, scrubbing his hands through his hair. "I require assistance, and after your uncouth behavior earlier, it is only fair that you be the one to provide it."

"In the middle of the night? Must not be for anything good."

"I assure you I have the most honorable intentions."

He snorted. "I'll bet you do. What is it you need me for?"

"A clandestine adventure."

"Is that so?" He lifted himself up on his elbows. "And what have we to gain from such an adventure?"

"Knowledge."

The expression with which he regarded me could have been politely called withering.

I sighed. "Yes, all right, it is not a particularly exciting excursion, but I could not think of anyone else to ask as it involves breaking and entering."

His eyebrows rose. "And where, exactly, would we be breaking into?"

"The library."

"Yes, well, goodnight." He fell back into the bed and drew the coverlet over himself. Then, when he realized I'd not moved, he flopped back toward me with an exaggerated sigh. "Are you still here?"

"I am. And I am prepared to be most irksome and remain here all night until you say yes."

"Good. Watch me sleep for all I give a damn." He pretended to snore quite loudly.

"You know I cannot ask Thaniel, nor can I tell Elyan," I said to the mound of blankets that was Arlo. "Please! I'll find a way to make it up to you, I promise."

"All right," he grumbled. "Fine. I'll go."

"Excellent!" I spun, whispering excitedly in the darkness. "Oh, and put on your pants. This particular errand requires pants."

I waited outside his chamber door until he had done as I asked, and when he emerged, hair sticking up at odd angles and his night-shirt partially tucked into his trousers, I grasped his hand and fairly hauled him to the door. "You do realize there are guards out there," he pointed out. "We'll not get far."

"Oh yes, we will. If we cause a proper distraction at one end of the corridor, we can escape down the other."

"So you were not, in fact, prepared to remain by my bedside all night."

"I was not."

Arlo cast a spell of muting upon the hinges, and together we peered through the crack of the doors, the vast emptiness of the corridor ahead flooded with moonlight. Arlo pointed. "There." Through the ornate panes of the windows at the far end of the corridor, I could make out the silhouettes of slender branches.

I nodded and whispered: "Perfect."

There came the sound of breaking glass, and branches slithered in through the broken panes. The guards yelped in shock and took off toward the broken glass and I took Arlo's hand in mine and yanked him in the opposite direction. When at last we'd put enough distance between us and the unfortunate windows, Arlo maneuvered us into the shadows that we might find our bearings.

I frowned into the darkness. "I don't suppose Princess Evolet mentioned anything about its location this afternoon and I missed it?"

He regarded me with incredulity. "You think I was paying attention during that tour?"

"Well, then, we need to find a servant."

We meandered about, several times forced to duck behind whatever pillar or corner was immediately useful when we heard the sound of voices. There seemed to be a great deal of coming and going even at this hour; achingly beautiful men and women in various states of luxurious dishevelment were traipsing about, clinging to one another, their trilling laughter lingering in their wake like perfume. Arlo several times looked as though he rather wanted to abandon my foolish quest and join them.

After nearly an hour of fruitless hunting, we happened upon a harried young man with a startlingly pretty face, hurrying down a hall, carrying a golden tray stacked with no less than twelve delicate porcelain plates; he looked positively exhausted. Arlo waited until he'd passed where we hid, then slid smoothly out from behind the pillar.

"Hello there," he addressed the servant.

"What are you doing?" I hissed, but he ignored me and strode forward.

The young man's shoulders stiffened before he turned, but then, beholding the sight before him, his posture relaxed, the corner of his mouth lifting in an appraising smile.

"I am mortified to cause you trouble," Arlo continued. "But I am rather hoping you could help us."

"I suppose I *could*, though I fear it will be a while. I have to deliver these to the kitchens, and then I'm off to the Thesa, and then to the princess herself—"

"No, no, no," Arlo rushed to assure him. "'Tis nothing of the sort. We seek the library. Would you be so kind as to point us in the proper direction?"

"The library?" He sighed. "How very tame."

Arlo nodded at me over his shoulder. "It's for her. Told a gentleman at court she'd meet him there but forgot to ask for directions."

The scoundrel! The servant's eyes flickered over Arlo's shoulder and took me in, clad in nothing but my nightdress; his eyes flashed and his smile widened, and I forced myself to appear ridiculous rather than enraged, blushing demurely at my bare feet even as I wondered what Arlo would look like if I burned off all his hair.

"Directions to the library," the servant mused. "That's all you require?"

Arlo winked, and we found ourselves in possession of what we sought.

Tucked away in a part of the palace that appeared little visited and oft neglected judging by the dust and cobwebs, we found twin scrolls carved upon an otherwise inconspicuous door. "This cannot be it," I whispered.

Arlo grasped the handle and turned it, then turned it again. It would not budge. "Well, shit."

"Indeed."

I'd never been very good at basic spellwork, but if there was one bit of magic I'd managed to master much to Elyan's good humor, it was how to unlock a door, and I did so now with gusto, the door slamming open with a shower of dust and echoing boom.

"So much for not bringing them down upon us," Arlo hissed, and grabbing me by the arm, he propelled us both into the library and shut the door.

We'd no need for Magefire for the room was already softly lit with Lumens. Set into chandeliers and sconces, they bathed us in a soft, golden glow.

It was a small library, smaller even than the one at the prison from whence I'd come, but this was, unmistakably, the resting place of Syr'Aliem's dearly prized knowledge.

Like those in the stillrooms, these books were primitively bound, aged, and looked as though they were very rarely handled by anyone. The shelves that held them were crafted of what might've once been considered finely carved wood but were now sagging with age and, to my chagrin, taller than I, taller than Arlo and with no ladder anywhere in sight.

There seemed to be no discernable order in which the books were kept, only that they were kept in very poor shape indeed, and there were shockingly few for a kingdom of such extravagant wealth.

'Twas Arlo who spoke first. "My expectations were quite low to begin with, being a library and all, but even I have to say this is... underwhelming."

There was a long table near a bank of windows and, save this and the shelves of books, the room held very little for how dearly King Anwar seemed to value the knowledge within. A number of large, crumbling tomes were displayed upon modest wooden stands at each corner, long forgotten for the thick layers of dust that lay over them; an industrious insect of some sort had even begun weaving a web upon one. Baskets lay beside them, scrolls piled within tied with moldering ribbon, and it looked as though something had nibbled at the edges of quite a few. They looked as though they would crumble at the slightest touch.

A series of shelves carved into the stone of one of the library's walls held a sorry collection indeed, but my curious eyes roamed the shelves and their contents with curiosity, for it was so very different than everything else I'd seen thus far in this gilded place. Dusty flagons and phials that may have once held ink now held little more than dried pigment at their bottoms, and I must've swirled the contents of a dozen before I found one that still held liquid, though my nose wrinkled at the pungency within. There were several animal skulls to be found, though I did not recognize their species. Their hollow eyes stared back at me, their pointed teeth and grins grotesque. I shuddered and left them well enough alone.

Behind an earthenware bowl that held an odd assortment of magnifying glasses was a pile of feathered quills and dried flowers; beside these, the carapaces of insects native to this world, and thus dear to my curious eyes, were encased within glass.

Dozens of brittle scrolls were piled haphazardly inside the remaining shelves with little thought to their fragility, some sealed with wax, some with ribbon, and all ancient. I would've dearly loved to examine their contents, but I did not know how much time we had, and I'd come for something most specific indeed.

"Right," Arlo said, surveying the crumbling tomes with distaste. "Where do we start? Do you even know if these are written in our language?"

"I'll save you the trouble," a surly voice piped up from behind the shelves. "*No.* They are not."

Arlo started. "Coleum's balls, who's there?"

"Me," the voice answered flatly.

The creature who emerged was half my height and stout with a long, hooked nose, enormous eyes, and tufts of white hair that stood straight up from his head. The green and gold brocade of his tunic and breeches might have once been fine but had been patched so numerously that they looked quite shabby indeed.

He stared down the length of his nose through a monocle with so many facets that a hundred eyes blinked at me in displeasure. "You are trespassing."

"Yes, well, I am exceedingly sorry about that, but it could not be helped. My name is Briony, and this is my companion, Arlo."

He puffed out the barrel of his chest. "My name is Meriwyn, and I am the keeper of this library. Leave at once, or I will throw you out myself."

Magefire flickered in Arlo's palm. "I rather think not."

I grasped his sleeve, and the small flame extinguished. "We mean you no harm, Meriwyn. Rather, I believe we require your help."

"My help?" he scoffed. "And how could you possibly require my help?"

"We seek information, and this seemed the most appropriate place to obtain it."

His enormous eyes narrowed to slits. "What sort of information?"

I lifted my chin, aware of both their curious gazes upon me. "An apparition. She appeared in my dreams last night, and just now at my window. I wish to know who she is."

"Well, I'm afraid you will need to be a bit more specific."

"Do you mean to say there is more than one apparition who frightens the wits out of Syr'Aliem's guests?"

"Yes. What did this particular one look like?"

"Oh, well, it was rather tall," I answered, taken aback. "And covered in white veils. And it had a crown atop its head made of branches."

Meriwyn's eyebrows disappeared into his hair and the heavy tome clutched in his hands plummeted to the floor with a loud thud. His mouth opened and closed several times before he found his voice, and it emerged as a rather undignified squeak: "You speak of the Dae Spira!"

Arlo frowned. "The who?"

"The Dae Spira," he repeated, and when we stared at him uncomprehendingly, he added breathlessly: "The Goddess!"

"A goddess?"

"No, *the* goddess!"

Quivering with joy, he fairly danced across the room, and before my very eyes, his legs grew and stretched, and up he rose; up, up, up toward the ceiling and the tallest shelves. With graceful, measured steps, he began to circle around them, dragging his thumbs across the moldering spines while Arlo and I watched with mouths agape.

"Never seen a Cluvian before, have you?" He winked down at us before resuming his search. "I was made to keep this library, you see."

"Made by who?" I asked.

"Why, by *her*, of course!"

We stared in awe for several moments while he glided about gracefully on the impossible stilts of his legs until he finally found what he sought. It was as sad and sorry a book as I'd ever seen, a thin folio gone nearly brown with age and bound with ropes of thin, knobby vines. Clutching it to his breast, his legs began to shrink until he was his previous size, and he rushed with his prize to the long table.

"The records of the Dae Spira are few and very old," he informed us, flipping through aged parchment. "Disgraceful, if you were to consult me upon the matter."

In fact, the entire state of the library was quite disgraceful, but we'd not time enough to speak of such injustice. I slid into the chair nearest Meriwyn, and by the light of the many Lumens that surrounded us, I leaned over to observe the page he'd opened to and quite caught my breath, for although the image was terribly faded upon the page and more impression than true likeness, I recognized her at once.

"That's her!" I exclaimed. "That's what I saw!"

"Ha!" he shouted, and in jubilation his legs stretched and grew, carrying him up in a dizzying arc to the ceiling where I feared the Lumens in the chandelier would set his hair alight. He peered down at us with crinkled, crescent eyes. "Do you know what this means?"

Arlo scowled up at him. "If we did, do you think we'd be here in the middle of the night?"

"It means that she has returned!" Meriwyn's joyful tones rang out through the library, and I shushed him furiously, for however wonderful this news might be, I'd no wish to be discovered before I learned why.

"No one knows we're here," I explained as his legs shrank back to their normal stature and he bent over the old book once more, tracing reverently the figure of the goddess. "And I would like to keep it that way."

"After all this time," he shuddered and sighed.

I studied more closely the sketch of the Dae Spira beneath Meriwyn's fingers. "They dress in her likeness—the Tacé."

"Of course they do, for they are made of her; for her."

I swallowed thickly. "And when did she make them, exactly?"

Meriwyn shrugged. "Before me, and that was long ago indeed." He turned the page, and Arlo and I looked over his shoulder at a crude drawing of a sphere held fast by coiling roots. "Ah, the greatest of her creations. Her gift to the people of the forest, whom she loved and took as her own. 'Tis a poor rendering, but I am afraid I have no other."

"This is the Incuna? I wish I could see it!"

"As do I," he agreed wistfully.

"Wait," Arlo said. "You've never seen it?"

"Of course I've seen it," Meriwyn answered witheringly. "But it has been hundreds and hundreds of years. You see, I cannot leave this place. Not anymore."

"Why not?"

The Cluvian sighed. "I wish I knew. I used to be able to come and go freely, day or night. Then, little by little, I found I could not leave at all, to say nothing of the fact that with the coming of the dawn, I sleep, whether I will it or no."

"But that's horrible!" I exclaimed. "Who would put such a spell upon you?"

He scratched his chin with one leathery hand. "Who can say? The answer certainly does not lie within these books; I have read them hundreds of times over hundreds of years."

Elyan had only that afternoon visited this place. To think, the library spirit had been there, sleeping, both unaware of the other.

"She showed me things," I murmured.

"Showed you things?" Meriwyn repeated, just as Arlo said: "What sorts of things?"

I shuddered. "Terrible things. Rotting crops and ruined dwellings in a field of dry grass. And the dying everywhere. She told me it's what is to come."

"She said that?" Meriwyn's voice was as sharp and startling as the Dae Spira's grasp, and I startled at the sound.

"Another prophecy," grumbled Arlo. "They're never of rainbows and kittens, are they?"

At that, my blood ran cold, for I remembered the warning of Garundel. Had the bones of my friends been among those upon which I'd trampled?

Meriwyn fretted and paced. "Oh, if only I could leave this place to warn the others," he muttered.

"Others?"

"All those whom she made. I may be the first you have met, but I am by no means the only one within these walls."

My body sank into the chair beside me, and despite the sudden lightness in my head, I was a stone.

"I don't understand," I croaked. "There is no famine here, no strife. And you've the Incuna! How could these things come to pass?"

Meriwyn surged forward, grasping my arms. "It is only the loss of the Incuna that could cause this devastation. She has shown you the end of all magic!"

"Why?" I gasped. "Why show me these things?"

"She must believe you can change them."

I was still mulling over that thought when something very odd happened.

It began with a tingling beneath my skin and a stirring of air that made the fine hairs at the back of my neck stand on end. Then the whispers came, just as they had in my dream, just as they had before the Dae Spira appeared at my window, but this time it was darkness they brought with them.

One moment, the library was filled with the warm light of the Lumens above; the next, it was as if someone had snuffed out a candle, and within the darkness, everything changed.

It crept forth from the shadows, wild and twisted, curling vines and branches that sank into the stone floor and stretched up the walls to the ceiling where it overtook the chandeliers. The gold and gilt were gone from the room, replaced with a luminous moss that covered walls no longer of carved stone, but of unpolished wood. And where the Lumen had been, the tips of the curling branches were gloriously alight with tiny flames with flickering, ragged edges and wreathed with black.

"What's happening?" I gasped.

Meriwyn looked up. "Why, 'tis only a blackout," he answered, settling his leathery hand atop mine. "Fear not—it will soon pass."

"We should go," Arlo said. "Right now."

Despite Meriwyn's casual dismissal, the legs of the chair upon

which he sat sprouted tendrils that began lazily wrapping themselves around his own. This, he paid no mind to, and yet I could do
little to quell my racing heart. I rose from my seat and sought the
nearest wall, stumbling over thick, gnarled roots, strong and solid.

Arlo likewise made for the nearest wall, seeking something solid
to brace himself upon, and as his palm met a vine, light bloomed—
green and beautiful and blinding. A violent tremor passed through
the Naturalist's taut frame before he wrenched his hand back and
stumbled to where I cowed.

"What is it?" I asked. "What did you feel?"

"Hunger," he answered with a shudder. "*Anger.*"

Throughout it all, Meriwyn sat happily with his book, humming
a lilting tune and turning pages as though it were not happening at
all. Then, as suddenly as it began, the Lumens returned and flooded
the room in golden light, which fell upon white walls and marble
floors and a lacquered table laced with tarnished gold. The shadows
and wild things seethed and recoiled and slithered away in a rush,
and I stood staring once more at the library as it had been before.

Had Meriwyn not named it, and thus given it truth, I might've
thought I'd fallen asleep reading an ancient, crumbling tome and
dreamt it, but no; the library had, for several minutes, been
overtaken by some wild, eldritch force that had utterly transformed
it and then disappeared as though it had never been.

Arlo looked about at the now-restored library with incredulity;
then, his eyes falling upon the library spirit still engrossed in the
book before him, he gave voice to my own thoughts, however
vulgarly: "What the fuck was that?"

"I do not know this word."

"What my companion means to say is, what is a blackout?" I
explained.

"They are quite commonplace, I assure you."

"Yes, but what are they?"

But he could not tell us because he did not know, because nothing of them was written in his beloved books.

Arlo gripped my arm. "We should go. I do not think it likely the others slept through that, nor our hosts."

The guards stared at us with mounting horror as we approached and they attempted to reason out how we were outside of our suite without their knowledge.

Arlo feigned insult quite convincingly. "We were Princess Evolet's guests at the gaming tables, do you not remember? Honestly, it's as if you two have been drinking and not we. Disgraceful."

They admitted us to our suite of rooms with slack jaws and confused gazes.

Clad in their nightclothes, Elyan and Thaniel stood before the hearth arguing, something I rarely ever saw them do. Our absence was, evidently, the cause of such unfortunate conversation, for the moment they saw us in the doorway, their voices stopped abruptly and the tension that had lined their faces gave way to relief, though Elyan's tall frame was still taut and guarded.

"Where have you been?" he snapped. "It's nearly dawn."

"The stillroom," I answered quickly, before Arlo could give us away. "I'd trouble sleeping and sought a posset. I did not think I should go alone, and Arlo was awake, and so he generously offered to accompany me."

Thaniel's eyes narrowed. "Is that right?"

Arlo nodded. "You know me—generous to a fault."

"We did not make it, though," I added, sick with guilt at the lie. "All of a sudden, branches and vines and green appeared everywhere. Wild, savage things. Was it thus for you?"

Elyan gave me only a curt nod in reply.

"On our way back, we overheard a servant call it a blackout," I continued. "She acted as though it were a perfectly ordinary occurrence."

"And so it is."

King Anwar had chosen that exceedingly unfortunate time to arrive, and it did not miss my notice that Elyan looked distinctly less than pleased to see him. He stood in the doorway of our suite of rooms, flanked by a pair of guards.

"My friends, I've come to inquire after your health," he said. "I do hope you were not too terribly frightened tonight."

Had he any inkling of what life in Asperfell had been truly like, he would not have spoken thus.

"Not at all, your highness," Elyan answered tightly. "We are well, as you see."

"Thank the stars."

"Even if it is benign," I pressed, "what exactly is a blackout?"

"A scourge," he answered darkly as he came in to stand before the hearth. "And one we are far too used to within these walls, for otherwise I might've thought to warn you upon your arrival."

"What causes them?"

"We do not know," he admitted. "They have baffled scholars for generations. Terrifying though they might appear, we've never known them to cause harm." He turned his eyes upon me then, and only a fool would've failed to see the way they softened in concern. "You are truly all right?"

I nodded and wished for nothing more than that he would leave and take his loathsome guard with him for I had much to say, and none of it to him.

After many repeated reassurances that we were, in fact, well and hale and in desperate need of sleep, he departed at last, and we were left alone with our mutual exhaustion and, in my particular case, a torrent of thoughts needing to be spoken.

As Thaniel led Phyra quietly away, Arlo ambling after them, I pulled softly at Elyan's sleeve. "Do you remember the dream I told you about? The creature in the white veils and the crown of wood?"

"I do."

"I saw her again, Elyan, only this time it wasn't a dream. She was in my chamber tonight, at my window."

"Your window," he repeated flatly, his expression inscrutable.

"She showed me another vision, only it was worse this time—so much worse." I drew a deep breath. "She said it was what's to come."

"Which is, I presume, why you and Arlo snuck into the library tonight?"

"I... what?"

He snorted derisively. "Do give me *some* credit, Briony."

I wanted to protest, but there was little use for it. "Fine. Yes, I snuck into the library, but you can hardly blame me, for it is utterly ridiculous that I was not invited in the first place."

"And what did you discover?"

He was angry, but he was also a scholar, and curious despite however much he wished to throttle me at that moment. And so I indulged him while he folded his arms across his chest and scowled down at me.

"I cannot believe you left our rooms tonight," he said when I'd finished, shaking his head. "What in Coleum's name were you thinking?"

"I just told you a goddess appeared at my window and gave me a rather horrifying glimpse into Syr'Aliem's future, and that is all you have to say?"

"My apologies. Perhaps you would prefer I praise your idiocy instead."

"How can you say so when it is knowledge I sought?"

"That I must explain it to you is regrettable."

Stung, I reeled back. "Then I shall save you the trouble."

My steps were swift as I crossed the great room to my chamber, flung open my door and made to slam it in his face—except that he caught it with one hand and followed me inside. "I wasn't finished."

"I was," I snapped, poking my finger into his chest. "How dare you barge into my room uninvited!"

He grasped the offending appendage in one large hand, and pulled me against his chest, unable to flee, unable to gain my proper bearings. Here in this borrowed room that was mine for however short a time, I'd expected to command the conversation, to command him, and my own response to him in turn, but he filled the space so quickly, so completely, 'twas as if it had always been his and never mine at all.

"Do you have any idea what might've happened were you and Arlo discovered?"

We were a hairsbreadth away from one another in our anger, my head tilted so far back to hold his gaze with my own that my neck ached. "'Twas not for idle curiosity that I went there," I insisted. "This kingdom is in danger."

His eyes softened. "Whoever she is, whatever it was she showed you, it is not our place to meddle in the affairs of another kingdom, particularly one whose help we are entirely dependent on to return home."

"If you'd seen it, you would not speak thus, Elyan. People here will die."

"People in Tiralaen will die—*are* dying—while we remain here. I agreed to a fortnight so that we might find the map, but even without it, we must leave these people behind us and save our own."

The reminder of home, of the suffering endured by our people at Viscario's hands, had the desired effect, and as the anger drained from me and guilt stole into its place, the weight of the last two days settled over me.

"You're exhausted." Elyan said gently. "You've not slept."

"She won't let me." I shivered and leaned into his chest as his thumb caressed my bottom lip.

"I've no desire for us to fight."

"Sometimes I rather enjoy it when we fight."

"So do I," he answered. "But not about this."

Before I could protest, he hooked his arm beneath my knees and lifted me as though I weighed nothing at all. "But we've not finished," I whispered, clinging to his neck. "I haven't won yet."

"And you won't."

I nearly pulled him down on top of me when he set me down upon the bed, for the loss of him meant defeat and I was by no means ready to agree to anything regarding the Dae Spira. But he pried my fingers from his neck and stood.

"Sleep," he told me. "Perhaps your dedication with regard to the library has earned you a night of reprieve from this goddess."

He moved toward the door, and I reached out and grasped his hand. "And if she returns?"

He looked down at me and smiled. "Well, are you an Orare or aren't you? Tell her to go fuck off."

13

I woke most unpleasantly to the sound of tinkling glass as a tray was placed with some force upon the table at my bedside.

Sitting up in a tangle of blankets and with feverish skin, I beheld a figure dressed all in green and white staring at me, her face twisted in anger as she jabbed her finger at the ruined lump of singed fabric puddled on the floor at the foot of my bed.

"I'm sorry," I managed to croak out. "I had a bit of an accident last night."

Her disgust palpable, Isri swept to the windows and began yanking the curtains open, the brilliant light assailing my eyes. I groaned and tried to burrow back beneath the covers, but found them unceremoniously pulled from me, gooseflesh rising upon my legs beneath the thin fabric of my nightdress. I was, evidently, defeated.

Had she voice, and had she hated me just a little bit less, I might've told her about my clandestine visit to the library and asked her all about the Dae Spira and the horrifying vision. But she did not, and so I said nothing.

A copper tub full of steaming, perfumed water awaited me before the hearth of my bedchamber, and as I sank into its depths,

I read the schedule Evolet had created for our pleasure, every moment of it set in stone, until the words blurred together and I sank beneath the surface that I might rid myself of it.

Isri's rough, impatient hands wrestled me into a gown of mauve and pale pink gauze with a bodice encrusted with silver, stiff to the touch and excruciating when I attempted to breathe. The collar of gems that accompanied it was even more ostentatious, my neck aching with the weight of so many stones; I wondered from what nearby river they'd been stolen. There was nothing on the schedule about traversing beyond the palace wall today, and I ached for some escape from the relentless splendor of the place. I resolved to ask about visiting the village of the common folk, for I had been told it resided but a mile to the east. To the best of my gleaning, this village and the palace itself were the entirety of the Forest Kingdom, although the princess seemed loathe to discuss anything outside the palace itself, and so my curiosity about such things had yet to find satisfaction.

Isri dusted the exposed skin of my shoulders and chest with shimmering silver powder, arranged sprigs of silver and gems in my curls, and departed, my nightdress bundled in her arms and her lips curled in disdain. According to the missive I'd been given, I was to join my companions in a half-hour for a splendid tour of the sculpture garden, followed by breakfast and lawn games.

The princess could wait; I had a much more pressing matter to attend to. I might not be able to pay Meriwyn another visit just yet, but that did not mean there did not exist within the palace other ways of obtaining information.

Outside the door to our suite of rooms, the guards regarded me with skepticism as I informed them that I was expected in Princess Evolet's receiving room and was already late.

"An escort will come for you," Longface rumbled. (I'd begun calling him thus for quite obvious reasons after he'd refused to tell me his given name for fear that the royal family might find it decidedly unbefitting.)

"Look," I said, thrusting a parchment that bore the princess's signature at him, the top folded down so that he could not see what preceded it. "She said she required my opinion on a matter of great importance, and she is not likely to be pleased that the two of you have delayed me!"

His companion (whom I'd nicknamed Grumble) stared down the princess's signature doubtfully, but ultimately they allowed me to pass.

I did not know the way to the kitchens from our suite, but it did not take long to spot a servant carrying a tray stacked with no less than twenty gold-rimmed plates and an even taller stack of matching bowls. I followed him until I reached the servants' hall once more and breathed in the comforting smells of broth and roasting meats that wafted down the corridor from the kitchens.

As I lingered at the threshold and watched the wonderfully familiar bustle before me, I eventually recognized a mop of golden ringlets barely contained beneath a white cap. Just the woman I'd been waiting for. She dropped several heavy sacks on one of the long tables, a white cloud of flour rising into the air, and through it, her eyes met mine.

"I am so sorry to disturb you," I said quickly, for her mouth had gone slack at the sight of me, and hers was not the only one. Evidently, members of the Court Eternal did not venture here often.

"And what's this, then?" The older woman from the other day approached us, hands braced on her full hips. "Can I help you?"

"I only wish a moment of your time," I explained.

"If you've a complaint about the food—"

"No, no, nothing like that. I simply wish to speak to you both."
I paused. "About the Spectre."

Their reactions were immediate and visceral. "Hush!" the older
woman hissed as the younger's cheeks turned scarlet. "Do not let
Perol hear you or I'll lose him to a fit of the vapors!"

"My apologies. Truly, I do not mean to cause you any trouble—
rather, I hope to help you."

"Hmph. How do you mean to do that?"

"I am a Mage of Tiralaen," I explained. "And in my world,
sometimes when magic born die, they leave a shade behind—an
umbra. I believe your Spectre might, in fact, be one of them." My
gaze slid to the younger woman. "And I believe you've magic in
your blood. The magic of my world."

I'd not thought it possible for her eyes to grow any rounder, and
yet I was proven wrong. "Me? Surely you are mistaken."

"Only magic born can see umbra," I answered gently.

The older woman's hand flew to her bosom as she slumped back
against the table. "I'd always wondered if you and Perol were
touched in the head!"

The older woman was named Mavis, the younger Iya, and after
I explained to them my talent for unbinding umbras from the living
world, I was promptly regaled with story after story of the Spectre
and the havoc it had wreaked upon the sanity of poor Perol, who
also must've been descended of my kind.

Evidently, there had long been rumors of a pearlescent shadow
with ghastly, cavernous black eyes that haunted a vaulted chamber
used for storage, but very few had ever actually seen it. In the six
months since Iya had come to the kitchens, it had begun to appear

more and more in the main storage rooms, hovering behind barrels and shelves, no longer a rumor but a menace.

"I will happily speak with your Spectre and, if I am able, ascertain how you might rid yourselves of the fellow," I assured them, and they quickly led me away to scout its usual lurking places. We found it in the vaulted chamber, lingering behind a moldering pillar. Mavis and Iya refused to set foot beyond the threshold, although only the younger could see it.

"Its eyes," Iya explained with a shudder, and in this, I could not say I blamed her.

"It's all right," I told them both. "I will be perfectly fine. Unsettling it may be, but harm me, it will not."

They did not seem convinced, but neither did they hesitate. With furtive, hopeful glances at me, they hurried back up the stairs into the warmth and safety of the kitchen, and I was left alone at last with my quarry.

The magic in my veins had begun to stir the moment I'd laid eyes upon the umbra, and as I crossed the crumbling chamber, I felt it rise, burgeon, flood me with light; oh, how beloved it was; how I'd missed it.

"My name is Briony," I said. "What's yours?"

It did not answer; I was not entirely certain it understood me, and so I tried again. And again, and again. After such an excruciatingly long time that I began to fear the umbra was too old and had forgotten too much, a rasping, hoarse whisper finally filled the space between us:

"*Mosag.*"

"Mosag," I repeated. "I am so very pleased to meet you."

Had he been born in Tiralaen, had he a Trial, he would've been named for what he was: an Elemental Mage with an inclination toward earth and stone. He had not been one of the prisoners who'd escaped Asperfell, but born perhaps two or three generations later, and had never been properly trained in his aptitude. But he knew he'd magic in his blood, cherished it, clung to it, even after death.

It took me nigh on an hour to ascertain this precious knowledge, and by the time I'd done so, I was sweating and shaking so badly that I sank to the ground lest I should keel straight over into the pillar. I'd not used so much of my magic in a very long time, and the effort had utterly exhausted me. I waited until the dizziness had passed somewhat, drew a deep breath, and spoke again.

"Why are you here?"

Another hour passed in arduous communion with the umbra. I learned that Mosag had married and started a family, and had grandchildren, and great-grandchildren, and it was then that he began to utter a single word over and over and over again: *Watch*.

"Watch what?" I croaked, my voice raw, clinging to the vestiges of my magic.

He said nothing more, but drew close to me, the hazy outline of him blurring into the warm, living skin of me, and so many images flooded my mind—faces, beloved faces, of all ages, throughout entire lifetimes.

'Twas not a *what* that he watched, but a *who*, and my joyful, delirious laughter bubbled from within me, echoing throughout the chamber.

Mavis and Iya were piping filling into delicate pastry when I emerged, held upright by sheer determination, for I had never wished more to sink into the blissful oblivion of sleep.

They rushed to my side and I slumped into their strong, capable hands. "I'm all right," I told them. "I only need a moment. I am still quite new to my magic and am easily given to exhaustion."

They clucked and worried and fretted, leading me into a small but cozy room off the main kitchen where they lowered me into a chair and pressed a hot cup of tea into my shaking hands. I took one sip, then another, then looked up at Iya.

"His name is Mosag, and he is not haunting you. He is watching you."

"Watching me?" she breathed. "But... why?"

"Because I was right about you being magic born," I answered. "Because he is your ancestor."

She blinked her enormous blue eyes and promptly sat down.

Mavis poured her a cup of tea as I explained what I had learned, and I watched with a curious sort of pride as emotions passed over her face: shock, joy, hope.

"I truly am one of them?" she asked me. "One of you?"

"Yes. For better or for worse, I suppose." I stood on unsteady legs. I'd been in the kitchens for almost three hours; no doubt the only reason no one had come looking for me is that they could not have imagined this to be the place I would've escaped to. I needed to return to my companions, and soon.

"What will happen to me now?" she asked. "How will I learn my magic? Can I be part of the Court or... or am I too old?"

She was wonderfully ambitious, her eyes bright, already envisioning a life for herself beyond the drudgery of the kitchens, but there was no one in Syr'Aliem trained in our magic enough to teach her even the simplest of spells. I suddenly felt quite melancholy at the thought and wondered how many others there were in this splendid place, both within the palace and without, who bore the magic of my world in their blood, the promise of power, but unable to claim it.

I'd no answers for her, only the vaguest of congratulations and the promise that, as unsettling as Mosag's umbra was, he only wished to watch over his family, his blood.

Mavis humphed. "I don't suppose you could relay that information to Perol? The very last thing I need is another fit of the vapors and a spilled vat of soup."

Hoarse, exhausted laughter erupted from my throat. "I certainly shall."

"Oh, mistress, however shall we thank you?" Iya asked. "You've done us such a service."

And here was why I had come.

"There is a way you might help me, if you like. I seek information—about the Dae Spira."

My heart sank at the blank look they exchanged between them. "Who?" Iya asked.

"No matter. What about the people of Syr'Aliem? What can you tell me of the lives of those outside of the palace? The villagers?"

"We do not know that either, mistress. We've never been outside of these walls."

I blinked. "What?"

"We were born inside the palace," she explained.

"But why should that mean you've never been outside of it?"

"No one within is allowed without."

"No one?"

Iya flushed. "No servant," she elaborated. "There are members of the Court Eternal who live in the Praela, but not us."

Mavis must've seen the disappointment etched upon my face,

for she reached over and covered my hand with hers. "I'm sorry we could not be of more help, mistress," she said. "But if there is ever anything else you require, you know where to find us."

I staggered up into the palace proper, my legs leaden and my skin hot and febrile. Curious eyes watched my excruciating progress, their voices calling out, asking if I might join them for lunch on the rooftop, or a stroll in the garden. I waved them away with assurances that I was quite all right and would join them another time, that I simply needed quiet, needed rest. So absorbed were they in their own pleasure, they did not question me.

I was supposed to be somewhere, although I could not recall where and with whom; there had been a bit of parchment, but I'd left it in the kitchens and the thought of going all the way back for it made me even more dizzy than I already was. Our suite—I simply needed to find our suite, and hope to every single god and goddess I knew in Tiralaen and in this world that Isri had not decided to choose this unfortunate moment to dust my chamber.

"Briony?"

Of course, of all the Court, it would be him. I turned to behold the King of Syr'Aliem, flanked by his guards. "Are you well?"

"I am perfectly well, your highness," I answered. "But I fear I am dreadfully late to... to..."

"An audience with my sister, no doubt," he finished gently. "Allow me to escort you, then."

"That will not be necessary."

Even as I said it, I swayed, and he was by my side in an instant, his hand warm and reassuring at my arm. "I insist."

I'd missed a morning stroll about the grounds as well as our luncheon. My companions were currently attending a concert in the music hall, and it was there that Anwar chaperoned me, steadying my arm even after he'd lowered me into the chair beside Elyan, left open all this time for me.

"I regret I cannot join you," Anwar whispered into the shell of my ear, and I shivered. "But I shall see you at dinner."

He left me to the lilting sound of strings and flutes and Elyan's positively murderous gaze, though whether 'twas meant for Anwar or for me, I could not say.

"You look terrible," he said flatly. "What is it you've gone and done now?"

Ah, so 'twas for me, then.

"I'll be all right by and by. Just used too much magic is all."

"And what in Coleum's name have you been doing that required so much of it?"

"There's an umbra in the kitchen storage rooms."

I heard his exasperated sigh, and sure enough, when I looked over at him, his long fingers were splayed across his temples. He did not speak to me for the remainder of the concert, but his irritation was palpable in the tense bunch of his shoulders, the rigidity of his jaw, the ice of his eyes.

Dinner was an equally uncomfortable affair. He spoke quite civilly with King Anwar and his family on all manner of subjects, though it did not escape my notice that they asked far more of him than they were willing to say of themselves. Anwar's eyes sought mine often, despite my fervent attempts to keep my attention firmly upon my plate, and he, for one, seemed to regret that my exhaustion held my tongue in check, at least for one night.

Elyan, I dare say, was not bothered by it in the least, and the Dowager Queen seemed to positively relish it.

14

Into my dreams that night stole the creature with a crown of branches, her weeping and whispers so loud, so persistent, that no matter how tightly I squeezed my eyes shut, I could not ignore them. There was anguish in them, the low keening of one in the throes of unimaginable pain, and so, sitting up, I glared into the darkness of my empty room and announced quite irritably: "I cannot understand you, so if you don't mind, please cease your endless whispering and let me sleep."

I waited, half-expecting her to emerge from the shadows and fly at me with her grasping, brittle fingers and bear me down upon the bed, but my chamber was still.

Sighing, I pushed the tangle of my hair away from my face before falling back against the mound of pillows. I had scarce closed my eyes when the whispers began anew; only this time, there was a word, one solitary word, and I understood it:

Come.

I was out of my bed in an instant, the skirts of my nightdress tangling about my legs as I rushed from my chamber into the room beyond.

Open the door, the whisper came again, clearer this time. *Come now.*

Compelled by her words, by the urgency in them, I hurried across the room to the door.

My hand upon the latch, I hesitated. Perhaps it was a trap meant to lure me from my bed and into danger. Perhaps it was a jest, a game played by the Court Eternal, and were I to open the door, I would find myself surrounded by laughing figures still in their finery, drunk and carousing until the late hours, reveling in my gullibility.

But it was not fear, nor doubt, nor the risk of possible ridicule that stayed me.

It was Elyan.

My exhaustion and his attention to it had prevented another confrontation with him that evening before we retired to our bedchambers, but I knew that to leave my room again tonight would be a violation of the tenuous trust between us, if I were to be found out.

Which meant I must not be.

I lowered the latch and opened the door.

At first, I saw nothing but shadows and the pale gleam of polished stone where shafts of moonlight poured through the windows of the long corridor. Then, movement: a ripple of white, a hand with too many fingers, and far too long.

Even though I'd seen her in my dreams, stood beside her upon a field of death, and felt her brittle hands upon me, nothing could have prepared me for seeing her at last with open eyes and the impossible weight of knowing who she was.

By virtue of my birth, I had stood many times in the presence of royalty.

Now I stood before a goddess.

She was tall, impossibly tall, and covered from head to toe in billowing veils that concealed her features from me, though I knew I would find no human face beneath, for the fingers that had scraped against my window and gripped my arm so tightly in my dreams had been made of wood.

Her magnificent crown of spindly branches rose like spires into the air, and flickering at the tip of each one was a tiny flame of vibrant green wreathed in black; strange, that, for they were familiar to me.

I fought to stay the trembling in my hand as I held my Magefire aloft. "You called," I whispered. "And I have come."

Slowly, the Dae Spira lifted its hand, and one long finger unfurled and pointed down the corridor.

"Show me the way," I told her.

She must've understood me, for the Dae Spira turned and glided down the corridor.

The palace was shrouded in silence and, though it was no less beautiful in the dark, it was of a melancholy sort, and I rather thought I preferred it to the endless glimmering gold and the intricate patterns of its tapestries and chandeliers and gildings.

I recognized our path somewhat; it was the same one I'd traversed on my way to the library. The sconces here were undusted, the walls unadorned, and the silence absolute.

She stayed well enough ahead of me, and from time to time the shape of her grew hazy and faded somewhat, slipping into the shadows surrounding us and reappearing just as suddenly. Was it a being of substance I followed or a spirit?

It would have mattered little had I known, for I was a creature entirely governed by irrepressible curiosity, and that curiosity sustained my courage as we reached a spiral staircase that fell away into darkness.

Deeper we traveled, and I lost track entirely of how many floors we descended. Although the stairs were of stone, many were cracked and brittle, and I feared losing my footing and plummeting to the bottom. I thought the air would grow cold as it had in Asperfell when I'd traveled to the lower levels of the prison, but instead, a lovely warmth suffused me. With each step, just as it had in the forest when we'd drawn near Syr'Aliem, my magic sang more loudly within my veins, and I knew then that my otherworldly guide was leading me toward the Incuna.

A rather narrow tunnel lay at the bottom of the stairs, even more ancient than the stairs themselves, and little by little, I began to notice curling vines and branches snaking along the walls.

At the end of the tunnel lay a door: a simple, wooden door with a handle of braided wood and surrounded by an arch of riotous green. My eldritch guide gestured that I should take the handle, and then, as I reached out my hand, the whole of her seemed to shudder as she sighed, a long, rasping sound that I felt within the very depths of me.

I opened the door.

No one had passed through it in an age, and the overgrown flora on the other side had formed a sort of barrier that I had to push through to enter the room. Once I managed it, I found myself in a sort of vestibule, though I could not see the floor nor walls for the roots—or were they branches?—that seemed to cover every inch, and yet they were not unorderly. In fact, they formed the most pleasing patterns.

From the vestibule, it was but a short distance down one last overgrown corridor until I emerged in a vast room with a high, domed ceiling, beautifully painted with the glory of the world above: the stars and the moon, encircled by trees and flowers and growing things, and between their branches and leaves, animals unknown to me staring with wide, wild eyes.

Here, in this breathtaking place, the natural world seemed to coexist quite harmoniously with the stone of the palace. Soft, thick moss dotted with tiny flowers and toadstools flowed over benches; vines encircled stately columns; trees with rich green leaves and brightly colored blossoms clustered together in the open spaces.

Across the grove before me was a magnificently carved archway and, in the darkness beyond its threshold, a pale green glow emanated. To each side of this extraordinary sight lay a door, and both were closed and so terribly overrun by creeping vines that they must've remained so for a very long time.

I turned behind me that I might ask my eldritch guide what I should do, but there was nothing in the tunnel beyond the door but darkness.

"And just what do you think you're doing here?"

I started in fright at the tiny, irritated voice behind me and whirled around, holding my Magefire high as I looked about for the source.

"Down here, if you please," said the voice again, and I dropped my gaze.

The creature was a diminutive thing indeed; even with the crown atop his head, a smaller and far less elaborate version of the Dae Spira's own, it only just reached my knees. Its skin was a bright, verdant green and glimmered in the same way that of the members of the Court Eternal did, but this was neither paint nor illusion.

It fixed me with enormous eyes and a pointed frown, its tiny

arms crossed over its chest. "Have you no voice? I asked you what
you think you are doing here!"

"I'm sorry," I answered, still quite taken aback at the sight of my
small accuser. "I do not mean to intrude. You see, she led me here.
The Dae Spira."

"Liar!"

A second creature poked its head out from behind a particularly
large root and fixed me with a frightful glare. Its skin was a rich
nut-brown, its hair a robust red not unlike my own, and it, too, was
crowned with twigs.

"Hello," I said brightly. "My name is Briony." Then I turned
back to the first creature. "And I am no liar."

"What did she look like?" squeaked a new voice, and I turned to
see a third tiny face peeking at me from behind a nearby urn. This
creature's skin was pale faun, and her curls were a shocking white.

"Well, she was very tall and covered in white veils so I could
not discern her features," I said. "And she wore a crown like yours,
only much, much taller."

All three creatures stared at me with wide eyes and absolute
silence, as though struck positively mute by my revelation.

"Impossible," the first creature whispered once he'd regained
his wits. "It cannot be!"

"It has been so very long," said the third creature in awe.

"Why her?" This from the second creature as he fixed me with
a most disapproving scowl. "No one has seen her in over a hundred
years, and suddenly she presents herself to an outsider?"

"She has presented herself to me thrice now, actually," I said.
"And shown me visions of what is to come."

The first creature started. "And what *is* to come? What did she
show you?"

I spared no detail in describing to them my dreams, though it did make the more delicate third creature nearly swoon, and when they regarded me still with skepticism, I pushed up the sleeve of my nightdress so that they might see the bruises their goddess's fingers left upon my pale skin.

The third creature gasped as she regarded me with tremulous awe. "It is true, then—you've come to help us! She sent you to tell us what is wrong with the Incuna."

"Tansy!" the second creature groaned.

My eyes went wide. "Something is wrong with the Incuna?"

"Introductions first," the first creature said, quelling Tansy's enthusiasm with a withering glare. "My name is Lark. That is Fife, and that is Tansy, and we are the Acolytes of the Dae Spira. There are more of us, but they are sleeping. They have been sleeping a long, long time."

"Disgraceful," Fife scoffed.

"I am most pleased to meet you all," I said. "Are you Cluvians?"

"Bah!" Lark said. "Do we look like we're from Cluvia?"

"I do not rightly know."

Fife squinted up at me. "Exactly! Why would the Dae Spira send you to this place? You're not even from this world. You're with the others."

"The visitors," said Lark.

Tansy whispered: "The prisoners."

"I don't know," I answered honestly. "But I wish to be of service, truly I do." Their doubtful expressions told me very well what they thought of that. "Well, why else would she have brought me here?" I paused. "And where exactly is here?"

Lark puffed out his chest. "This is the Ita Locrum: the Place of Ways."

"Indeed? And where does that way lead?"

His eyes followed mine to the center chamber and the strange glow within. "Why, that is the Incuna, of course."

My heart fairly leapt into my throat. "The Incuna!"

Lark quite ignored my excitement and continued, "The door to the left is the Ita Hypogaeum, and to the right is the Ita Hominaeum."

"Where do they lead?"

He tilted his head to one side. "We knew once, but no longer."

"Locked for centuries, they've been, and our memories with them," Fife grunted. "A state most shameful."

I frowned down at him. "Who has the keys?"

"The king, I expect," he said, scratching his beard. "He is the chosen one, after all."

"But the way to the Incuna is not locked."

"*Never* the Incuna."

I did not realize Tansy had crept forward until I felt her tiny hand slip into mine. "Are you ready to see it?"

Lark spluttered. "Tansy!"

"Outsiders are not permitted within the Incuna chamber," Fife reminded her firmly. "Not anymore."

"Why not?" I asked. "And what do you mean by *anymore*?"

"That is neither here nor there," he scowled.

"If the Dae Spira sent her here, how is she to find out what's wrong if she is not permitted to see it?" Tansy pointed out.

After a great deal of bluster and sputtering, Fife cited my status as an escaped prisoner, my alien magic, the entirely unexpected nature of my arrival, and even my wild appearance (for I'd given little thought to the taming of my hair nor the bareness of my feet when absconding from my chamber) before Lark decided that they should put the matter to a vote. The Acolytes turned their backs on me, put their heads together, and a furious whispered discussion ensued between the three of them during which Fife looked up every now and again and fixed me with a disapproving scowl. I waited with as much patience as I possessed, which was, unfortunately, very little as the magic within my veins seemed to be suffering a helpless pull to whatever lay within the chamber of the Incuna.

At last, they faced me.

Tansy positively beamed as she informed me: "We've decided."

Lark added: "After much deliberation."

"To allow you to see the Incuna."

"And see if you might be able to tell us what is wrong with it."

Fife grunted.

I could scarcely breathe as Tansy took one of my hands, Lark the other, and together they led me forth, Fife shuffling his feet behind us and grumbling all the while.

The resting place of the Dae Spira's gift to Syr'Aliem was more extraordinary than I could've possibly dreamed; even possessed as I was with an overabundance of imagination, I found the sight of it stole my breath.

Water, its surface glassy and still, filled the enormous chamber, stretching from the threshold where we stood to a dais in the distance. Upon the dais, something glowed, luminous and ancient, the light dancing upon a great domed ceiling comprised entirely of roots rather than stone, as were the walls that surrounded us— thousands and thousands of them entwined together in breathtakingly beautiful patterns. But even more remarkable were the shimmering threads of light woven throughout them.

Curious... they glowed brightest above, but upon the walls around us, they were so faint I could scarcely make them out.

The only way forward was a path of stones set into the water. I looked down at Tansy. "What should happen if I fall?"

"You'll get wet," she answered, quite seriously.

"That's all?"

She nodded, just once, and I stepped forward, holding the hem of my nightdress that my feet might carry me safely across, for the stones were unevenly placed. Within my breast, fear had begun to mingle with excitement, rendering me as clumsy and awkward as a newborn foal, but I reached the dais and lifted my head, and beheld a most glorious sight.

Carved in stone was the likeness of the Dae Spira, and still it was covered in white veils. I could nevertheless see the edges of her strange, ethereal features. Peaceful was her expression, but there was such power in her, such ancient and undoubted power, that I stood in thrall even before the statue of her with her arms held high and her impossibly long fingers splayed above her head.

And in those fingers, cupped lovingly by palms of stone, was the Incuna—a sphere of incandescent light being received by roots that curled down from high above.

And I recognized at once what shape those hanging roots took far above the surface.

The throne of Syr'Aliem.

I frowned as I took them in, for there was something strange about them, something wrong; the roots extending straightest and highest were thick and thriving and green as they rose up to the throne, but the sprouts and tendrils that spread outward from that vigorous shaft became thin and shriveled and brown as they traced their way down the domed ceiling in beautiful, intricate patterns and disappeared into the walls.

Tansy had climbed upon the dais and she stole to my side,

slipping her tiny hand into mine. "Something is very wrong with them," she whispered.

"Why are they less bright than those above?"

"That is precisely what we hoped you could tell us," Lark called, carefully picking his way across the stones. "That is why she appeared to you, is it not?"

I looked back to the statue of the Dae Spira and the sphere of power that was the Incuna, then to the roots of the throne and their strange, withered ends.

"This is their symbol," I said, realizing that I had seen the likeness of the Incuna and its living connection to the throne painted upon shields and embroidered on tunics before I'd ever stood in King Anwar's presence. "But not her. They do not include the statue. Only the power. And the throne."

"Not the Dae Spira?" Lark squeaked, nearly toppling off of the last stone. I reached out and helped him onto the dais. "It is unconscionable!"

"I spoke to the library spirit of my visions. He told me that what I saw was the loss of the Incuna. The loss of all magic."

'Twas as if I'd shouted a litany of the most profane curse words imaginable in the middle of Aunt Eudora's parlor during a visit from the king of Tiralaen himself. Their mouths fell into perfect roundness before Tansy squeaked and toppled over while Fife fell to his knees and made a series of movements with his hands before him.

Lark recovered first. "The Incuna cannot be lost. 'Twould be *impossible.*"

"Yes, but if it *were—*"

"But you can stop it, right?" Tansy squealed, wringing her small hands. "You can tell us what's wrong with it!"

As vibrantly as my magic sang within my veins, I felt as if I could command an entire army of umbras to conquer the world for me. And I knew this power came pouring into me from the Incuna as surely as I could tell the direction of the sun if I stood in a desert with my eyes closed. But I could not find any purchase for my particular magic within the Incuna itself. I could not *speak* to it, for it only gave and gave of itself, and it would not take anything from me, not even my words.

"I cannot," I answered. "I think it is because the Incuna has no will of its own—because it was a gift from the goddess to the people to do with as they would—and so it cannot speak to me in the way that our own magic does."

"Then you can do nothing to help us!" Fife accused.

"Perhaps I cannot," I admitted. "But I believe I know someone who can."

As I'd feared, the journey back took far longer than the journey to, and I became hopelessly lost several times, requiring me to retrace my steps and start again, wishing fervently all the while that some Mage or other had died a horrible death within the palace walls so that their umbra might be convinced to guide me. At least these walls and stairs did not move and change as they pleased as those in Asperfell had, depending on the time of day, or the season, or the moods of those within.

Eventually, I began to recognize certain columns and stairs and corridors, and at last I'd reached the part of the palace where we were housed when a lilting voice rose in the darkness behind me.

"My goodness, Mistress Briony—is that you?"

Dismayed, I turned to behold Princess Evolet holding a delicate lantern of gold filigree in which a glowing Lumen floated. She was still clad in the gown she'd been wearing that evening, and I wondered if she'd been at some amusement or other all this time.

"It is, your highness," I managed to answer.

"And why in the world are you here all alone, and so late at night?"

"I could not sleep." Well, it was not exactly a lie.

"You could not sleep," she repeated. "And so, you somehow found yourself wandering the palace alone?"

I took in her pale countenance. She looked positively exhausted; keeping pace with the extravagance of the Court Eternal must've cost her dearly, and no matter how ridiculous I found it, I did feel sorry for her. "If I may, what are you doing here so late at night?"

Her smile was bright, yet it did not reach her eyes. "Why, I've come from the pleasure garden, of course."

For what I imagined was quite a sumptuous affair, she seemed strangely indifferent. Perhaps she'd simply experienced its hedonisms so often they'd become perfectly ordinary to her now.

"You should be abed," she continued. "Please, allow me to escort you."

I was scarcely eager to return with her should she continue to press me about my late-night wanderings, but she was watching me expectantly, her lantern held at the ready. And so, with great reluctance, I followed her. Thankfully, she chattered on about the pleasure gardens, which she and her brother were most anxious that we should sample the delights for ourselves.

"It will be enormous fun," she promised. "You'll see."

"I can scarcely wait."

At length, we arrived at our suite of rooms where the princess beheld the sight of our unguarded door with consternation. "Why are the guards not at their post?"

"I do not know, your highness."

"Well, I shall certainly have to see to that straightaway. Do sleep well." She made to leave, and then, perhaps thinking better of it, turned back to me, her face illuminated by the Lumen in her lantern. "Oh, and Mistress Briony? Guards or no, do try not to wander the palace at night. My brother would not approve."

"I will try to remember," I told her politely, knowing very well that I would not.

"Excellent," she answered, and I thought perhaps she knew it, too.

Under Princess Evolet's watchful eye, I let myself into our suite. No doubt the hour was late, close to dawn. The Lumen had shrunk to nearly nothing in the grate, as had the excitement that had kept me from realizing I'd been out all night and was properly exhausted.

No doubt Isri would see to it that I was awakened obscenely early, and the princess had already promised us a day full of untold delights, several of which I imagined would require every ounce of patience I possessed.

A servant had left a decanter of water on the sideboard beside the bottle of Calique, and as I moved to pour myself a glass, I heard a muffled thud against the door.

I tensed, wondering if there were any way I could use the decanter as a weapon, save throwing it at the heads of whomever came through the door as my magic was far too unpredictable to be used reasonably to defend myself. As it happened, I needn't have worried. Arlo, slightly disheveled and unsteady on his feet, stumbled into the suite a moment later. When the door closed loudly behind him, he turned and shushed it.

"Arlo!" I hissed. "What are you doing?"

He started with a yelp and pressed his hand to his heaving chest. "Coleum's balls, Briony!"

"Quiet, or they'll hear you!"

He jabbed a finger at me. "No, they'll hear *you*!"

He really was quite vexing when he was intoxicated. I pulled the stopper from the decanter and poured him a generous glass of water, which he refused. Instead, he reached past me and seized the Calique. "Should you really be drinking more of that?" I asked him warily. "Haven't you had enough?"

"Gods, no," he answered, raking a hand through his already disheveled hair. "What time is it? What day is it?"

"Near dawn, and I have no idea. Where have you been?"

"Playing Trills."

"I have no idea what that is."

He flopped down dramatically on one of the couches in front of the hearth. "It's better that way, trust me."

"No." I sat directly opposite him and fixed him with my most determined glare. "Tell me."

He took a long swallow directly from the bottle. "It's a game."

"Well, that doesn't sound so very scandalous to me."

"That's played in the nude."

Of course it was.

"Arlo, you really must be more careful. You will expose us to scrutiny with such behavior."

"Oh, I exposed them to something, all right."

"Scoundrel!"

"Prude," he hiccupped. He set the bottle of Calique down and scrubbed both hands over his face. "I've been trying all night and I cannot seem to drink this away."

"Drink what away?"

"All of it." He waved his hand aimlessly at our surroundings. "This place does the strangest things to my magic. Makes me feel restless. Like I'm supposed to *do* something." He paused. "I hate it."

"Why?"

He grunted dismissively and took up the bottle again.

"You are exasperating," I told him.

"Yes, and so is the urge to do something," he shot back. "I don't do things."

"Oh, I would argue that you do things."

"No, not *those* things," he exploded, leaning forward, his elbows braced on his thighs. "I mean real things. Things you people do."

You people. He'd spoken thus before, of the rest of us, and what he believed were our worthless crusades.

I gestured to the bottle. "So you do this instead."

He scowled. "I never had to so much before. Before all of you. Before this place."

"Far be it for me to judge a man his pleasures, but perhaps you might instead try a bit more of what *we* do if you wish a respite."

"No. I'd have to use my Gods-forsaken magic, and that I simply cannot tolerate."

"Oh yes, Gods forbid. Why do you hate it so?"

"Because it is utterly pointless."

"It most certainly is not," I told him, and for a moment I felt magic in my voice. "You helped us defeat the Sentinels and sheltered us in a forest where we otherwise would have died."

"With leaves," he answered. "Leaves and vines and twigs and other nonsense."

"Not nonsense!"

"A Battlemage could've done far more for you, or even an Elemental of some repute, not some soft green boy with a pea shoot."

I had heard Arlo swear, heard him lie, heard him charm and laugh, but I had never heard him speak so, with such vehemence against himself. He had expressed hatred of his magic before, but removed from himself, a thing outside.

A soft green boy.

Someone had called him thus, once; I was certain. And he carried it with him still.

"Your magic is not soft," I told him quietly. "Nor are you."

But he was done with me and, I strongly suspected, with himself. He stood, swaying slightly, and returned the bottle of Calique to the sideboard.

"If any of those silent women wake me up before noon, I will not be responsible for my actions," he said, then stumbled down the corridor to his chamber.

15

Despite my long nocturnal wanderings and my lack of sleep, my heart was so full to bursting with purpose that I rose with the sun.

Blessedly free of Isri due to the early hour, I rushed from my chamber clad in nothing by my nightdress with my hair braided and slung over one shoulder. I rapped upon Elyan's chamber door until at last he appeared, hair mussed from sleep, one arm braced against the frame.

Before he had a chance to chastise me for waking him, I announced: "Last night, I followed a goddess no one has seen for hundreds of years through a secret tunnel to the Place of Ways and met her Acolytes."

He blinked slowly. "What?"

I ducked under his arm and into his room. "It was all rather marvelous, though they were quite impolite at first—"

"Who was?"

"The Acolytes! And they were ever so small—just so." I leveled my hand at my knee. "And they had green skin! Well, one had green skin. They were as varied in their appearance as you can imagine. Well, except for their crowns."

"You left our chambers again," he said flatly.

"I did. But I had a very good reason to do so."

"We spoke of this—"

"No, *you* spoke of this," I pointed out. "I promised nothing. And even if I had, I still would have gone because, Elyan... I saw the Incuna."

His hand flexed at his side, and I wondered if he were considering strangling me with it. "Gods, I am certain I will regret this, but tell me everything."

I clambered onto one of the chairs before his empty hearth, tucking my chilled feet under my nightdress as he lowered himself into the chair opposite, and out it poured: my midnight visitor and our journey below, my strange new friends and the mysterious doors locked for centuries, and the Incuna! I described its splendor as best I could, though my words rang hollow for how could I ever hope to capture the wonder of what I'd seen?

"Whatever it is that ails the Incuna will cause the devastation that the Dae Spira showed me in her visions," I said. "But I cannot speak to its magic, which is why I am here."

"I must say I am surprised it took this long for you to involve me in your scheming."

"Why, thank you. Does that mean you'll help me?"

He scowled. "I ought to refuse, considering what little regard you have thus far shown for the promise you made me."

"I hope you know I would never do so lightly."

"And what if our hosts find out that we've been carousing with their sacred deity, and at the source of their magic, no less?"

My skin grew uncomfortably warm at the recollection of Princess Evolet's lovely face emerging from the darkness.

"They won't," I said.

"You are hardly known for your subtlety."

"I am, however, known for my persistence. Will you help me?"

The door to his chamber opened before he'd a chance to answer, and the scowling face of Isri appeared at the threshold.

"Oh no, she's found me."

Elyan rose. "We shall speak further upon the matter," he said as she marched me forcefully away. "In the meantime, do nothing, Briony. Do you understand me?"

I did not answer.

Back in my chamber, Isri bundled me into yet another new gown, this one the finest I'd worn yet, made of deep umber that faded to gold with a kirtle of flowering vines in shades of green and burgundy, the embroidery done by a masterful hand, for I found tiny jewels at the center of each flower. A headpiece of the same was placed carefully atop my brow, for, of course, no one in Syr'Aliem would ever deign to wear something as provincial as real flowers in their hair, and my curls were pinned around it.

I thought surely I was to be summoned by Evolet, or perhaps her brother, to further discuss my nighttime wanderings, but when Isri thrust a piece of thick, creamy vellum at me, I beheld an invitation from the Dowager Queen herself.

"Why does she wish to see me?" I choked.

The Tacé fixed her face into the most determined frown and continued to tug at my hair.

Had she ever behaved toward me with even a modicum of civility, I might have shared the secret of my summons the night before. But I could easily imagine that any smile it brought to her face would be at the thought of betraying me to her king, and not for the return of her goddess. And so, I pressed my lips into a thin, flat line.

I'd expected the Dowager Queen to receive me in a room to rival any I'd thus far seen in its opulence.

Instead, she received me in a shrine.

Her ivory throne, modest in comparison to others I'd seen in the palace, was flanked by two enormous gold statues: one her husband, one her son. To the left and right, shrines to both were heaped with fresh flowers and offerings of fruit and gemstones, and everywhere were sticks of smoldering incense, their cloying perfume a cloud that set my eyes watering.

The Dowager Queen held her customary doll in her lap as though it were a child, stroking its hair absently. "Good morning, Mistress Briony."

I curtseyed absently, still absorbing with horrified eyes the sight before me. "Your highness, it is an honor indeed."

"Come closer, child."

I did so, willing myself to remain still as her penetrative gaze swept every inch of me, from the sweep of my gown upon the marble floor to the cinch of my waist to the flame of my hair, a trifle wild even after the care Isri had taken with it.

"You are pretty, I suppose, in a sharp, small sort of way," she said at last. "But you are not beautiful. Not as we are beautiful."

I did not disagree in the least, but still, it stung to hear it spoken aloud. I opened my mouth to inform her that the Court's perception of my beauty was of little consequence, but she cut me off with a sharp snap of her wrist.

"Your hips are far too narrow—I cannot imagine you will breed well. And all those unsightly marks." She shuddered as if my freckles had personally offended her and she must therefore duel them in the village square. "You are far too outspoken, and far too self-absorbed. To best serve your king, you must put his needs above your own, and be grateful for the opportunity to do so. You must be demure; obedient; servile."

Anger rose like bile at the back of my throat as I realized someone was watching and reporting upon my personal dealings with my companions to the Dowager Queen. Isri, most likely, the loathsome woman. "My relationship with Prince Elyan is not a matter for discussion amongst your staff, nor are you entitled to—"

"I do not speak of your prince, Mistress Briony. I speak of my son."

I was, momentarily, struck quite dumb by her words, and I gaped most unbecomingly before I gathered my wits. "Your highness, I fear you are mistaken. Your son and I... That is to say, we are not—"

"I would believe him utterly without sense were it not for your power," she agreed, her fingers trailing over the effigy's cheeks. "For you do not understand what it is to serve. You see, it is rather like being a mother. Whatever it is he requires, whatever it is he wants, you must give it to him however you can, even to the detriment of yourself."

"Is that what you did?"

"Oh yes." She smiled dreamily and rested her cheek against the effigy's hair. "My Raolin wanted for nothing; *still* wants for nothing. It was the honor of my life to devote its full measure to his own."

I shook my head. "I could never do that."

"And I doubt you shall ever be needed to," she said as she reclined in her throne. "I fully expect that my son's momentary lack of judgment will swiftly pass, and we need never speak of it again. However, it would've been remiss of me not to address your shortcomings, for I will certainly not be the only mother to question your suitability, Mage or no."

"You yourself have catalogued my thoughts quite thoroughly, and thus I could never hope that, such as I am, I might find favor with your son."

She gestured to one of the servants behind her throne, and when he approached, he took a heavy scroll from her and presented it to me while she watched. 'Twas a heavy thing indeed—layer upon layer of parchment rolled together and sealed with a wax stamp of the throne of Syr'Aliem and the Incuna.

"You've proven yourself a studious young woman," she said. "If my son does persist in his attentions, you must educate yourself regarding our ways so that you might hope to please him. These are an excellent place to start."

I clasped the scroll to my chest awkwardly. "Your highness, I really do not—"

"That is all."

She waved, and I was dismissed.

I did not know whether to scream or collapse upon the ground laughing, but I had the chance for neither before the guards swept me from the twin shrines and back into the airy hall. The smell of incense lingered in my nose and upon my gown, but my request to return to my chamber was refused; my presence was expected in the princess's receiving room.

After what I had just endured, I could not abide the thought of being anywhere near her or her brother, or any member of the Court Eternal for that matter. There was only one person I wished to see, and only one thing I wished to do.

"Where is Prince Elyan?" I asked the guard.

"With King Anwar in the north gallery, Mistress."

"Then it is there that I wish to go."

He shook his head, face impassive beneath his gleaming helm. "I am afraid I cannot do that, mistress, for I am under strict orders to take you to Princess Evolet's receiving room."

Already quite frayed after enduring both Isri and the Dowager

Queen, my temper stretched taut and finally snapped. "I've had enough of orders for one day," I fairly growled, thrusting my chin up and advancing upon him with one finger stabbing at his liveried chest. "Take me to Prince Elyan this instant or I shall go myself."

Fearing Evolet's retribution far more than he did me, he staunchly refused, and so, naturally, I did what any respectable, well bred young woman would do under such circumstances.

I turned on the heels of my ridiculous shoes and bolted the other way down the corridor.

Thankfully, the guard—whom I decided in that moment to nickname Vile Betrayer—was a lumbering sort, and even with my feet as encumbered as they were, I still managed to lose him quite easily. After begging directions to the north gallery from a passing gentleman whom I was quite certain was thoroughly intoxicated despite the early morning hour, I made my way there without further incident. Concealing myself behind a pillar, I surveyed the ostentatious room, looking for a familiar head of black hair that stood high above the rest.

Elyan, King Anwar, and several other men I recognized in passing stood before an enormous gilded map upon the marble wall. It appeared to show the forest surrounding the palace, and I should've liked to study it myself, but it was for another reason entirely that I had come, and I was not about to be deterred, no matter how curious.

He caught sight of me then, and I must've looked a fright, for his eyes widened in dismay before he schooled his face with all the grace his royal education had afforded him. Excusing himself from the conversation, he made his way over to me.

"What's happened?" he asked, his eyes flickering down to the scroll in my hands. "What's this?"

I grimaced. "An unfortunate audience with the Dowager Queen is what happened, but that is not why I am here."

"Oh?"

"Come with me to the Incuna."

Glancing swiftly back at Anwar, he pulled me into the shadows behind the pillar, crowding me against the cool stone. "Have you gone mad? This is not the time—"

"Actually, I think you'll find it's the perfect time. No guards outside our doors to distract."

His eyes narrowed at that. "Speaking of guards, how did you get here, anyway? Aren't you supposed to be supping with the princess this morning?"

"Both excellent questions. Are you coming with me or not?"

"Briony," he exhaled.

"Please," I begged. "The Acolytes—they deserve to know. Maybe once they do, they can fix it. And if you won't help me, I'll ask Arlo. As you're well aware, he has no aversion to clandestine adventures."

"Is there anything I can say to deter you?"

"There is not."

He sighed. "What choice do I have?"

For the first time that morning, I smiled.

Lark stared wide-eyed at Elyan as he emerged from the shadows of the ancient tunnel behind me, and for a moment I was afraid he would flee in terror, for Elyan was imposing enough to one of my stature; to Lark he must've appeared terrible indeed.

I knelt down before him. "It's all right, Lark. This is Prince Elyan, and he is a friend."

"He does not look like a friend."

My lips twitched. "And what does he look like, then?"

"A Larimaq," he whispered.

"And what is that?"

"A bog spirit, taller than a tree, covered in mud and bracken."

No doubt Elyan appeared thus to Lark as he ducked and folded himself through the door, rubbing the back of his neck as he stood and took in the breathtaking sight of the vestibule around him.

"This is a sacred place," Lark said. "The home of the Ways, and the Incuna. You must swear never to defile it, nor to divulge it."

Elyan's lips twitched as he placed his hand over his heart. "I swear it."

The other Acolytes were waiting for us, and they stared agog at the sight of Elyan standing beside me. Quite a bit of explaining was required before Fife sheathed his axe and Tansy picked herself up off of the floor where she'd collapsed into a squeaking heap, but eventually, they accepted him into their sanctuary, though they did make it perfectly clear that I would no longer be welcome should Elyan prove as untrustworthy as his appearance evidently suggested.

I knelt down beside Lark, tucking a thick fall of hair behind my ear. "Elyan has an unusual aptitude that may allow him to divine what plagues the Incuna. Will you allow him to see it?"

Lark resisted at first, bolstered by Fife's protestations, but by and by, my pleas wore him down, particularly when I took care to mention how very important Elyan was back in our world. Then, his chest puffed with pride at being the one to show the heir to the throne of Tiralaen the heart of Syr'Aliem's power.

I watched with delight as Elyan took in the marvelous sight, wishing in that moment that I was him, seeing it for the first time.

I turned and grinned up at him. "Isn't it glorious?"

"It is that."

He traveled the path of stones gracefully and with purpose, and once he came to the dais, he stared up at the Dae Spira's towering visage with the same awe and reverence that I had when first I beheld her.

"This is what you've seen?" he said. "Who you heard?"

"Yes."

"What strange company you keep."

"You've no idea." I grimaced; the ring of bruises left by the goddess's brittle fingers still encircled my arm.

Elyan asked, and was given permission, to touch the withered roots upon the wall at the back of the dais, and Lark and I watched mesmerized as he laid his hand gently upon them and called his magic, probing the threads of light with his long fingers.

"So much power," he murmured. "But its pathways have been strangled."

"Strangled?" Lark squeaked.

"It's similar to the way I siphon magic," Elyan explained. "These roots serve as pathways between the Incuna and the land, but they are shrunken. Some have collapsed altogether."

Elyan did not pull away then, but held himself perfectly still, his brow furrowed in consternation, head tilted.

I brushed my fingers across his in concern. "What is it?"

"Magic," he said. "Our sort of magic, but not yours nor mine."

"There are many in the palace whose blood is mixed with ours."

"No, it's here. Right here. Gods, you'll think me mad, but it feels like being in Tiralaen again."

"I don't feel anything at all, save you," I grumbled. "Must be your aptitude. That, or you actually have gone mad."

Elyan laughed and took my hand as Lark led us back over the stones and into the antechamber where the other Acolytes waited. I realized suddenly that there were several more tiny sets of wide eyes staring at us from behind the columns of vines and stone. They wore the same crowns as the other Acolytes, but otherwise, they were as different from one another as could be. The colors of their skin, their hair, their eyes—it reminded me of every manner of tree and earth and stone, from the herbs in the greenhouse at Orwynd to the woods beyond Asperfell. They were as varied as the denizens of the Court Eternal, but far lovelier, their ornaments treasures of the living world: flowers and nuts, berries and smooth stones, and moss.

"Since you first set foot in this place, the Dae Spira has seen fit to rouse them from their long sleep," Tansy piped happily.

"But I had nothing to do with it, surely."

Whether yes or no, the newly awakened Acolytes were clamoring to meet me, and all of them had ever so many questions about Elyan. They begged of him a demonstration of his magical skill, and for every wondrous bit of spellwork he performed, they bestowed upon us both a most unusual story: their own.

It was told in bits and pieces, for not a one of them knew the entirety of it. Instead, we pieced it slowly together from the cacophony of tiny voices clamoring over one another to interject whenever they could, until my head spun and, laughing, I begged them to stop.

The Dae Spira, as it happened, was not the only ancient deity to haunt the forest surrounding Syr'Aliem. She'd had an admirer once, destined to love her unrequitedly, for she was a wandering thing, an ungovernable thing, and would suffer no master save herself. Still, he sighed and pined and made her the most marvelous things, for he was a craftsman of unrivaled skill even amongst his otherworldly kind. For her head, he made a crown as wild as she; for the people with whom she shared her magic, he crafted a throne; and for the singing of her praises, he created the Acolytes.

From forest ephemera, they were crafted by expert and tender hands, and when at last they were complete, it was the light of the Incuna that filled their lungs and hearts and eyes, and they were as alive as any fellow creature of the wood, however strange their origin.

He had hoped perhaps this gift would please her so much that she might stay her wandering feet in the grove beneath the earth where he dwelled, but alas, not even the Acolytes' shining eyes and lovely songs could tempt her. She returned to wander the woods, taking her Acolytes with her, and he remained in his grove, his roots slowly sinking into the soil until it became his tomb.

They could tell us little else besides, for with their long sleep had gone most of their memories, save songs. As the hour grew late, Fife exchanged his axe for a wide-bodied string instrument, which he plucked at, while another Acolyte blew into a set of pipes and another beat expertly with his fingers upon a drum. Tansy proudly bore a clay pitcher, the contents of which she poured into tiny cups that we passed around amongst us, and we shared a mossy bench, Elyan and I. I leaned against his shoulder, his fingers stole into my hair, and we watched the Acolytes dance to the lovely tune with such joy that not a single moment in Syr'Aliem that had come before could compare.

16

The pleasure garden of Syr'Aliem lay at the center of a great hedge maze, and it was at the entrance that evening that my companions and I were met by King Anwar and Princess Evolet; thankfully, the Dowager Queen was not in attendance.

The moment he caught sight of me, Anwar strode forward, his face a knot of worry. And to my great surprise, he took my hands in his. "I just found out not a moment ago what my mother did this morning. How can I begin to make amends for such behavior?"

My face aflame, I tried to tug my hands free, but he held them fast. "I am perfectly fine, I assure you."

"It was unforgivably rude."

"It is already forgotten."

He studied my face intently. Whatever he found there was enough to convince him of my sincerity, and as I felt his fingers begin to slacken, I freed my hands at last, thrusting them into the skirt of my gown. "

"Shall we?" I asked, my voice too bright.

The hedge maze seemed to go on forever, and I wondered aloud how many poor drunken fools had found themselves utterly lost within its depths.

"Too many," Anwar laughed. "Don't worry. We send servants in after them... eventually."

The sounds of tinkling glass and laughter and music grew louder until, at last, we emerged from the shadows of the maze. Before us, to the otherworldly strains of an orchestra playing instruments of gold, the Court Eternal strolled at their leisure up and down a wide, tiled thoroughfare lined with low hedges, meticulously trimmed, and pedestals bearing Lumens that set the night ablaze. On and on it stretched, with smaller paths branching from the first, winding around fountains and statues, groves, and bowers. At its end, a fantasia, the largest I'd ever seen, shone silver in the moonlight, and beyond it, the still waters of a lake surrounded by trees.

Tents dotted the landscape, lights twinkling beneath the billowing silver of their canopies, and within, games were played at tables—games with intricately painted cards and boards piled high with glass pieces. Beyond, upon a spacious lawn, a different sort of game altogether was being enjoyed, with balls and cunning little clubs, and joyous shouts arose from the men and women dashing to and fro about the field, though decidedly more men than women.

Refreshment could be found everywhere, though I suspected they were meant to be decorative rather than provide any real sustenance, for each was a work of art less to be eaten than to be admired, which suited me quite ill indeed, though the Court Eternal seemed not to mind, for they hardly noticed the food. They quite preferred drinking, then dashing behind hedges for the purpose of retching without an audience, only to emerge moments later laughing and calling for more. I found myself growing slightly ill at the sight of them swaying and staggering back to their friends with glasses full and smiles wide.

"What do you think of our little garden, Briony?" Princess Evolet asked as she slid her hand in mine. "Is it not charming?"

"Indeed," I answered, wondering at her choice of words: the pleasure garden was many things; little was not one of them. Nor charming.

"People attend to see, and to be seen," she continued, "so they are always in their very best looks. There is nothing worse than attending the garden wearing something you've already been seen in, though some certainly do. Alorah is particularly terrible about trying to pass off old gowns as new, as if we can't all tell she's simply changed the color of the fabric and left the cut exactly the same."

One could sympathize with the unfortunate Alorah.

We approached a path that led down to a fountain with a statue of gold at its center: a couple caught in a passionate embrace. Surrounding the fountain were paintings set upon easels draped in silk, and though they were beautiful, the men and women who observed them did so indifferently, moving from one to the next with little care, as though it were a tedious chore indeed to endure them.

Hovering nearby, watching anxiously as his work was appraised, was Yveme. When he caught sight of me, he called out: "Mistress Briony! Your highness! Please, do join me!"

Evolet glanced over at me. "I did not know you and Yveme acquainted, you sly thing. Perhaps you hope to sit for a portrait while you are here."

I laughed. "Gods, no! Why would anyone want to paint my portrait? We met one afternoon while he was painting a woman in a fountain."

"Ah, yes—Cezann. She is quite a favorite of his."

Yveme bowed low as we neared. "Well? What do you think of it?"

The scene upon the canvas was so unlike the fifty-eighth iteration I'd seen two days before that recognition came slowly, followed swiftly by chagrin.

"Oh," I said.

He had evidently decided that "more" meant Cezann becoming the fountain rather than frolicking in it, painted entirely in gold and wearing a headdress from which no less than twenty streams of water arched into the air. Members of the Court Eternal dressed in white tossed handfuls of pearls at her feet, and I remembered the strands he'd torn in his despondency.

Looking around, I noticed that the rest of his paintings followed much the same scheme: all featuring members of the Court as places within the palace. No wonder they inspired such boredom.

"They do not like them," Yveme sighed, as though I'd spoken the thought out loud. "Try as I might, I cannot seem to captivate their interest. They pass them by, but their eyes do not linger."

"I do not think you lack talent," I answered delicately. "'Tis only... well, perhaps they have tired of seeing the same thing over and over again."

He slumped down upon the edge of the fountain, his head between his jeweled hands. "I have painted every crystal within the palace and every leaf thereout. There is simply nothing left that they have not seen."

At his feet, I noticed a discarded sheaf of papers, and an idea blossomed suddenly within me. "Pass me a piece of parchment, please—and do you have a bit of charcoal? Fine tipped would be best..."

As Evolet sipped Calique with a group of men and women nearby, Yveme peered over my shoulder while I sat with my knees drawn up and sketched a place so beloved to me that I nearly blotted the parchment with my tears as it took shape beneath my shaking fingers: the garden at Orwynd, and the Morwood beyond. There were the rickety trellises and the poles for the beans wound together crudely with rope that would not survive another year were the crop as heavy as the last; there were the bushes of lavender that hummed perpetually with fat, yellow bees from spring to fall; there was the apple tree that had stood for two hundred years and still produced the sweetest fruit. And there were the ancient groves and shadows of the place that had been my refuge, treasured and feared in equal measure; I wondered if I would ever see it again.

I handed Yveme the finished sketch and scrubbed my fingertips clean of charcoal with a bit of water from the fountain. "It's the garden where I grew up, and the woods beyond," I explained. "I know it isn't terribly clever, but it is one of my most favorite places in the world, and you *did* wish to see something beyond the walls of the palace."

It seemed my simple drawing had left him quite speechless for all he could do was stare down at it, blinking occasionally as though he were wrestling with something quite elusive. His mouth opened and closed several times as though he would've liked to say something to me, but no sound came out and, eventually, I bid him farewell and returned to the princess.

"Music, then," declared the princess, dismissing Yveme with a flick of the wrist. She led me back to the main path and to her brother, expounding upon the excellence of the kingdom's composers. "Roven was overly fond of flutes, but Twillian was quite entertaining—always coming up with the most wonderful things. I've not seen him in an age. What happened to him?"

Anwar rubbed his chin. "Wasn't he executed for treason?"

"Was he?"

"He was a deserter, don't you remember? Wanted to run off and join the people of the forest."

"Oh yes!" she laughed. "I'd quite forgotten! A shame, really. His concertos really were quite clever. Well, never mind the music, then. *My* favorite is Lady Fate, who tells fortunes, or do you prefer the water? The boats are tremendous fun, too, unless they capsize."

"Honestly, it's only tremendous fun when they capsize," her brother whispered to me, and when I looked up at him, he winked conspiratorially.

I was, unfortunately, rendered quite speechless by their cavalier exchange, their dismissive laughter at the loss of a man's life. "Why would anyone want to join the people of the forest?" I asked.

This brought an end to their laughter, and rather abruptly.

Anwar recovered his smile first. "Artists," he sighed. "Who can understand them, eh?"

"What should you like to do first?" Evolet asked, gripping my hand all too tightly. "Shall we have our fortunes told or play games before? I do believe there is a concert later, perhaps a play..."

"First, she shall meet the Court," Anwar laughed. "Come—I should very much like you to make the acquaintance of some of my dearest friends."

A trio of men stood beside a fountain of pure crystal, from which poured not water but Calique; they held their glasses below the pale green streams until they were full, drank, then filled them again.

"I wish you to meet Wynsel, Braesor, and Carlew," King Anwar said, as he and his sister propelled me toward them. "They are as excellent of friends as you could possibly hope for, though they are often drunk and therefore extremely unreliable and frequently inappropriate."

Wynsel had a long, pale face and hair to match, braided

elaborately down his back and studded with clear gemstone pins. He appeared entirely out of place at such an indolent gathering, surrounded by such color and fire and life, for he did not smile at all when he bowed stiffly to us. Despite the dizzying array of fashions on display around us, he was wearing what appeared to be a dressing gown that was as white as the rest of him, with a train of feathers that left a trail upon the grass wherever he walked.

"How do you do," he greeted us. "I hope our gathering meets with your approval."

"Approval!" Braesor roared with laughter. "The whole point of the pleasure garden is to *not* meet with anyone's approval!" He was far more jovial, with a pleasant smile, round cheeks, and kind eyes. "Ignore old Wynsel. He has no idea how to act like a person."

"I am merely being polite," sniffed Wynsel, his nose upturned. "Perhaps you should try it."

"Ignore the both of them," the third man cut in, "as I am the only person here whose acquaintance is worth making."

He was a tall man with a head of wild brown curls and a shrewd face. He regarded us with the air of one whose humor was itself a constant riddle and one was never sure if one was in on the joke or the unfortunate victim of it. His robe was even more ridiculous than Wynsel's: deep purple velvet, with a neckline that plunged to his navel and an enormous hood lined with golden tassels.

"Forgive me," I said, stifling a laugh. "But I must inquire after your robes."

Braesor groaned. "Please do not encourage them! They decided upon a friendly wager some time ago as to who could annoy Princess Evolet the most by wearing a dressing gown to one of her balls, but she took no notice of them whatsoever and now they wear them everywhere, each worse than the last."

"How long has this competition been going on, exactly?"

Wynsel glanced over at Carlew, his brow raised. "Six months, perhaps?"

"Seven," he answered. "You know, I think I'm going to wear them forever. They're terribly comfortable and clothes are such a bother when you cannot get them off fast enough. But enough about that." He waved his hand airily. "You're going to absolutely love tonight. Though, mind you, drink the Calique, not the punch."

Here, Arlo peeked his head into the conversation, for he'd finally found a topic of interest to him. "Why?" he asked.

"The punch will treat you very well at first so you will fall desperately in love with it, consume far too much, and wake up the next morning completely nude, cradled against the bosom of the statue of old King Dolin in the northeast courtyard."

"Do you ever partake in this punch yourself?"

"All the time."

King Anwar fixed him with a pointed stare. "Not tonight, Carlew. I expect you to be a most charming host to our guests."

Carlew waved this away in irritation. "I promise nothing. I came here tonight solely to drink, dance, and generally make a complete fool out of myself."

Braesor shook his head. "Idiot."

"Honestly, they are all idiots," Princess Evolet whispered to me.

"Bring forth the punch!" Carlew bellowed.

Once we'd been furnished with glasses full to the brim, we watched a short play depicting a scandal that had apparently divided the Court Eternal some decades ago: a woman was caught between three men, and so she set them to tasks of increasing impossibility that they might win her heart. The actors and actresses all wore masks that, by the grace of a wondrous bit of magic, altered with their emotions, though I took little pleasure in it, for no emotions played on the faces of the audience but laughter, even when the play ended in heartbreak and tragedy for all. I clapped politely when the play drew to a close and the actors took their bows.

Evolet clasped my hands as we rose from our seats. "You must come with me," she said. "I have ever so many people who wish to meet you! May I steal her away, dear brother?"

That she should ask it of him and not of myself was most vexing, but nevertheless King Anwar inclined his head in acquiescence, and I was swept away in a flurry of skirts as she fluttered her fingers at her brother in farewell.

"Now that's better, isn't it?" she said. "Let us seek out far better company."

Far better company turned out to be a dozen women seated around a low table in a small grove strung with thousands of tiny Lumens. Between them they passed a small, clear bowl overflowing with tendrils of lavender smoke that they lifted to their faces and breathed in, long and slow and deep. Languid smiles and throaty laughter followed, and the undulation of limbs, fingers caressing the air as though it were silk.

Two of the women stood immediately at the sight of the princess, and we took their seats while they scurried to stand behind us in fawning deference. I thought perhaps I recognized several of their faces from the concert we had attended the night before, but their paint and decorations were so convoluted that they might've been anyone; they were, all of them, like jewels glittering in a velvet case, posed just so that the light might strike them perfectly.

"Do show us your magic," the woman beside me said, reaching out dreamily and running her delicate hand down my arm. "You must be able to do a great many things."

"Yes, show us," another said. "We are ever so bored."

Well, that was hardly surprising. I'd only spent a week in Syr'Aliem and already I was thoroughly exhausted with the foolishness of it all, the saturation of gilt, the endless veneer of beauty that concealed nothing but air. My mind had grown quite restless the more of it I was inclined to endure.

"I can do basic spellwork only without a magical source," I told them regretfully. "But if you insist..."

The smoke they'd inhaled had, evidently, mucked about with their wits for they found the conjuring of a small flame in my palm the most extraordinary thing and the levitation of a silver bowl full of plump, deep red fruits some feet above the table before us even more so, and they collapsed upon one another with squeals and gasps. Calique splashed upon their gowns and painted skin, though they hardly seemed to notice nor care.

"My brother tells me you grew up at the court of your own kingdom," Princess Evolet said to me. "Do tell us all about it. Was it so very different than the Court Eternal?"

"I hate to disappoint you all, but I was only at court as a child, and not for very long," I answered. "But, yes, it was very different."

I thought perhaps they wished to hear of our customs or politics, but instead they asked after the fashions of King Keric's court, and of the way they conducted their flirtatious and amorous affairs, of which I knew positively nothing save what Livia had written in her letters, and they pouted with their beautiful lips when I could provide little to entertain.

"You've never had a lover?" said a woman with rich bronze skin and tight black curls. "Not even one?"

"Not even one."

"Then we shall find you one."

The woman beside me scoffed. "Fool, she already has one. Or had you forgotten the prince?"

"*I've* not forgotten him," someone else said slyly. "Such eyes..."

"Such hands!" the woman beside me exclaimed, and looked over at me with a sly smile. "Come now, do tell us if he is as talented with his fingers as he is with his magic."

Titters of laughter erupted at this, and I could scarcely breathe for the mortification that suffused my person.

"We've not..." I stammered. "That is, in our kingdom, it is considered highly improper for a woman to engage in... well, *that*, outside of marriage."

"Why?" the woman asked, and it took me far too long to realize that she was in earnest. And she was not the only one. All around me, the women of the Court Eternal watched me curiously, waiting upon my words.

"She would be considered ruined," I said.

"By whom?"

Princess Evolet had been watching me silently throughout the entire, excruciating exchange, and now she smiled and gave voice to my thoughts: "Men."

We regarded one another over the bowl of smoke. I should have liked to contradict her, so smug did I find her expression, so odious did I find her kingdom in that moment; I should have liked to.

"Yes," I said softly.

A woman with an elaborate headdress leaned forward. "Why bother with the judgment of men at all? We certainly do not!"

They erupted into laughter at this, the women who surrounded me, and I smiled weakly. "Well, we must, you see, for otherwise we become a burden to our parents, for there the matter of employment and the ownership of property—"

"How I feel for you, dear Briony, to be so bound by convention," Evolet interrupted with a voice of syrup, her hand upon my leg as she leaned forward and fluttered her eyelashes. "And love does not come into it, I suppose."

I could not tear my gaze from the gentle part of her lips, plush and gleaming pink. "I imagine it does, from time to time."

"From time to time?"

I fumbled with the glass in my hands and fixed my gaze most determinedly upon my lap. "Yes, well, enough about me. Perhaps you will instead tell me about you? How do you fill your days at court?"

"Days?" The woman beside me laughed. "I do not rise until noon!"

"And you do not go to sleep until dawn, Lasia, so I suppose your day is, in fact, your night!" This from her friend beside her, and they collapsed in a fit of giggling.

Another woman had, I suspected, inhaled far too much of the lavender smoke, for she actually reached out to touch my cheek with one, dainty fingertip, then exclaimed, "They're not dirt!"

As her friends began to whisper behind their jeweled hands, I realized that she meant my freckles.

"There are ways to remove them, you know," the woman with a head full of dark, tight curls whispered to me. "Princess Evolet could show you how."

"Why would I want to?"

"Indeed, why should she want to?" Evolet agreed, taking up my hand in a show of solidarity, and though I suspected the gesture more ceremonial than sincere, I was grateful, for there was no further talk of altering my appearance.

We were summoned by King Anwar not long after to play several rounds of a game upon the lawn, and this I liked much better, for as I darted about the field beneath the warm night sky, a long club gripped in both of my hands, my muddled head began to clear.

I was far too short, and encumbered by the long skirts of the pale sea green gown Princess Evolet had chosen for me that night, but it was with the enthusiasm of one who had not had such freedom since childhood that I played, and I shouted with delighted laughter when I finally managed to score a goal, and then another, against our opponents.

"Excellent, Briony!" Princess Evolet clapped and beamed from where she sat upon a blanket with several other women of the court. "You are, indeed, a natural!"

"Beginner's luck," grumbled Thaniel good naturedly, for it was his team that was losing, and he appeared none too pleased at the fact.

King Anwar cuffed him lightly on the back as he passed. "Don't worry, my friend, you may win yet, though I do believe you'd stand a better chance if old Carlew stopped drinking the punch."

Indeed, I was not even sure why he'd agreed to play, for all he did was stand in the middle of the field with his club hanging loosely in his fingers as he drank from his cup and shouted at the lot of us that we were breaking rules that, frankly, I doubted existed at all.

"Idiot! Get out of the way!" Braesor bellowed at him, and when that failed, he began thwacking him in the legs with his club every time he passed.

"Can we not replace him?" Thaniel asked hopefully.

"Against the rules," hiccupped Carlew.

I could scarce play properly for laughing, but in the end, it was my team, the king's team, which emerged victorious, and a great deal of cheering and clapping arose from the spectators who had watched our unruly game with interest. Thaniel flopped down on the field and threw a hand over his eyes with a groan as I rushed over to where Elyan stood, an irrepressible smile upon my face and a lightness in my heart.

"We won! Did you see?"

"Indeed," he said. "You play the way you dance."

I pulled a face at him. "Unladylike?"

"Joyfully."

We supped then, for after such excursions we were quite famished. In a bower hung with lanterns of every shape and size, we sat at a long table set with silk and silver and crystal bowls overflowing with lush, fragrant blooms in shades of blush and aubergine, while food that better resembled art than sustenance was paraded before us by an endless stream of servants. They lingered only briefly, lowering the platters they held upon one hand, and I was scarce able to serve myself before they'd gone. Like every meal I'd had in Syr'Aliem, it was utterly delicious and utterly unsatisfying.

While I ate, I rested my eyes from the kaleidoscopic costumes and chaotic revelry of the people by staring absently at some refreshingly plain shrubs, when the sudden appearance of white fabric between the leaves gave me pause.

Frowning, I slid unnoticed from my chair and approached the spot where I thought I'd seen it and crouched down. Hidden within the waxy green, a tiny face peered out at me, crowned with golden curls.

"Hello, there," I said, my voice warm and cheerful so as not to frighten her away. "And what is your name?"

"Rosael."

"I am most pleased to meet you, Rosael. My name is Briony."

"Don't tell her I'm here," the little girl whispered back, her voice small and sweet. "Please."

"Who?"

"Nanny."

"Well!" I said brightly. "Having spent most of my childhood avoiding each and every nanny and maid and tutor assigned to look after me, I give you my word."

"I want to go home," she said.

"Is not this your home?"

"My real home."

I brushed an errant curl back from her face. "What do you mean?"

"Rosael!" cried a shrill voice across the clearing, and the child's fearful eyes met mine.

"Nanny, I presume?"

She did not answer me; rather, she bolted, the sly thing, darting back into the hedge and running at full tilt out the other side, blundering upon her little legs through a crowd of drunken revelers.

"Nanny!" the princess demanded. "What have you done? What is that child doing here?"

"I'm sorry, your highness," Nanny huffed, for it was quite evident given her age that she was not used to running after her charges. "This one's been trouble from the start."

A child escaping her nanny did not seem an offense worthy of the royal guard, but Princess Evolet immediately set them upon the girl, and she was caught with disappointing swiftness; I did not much like the look of Nanny, nor her tone, and I'd rather hoped Rosael might inconvenience her a while longer.

"Let me go!" the child cried, kicking and struggling as mightily as one of her age and stature could, but a guard held her tight by the wrist.

Nanny approached her with a face full of thunder and something clasped within her hands. "You've caused quite enough trouble for one night, little miss," she said, and as the guards held the girl still, Nanny poured the contents of a small phial into Rosael's mouth.

The effect was nearly instantaneous; one moment the girl howled with righteous fury, and the next she was slumped against Nanny's stalwart form, her eyes glazed and slightly unfocused.

"Now, then," Nanny huffed. "Back to bed with you."

"Yes, Nanny," Rosael mumbled, and she allowed herself to be led away by the hand.

King Anwar was studying me intently, and I must have looked as nauseated as I felt. "You seem troubled," he said. "She is a child who does not care for the nursery, nothing more."

Given my own fervent dislike of my own nursery and the long-suffering mistresses who cared for me there, I understood perhaps better than anyone, and yet there was something odd about this particular child, something desperate.

"Of course." I shook my head, affecting what little of a smile I could for him. "I did not care much for mine, either."

He grinned. "I have no difficulty imagining it."

"What was it that Nanny gave her?"

"A sleeping draught, nothing more. Kevren brews them for any who cannot find rest." He offered me his arm. "Come. Walk with me."

I hesitated, looking about for Elyan, but I did not see him, nor did I see Thaniel or Arlo. (Phyra, of course, had declined the throngs in the pleasure garden in favor of the solitude of our suite). Even the princess had disappeared, no doubt by design. Reticently, I rested my hand in the crook of his elbow.

"I do not think it is a wayward child that has you so troubled, Mistress Briony. I believe I am at fault," he said as we walked, and when I turned abruptly, denial upon my lips, I found him watching me with amusement in his eyes.

"What fault is that, your highness?"

"My talk of marriages and alliances the other day," he clarified. "The matter continues to upset you, I think."

"Not at all," I lied. "You gave me much to think on is all."

"Not pleasant things, I fear."

"Necessary things," I answered, and wished fervently to say no more about it, for unease had begun to unfurl within me at the very mention of the odious subject.

"Do you view marriage as a necessity, then?"

Had my binding succeeded in hiding my magic forever, my Aunt Eudora would by now have likely seen no less than a dozen suitors from the most ancient noble families of Tiralaen paraded through the halls of Orwynd for my benefit. Of course, she was also quite certain that my unruly nature would repel any man of quality. Should I find my way home and into her company again, rather than rejoice at Elyan's affection for me, she likely would ask him if his imprisonment had thoroughly muddled his senses.

"For me, I could not say," I answered him at last. "For others... most certainly."

"I was right, then. My words continue to trouble you."

We'd drawn near a bench along the path, and he gestured for me to sit. For a moment, there was nothing but silence between us as we watched a laughing woman stagger about blindfolded, her hands held out before her as a group of men teased and taunted her, darting about just out of reach. When at last she managed to grasp one of them by the sleeve, she flung the blindfold away in triumph and welcomed him for a kiss, as the other men groaned in good-natured disappointment.

"I hope I am not incorrect in my assumption that you have enjoyed your time in Syr'Aliem, however brief," Anwar said. When I looked over at him, his gaze was still fixed upon the kissing couple across the lawn.

When first we'd arrived, I would've agreed most enthusiastically; all was splendor and delight. I decided to pretend as if nothing had happened since, and said: "I quite adore it here."

His relief was evident, and his easy smile returned. "Then may I ask you something?"

"Of course."

"Are you certain beyond doubt that your cave exists and that it will lead you back to Tiralaen?"

"Very certain," I lied. After all, I'd been told of the cave by the shade of a man long dead who had never actually seen it. "Why do you ask?"

He tilted his head thoughtfully. "Only this. If it does not and you are forced to remain in our world, would it be so very terrible?"

I jumped to my feet. "Yes! If Elyan does not retake the throne, countless more lives will be lost."

"Peace," he said. Taking my hand, he drew me back down beside him. "Tell me, how much time has passed since you last set foot in your homeland?"

"Half a year, maybe more. I cannot truly say," I admitted. "I lost count of the weeks in the Heimslind."

"And in that time, do you not think that others have taken up your righteous cause?"

"Some may fight," I said slowly. "But when I left, the resistance was a shamble. With my father's death came also the loss of hope that Queen Gwynliere of Sidonia might openly join our cause. And besides, no one there even knows the name Viscario, much less his role in Keric's madness. His magic is beyond anything I've ever known or read about. There is no hope of victory against him unless we can return."

"I know little of the grandeur of kingdoms such as yours," Anwar said. "We are very isolated here in the forest, but I have studied the nations beyond the northern mountains, and among the islands to the east, and it seems to me that empires rise and fall as the tides. There is no such thing as victory, for the game never ends. It will be played forever so long as men seek to rule one another."

I shook my head adamantly. "I cannot believe that. I won't."

"Suit yourself." He stood and walked to the edge of the balcony, his hands laced behind his back. "May I ask you a hypothetical question?"

"Of course."

"If your prince must marry another to secure his crown, and it is your unfortunate fate to witness it, would you not consider an alternative, one that may prove less painful to you?"

"I'm afraid I do not understand you."

"Stay here," he said softly. "In Syr'Aliem."

Remaining in this world had never burdened my thoughts, however hopeless our task had seemed. I would succeed or die in the attempt, and no other fate existed for me. Foolish bravado, some would likely say, or naïve stupidity, though perhaps they often clasped their arms as friends.

I drew myself up and met his gaze squarely. "You are right that I care for Elyan, and deeply. But there is no force in this world or

my own great enough to tempt me from the task to which I have
been set."

"And if there is no cave at all?" he asked. "What then?"

"Then I will simply have to find another way."

His smile was wistful. "I expected you to say that. But, still,
something to think on."

Desperate to look upon anything but his handsome face, his
probing, inquiring eyes, my gaze fell upon the fantasia in the
distance, awash in starlight.

"Would you care to see it?" Anwar asked, for he had followed
my gaze. "It really is quite remarkable."

In fact, I did wish to see it, and so, despite my misgivings as my
companions had not reappeared, I allowed him to lead me down
the brightly lit path. Within the shimmering pavilion was an
endless dance, courtiers whirling past me in a glittering haze of
color, all spangles and sparkles in the golden light of Lumens
reflected by crystal, fractured and blinding.

We watched them for a time, weaving their patterns upon the
floor as we sipped from our glasses, and I hated their eyes upon me,
so many eyes, and I wondered if when they looked upon me, they
saw a grasping, devious stranger beside their sovereign.

Drink flowed with the music, and a man and woman, giggling
madly, decided to swap their clothes. He was much taller than she
and far more robust; the bodice of her gown barely covered the
expanse of his chest, which everyone found terribly funny, and to
thunderous applause he staggered onto the stage beside the
conductor so as to regale the assembled with a song. He managed
a verse, a chorus, and part of a second verse before toppling
unceremoniously into the orchestra, and I could not help but laugh
at his flailing limbs, one leg stuck firmly inside an enormous horn

and his arm hopelessly entwined in the strings of a rather lovely standing harp, the owner of which commenced smacking him over and over again upside the head until he slid free.

The men and women around me, their king included, found the spectacle uproarious; laughter pealed and shrieked around me until it became a persistent drone that made my head ache and my teeth clench. I could stand it no more, and so, as stealthily as I could manage, I slipped from Anwar's side, a wisp of smoke disappearing into the night air.

I wandered alone, far away from the fantasia, swallowed up by the darkness and grateful for it. My feet led me nowhere in particular, and the raucous noise of the pleasure garden faded into blessed silence. I could breathe again, and as my head cleared, I thought of Tiralaen.

Had Gavreth remained king, had none of it ever happened, I might've spent that night in the pleasure gardens of another place. I would've worn an entirely different gown and danced to entirely different songs in the arms of an entirely different man; my husband, perhaps, but I would have been home, and I would've been among my people. My future would've been exactly the torment that the women of the Court Eternal imagined it to be, but I would have had them once more: my parents, Livia, Uncle Geordan, Aunt Eudora and Layn and Mora and Saren and even the odious Sturgus, and Master Aeneas, and... and...

A shadow poured down like sand from the heavens before me, at first nothing more than a gray, indistinct shape against the distant lights. It shifted and shivered and became a man, although I could not discern his features.

It terrified me so that I gasped, stumbled, and the figure dissolved, dissipating into the air as if it had never been.

In the darkness, I stood and tried to remember.

Master Aeneas and... Master Aeneas and...

A cry escaped unbidden from my lips as images overwhelmed me: a scaffold; a block; a sword gleaming in the sun; the Gate; and then darkness.

I stumbled off the path and pitched forward, seeking anything I could to break my fall. My hands found stone: an urn full of night-blooming flowers, their delicate scent surrounding me as I closed my eyes and breathed slowly in and out, in and out, until my heart no longer thrashed in my chest like a wild thing.

When at last my head began to clear, I became aware of voices drifting across the lawn, one familiar to me. Their words were hushed, but the urgency in them roused my suspicions. I lifted my head and beheld two figures some yards away, a woman of the Court... and Kevren.

"Please," the woman begged, her hands fisted in the healer's tunic. "Please, Kevren, you must help me. I cannot go through it all again, I cannot!"

"You must keep your voice down, Cylene," Kevren answered, gently unraveling her hands and looking around. "This is neither the time nor place to discuss such things."

"Help me get rid of it. You know what is at stake if you do not!"

"What you're asking me to do is forbidden. If we should be discovered, it would mean both our heads."

Cylene let out a choked sob. "I will not survive if you do not."

And with those words, they were gone. Kevren led the weeping Cylene beyond the reach of my ears, and it was not for me to follow; I was not one of Princess Evolet's gossips.

And yet, though I had the strength to stop my feet from following, I could not stop my mind from racing. What in Coleum's name could this Cylene be asking of Kevren that the price of discovery would be their lives? Evolet's composer had been executed for desertion, for wanting to join the people of the forest... but if this were Cylene's desire, what need she rid herself of in order to achieve it?

Could she possibly mean her magic, her connection to the Incuna? The Court Eternal served the crown by virtue of their magic—perhaps if Cylene could rid herself of that, she would be dismissed from service. But before I could think longer on the matter, raucous shouts and laughter drifted across the lawn, drawing close.

I hid, for I did not wish to return to pleasure garden; the very thought of it turned my stomach. Only days ago, I'd been so looking forward to seeing it, but like everything else in this achingly beautiful place, it had left me wanting, hollow. And I thought perhaps Elyan had been wrong when he said that nothing in Syr'Aliem was as it seemed, for its glittering surface held the truth in its entirety, and to look beneath would reveal nothing but nothingness.

17

"When might we see the village?"

My question took Princess Evolet quite by surprise.

"The village?" she repeated. "There is very little to entertain in the village. I cannot imagine why you should wish to see it."

We were all in her receiving room with no less than thirty ladies of the court present, all splendidly dressed, sipping dainty cups of lavender-colored punch and nibbling on delicacies passed by servants so silent and unobtrusive that I might've thought them phantoms. The princess had summoned us here to announce that she would be hosting a grand ball in our honor to celebrate the passing of our first week in the palace, and at the news, the ladies of the court had let out a collective sigh of delight and began to fan themselves in earnest.

I could not imagine why; their very existence was a ball.

"A kingdom is comprised of more than its nobility, is it not? I think the village a splendid idea," Elyan said.

Princess Evolet lifted her beguiling eyes to his face. "Have we so failed to captivate you that you would seek your pleasure elsewhere?"

"Not at all."

She snapped her slender fingers, and a servant appeared with a silver tray bearing nests of golden pastry filled with cream and dusted with glimmering flakes of gold. "These are my absolute favorite," the princess gushed. "You simply must try one."

I required no further urging. The buttery crust melted in my mouth, the cream a revelation of savory and sweet, and I'd scarce finished swallowing before I seized another from the tray before it was whisked away.

"And the village?" I pressed, as the servant bowed and moved on.

She had clearly hoped the pastries might prove a distraction, for her smile was now decidedly more fixed than it had been a moment before. "Goodness, but you are persistent!"

"Indulge us."

"In this, as in all things, I shall have to consult my brother."

She left us, floating away on a cloud of silk and scent, and I knew we were as likely to see the village as we were to be given a personal tour of the Incuna itself.

"Has it occurred to anyone but me that there is, in fact, no map, and this whole thing is one enormous jest?" Arlo looked about at the rest of us. "No? Just me?"

"Patience," Elyan said through gritted teeth, though it was clear his was slipping with each passing day.

My own patience was frayed to a gossamer thread, ready to snap, for I could find no peace at night and very little sleep.

The Dae Spira came and went as she pleased, appearing one moment wreathed in the fog of a distant horizon, and in the next moment looming over me in my bedchamber, with her accusing fingers and mouth stretched wide.

Those were the good nights; the worst of my nights were haunted by another specter entirely.

Ever since the day I'd worn the gown with the bodice of leaves and imagined Elyan upon his knees before me, the idea had taken root and grown until I could not escape it even in sleep.

In such dreams, his long fingers ghosted across my untried flesh until I writhed and begged, his black hair clutched between my fingers. His extraordinary eyes always looked to me, then he pressed an open-mouthed kiss to the soft skin of my inner thigh, seeking permission.

I gave it, always.

I was not myself in these moments, and I could not remember my own name as I squirmed in the dark and woke a shivering, sweat-slicked tangle. A hot, persistent throbbing remained that my shaking fingers attempted to assuage, but inexperienced was I, and afraid, and when the sensation grew to a tempest that threaten to drown me, I recoiled from it, gasping, and tears of frustration and longing leaked from my eyes and stole into the tangle of my hair.

It had, therefore, become quite impossible to hold his gaze, for I was certain that my eyes would betray my wicked thoughts and he would find me even more of a disappointment than he already did.

If my behavior perplexed him, he said nothing of it, and for that at least, I was grateful.

To escape the unbearable warmth of Elyan's presence, I began to wander about the room, where card games were being played at low tables and conversations mingled with the sound of tinkling glass, and then I saw her. The woman from the pleasure gardens, the one who had begged Kevren for help.

She was sitting upon a velvet chaise with another woman who appeared to be comforting her, although she seemed distracted by the very notion, nodding every so often and sipping from her cup of punch, her gaze wandering much as my own had done. Evidently the misery of her friend was of little interest to her.

I rose, pressing my hand upon Phyra's shoulder. "Will you be alright here for a moment?"

"Of course." She blinked up at me, and a sweet smile spread across her face, sweet and a bit bewildered. "I'm having rather a nice time, actually."

I crossed the room to where the two women sat, and as I drew near, they both looked up at me; the woman I'd seen in the pleasure gardens swiped quickly at her eyes, and I realized she'd been crying.

"I am so very sorry to interrupt you," I said, turning to the other woman who had been such a poor source of comfort. "But Princess Evolet wishes your company."

The woman's eyes widened, and she stood so fast that she nearly upended the contents of her glass upon herself. "Really?" she breathed. "Oh, I do apologize, Cylene, but I must..."

Cylene watched me with red-rimmed eyes and pursed lips as her companion hurried away without a backwards glance. Her luminous skin was the color of fresh cream, and dark curls spilled over one bare shoulder, woven through with diamonds.

She caught me staring and raised her eyebrows at me, which I decided to take as an invitation and swiftly crossed to her side. "I was hoping to speak with you," I said. "May I sit?"

"Me?" She studied me for a moment, and I feared she meant to refuse me until she gestured to the seat beside her listlessly. "If you must."

"My name is Briony—"

"I know who you are."

"Ah. Well, I do not know who you are, but I saw you the other night," I said. "In the pleasure gardens."

She sighed, clearly disinterested.

"With Kevren."

It was as if I'd called lightning down from the heavens and struck her with it. Her posture went positively rigid, her eyes wide and fearful. "Leave. Now."

"I only want to help." I reached out and grasped her hand, a mistake for she immediately drew it back. "I promise, I am a friend."

She snorted. "There are no *friends* in this place."

"It is quite fortuitous, then, that I am from another world entirely."

"I've heard rumors about you," she said slowly, "that you are remarkably uncouth and ill-mannered."

"Oh?" I answered faintly.

"And sweet. Far too sweet for your own good. I am both surprised and impressed that Syr'Aliem has not eaten you alive."

"Well, I survived a private audience with the Dowager Queen in her shrine of a receiving room, so I think you'll find I've a strong constitution."

The hint of a smile tugged at her lips, but was quickly smothered. "What is it you want, Briony who is not of this world?"

"You seemed to be in some distress last night, and I thought perhaps I could help you in some way."

"Help me?" Her laugh was mirthless.

"What troubles you?" I asked gently. "Is it your connection to the Incuna?"

She started. "The Incuna? Why would you think it had anything to do with the Incuna?"

"You mentioned ridding yourself of it—"

"Stop," she hissed, and gripped my wrist so tightly that I gasped. "Do not speak such words aloud."

I drew back, rubbing my smarting skin. "Fine. Let us make a deal, then. You tell me why you sought Kevren's help, and I shall not forget myself and mention it in polite company."

It was a cruel compromise to force upon her, but I was angry at her for the pain in my wrist, and the words were out before I had considered them. Her eyes narrowed into glittering, hateful slits. But she rose, beckoning me to follow.

I glanced toward my companions. To my surprise, I found Phyra engaged in a card game—and winning, it seemed, for the scowl on her opponent's face. Thaniel was at her side, while Elyan was in a quiet corner of the room, enduring the tittering conversation of the princess. Across the room from the rest was Arlo, who had quite captivated the attention of three lovely young women with some story or other that I felt certain was inappropriate for their ears. None of them were looking in my direction.

"Right," I exhaled. "Let's go."

If the guards thought anything untoward of us leaving the gathering, they did not show it. As she led me down corridor after corridor, Cylene tucked my arm into hers, and I could feel the tension vibrating through her body with each swift step toward our destination; outwardly, no one would've ever imagined the tumult within. She greeted everyone we passed politely, demurely, but I did not attempt to do the same, for I could not possibly have managed it with the same grace. I'd thought her a flower like the rest of them were flowers: exquisitely beautiful; delicate; fragile; quick to wither with the fading of the light or the slightest rime of frost. Not so. An herb amongst flowers was Cylene, the green spires of rosemary, the enduring thyme.

Her suite was light and airy, with a lovely balcony overlooking the courtyard in which I'd passed my first afternoon in the palace. She drew the curtains, afraid of prying eyes even here, and poured us each a glass of pale-yellow wine from a crystal decanter.

"I know a little of your reputation, Briony of Asperfell," she said.

"Yes, so you said. Uncouth and entirely too sweet."

"That, and you've an insatiable desire to help anyone you come across. The servants do talk, you know, and sometimes we listen when they do. But this is no spirit in the kitchens. If you breathe a word of it, it will cost far more than my reputation."

"Why? If there's a way to rid yourself of your connection to the Incuna, why should such a thing not be allowed?"

Her laugh was a harsh, incredulous bark. "You believe it is my magic I wish to rid myself of? Oh, but you are as fresh as they say."

"Then what could you possibly require Kevren's help to—oh."

She'd not yet begun to show, though it could've simply been the cut of her gown, the cunning way it was cinched and draped; still, there was a roundness in her face, a heaviness in her breasts that betrayed her condition; a condition she'd sought a healer to rid herself of.

"*Oh*, indeed. I see you've caught on at last; well done."

"Is this truly what you want? To rid yourself of your child?"

Her face hardened. "I believe we are finished here."

"No, wait—please. It's just that last night you sounded... distraught."

She turned from me, slamming her glass so hard upon the table that it shattered; her fingers still gripped the ragged stem, and I was shocked to see thin rivulets of blood trickling over her knuckles. "Of course you would imagine such a thing of me; of any of us."

"I would not," I answered honestly, unable to tear my gaze away from the spreading stain of red and shards of glass. "I could not imagine how anyone could wish for such a thing."

"You understand nothing of our way of life," she snapped.

"Then tell me," I said.

There was such fury in her eyes that I thought she might throw the jagged stem of her broken wine glass at me or jab it into my throat. But then the moment passed, and she only shook her head. "What you saw last night was a moment of weakness, and I have moved past it. I suggest you do the same."

"Please, there must be something I can do," I begged.

She smiled then, because she'd expected it of me, and thought me a fool for it. "In less than a fortnight, you will be gone from this place. The best thing you can do is to forget all of this and greet me as a stranger when next we meet."

I would greet her as a stranger as she wished, but I would not forget her predicament, and I certainly would not remain still. She'd sought the healer's help before; I would do so now.

The stillroom was empty when I arrived, but then Kevren lifted the curtain of moss and entered with a tray of shining silver instruments. There was such grace in his movements, such ease and assurance that it was no wonder he was such a skilled healer. When he saw me lingering at the threshold, a warm, welcoming smile spread across his face. "Good afternoon, Briony. Do come in!"

Then, through the curtain of moss, a familiar voice said: "Is that Briony?" Thaniel's golden head emerged, and he grinned at the sight of me. "I had to sneak away, I'm afraid. There's only so much gossip I can take, especially about people whom I know little and care less."

"Oh," I started, deflating a bit at the sight of him. "I do not wish to trouble you if you are otherwise engaged."

Kevren offered me an easy smile. "As you can see, I am unencumbered by patients, as usual. In fact, Thaniel and I were just working on a spell to induce a healing sleep."

I looked to where Thaniel stood rubbing the back of his neck, a proud smile upon his handsome face. "We haven't cracked it quite yet, mind you—this bit of spellwork was originally intended for more... nefarious purposes."

"We'll manage it yet. Now then," Kevren said, turning to me. "How may I be of service?"

"I wish to speak with you about someone at Court."

"Ah," said he, and his smile faded somewhat. "I hope this does not concern their health, for I am not at liberty to discuss my patients with anyone."

"Yes, but in this case, she isn't really a patient."

He tilted his head. "Is that so? Well, now I am intrigued. Of whom do you speak?"

"Cylene."

Kevren's smile disappeared entirely. "Briony, I do not know what you might've heard or from whom—"

"You, as a matter of fact. Last night in the pleasure garden."

Kevren's eyes went wide as a rabbit's in a snare. "Not here," he said, then ushered me from the main room though the mossy curtain into his workroom, Thaniel on our heels. "What she asks is forbidden, Briony."

"To rid herself of her baby."

He sighed brokenly, dropping his face into his hands. "Yes. The Incuna take me, yes."

"Oh Gods," Thaniel choked.

"But she does not wish to be rid of it; not truly—she told me as much herself. Why would she ask you to rid her of it if she wants it?"

"You do not understand—"

"Then *tell* me," I begged him. "Tell me so that I might understand."

He seemed to consider his words very carefully. "As much as I believe you mean well, both of you, there are reasons beyond Cylene's predicament that prevent me from revealing what I know."

"What reasons could possibly be worth more than a child's life?"

"The lives of many, many others." He slumped, defeated, onto a nearby stool, his hands hanging uselessly between his knees, and Thaniel rested a heavy hand upon his shoulder. "I am truly sorry, but the risk I face is too great."

"She said she couldn't bear for this to happen again," I said. "Did something happen to her first child?"

Kevren dropped his eyes from me. "He was taken from her. Just as this one may be also. It remains to be seen."

The breath was stolen from my lungs at his words. "Why?" I gasped.

"Only those with magic may join the Court Eternal."

The full meaning of his words fell upon me like a blow to the head, leaving me dizzying and staggering.

It was Thaniel who asked, "What happens to those who do not?"

"They are taken to the village."

"May not a mother go with her child to live in the village, then?" I asked, though my words were muffled by my hand over my mouth. "Can Cylene not abdicate her position among the Court Eternal?"

Kevren met my eyes then, and said softly: "Leave the palace? Have you not pieced together the answer to that question by now?"

"Is there any way at all that we might help her?" Thaniel asked. "Take her in secret to the village, that she would be able to keep her baby?"

"There is no place in Syr'Aliem they will not find her."

"Then she must leave Syr'Aliem," I said.

The answer hung between us all, suspended in the heavy silence, and when Kevren did not immediately dismiss the idea, the smallest seed of hope began to flourish within me that perhaps there was a way yet to help Cylene.

I knelt before Kevren and reached for his hand; a shiver passed through him when I took it. "If there is a place where mother and child might both be safe, please tell me. Let me help her."

He sighed, a deep and heavy thing. "There is a place, deep within the forest, and people there who will take her in."

"People there..." My eyes widened. "You cannot mean the magic thieves?"

"They are not as Anwar would have you believe."

"But how could you possibly know that?"

He looked to Thaniel, standing stalwart at his back, then back to me. "I know this because I am one of them. 'Tis where I was born."

Thaniel had known, and not told me; not told any of us. Still, I could hardly fault him for it when I'd been keeping secrets of my own. It seemed I was not the only one of Elyan's entourage to be making the most of my time in Syr'Aliem by involving myself in the locals' intrigues and mysteries.

"How?" And then, quite suddenly, I understood: "You're a spy."

"I would hardly use so dramatic a word," he said. "Informant, perhaps."

"How long?"

"I presented myself to Anwar five years ago under the pretense that my healing skills could not flourish under the cruelty and ignorance of the wild people of the forest. I found him quite eager to believe my stories of how desperate and abysmal my life had been there, and I have worked tirelessly ever since to gain his trust. Even now, I am never certain I've succeeded entirely."

He refused to tell us more of his purpose, and begrudgingly I agreed that he'd be a poor spy if he did. Still, he had earned Thaniel's trust, and that was no easy feat. Therefore, I swore to keep his secret, even from Elyan, if he would agree to help smuggle Cyrene from the palace and into the forest.

"If she'll go," said Thaniel.

I remembered her white knuckles wrapped around the stem of her broken glass, her blood mingled with shards of crystal, pooling on the table. "I believe she will."

"Still, there is the matter of how," said Kevren. "This is hardly the first time someone has decided they've had enough with life at court and tried to escape into the forest. It rarely ends well."

"I can handle a few guards," Thaniel declared.

Kevren raised a skeptical eyebrow. "No doubt you can. And what will happen to you and your friends after you do?"

A wild thought entered my mind, and I flashed them a wide grin. "It's not a soldier we need, but someone a bit more... humble."

Thaniel frowned. "Briony? What is it you are thinking?"

"That someone in the kitchens owes me a favor. And I think I know exactly what to do with it."

18

The night of the ball, Princess Evolet's foremost seamstress herself delivered the gown she'd created for me to my chamber: layer upon layer of ivory gossamer studded with ever so many stars, gold and silver and gleaming. My trembling fingers slid over the fabric as Isri opened the velvet-lined case that had accompanied it, revealing not a mask, but a dozen jeweled stars that her deft hands wove into my hair, a crown rising from my flaming curls.

There was a necklace as well, a delicate constellation that fanned out across the expanse of my chest, and I shivered as Isri fastened the clasp and settled the cold metal against my skin. Pronouncing me suitable with a curt yet satisfied nod, she took my hands and attempted to draw me to the looking glass in one corner of the chamber so that I might see the splendor upon my person for myself, but I would have none of it.

She fixed me with a most irritated expression indeed and gestured sharply to the mirror, but when it became perfectly clear I would not be moved upon the subject, she gave up and let me be.

The unfortunate truth of the matter was that I found I could not bear to look upon myself, for rather than rueful resignation, I'd found myself increasingly pleased by the creature reflected back at me, and this I simply could not abide.

I'd never thought myself possessed of anything remotely resembling fine looks, nor had I ever cared, for a curious sort of cage was beauty: sought, prized, and then inevitably lost, and the losing of it akin to a different sort of cage altogether, for what remained when nothing more had ever been cultivated? In my limited experience, beautiful women were seldom clever, as they'd never had cause to be, and the squandering of such potential I found abhorrent, for how could they seek to care only for outward appearances and let their minds atrophy most disgracefully?

And yet, it was not only the esteeming of beauty to the detriment of all else I feared, but what terrible havoc beauty had wrought upon my ignorance, and my peace. Had I known where the gown with its bodice of leaves had ended up after being whisked from my body by Isri, I would have hunted it down and burned it to ash so thoroughly did I rue the day I'd worn it. I'd learned that day, and suffered each night thereafter, that I knew little of love, and absolutely nothing of desire.

One I believed to be a friend, but the other... the other was a stranger at my door with flames in his hands, and if I let him in, he would set fire to me, consume me.

And worst of all, in the darkest, most secret corners of myself, I whispered that, perhaps, I should like to be consumed, so that I might see what emerged from the embers.

What a wicked thing I was, wanting such a thing, for proper women did not want and I was, my Aunt Eudora insisted, despite my willfulness, my wild, ungovernable nature, a proper woman.

And I was dreadfully late.

I'd nearly made it to my chamber door before Isri put out her arm and stopped me. She held up a small pot of gold paint and gestured to my eyes. I realized that I'd not yet donned a mask.

Although I was already quite late for the princess's ball in our honor, I knew better than to argue, and so I sighed and closed my eyes, and waited to feel the cold paint on my face.

She drew the wide brush from my left temple to my right in a single stroke, and when I opened my eyes, my vision was a glorious haze of light, glittering and gleaming, and it was some time before my eyes adjusted to the unusual heaviness of the paint.

Another brush appeared in her hands, but I could not bear any further ornamentation, and so I ducked under her arm, proclaiming myself quite ready to attend upon the Court Eternal, and stifled a smile at the exasperated sound of her sighs.

A Lumen glowed within the fireplace of the great room, newly conjured and blindingly bright, and a fresh decanter of Calique sat on the sideboard with five pristine crystal goblets beside it, but I was entirely alone.

"They've gone on, mistress," said a servant near the door, watching me expectantly. "If you are ready, the guards will escort you."

"Even Phyra?"

The derision upon the servant's face when I said her name did not escape me. "The Death Mage has declined to attend the gathering this evening."

I'd not truly believed she would attend; at Asperfell, she would not even attend the Serus feasts, but still I'd hoped. I made my way to Phyra's chamber, and when I knocked softly upon her door, she called from within: "Come."

The room was utterly dark, save the moonlight spilling coldly through the windows; not even the hearth had been lit. Phyra sat wrapped in a blanket, an untouched supper tray upon a small table beside her. "Briony," she greeted me with a small smile. "You look lovely."

"Thank you, but I feel ridiculous," I said. "Perhaps I should stay here and keep you company."

"No, unlike me, you would be missed. And I fear I would be poor company at the moment."

There was a second chair beside the untouched tray of food, and I smoothed my skirts so that I might sit facing her. We regarded one another silently. Where she saw my splendor, I saw the dark circles beneath her eyes, the strain about her mouth.

"What troubles you so?" I asked. "Are you so very frightened here?"

"I am not frightened," she said, and her lovely face became cold suddenly, and brittle. "I am angry."

Her brown irises had gone black before, when she'd raised the Phaelor in the forest. It might've been a trick of the shadows now, but I thought her eyes darkened ever so slightly. I swallowed, found my voice. "At the court?"

"No. At those who have taught them to fear death. It is fear that breeds hate."

"And do you no longer fear your own power over death?"

"On the contrary, I fear it more than ever."

Phyra had spent seven long years in Asperfell refusing to raise the dead, so terribly did she fear her power, fear what she might become in embracing it. For me, and for Tiralaen, she had raised Elyan. I had not expected her to ever do so again.

And yet she had, and so soon afterward.

"Once you told me you must bargain with Death's envoy to return a soul to the living world," I ventured.

"It has always been thus."

"And how do you reach such an agreement?"

She did not answer me right away, and I feared I had pressed my curiosity too forcefully upon her, particularly in her weakened state.

"I'm sorry," I said. "I do not mean to cause you distress. I know so little of magic, but I want to."

"What is it you wish to know?"

"Everything."

Her slender hand emerged from the blanket and grasped mine tightly, palm to palm, our fingers threading together. The air stilled around us, and the steady beat of the filigreed needle of the timekeeper on her mantle slowed, then stopped altogether. My eyes grew heavy and closed though I had not bid them to do so, and when I opened them, a monumental effort, I was no longer in her chamber.

"Oh!" I exclaimed, and in my shock, I nearly let go of Phyra's hand. She held me fast, tethering me to her magic, and to what I recognized as her Deathscape. She'd described it to me once, but never had I imagined I'd see it.

We stood together in shallow water that stretched on and on, perhaps forever, for the horizon was shrouded in thick fog, though I thought I saw dark shapes and shadows moving amongst the gloaming. I should've felt the cold shock of the water seeping through the velvet of my slippers; the hem of my gown of stars should've been soaked through and through, utterly ruined, and yet it felt as air; it felt as nothing at all.

A low rumble of thunder sounded far off in the distance; above our heads churned a river of gray clouds.

"Phyra!" I gasped, gripping her arm. "What have you done?"

"We are in my Deathscape."

"Well, I know *that*, but how is it I can be here? I am no Necromancer!"

"Were I using my magic to raise the dead, you could not be. Still, we do not have much time."

"Are you sure it's safe?"

"No. But you've never been one to prize your safety over your curiosity."

I grimaced. "What a splendid reputation I've cultivated."

"Indeed."

Before us, a short distance away, I beheld a rather odd sight: a simple wooden desk of the sort which I used to sit at before my little window at Orwynd, penning letters to my father and to Livia, and before it, a chair. A petitioner's chair.

"That is where I meet him," Phyra said, following my gaze. "Death's envoy. He sits there, at the desk, and I in that chair, and we speak, the two of us."

Upon the desk sat a single piece of parchment, a pot of black ink, a feathered quill, and a single candle, its wick blackened with use though it had never burned long enough to collect droplets of wax upon its body.

"What are they for?"

Phyra rested her hand on the back of the petitioner's chair. "If we are in agreement, the name of the dead is written, and then the candle is lit, returning the spirit to the living world."

"And if you are not in agreement?"

"I do not know. We have never been before."

I remembered Livia's letter from court so many years ago telling the story of the night a young Necromancer and her brother were brought before the king, her remarkable and terrifying gift intended to entertain a gathering of courtiers. Her aptitude, kept a secret since her childhood, had been brought to his attention only by tragedy, by a death, and Phyra's uncontrollable grief and longing.

"What about the first time it happened? I thought your grandmother was raised by accident."

"She was," Phyra answered. "In grief and desire, I found my way to this place quite without intention, and Death's envoy wrote her name and lit the flame before I could comprehend what it was, and before I realized I did not want it after all. For the others, there have been words spoken, and an agreement struck."

"What sort of words?" I wondered, as my eyes roamed the blank parchment, as weathered and aged as any in Asperfell's decrepit library.

"I ask for their lives, and I am either favorably met or I must further plead my case. Death's envoy must agree that the gift of a second life maintains the balance between all things living and dead."

"Balance," I echoed. I'd not realized until that moment how terribly complex Phyra's magic was, and I felt a modicum of foolishness that I'd been so ignorant of how vast the responsibilities of those who trafficked in life and death truly were. It was with greater understanding, and great sorrow, that I looked at her then, and what I saw snatched the very breath from my lips.

The rich brown of her irises had turned black and it was spreading, stealing into the whites of her eyes; thin, curling tendrils like drops of ink in water.

My voice, when I found it at last, was little more than a whisper: "What was it like when you raised Elyan?"

"His highness has a role yet to play in the fate of many. His was an easy case to plead."

"And if the one you sought to raise was not destined to be a king?"

"Less so."

I longed to hear more, but at that moment, I felt Phyra's hand grip mine tightly. I followed her gaze toward the distant fog, and this time I was certain I saw something moving there, the hazy outline of it growing larger as it drew closer. Before I could ask her what it was, the world around us dissolved, and I found myself back in the chair before her chamber window, nothing remaining of Phyra's Deathscape but the memory of endless water and the blackened wick of a candle.

Phyra released her punishing grip upon my hand and retreated back into the shroud of her blanket, drawing it up around her chin. The effort to bring me into her Deathscape must've been great indeed, for she looked even paler than she had when first I'd set foot in her chamber.

"Go," she murmured, a gentle dismissal. "Enjoy this night. Think not of me for I am weary."

I left her staring out into the abandoned courtyard, her delicate fingers splayed against her face, and I could not see her eyes by the light of the moon.

I'd been but a child when my family lived at court, and my father had sheltered me most thoroughly from what he believed were the unsightly bits: forbidding me from most gatherings and, even when I was permitted to attend, sending me to bed when the hour drew late, for with darkness and drink came that about which he was most insistent I remain in ignorance.

As such, I'd never seen a ball, let alone one in which the guests wore costumes and masks, but my sister had, upon her return to court, been present at a mask that Keric had thrown in honor of the visiting Princess of Cyr. He'd briefly entertained the idea of marrying her as a way to increase his support in the east, despite the fact that she was several years older than he and said to be quite pious and restrained. In the end, her vast fortune could not make up for the fact that he found her to be a crashing bore. She did not even attend the mask, preferring to cloister herself in prayer. He'd not noticed nor cared.

Ever the proper and sweet young woman, Livia's letter describing the mask had been mostly been concerned with what songs had been played and who had danced with whom and how very handsome the king had looked, but she had at least taken the trouble of describing the way the guests wore blue and white, the colors of the visiting princess's house, as well as the enormous wheel of gold at the center of the throne room crafted by Alchemists and bearing hundreds of masks.

Upon entrance to the gathering, each guest took their turn at the wheel, and whatever mask was bestowed upon them by the fate of that spin, they were made to wear unless they wished to pay for a second turn, the price of which was a kiss upon the ruddy cheek of the attendant, who was well and truly drunk by the time Livia arrived on our Uncle Geordan's arm. His turn yielded the mask of a merry fool, which he accepted good-naturedly, but my sister received a death-mask, a hideously grinning skull, and she recoiled from it in horror, much to the delight of the gathered gentry. My sister's face burned as she surrendered the necessary kiss, then hid behind the mask she received in return, a delicate, feminine countenance, even as the nobility roared with laughter.

The Court Eternal followed no such scheme; they'd chosen their costumes and masks with seemingly no purpose save to outdo one another, and in that, they'd succeeded spectacularly. My delighted eyes darted this way and that, unsure where to settle, for everywhere I looked was splendor and whimsy and delight, a feast I wished to savor, but that whirled past me so quickly I thought it surely a dream.

Though the animals and insects were unknown to me, I marveled at jeweled carapaces and wings, at beaks and feathers. One woman glided by in pale blue with endless ruffles of white the same shade as her hair, piled high like the softest of clouds atop her head and threaded through with strands of gleaming blue gems. She stopped to talk with a man whose person was covered in glimmering scales that changed color with the shifting of the light. Beside them, a group of women were dressed as the seasons as they passed through the woods beyond, stretching toward the Heimslind: one the rich green of summer, one the burnished copper of autumn, and the other the pale frost of winter. As they gossiped and tittered behind their hands, glitter rained from their towering wigs, covering the floor around them.

Someone brushed past me, a man in plum velvet with a mask that resembled a soldier's helm, and when he looked briefly over his shoulder to mutter some distracted apology, he stopped and a slow smile spread across his lips.

"My apologies," he said. "I appear to have stumbled upon the very heavens above."

"I'm perfectly fine," I stammered.

"You're one of the Mages, yes? I thought I recognized that hair of yours. Come and tell me all about your little prison, for I find it utterly fascinating." He'd drawn so close that the cloying scent of his perfume filled my nostrils, and he reached out with one hand and touched the stars in my hair.

"I spent most of my time at Asperfell conversing with dead things," I told him. "And I find I quite prefer their company to most I've met here."

His laughter echoed in my ears as I turned and was promptly swallowed up by the sea of gowns and masks, grateful for the thick press of bodies.

I sought refuge beside one of the many columns that lined the room, searching what little I could see of the faces around me for anyone familiar and wondering if I should not have stayed behind in our suite of rooms with Phyra after all. How had the flame of my delight in the costumery flickered out in one brief conversation? I understood this place all too well now; a few words were all it took to crack the façade and expose the vacuous interior.

A voice, soft and deep, spoke close behind me:

"Good evening."

I gasped and turned to behold an exceedingly tall figure looming over me, wearing a mask of black feathers with great, fearsome horns and a long, pointed beak of silver. I need not see his beautiful, angular face to know my Elyan. He cut a truly dashing figure in the colors of House Acheron, eschewing the jewels that ornamented the other, lesser men in favor of the feathers and thorns of his sigil. He lifted the mask to reveal a smear of silver on the sharp angles of his cheekbones; it glimmered in the glow of so many Lumens, and my breath caught at the sight.

Mere weeks before, we'd been prisoners within ancient walls, crumbling and forgotten, and now we wore silks and jewels, guests of royalty, attending a ball given in our honor. How very strange the world was.

Taking both of my shaking hands in his warm, steady ones, he bowed and pressed his mouth softly upon my knuckles.

"Look at you," he murmured. "So beautiful."

"Where are the others?" I asked, desperate to distract myself from his devouring eyes, for in my thoughts he was on his knees again and I felt as though my skin could no longer contain me.

Elyan pointed, and across the room, I saw Arlo standing with a glass of Calique in his hand and a distant expression upon his face. Princess Evolet had chosen for his costume a morning coat of the deepest jeweled green with a gallant, embroidered collar, his mask a riot of gold thorns that grew into a halo redolent with gems. It exuded the riches of the natural world, a fitting tribute to his aptitude; no doubt he hated it.

A group of men and women, lavish and most animated in their laughter, clustered around him, and yet their attempts to coax him to share their merriment were met with vague interest and brief, polite smiles; strange, that. Gatherings of any kind in which there was drink and laughter were, indeed, as natural to him as breathing, yet he appeared distracted.

He caught sight of us then, and I waved cheerfully. After swallowing the contents of his glass and setting it on a passing tray, he abandoned his admirers and pushed his way through the crowd toward us.

"Where is Phyra?" he asked, looking to the entrance of the ballroom expectantly. "Did she not come with you?"

"Phyra declined to attend this evening," I answered, and watched him deflate somewhat. "You've no cause to worry. She is merely tired, and you know she abhors gatherings such as this."

"And his knightliness?"

This I could not answer, for to do so would reveal the secret I'd been keeping for several days now: our plan to take advantage of the glorious chaos of the ball to spirit Cylene from the palace.

It had been no easy thing to convince Mavis and Iya to help us. Asking them to bring cups of wine to all the guards along a particular path out of the palace was a peculiar and suspicious favor to request, and when I warned them that the wine would contain a particularly potent sleeping draught, I feared they would run straight to the king himself to betray me.

It was Iya, made newly bold by the discovery of her remarkable ancestry, who rose to my defense, her blue eyes blazing with the thrill of clandestine adventures beyond the drudgery of the kitchens.

"Briony is not of the court," she reminded Mavis. "She's not like the rest of them. She's a friend, and I trust that her cause, whatever it may be, is a righteous one."

Thaniel was with Cylene even now, making their way through corridors Kevren assured us were rarely used.

"I believe he suffered a tear in his costume and had to visit the Thesa," I told Arlo. A servant appeared with a tray of Calique, and I seized glasses for us all, grateful for the distraction.

As we sipped, my eyes fell upon the royal dais.

The Dowager Queen had dressed Raolin's effigy splendidly for the occasion, in shades of silver and slate to match her own gown and ever-present necklace. He sat upon his customary cushion in Bean Pole's arms while his widow surveyed the room and leaned her head toward him occasionally to whisper some mad thing or another into his ear.

Beside her, King Anwar sprawled in his throne, deep in conversation with Princess Evolet. The king had chosen the sun as the inspiration for his costume that evening, and I wondered that he had done so when I myself bore so many stars upon my person, and then Princess Evolet's eyes met mine, and I wondered no further. The sly smile she gave me told me very well that she had been the architect of our counterpoint.

She herself had dressed as the moon, and her gown was the most magnificent of all. Sheer black gauze only just covered the pale expanse of her chest and arms and fell in layer upon layer in a magnificent train, the whole of it scattered with silver spangles and embroidery that showed the lunar phases as they passed across the night sky. A circle of crystals adorned her head, rising like the spires of the Sundering, and a glittering crescent moon cradled her brow.

King Anwar must've felt my appraising eyes upon them both, for he smiled broadly when he beheld me. I was quite loath to admit the sun suited him, his sunburst crown and garments gleaming. My cheeks aflame, I stared down at the Calique in my glass as he pushed himself off his throne and bounded down the steps of the dais to meet us, the princess following close behind.

"Welcome, my friends!" he said, then lifted his palm suddenly to rest above his heart. "Why, Mistress Briony, you are beauty personified."

My cheeks flamed as I felt the eyes of my companions upon me, particularly Elyan's. "I thank you, your highness."

"And look at the prince, come into his glory!" Princess Evolet slid her arm through her brother's, beaming at Elyan. "When you told me of the raven and thorn of your family's sigil, I knew it would fit you perfectly. You know, I had *such* a cunning scheme for your Necromancer, as well. A pity she's decided to waste it all, though I daresay her presence may have frightened quite a few people out of their wits!"

"And is this your design as well?" I asked, brushing the fabric of my gown with the back of my fingertips.

Her laughter chimed like the peal of bells. "Between you and me and my brother, we make a merry celestial trio, do we not?"

Even as King Anwar and Princess Evolet regarded me with satisfaction, the eyes of my companions were far less kind. I longed to shout at them, to laugh with the absurdity of it all. Did they not know me at all? Surely, they did not believe I had conspired with the king and his sister to fashion myself as one of them?

King Anwar cleared his throat and straightened to face me. "And how do you find the festivities? They are, after all, for you."

"You needn't have gone through so much trouble on our behalf," I answered, my face well and truly flushed. "But it truly is splendid."

"It is about to become more so," he promised. "Now that you are here, the dancing can commence. Music!"

From one of the balconies high above us, glorious strains burst forth at his command. Musicians, dozens and dozens of them, took up their harps and drums and flutes, and the tune was so lively and wonderful that I could not help the smile that spread across my face.

King Anwar held his hand out to me. "Shall we?"

My brief moment of merriment was dashed at once. "I don't know this dance," I told him. The very thought of my exuberant and, quite frankly, uncivilized dancing being observed by the Court Eternal made me positively sick with panic.

"Fear not. I am an excellent partner."

"You do not understand," I answered, the pitch of my voice rising as a servant appeared at my elbow quite unbidden and took the glass of Calique from my fingers. "Even when I do know the dance, I am hopeless."

He took my hand despite my protestations, and I cast one last, helpless glance at Elyan, only to see that Princess Evolet had claimed him as her partner. When Arlo accepted the proffered hand of the woman I'd seen earlier dressed as a sky filled with clouds, I forsook all hope of rescue.

"Your highness, I am bound to do you bodily harm," I warned as the king slid his hand about my waist, my own settling nervously upon his shoulder.

"Then I shall have to have you beheaded."

The dance was, to my immense relief, not nearly as complicated as those I'd been forced to learn in Iluviel with Mistress Precia and her horrid stick, but still I stumbled. I trod soundly on King Anwar's foot once, but he merely feigned outrage, then chuckled with a smile so infectious that I could not help but return it, and gradually, I began to enjoy myself.

The dance ended with a flourish of skirts and excited ovations, and before I could catch my breath, the king took my hands in his and we began again, much to the irritation of a cluster of women nearby who had obviously hoped to dance the next with him. Their eyes narrowed to slits behind their masks, and I felt the full weight of their disapproval well enough.

Over King Anwar's shoulder, I glimpsed Elyan, who had managed to extract himself from Princess Evolet and was leaning against a column, gazing about at the company, his eyes missing nothing, and betraying nothing.

How I longed to dance with him, but immediately after the second dance ended, a gentleman I recognized as Braesor asked the king if he might claim me for the next, and he, too, was a splendid partner, good-humored and forgiving of my gracelessness. Indeed, he was nearly as enthusiastic as I was, and I found I quite enjoyed his company for there was a genuineness to him I'd yet to encounter in any other member of the Court Eternal.

"Do you know, I think that was the most I've enjoyed dancing in... oh, forever!" he told me as we clapped heartily together for the musicians.

Another gentleman claimed me for the next dance, and another for the next. As the evening wore on, I could no longer contain my vexation at not having yet enjoyed a single dance with the only man present in whose arms I cared to be. He was a splendid dancer for all he feigned disinterest in the pastime, but even as I wriggled free from one overenthusiastic partner after another, Elyan eluded me.

"Briony!"

Evolet's sparkling laugh was at my back, and a moment later, she had my arm in a vice.

"Have you seen Elyan?" I asked.

She fluttered her lashes, eyes wide and guileless. "Why, I thought he'd left!"

"Left?" I stammered. "But why would he... We've not yet—"

"Who can ever understand why men do anything at all? I certainly do not. But I could have sworn I saw him leave with Alorah some time ago. Cheer up! I've suddenly had the most brilliant idea. We'll dance a Gambral!"

I'd no idea what a Gambral was, nor how one danced it, but this suggestion was met with so much enthusiasm by the members of the Court that I was immediately suspicious, particularly of the way they looked at me: ravening and feverish, conspirators to something I'd not yet figured out.

The princess skipped to her brother's side and she clasped his hands, her face alight as she told him of her idea; he turned to me, his face splitting into a broad grin.

"Friends!" he shouted, and as he strode across the marble floor to where I stood, the sea of his court parted for him as though he were a Mage himself with the elements at his fingertips. "My sister has had the most marvelous idea!" At this, he turned and looked up at the musicians in the balcony. "We will dance a Gambral!"

A great cheer went up. Then, with his handsome grin and cheeks flushed from drink and dance, Anwar held out his hand to me.

I hesitated.

"Oh, go on!" Evolet laughed, as she pushed me none too gently into her brother's waiting arms. Anwar's hand slid deftly to my waist, strong and sure.

"I think after all I am too tired to dance," I told the king. "Please excuse me."

He laughed softly, gripping my hand. "Stay, for I will dance with no one but you, and I should hate to miss this one."

My gaze traveled about the perimeter of the room, searching once more in vain for Elyan; indeed, for any of my friends that I might affect some excuse that would not insult our gracious host. Only Braesor's kind eyes met mine, and he appeared uneasy, on the verge of saying something, but then the musicians struck the first chord, and we began.

Round and round we slowly turned, Anwar and I, our hands locked high above our heads, and unlike Elyan, he governed his passions not at all; I could scarcely breathe for the desire in his eyes, nor could I seem to tear my gaze away. The stranger with hands of flames knocked upon my door, distantly.

And then the beat of the drums quickened, and I was twirled into the arms of the man to my right, while Anwar took the woman to my left for his own, and we began anew, only a bit faster this time, a bit wilder. My new partner's hands clasped mine, and I was afraid to look at him, afraid of what lay beneath his mask, within his eyes, and so I kept my red face adverted until I was handed off to the next man, and the next.

As the musicians' tempo increased, so too did the boldness of the men around me, and the women responded in kind, writhing under their hands, whosoever's hands they may be, every bit as willing and pliable for one as the next, and the next, and the next. I wondered then how familiar they all were with one another; how often these notes had been played and how many times these patterns had been traced upon the floor.

Laughter swelled in my ears, laughter and gasps and murmurs, and it was obscene, all of it, the grasping and undulating and feverish smiles. Lips began to dance across skin, quickly, clandestinely, and I thought I saw from the corner of my eye a bodice tugged low, a breast revealed, a rosy nipple, and a pair of lips closed around it. I averted my eyes, shame flooding my face though I wondered why, for it was not I who had pulled my gown down, who had welcomed such an intimate act. And yet the sight of it, of the expression of ecstasy upon the woman's face, had emboldened my own stranger with his hands full of flame.

The air grew heavy with the scent of warm, awakening flesh, and above us all, large flowers, the color of blood welling to the surface of pale skin, began to blossom, their perfume heady and intoxicating. My body was a stranger to me, heavy and febrile, and I felt everything, however subtle: the brush of fabric against my skin, the warmth of hands upon me, palm to palm, gripping my waist, sliding up my back to graze my neck, and so shocking was the intimacy that I wrested myself away, stumbling as I abandoned my partner and the dance.

Hands reached out, grasping hands; hands I did not recognize nor welcome.

I shoved at them, and was met with laughter. But the flame I called to my hand quelled their good humor at once, and then they let me pass unmolested.

I'd nearly made it to the outer edge of the circle, to freedom, when a pair of arms grasped me tightly from behind, and I found myself held securely against the hard body of a man, his scent familiar to me. One hand climbed my chest and snaked around my neck until I felt the tangle of fingers in my hair. The other pressed into my hipbone, holding me fast against him.

It was wrong; everything about it was so very wrong. I had not given him my consent; he had not asked. A familiar voice chuckled near my ear, and King Anwar murmured. "Peace, Briony, it's only me."

But it was not peace I felt, nor did I appreciate the laughter in his voice, the surety that I welcomed his advances, that whatever intimacy lay between us allowed him such liberties.

"Please release me, your highness," I said calmly, and it cost everything within me not to rake my fingernails down his handsome face.

His grip upon me tightened, and as ever, there was laughter in his voice. "Come now, Briony. We are friends, are we not?"

"We are."

"Then stay with me. Dance with me." His mouth was close to my ear; too close. His breath ruffled my hair.

"We are not dancing, your highness."

"Is this not another sort of dance?"

Anger, hot and ripe, bloomed under my skin and my magic rushed to meet it; it longed to be used, and I felt the tendrils of my power wrap about my throat, becoming a collar of iron, and I held my head high. Words began to take shape within me, and yet they were not only words, they were spells. How... how could this be? I'd never been taught magic such as this.

The make of them was strange; and I grew afraid, for the path they beckoned me down was one of devastation. Walls crumbled beneath such words, forests burned, and cities fell. It was beyond anything I'd ever imagined my magic capable of; indeed, any magic at all.

And in that moment, I wanted it.

Wrenching my arm from Anwar's grasp, I was furious to see that he dared *smile* at me, at my fury and indignation. The spells grew louder and clamored about inside my skull, inside my throat, filling my mouth, demanding release. If he only knew, if he could only hear them, *taste* them as I did, he would not smile so.

The rushing grew louder, and I opened my mouth.

A hand, large and solid, grasped my own, and I knew him at once, for when we touched, the spells quieted, and the dreadful clamor in my head began to recede. I was pulled mercifully from the thick, hot press of bodies that I might breathe, and King Anwar watched me go, a smile still playing about his lips.

Elyan led me far away from the dance, to the outermost part of the room, and when he released me at last, I pressed my feverish face and hands against a stone pillar. Oh Gods, what had very nearly transpired? I'd only ever used my gifts as an Orare to speak to the magic that dwelled outside myself; I'd not known such spells might be contained within my own voice. Had I power enough, I could've used them not merely to shatter glass as Elyan had done, but marble and stone as well, I was certain of it; certain in the very depths of myself.

I felt Elyan's hands close over mine upon the pillar, and heard his voice, rich and low and steady. "Breathe, my love. Breathe."

The dance had gone on without me, the drums beating ever faster. King Anwar must've found another partner, for he had not followed me; a small mercy, that.

"There were spells," I whispered, my cheek still pressed against the cold stone. "Spells in my head and on my tongue."

"I know," he said. "I felt them."

"Oh Gods, what were they?"

"Not here," he answered.

"Elyan—"

"Walk with me."

19

That we made it from the ballroom and into the hall beyond was a wonder, for my limbs were infuriatingly unsteady and my knees threatened to collapse with every step. The ebbing of such potent magic from my person brought exhaustion unlike any I'd known since performing my first spell.

"You must think me a perfect fool, panicking the way I did," I said miserably, once we were well enough away. "No doubt I've insulted the king most thoroughly."

"I doubt it," Elyan answered. "The king seemed in high spirits when we left. It's unlikely he will give it a second thought, so natural is profligacy in his kingdom."

I shuddered, remembering the feeling of so many uninvited hands upon my person. "If that is what I missed living away from court all those years, then I am not the least bit sorry for it."

"My father's court possessed less than half a brain between the lot of them, but they did at least have some sense of propriety."

"Have a care. My father was a member of his court."

"Your father was an exception."

"Did you know him well?" I asked. "My father?"

We'd not spoken of him since the day I arrived at Asperfell and

Elyan recognized my surname. He'd expressed surprise that my father had lived as long as he did, rare amongst good men ruled by worse. I'd thought him heartless then; he had been right, if insufferably blunt.

"Not as well as I should have," he admitted. "I was not yet a man and much occupied with trying to become one. But he was always kind to me. Whenever he came to court, he brought me books."

A thought struck me then, and I looked up at the unforgiving slant of his jaw. "Do you remember me at all? From before? We did not come to live at court until your brother became king, but we did attend several feasts..."

"It was Serus, if I recall," he answered, tilting his head. "Almost a year before it happened. It is only a vague recollection, mind you, but you were not inclined to remain within your own clothing."

"What?" I spluttered.

His laugh was rich and warm. "You traded your gown to one of the kitchen boys so that you could sneak around the servants' hall."

"I did no such thing!"

"You absolutely did."

"How can you possibly remember that?"

"One does not easily forget the sight of the king's closest advisor carrying his daughter over his shoulder dressed in breeches."

I turned my face into his arm and groaned. "No doubt you found me ridiculous."

"Actually, I quite admired your determination."

We walked on, and as the sound of drums gradually faded into silence, my anger began to ebb, and with it, the spells that had clamored so desperately for a voice; for *my* voice. I wondered if I would ever feel it again.

I hoped I would not.

If the price of such power was anger born of helplessness, I could do well enough without it.

"What happened to me," I asked, "During the dance? I've never felt such magic before, such spells upon my tongue."

His brows drew together in a frown. "In Master Aeneas's books, there were mentions of very old spells in the Veta Ora—that is, the ancient language of magic."

"But our magic requires no words," I said, most perplexed.

"Not now," he agreed. "But long ago, when magic was but newly gifted us, conjuring was a spoken art. The words are lost to us now, but perhaps they are still remembered by magic itself. If so, the ancient spells might still be heard by those who can listen. Perhaps you are one such Mage."

Orare, Phyra had once told me. *From the old tongue meaning* orator: *to speak.*

"And tonight?" I whispered.

He shrugged lightly. "It is possible that your magic, such as it is, still retains some memory of our first spells such as they were: spoken."

"I was frightened of it," I admitted softly. "Frightened of myself."

His hand, warm and solid, moved to cover mine where it rested at the crook of his arm. "Believe me when I say I mean no disrespect, but such spells have not been performed for centuries. They require power which only the strongest among us possess. Hear them you may, but fear them you should not."

I wanted very much to believe him, and yet I also felt a keen stab of disappointment, for although I'd feared it, there had been power within such words, power that, for a moment, I had craved.

We walked in companionable silence, his strides slow and obliging of me, and I wondered whether or not, if I said such things out loud, he would regard me less for the wanting of such power. We reached a part of the palace that was less traveled than the rest and, as such, was somewhat neglected. Here, the tapestries were worn yet still achingly lovely, depicting lovers stolen away, taking comfort in one another amongst the forest. Farther down the corridor, nearly hidden in a swath of darkness the Lumens could not reach, I saw an archway hung with thick, velvet curtains.

"What do you suppose is in there?"

Elyan raised one eyebrow at me. "I haven't the faintest. Would you like to find out?"

He lifted the drapes so that I might pass beneath them, and for a moment, I could see nothing at all. Then, as my eyes adjusted, I realized we stood inside a small room, circular, and made entirely of windows, tall and stately despite the dust that coated their panes. Beneath each one was a bench of white stone, and between them hung gold sconces bereft of Lumens, so that we were bathed only the pale glow of moonlight. As such, the room felt forlorn and forgotten despite its beauty.

I adored it.

"Shall we light them?" I whispered.

Elyan merely waved his hand and tiny, brilliant fires bloomed where he bid them, and soon the room of windows was softly lit and utterly beguiling—a place of quiet beauty, entirely unlike everything that surrounded it; a place for lovers.

And now, Elyan stood before me in his usual repose, as he had so many times on our journey, hands clasped behind his back, staring up at the stars, and I stared at him unabashed, drinking in greedily the towering height of him, the shape of his back, his shoulders, his jaw, his angular face. By the Gods, he was beautiful, and I wanted him.

I wanted him.

Elyan had kissed me many times before, but I had never kissed him; strange, that. Of course, once initiated and accepted, a kiss became a moment shared, and we had shared many. Why should I fear to make such an offer myself? Giddy at the thought, and brave, I made up my mind to do so, for in that moment, the stranger with his hands full of flames stood at my door, and my own rested upon it on the other side.

"What is it you are thinking?" he asked softly.

"That I want to kiss you."

The hint of a smile appeared upon his face. "Where?"

"Here." My fingers stole to the place just below my ears where my jaw met my neck, trailed down past my collarbone until they reached the fabric of my bodice, lingered there; I could feel my heart hammering beneath my fingertips.

"Yes," he said, his voice rough and unsteady. "Yes."

Even on the tips of my toes I could not reach him, but he understood at once what I sought and lowered his head so my hands might slip round his neck, sinking into the hair at his nape; I tugged lightly, his soft gasp my reward.

Emboldened, I pressed my lips, trembling and feverish, to his skin and felt him shudder, heard the catch of his unsteady breath, and I marveled at the power I held in that moment, for it *was* power; strange that I'd ever thought myself without it. This was power of a different sort, and I found I preferred this sort to that which had nearly overcome me in the ballroom of Syr'Aliem.

"Stay still," I murmured, for I was not yet ready to relinquish it. He obeyed.

My lips traveled the path my fingertips had taken, delighting in the way his fists clenched at his sides in the effort to obey my command, in the unsteady rise and fall of his chest, and I took my time discovering the warmth of his skin, the scent and taste of him. The collar of his tunic was high, too high; my shaking hands fumbled with the jet buttons until I'd bared the skin of his throat, his collarbone, to the golden light of Magefire, and I kissed him there, too, my palm splayed against his chest. Beneath my fingers, his heart beat wildly. I raised my face and our eyes met.

"Must I remain still?" he rasped, and there was such desperate longing in his eyes.

Mutely, for all words seemed to have escaped me, I shook my head.

With a groan, his arms went around me, lifting me against him, and our lips met with a desperation that left me feverish and trembling. I'd never known such want, never thought it possible to crave the touch of another so desperately.

Elyan's hands gripped the back of my thighs and lifted me as though I weighed nothing at all, and I experienced then the most marvelous and unexpected sensation of looking down upon him, for it had always been I who had stood upon my toes before him or tugged lightly at his collar until he bent. I framed his face with my hands, drinking in the part of his lips, the sharp planes and angles of his face, the desire in his eyes, pupils so wide little color remained.

He walked backwards until his legs hit the edge of the stone bench behind him, and he sank down, and I sank with him, gasping at his hands, large and warm and solid upon my hips.

Dazedly, I thought perhaps I should have been mortified at allowing a man such intimacies, but it felt so wonderfully good that I could scarcely think at all, save that I wished it would never end.

With joyful abandon I'd thrown open the door, and with a smile upon my face, I had stepped into the flames. An ache so very sweet had gathered at the very core of me, and I knew not how it might be soothed other than that I wanted his beautiful hands upon me, upon every inch of me.

"Touch me," I heard myself say.

He looked at me, eyes dark and lips parted, and heat dappled the bare expanse of my chest such that it was suddenly very difficult to breathe. Perhaps he found me wanton, and why shouldn't he? No young lady of good breeding would possibly be found writhing with feverish need in the arms of a man alone in a secluded bower, to say nothing of what I had asked of him.

My fear vanished entirely with the soft, open-mouthed kiss he pressed just below my ear, and as his teeth gently grazed my jaw, his name tumbled from my lips. A shudder passed through him, and then he was kissing me as though I were the answer to every question he had asked, every riddle he had ever pondered, every lesson he had ever learned; as though I were everything.

My fingers sunk into his hair and I gasped into his mouth, shivering as his tongue slid against mine and his beautiful hands mapped the shape of me slowly, reverently; when his thumbs brushed over the hardened peaks of my nipples beneath the sheer fabric of my gown, I keened.

"Please," I whispered, not knowing what it was I asked for, only that I wanted it, desperately.

"How I want you," Elyan rasped. "But, by the Gods, you'll have my name first. I swear it."

His name.

'Twas both a question asked, and a promise made.

Oh, but I wanted it, wanted *him*, and for a fleeting moment, I felt naught but joy at the thought of us cleaved to one another, of the life we might share, of what might have been if he were but Elyan and free.

But he was neither.

He was a prince; a king; and he was not free to wed me. Not if he wished to reclaim his throne.

He regarded me with confusion as I slid off his lap, and I felt acutely the loss of his warmth, for the lovely, secret room had grown cold as desire ebbed from my body, replaced by the cold, ugly heaviness of truth.

"What is it?" he asked me, concern darkening his eyes. "Have I frightened you?"

"No, I am not afraid."

He held out his hand. "Come back, then, and tell me what troubles you."

I should have known what to say, at the very least for the magic in my blood and more because I'd always thought myself clever, but I found that my words utterly failed me. Why did I fear so to say what I must?

I love you. I want you. I despair at the thought of a lifetime in which you must bind yourself to another to save our kingdom, our people.

Because I knew what I must also say.

And so, we can no longer be as we are.

But I could not. Not yet, for I was not strong.

I said instead: "You must marry."

Had my heart not lodged itself in my throat, I might have laughed at the expression on his face. It was a merry war waged between desire and confusion, and Elyan, who never appeared unsettled nor lacked the proper words, even when they were far too true to be acceptable in polite society, seemed quite unable to form a coherent thought. "Yes," he answered slowly. "I believe I just made my intentions quite clear on that particular point."

My hands shook; I folded them into my skirts and clutched the fabric tightly. "When we return to Tiralaen, you must marry, and you must do so strategically for you cannot hope to reclaim your throne without support."

This, he had not expected.

"Briony—"

"You have no army," I continued. "No funds, and your good name has been sullied over and over again by Keric and Master Viscario and their lies. To unseat them will be a feat impossible without proper support and allies."

"Yes, I have given it a great deal of thought," he answered drily. "After all, I've had nearly thirteen years to do so."

"If that is true, then you know as well as I do that your best chance for success is to marry someone in possession of such necessities." I drew a deep breath. "And you should also know it is not me."

All mirth had gone from his face.

"Elyan, I have nothing," I pressed on. "My father is dead, my mother and sister traitors, and even if Keric has, for some reason, allowed House Tenebrae to retain their lands and holdings, the sum of them together could not buy you the armies you need to defeat him. I am a poor choice for any man, let alone a king."

"Well, that is most unfortunate as I have already chosen you, and I will have no other."

I should have rejoiced to hear it. I should have kissed him and tumbled back again with him upon the bench.

"The choice may not be yours to make."

"Of course it will."

"And the men who pledge themselves to you? Who give you their coin and their Mages and their swords? What if they object?"

"Then let them object."

"And withdraw their support as well."

"By the Gods, what has brought this on? Never mind, I believe I can guess well enough," he said in disgust, rising from the bench. "So, this is what Anwar has been filling your head with while he hides you away in secret gardens."

I flushed at the insinuation. "King Anwar and I did speak on the matter several days ago, if you must know, and I am only ashamed it did not occur to me sooner. Or perhaps it did and I simply refused to think on it, for all I wished it not to be true."

"What an excellent service he has done you, then."

"You doubt his sincerity."

"Entirely."

"Why?"

He laughed then, though there was no humor at all in his eyes. "Come now, Briony, you are far too clever not to be aware of his intentions, or is it that you are simply too inexperienced to understand them?"

His words cut me, deeply.

"You are mistaken," I answered, my throat uncomfortably tight. "He wished only to help me as any friend might."

"It is no friend who would seek to sow discord where there should be none. He asked you to stay here, didn't he?"

I wanted him to be wrong; I wanted to lie to him. But I could not.

"He suggested that, should I find the prospect of returning too painful, I would be welcome to remain within the Forest Kingdom. That is all. I'm sure he only offered out of polite obligation and would never expect me to agree."

"On the contrary, I believe he quite hopes you will."

"Utterly ridiculous," I scoffed.

"Yes, it is," he agreed, and when I opened my mouth to shout at him in outrage, he went on: "Do not mistake me! There's no doubt that he desires you, and I do not blame him for it. But this is not some tawdry play with a trio of fawning lovers dancing about each other in circles! It is ridiculous to think that I might be jealous of that imbecile, and even more so to think you might fall for his charms. You are without equal, my Briony. You are wise in all the ways I am not. It's you that I need by my side—not just to claim my throne, but in all things and every way. Of what worth is an army if I do not have you?"

One day not so very long ago, I'd thought that I might spend the blush of my youth collecting proposals and turning each and every one of them down in ever more elaborate ways, so that my Aunt Eudora might know that she could not make me marry. I had despised the very idea of marriage then.

But in this moment, with the word *yes* begging to be released from my lips, I realized that I'd never truly understood what a marriage could be. A partnership of hearts and minds and purpose; a partnership of equals in awe of each other. That is what we were, Elyan and I, and what our marriage might be.

It cost me everything to say it: "You cannot marry me, Elyan."

"Of course I can."

"You should not, then."

He pinched the bridge of his nose and sighed. "By the Gods, you are exhausting. We'll find other ways to secure support for my campaign."

"It is not only your campaign, and you well know it."

"Well, then, by all means: enlighten me. What other ridiculous reason have you for your refusal, for I know you desire me. I hope that you love me."

That he should doubt it was worst of all. "Of course I love you," I whispered desperately, and my voice broke in the telling.

"Then marry me."

"It is not that simple, Elyan! Can you imagine me upon a throne? I cannot even hold my tongue long enough to eat a meal without saying something scandalous, and eventually you would grow tired of a wife more suited to living amongst wild things in a forest than at court."

"It might be difficult, for a time," he admitted. "But you would learn, as those who have come before you have done."

"And cease to be myself."

"No," he said, but something flickered across his face ever so briefly before he schooled himself against it. It mattered not; I'd already seen.

"It would be a misery," I said. "And we both know it."

"Then what will you do? Stand by my side while I marry another? Or leave me and live as a recluse at Orwynd until the war is decided one way or another?"

"You know I could never stand idly by." My tears at last had fallen, and they slipped down my cheeks with abandon. "But I cannot watch you marry another. I fear I will not survive it."

"Then marry me."

His words hung between us, and what I would've liked to say was: *I will.*

What I said instead was: "If I am to see those I love in Tiralaen safe from Keric, I must do everything I can to see you restored to your throne."

"Say it. Say you'll marry me."

What I wanted to say was: *I'll marry you.*

And what I said instead was: "I'll not risk everything for love of you, and I'll not let you do the same for me."

Any power my voice might've held that night had long since bled out of me, leaving my words hollow and spent.

He loomed over me, so close that I could feel the warmth of him through his clothes, and through mine, so close that I could smell his skin. I tasted him still upon my lips, my tongue, and for the briefest moment, weak that I was, I wished we could return to that moment, when I'd asked him to put his hands upon me, for I realized now how very wrong I had been.

Desire was, indeed, consummation and ascendance, but it was simple and uncomplicated. It was want and need; it was human.

No, it was love that had fooled me, for it was no friend. Love was the stranger outside my door with hands of flame, and now I stood in the smoking wreckage.

"Say it," he whispered, and when finally I raised my head, I saw in his face the forlorn, frightened boy he'd been on the scaffold of the Tower of Maer so many years ago; my heart cleaved in two then, and I feared it would never fit properly back together.

"Oh Gods," I said, and tasted bitterness on my lips. "I've spoiled everything."

I turned then, and fled.

"Briony!"

He chased after me; his long legs were faster than mine, and though he had to duck to pass through the stone archway, he drew close, reached out. I whirled around to face him.

"No!"

I threw my hands up, the purpose and desire of my will upon my magic clear and strong. A shield erupted spectacularly between us, and Elyan skidded to a stop in time to avoid the shimmering veil.

We stared at one another across what seemed like miles until I could bear it no longer. I turned my back on him and fled once more.

He did not follow.

20

My vision was utterly blinded by furious tears by the time I reached our suite of rooms, and when I approached the guards, I did not so much ask as make a threatening gesture that meant absolutely nothing so far as magic was concerned to demand they open the doors. They fell upon themselves in haste so as not to find themselves on the receiving end of whatever spell they imagined I sought to conjure.

On opposite couches before the hearth sat Arlo and Phyra, the latter of which was so wrapped in blankets that I could only see her face, but she looked far livelier now than when I'd left her. The game with pieces of glass, one side clear, the other side black, sat on the low table between them, and her dark eyes watched as Arlo considered his next move. When he made it, she reached out a long, delicate arm from her blanket and moved her own piece over his thrice, and thrice again.

"Damn," he grumbled as she dropped his pieces among a pile twice as high as those he'd captured from her. "Why can I not beat you at this wretched game?"

Phyra fixed him with a thoughtful expression. "Because this is a game of skill, and not of charm."

"You know, you're so right. Perhaps we should play a different game?"

"I like this game well enough."

"Because you're winning."

"Yes, so let us play again, and perhaps I shall let you win this time."

"No, you won't."

"No, I won't."

"You know, you're rather good at gaming. I should teach you how to play Flisket. No, *strip* Flisket," he mused. "I know what you're thinking, that *I'm* the one who will be losing all my clothing, and I am absolutely fine with that."

Phyra fixed him with a withering stare. "I most emphatically decline your offer of tutelage."

He laughed heartily and, as he moved to reset the board, saw me lingering at the threshold. "Is the ball over, then?"

"No," I answered, forcing a smile upon my face. "In fact, the evening was turning quite... interesting as I left, so I'm surprised to find you here."

"Ah," he said, and his glance flickered across to where Phyra had begun to organize the glass pieces on the board. "Well, once you've seen one royal ball, you've seen them all. And I thought perhaps Phyra might like some company."

Phyra looked up at me, and Arlo busied himself suddenly with his empty glass of Calique, though he did not refill it but pushed it aimlessly away. "Would you like to play?"

"No, thank you. I don't suppose either of you has seen Thaniel this evening?"

"Not yet," Arlo shrugged. "Must still be at the ball."

Fear gripped me, for I'd not seen him at all that evening, and if

he had not yet returned to our rooms... "I need to go to the stillroom!" I breathed, only realizing I'd spoken aloud when they both looked up at me with concern in their eyes.

"Are you unwell, Briony?" Phyra asked.

"Restless is all, and in need of sleep. I'll ask Kevren for herbs to make a posset."

Arlo offered to escort me, though his gallantry was halfhearted; 'twas clear he did not wish to leave our suite of rooms nor his game with Phyra. They were setting the board up once more when I slipped quietly out, laughing and speaking with quiet ease; I envied them their peace.

The revelry had by now overborn the ballroom, spilling into the corridors and alcoves, and though many called out to me to join them, to perform a bit of magic for them, I pressed on, seeing nothing but the task ahead of me, for it kept me from wondering where Elyan was at that moment. Perhaps he was still where I'd left him, mourning me or angry at me or very likely both; perhaps he'd gone back to our suite of rooms and locked himself away.

When at last I reached the stillroom, the door was slightly ajar and all was dark within. Magefire bloomed in my hand, illuminating the pristine tables and white linens, unblemished by ill and injured, and beyond them, the dusty bottles and ancient texts sat forlorn on their shelves.

No one was there.

'Twas possible that Thaniel had made his way to the ball after seeing Cylene safely delivered to Kevren's people and that all was well. 'Twas also possible that he was now languishing in whatever gilded cage passed for a dungeon in this place. I did not relish the idea of returning to the ball to find out, but until I knew him safe, I must exhaust all possibilities however unpleasant.

I'd told Phyra and Arlo I'd come for herbs to make a posset, and I did not wish to invite their suspicions by returning emptyhanded, so I fingered quietly through several stoppered bottles until I found what I sought: Vanda. Kevren likely knew it by another name entirely, but it was the very same herb that the Asperfell Healer had used to make a sleeping draught, though she'd mixed it with valerian and lavender and chamomile flowers, which Kevren, of course, did not possess. It would have to do. I also found a bottle of something that smelled very much like Solberry extract, which kept dreams at bay, and I took that as well in case the Dae Spira decided to visit me once more.

My gown, of course, had no pockets and I'd brought nothing with which to carry my burden, and so, holding my flames aloft, I searched about in the shadowy corners for something that might suffice, but found little. Crouching despite the protestations of my over-tight bodice, my hand had hardly rested on the handle of a cupboard when I heard a sound from over my shoulder, in the storage room with the curtain of moss. From within, I heard the sound of a foot scraping across the floor, and then a soft voice murmuring.

I lifted the Magefire in my hand and drew back the curtain but an inch.

At first, I could see very little, as I did not dare risk setting fire to the verdant drapery, but my eyes grew used to the shadows and I could see two figures standing entwined in fierce embrace, one pale with golden hair and the other as dark as ebony. It was with dawning horror that I realized it was Thaniel I was seeing; Thaniel and Kevren kissing and clinging and tasting, wrapped around one another so that in the moonlight they appeared as one.

Shock had rendered me quite unable to move, and so I watched

Thaniel's lips seek the skin of Kevren's neck below the curve of his ear, much I had with Elyan, and Kevren let out a low chuckle. He threaded his hands through Thaniel's hair, resting them at the nape of his neck, and said, "You really should go to the ball. They'll be wondering where you've been all night."

"Oh, I like it here well enough," Thaniel answered, lifting his head, his lips curved in a sweet smile. "I never was a very good dancer."

"Liar," Kevren said, and their lips met again, briefly. "I'd wager you dance beautifully."

"Come with me, then, and see."

"Me, at one of their balls?" Kevren laughed.

"Why not? It's no more ridiculous than me at one of their balls."

"Ah, but see how they've dressed you up?" Kevren ran his hands down the length of Thaniel's finely embroidered sleeves. "Were it not for these callouses—" Here, he paused and brought Thaniel's hand to his lips, pressing a delicate kiss on the tips of each of his fingers— "I could easily mistake you for one of them."

"'Tis but a costume. I would rather be rid of it, truth be told."

"Let me help you, then."

Kevren let go of Thaniel's hands and slowly began to undo the clasps of gold at his throat.

The Alchemist's unsteady breathing filled the small space, scraping against the darkened walls; his eyes never left Kevren's. I knew I had lingered far too long, intruding on this most intimate moment, and I slowly let the curtain fall and tried to back away without sound. But Thaniel, ever a warrior, stilled suddenly, and I knew he'd heard me.

His head whipped around and he peered beyond the curtain of moss. I smothered my Magefire with a shake of my hand and made for the door as quickly as the darkness and my attire would allow, but I was not fast enough.

"Briony!"

I turned. Thaniel emerged into the darkened stillroom, Kevren just behind him, and we stared at one another. An entirely inadequate apology bubbled up to my lips, but when I saw the expression on his face, any words I might've spoken were forgotten. It was fear I saw in his eyes, and I thought perhaps in that moment that my heart stopped beating entirely, for the thing he feared was me.

"I'm so sorry, I was... That is, I wanted to make sure you and Cylene... That all was well. I should've... Gods, I'm sorry." It all came tumbling forth in a rush and I cursed myself for my ineloquence, but his face—oh, his face.

"Briony—"

"I'm so sorry," I whispered miserably, then turned and blundered from the stillroom up into the corridor.

"Let her go," I heard Kevren say.

I cared little where my feet took me, only that I put as much distance between myself and Thaniel as possible, and so I walked on and on until I was quite lost, and glad of it, for I could not rid myself of the sight of them entwined together. Thaniel, the most honorable man of my acquaintance. How could he do such a thing, for he was Phyra's and she was his; the love they shared was palpable to anyone who laid eyes upon them. They'd even shared a chamber from time to time at Asperfell, an occurrence that surprised no one at all and thus I'd assumed...

I'd assumed. I'd never asked.

Ever since we had arrived in Syr'Aliem, Thaniel had never concealed attentions toward Kevren, his obvious admiration. I had seen it that first day in the stillroom in his smile, and felt it in his frequent absences when they'd been together, discovering a side of his magic that he'd not dared to explore before now.

But if he and Phyra were not bound to one another as lovers and I had not caught him in a moment of indiscretion, why had he looked upon me in fear?

It was too much; everything that had happened that night was too much.

I moved on unsteady legs to the nearest wall and slid down the length of it until I was sitting, quite unladylike, on the floor surrounded by my skirts. The sounds of revelry, hedonistic and blithe, floated down the corridor, and I despised them suddenly for their pleasure, for I had robbed myself of mine twice over that evening. I closed my eyes, and waited; waited to feel less; and in my waiting, the world around me changed.

As with each blackout that had come before, I felt a prickling beneath my skin, heard a rush of whispers, smelled rich verdant soil and the promise of a world transformed. I opened my eyes to wild things. Beneath my hands, roots crept from the walls, curling into the corridor, framing the windows with leaves that unfurled quite unhurriedly to reveal their shape.

To say that the first blackout had not frightened me would be a demonstrable falsehood for it certainly had, at least for the first few moments. Now, it brought a strange, but blessed, relief—for my restlessness, my anger, the churning sea within me that thrashed unrelentingly upon the pitiful shore of myself, became silenced by my sudden determination. Here was a mystery and a calling to which I could apply myself, and with which to distract myself, and I seized upon it desperately. I pushed myself up from the floor, and as roots and vines lazily took my place, I set off down the corridor.

21

This was the fourth blackout I'd experienced in recent days, and the previous ones had been relatively short, none more than a quarter of an hour. This one, it seemed, would not relinquish its hold upon Syr'Aliem so easily, and for that I was grateful: reaching the Incuna would take time, and still more time would I require if I were to study the mystery of its withered roots while the world was changed.

Unfortunately, the transformation of the palace's corridors and staircases made it quite difficult to remember the way to the secret tunnel, and the ball made it even worse. I encountered several members of the Court Eternal on my way, traipsing drunkenly, some laughing, some grumbling, sloshing great quantities of Calique all over the writhing roots.

I began to despair of finding the neglected corridors that led to the ancient spiral staircase, for who could tell which hallways might have been covered in dust and adorned with faded tapestries when all the world about me was now a savage wilderness, but then I heard an impossibly small voice:

"Mistress Briony! This way!"

Tansy's tiny face peered out at me from behind a tangle of vines, and she gestured to me with a fluttering hand to join her.

"I've come to fetch you, I have!" she squeaked. "It is time!"

"Time? Time for what?"

Her voice fairly quivered with excitement. "The Ita Hypogaeum has opened!"

"Show me."

By the light of Tansy's crown and my magic, and we wove our way together through the transformed palace until we reached the spiral stairs, and down we went, until at last we tumbled through the door at the end of the ancient tunnel.

Lark waited for us. His tiny hands were crossed over his chest, his frown an exaggerated attempt to inform us at his displeasure (yet I could not help but find it endearing). "You're late."

I dropped to my knees despite my attire and folded my hands in my lap. "I am truly sorry. I'm afraid the blackout made it a bit difficult."

"Well, never mind that. We cannot know how much time we have!" He bid me rise, and together we approached the Ita Hypogaeum to the left of the Incuna chamber, and though it remained deeply buried in tangled vines, there was a gaping blackness behind them now, and not a closed door.

"Lark," I asked, as we peered into the darkness. "How long has the longest blackout lasted?"

"This *is* the longest blackout," he answered.

No time to waste, then.

I called Magefire to my hand, and under the mess of thick vines I could just make out an archway, elegantly formed, and... Was that a face? I drew closer. Twin statues, both women from what I could tell, flanked the entrance.

"Who are they?" I asked Lark.

He squinted, then shrugged. "Can't say. Too overgrown."

"We'll try to clear some of it while you're within," Fife said, hefting his small axe onto his shoulder.

"Thank you," I answered. They stared up at me, and in their overlarge eyes and wringing hands, I saw fear; fear for me, and perhaps fear for themselves. I tried to smile as reassuringly as I could. "I'll be all right. But if anyone should happen upon this place while I am within—"

"We'll fight them off, we will!" Lark declared, swinging an imaginary sword in the air.

I laughed. "I do not doubt you the fiercest warrior in all of Syr'Aliem, but you mustn't put yourself at risk. Try to warn me if you are able, then hide."

Their pointed chins nodded in unison. And so, I pushed my way through the heavy vines and into the open door.

The air inside the tunnel—for it was a tunnel—was far colder than without, and it smelled of loam and green rot, though not unpleasantly so. The ground was made of round, smooth stones set into patterns that, although woefully lost to time and decay, must once have been beautiful, and empty fountains that depicted strange, wonderful beasts lined the walls. The water that had fed them had long since dried up, and I touched my fingertips to the stains left by their gradual decline.

Between the fountains were alcoves that I supposed were meant to hold Lumens but would have to be satisfied with Magefire, as it was all I had. I carefully set handfuls of flames into each one and took stock of my surroundings. The tunnel opened into a large rotunda with a vaulted ceiling over a large stone basin on a pedestal of wood, and this, too, I filled with Magefire.

I faced two passageways, both horribly overtaken by the vestiges of dried, brittle branches clinging to the stone archways, and yet they were beautiful. A thrill rushed through me at the promise of discovery, even as I feared that I'd already tarried too long; the blackout could end at any moment.

"Right," I whispered to myself, as much to bolster my courage as to remind me that I had precious time to waste. "Let's to it, shall we?"

The archway to the right seemed somewhat less overgrown, and so I decided to start there. But when I lifted my handful of flame to better see what lay before me, I was met with a sight so frightening that I could not help the scream that burst from me; for a moment, I was back at Asperfell, staring up at the sightless eyes of a thousand skulls set in hideous tableau.

But this was not Asperfell, and these slumbering souls could not hurt me.

I drew a deep breath and called Magefire to my hand once more.

I was standing inside a crypt.

Lining both walls as far as I could see were alcoves carved into the stone, and within each rested the mortal remains of whom I knew not, but they must've been of great importance to have been afforded such treatment after death. With hands folded peacefully across their breasts, they numbered in the hundreds, covered in the dust and cobwebs of age and abandonment. That Syr'Aliem should honor their dead in such an elaborate way was hardly surprising, but that they should conceal and neglect it was certainly unexpected.

In Tiralaen, many noble families had crypts on the grounds of their country estates and, of course, there were the royal crypts below the Citadel. House Tenebrae, in fact, had its own crypt at Crenswick, but I'd never managed to get past Old Bram to see them, no matter how hard I tried, which was infuriating when one considered the fact that Old Bram was blind. And yet, he spent hours below ground every week lovingly tending to the ancestors of the family who employed him. Should the grave of any Tenebrae have fallen into such ruin as that before me, he would have promptly surrendered his position in disgrace.

Whose remains were these? And why had they been hidden and forgotten for so long?

I wiped the dust away from the letters carved below the alcove nearest me, but it was in a language unknown to me. A name, most likely.

All those I'd encountered in Syr'Aliem spoke the tongue of my homeland with such ease that I'd not thought to wonder what they'd spoken before our kind had appeared among them. Why had they abandoned their native tongue so completely in favor of one spoken by a ragged band of escaped prisoners? There was something deeply frightening in that fact, but I could not pause to ponder the mystery just now.

As if to remind me of the tenuous nature of my investigation, there was a sudden flickering of light and whispers crept into the darkest corners of my mind. It lasted little more than the space of a breath before the darkness returned, but I was reminded all too well of how little time I might possess.

I burst out of the crypt and into the rotunda once more and made for the second passageway, stumbling over my gown in my haste to discover what secrets lay beyond before I was shut out of the tunnel, or worse, shut *in*.

Oh, why had I not told anyone where I was going? It had all seemed quite daring at the time, and now, my bravado ebbing, I was quite unfortunately faced with the fact that, should I continue in my dogged attempts to unravel the secrets of the Dae Spira and the Incuna, I might be trapped indefinitely with only bones for company until I joined them myself.

There were no bones here; there did not seem to be anything at all but an empty hall. Then, a face emerged from the shadows.

It was a woman's face, a delicate, pale oval, and as I approached the wall upon which she was painted, her beauty was revealed: fine eyes of deepest amber, a blush about her cheeks, and upon her dark curls...

She wore a crown.

A crown of branches. A crown of light.

I gasped, the sound echoing in the vast hallway.

The Dowager Queen herself had told me that no woman ever ruled Syr'Aliem, and yet was this not proof one had, for what else could she possibly be but a queen?

The words carved below her image were in the same alphabet as those upon the stone slabs in the crypt: her name, I supposed, or perhaps the date of her rule. I pored over every detail of her person, as if any of them might tell me what I longed to know about this remarkable woman, long forgotten and left to decay beneath a palace of splendor. Her garments more resembled robes than a gown, simple and modest, with a kirtle of leaves and simple jewelry upon her neck and ears made of colored stones and hammered metal.

At her waist hung a ring with two sturdy bronze keys.

As I moved closer to inspect them, the light of my Magefire fell upon another portrait beside the unknown queen, this one a man. He was much older than she, with steel gray hair and stern, hawk-like features. He, too, wore the same crown, bore the same keys.

Her successor? They looked absolutely nothing alike.

I walked farther down the long hall.

Faces, endless faces, stared out from portraits that lined both sides of the gallery, and I blinked in wonder at the sight, drawn helplessly forward.

After the old man came a boy no older than I'd been when I'd left the Citadel, with skin as dark as Kevren's. His crown rested heavily upon his brow, too big even in portrait. Two more women reigned after the boy, one a round-faced woman with a long, thick braid and nut-brown skin, and the other as austere in her expression as in her coloring: pale, nearly white, and with a sheet of silver hair.

On and on I walked, and all around me, painted on both sides of the hall, were men and women from the blush of youth to the wisdom of age, as different from one another as the seasons; indeed, there was no discernable pattern from one ruler to the next, other than the crown they all shared and the keys at their waists. As I passed through the long years of their shared history, their fashions changed, though their garments remained simple, homespun yet lovely, their jewelry made of stone and crystal and hammered metals, nothing like the splendor of the Court Eternal.

If these were in fact portraits of the rulers of Syr'Aliem, surely King Anwar's forebears would be amongst them. I quickened my steps, holding my fire aloft, the faces of more and more men and women, girls and boys, blurring until I saw only the crown and the keys.

And then, suddenly, there was nothing at all; nothing but stone. I turned and held the Magefire aloft so that I might see the last portrait in the tunnel.

A woman only a few years older than myself stared back at me, fair-haired and freckled, a sun-kissed beauty with long, golden hair and bright blue eyes.

I frowned and walked farther into darkness. There were no more portraits to be seen beyond hers. But how could that be?

And then the light I carried fell upon the man before her.

Ah, there you are.

His jaw was not as square as Anwar's, nor were his brows as thick, but I recognized his amber eyes, his curling hair, the hint of a smirk upon his lips. This man was Anwar's forebear, I was certain of it.

The Dowager Queen had told me that five generations of her family had sat upon the throne of Syr'Aliem in succession, and yet a woman's portrait followed the man who very much resembled her son. A mistake, perhaps. And yet, as I stared at their portraits side by side, an uneasy feeling stole over me, as though I were reading a book from which several chapters had been torn from the middle and burned.

The Acolytes had told me that the Ita Hypogaeum had been closed for hundreds of years; perhaps, in that time, history had been forgotten. Even as I wondered at the thought, I knew it to be false. There was a reason this place had been shut away for so long, and the last two portraits held the answer.

"Mistress!"

I'd forgotten entirely that the Acolytes waited for me; that I'd asked them to alert me should any danger approach. I could not see her at the far end of the tunnel, but Tansy's high, panicked voice was unmistakable.

"The king is coming! The king and his sister!"

22

There was no time for me to get out unseen, and if I should be seen, particularly after Evolet had warned me against any further late-night wanderings, I did not imagine I would be favorably met, but what choice did I have? Like a fool, I'd not thought to look for another way out before letting my curiosity overtake me. I had no choice but to hide.

There was nothing for it; the bones of the kings and queens of old would have to shield me until I could make my escape.

The alcoves I'd set alight in the tunnel had long since gone out, my control over my magic not yet strong enough to sustain them without constant attention, but the Magefire in the white stone bowl was still ablaze. I extinguished it as quickly as my skill allowed, and as I did so, I heard footsteps in the distance, and voices.

They were coming.

Into the crypt I went, feeling along the wall for a slab, any slab. My hand found bones—a ribcage, I thought. "Oh, I am sorry about this," I whispered. Then I clamored over the bones, ripping my gown as I went, and pressed myself against the wall.

"It's never lasted this long before."

Princess Evolet's voice was tight and sharp, quite unlike the way in which she usually spoke, and I realized that I was hearing her true voice for the first time since we'd met.

"It will stop soon enough," her brother answered. "They always do."

"It's been an hour," she snapped. "Nidaan reported riots in the village. How long until they storm our gates demanding our heads?"

"Of all the nights for it to happen."

"That it should ruin your precious ball, you mean," Evolet replied witheringly. "I'd say you accomplished that already with your behavior during the Gambral. You were meant to initiate her gently, not maul her, dear brother."

"A misstep, I'll admit. Still, what spirit she has!"

"Far too much spirit. Even if you do somehow convince her to stay here, she is no fool."

"I rather like that about her, don't you?"

"Be serious, Anwar."

"I am being serious," he shot back.

"And then there is the minor obstacle of her being in love with another man."

"Wait," he said, and their footsteps stopped abruptly. "Evolet, look."

They'd seen it: the open door.

"Was this you?" he asked.

"Of course not! It must've been the blackout."

"The blackouts can open doors now? Wonderful." His voice sounded closer, near the entrance to the Dae Hypogaeum; I pressed myself against the cold stone of the crypt's wall. "No, look at this!" he hissed. "Someone's been cutting away these vines."

"Impossible," Princess Evolet said, and I heard the rustle of her skirt as she moved. "This is not as it was the last time I was here."

"Was that recently, or have you been neglecting your duties, then?"

My eyes widened in the dark. *Her duties?*

"I'm here every morning," she snarled. "This was done tonight."

"Check inside," King Anwar ordered.

"I beg your pardon? I still plan to return to the ball. I'll positively ruin myself in there."

"Do it."

A long, drawn-out sigh followed, but then I heard Evolet's heels clicking on the stone floor of the tunnel.

My mind raced, furiously seeking some way to avoid the inevitable moment when I would have to untangle myself from the skeleton and present myself, red-faced and ashamed, to beg for their forgiveness. I knew no spells of concealment; indeed, I did not even know if such enchantments were possible. What I needed was someone to help me, to call the king and his sister away or to distract them long enough to allow me to escape. Someone who knew of this place and knew how to reach it.

There was only one such person, and not only did he very likely want nothing at all to do with me, but he was, most inconveniently, located several stories above me at that moment. Still, he was my only chance at avoiding discovery, and I would much rather have to suffer his annoyance at having to rescue me than his anger should I be caught. Of course, this assumed he could even be called at all.

I'd only ever spoke to the magic within a person once before, and my success had been owed entirely to the fact that the man in question had not been in possession of all his faculties, for I was still so very new to my aptitude. Elyan was not only as unincapacitated as a person could be, but had very likely learned how to shield himself against such intrusions long ago.

Princess Evolet's footsteps neared the entrance to the tunnel, thunderclaps against the stone that threatened to grow into a tempest the nearer she drew to me. Needs must, though failure was almost certain, I prayed to Thala a world away that my magic was strong enough to save me.

I closed my eyes and, despite the racing of my heart, bid my breath to stillness. My magic stirred beneath my skin at my call, languid, roused as if from a long sleep; it had been too long since I had called upon it.

Rushing fast beyond me and into the rich air of the Incuna, it swelled, stretched, and I with it, reaching high into the halls of the palace, searching for him, for the familiar feeling of the gift within his blood, that which I could speak to.

Here and there I felt the conversant thrum of power like my own and I realized there were far more souls within this gilded place like me than I'd known, and yet none of them were him. Oh, but he was stubborn. Like as not, he'd learned long ago to smother his magic as he did his secrets when he did not wish them known; insufferable man!

Elyan.

I waited in the dark, waited for the pull at the other end of my magic, but was met only with silence. Had he heard me? I closed my eyes and tried to picture him, as though it might help me reach him in some way; a study in opposites was Elyan. The sharp line of his jaw, the softness of his lips. His face shimmered just out of reach, shrouded in shadow, and then I saw him clearly: head bowed, elbows braced upon his knees, hands clasped in contemplation. My magic faltered with the fluttering of my heart, like the sputtering of a candle in the breath of a word; I seized it back.

Elyan, I tried again. *Please.*

She was in the rotunda now, walking slowly. The heels of her shoes struck the stone and echoed throughout the darkness, each one a torment. Soon she would reach the white stone basin and fill it with the warm, golden light of a Lumen, banishing the darkness that protected me.

It was hopeless; I was simply not strong enough, not skilled enough for my voice to be heard. I slumped back against the stone in exhaustion.

And then, suddenly, an answering tug at the end of my magic; I became aware of him, and he of me, and I felt his surprise as he realized what was happening, what I'd done.

How are you doing this?

Relief poured over my feverish skin, and I exhaled. *You can hear me!* The connection, tenuous at the offset, was weakening. Already I could feel him slipping away. *I need your help,* I thought hurriedly. *Please—the Incuna—hurry!*

Briony—

But it was gone, and I was alone once more.

All I could hope for now was that the princess would be disinclined to diligently inspect the crypt, which, given her extreme dislike of anything unpleasant, was a distinct possibility.

"What do you see?" King Anwar called to his sister.

"Very little but gloom and rot," she answered. "Must I really go any farther?"

"You must."

She sighed. "I rather liked this gown."

"You'll have another tomorrow."

I waited, curled in my bower of bones, as her footsteps grew ever closer.

Then, from outside the tunnel came the distant, rumbling sound of splitting rock and falling stone, and I gasped as the ground beneath the slab shook with the force of it.

"Anwar," Princess Evolet gasped. "What's happening?"

"Get out of there, damn you," he shouted back. "Part of the main passage above the stairway is collapsing—help me!"

I did not hear her footsteps right away, and I wondered if she hesitated, thinking that whatever she might discover within the Ita Hypogaeum was worth being trapped along with me. Evidently, she decided not, for I heard at last the sharp, swift snap of her heels as she rushed out of the tunnel. They were shouting to one another, rushing up the staircase that led back up the palace, but I could not understand what they were saying.

Eventually, their voices faded away, and I was left in darkness and silence once more. I did not dare move; they might return at any moment. And so I waited, and at last I heard footsteps in the tunnel once more, only this time they did not belong to Princess Evolet.

The footsteps stopped at the slab, and then Elyan crouched down, his face illuminated by the Magefire he carried. "And just how exactly did you get yourself into this mess?"

I was so relieved to see him I did not mind the obvious exasperation in his voice as he beheld the result of another of my foolish impulses.

"You heard me," I whispered.

"A fine bit of magic, that. However did you manage it?"

I could only shake my head as I scrambled over the skeleton and off of the slab. "The king and his sister would have discovered me. Perhaps it came from desperation."

As I dusted off the sorry remains of my skirt, Elyan held his hand out and looked farther down the tunnel. "Where are we?"

"The Ita Hypogaeum," I told him.

"By the Gods, it's a crypt!"

"A royal one, I think."

I'd hoped to show him more of my unusual discovery, but it seemed as though our borrowed time was, at last, at an end.

"No," I whispered as my skin began to prickle. "Not yet."

"I feel it too. Come on."

Elyan and I raced down the tunnel toward the antechamber. Beyond the door, I could see the anxious faces of the Acolytes watching our progress, gesturing frantically with their small hands.

"The blackout is at an end!" Lark shouted. "Hurry, or you shall be trapped!"

We tumbled through the door just in time to watch it slam shut behind us, lost to time once more. King Anwar had been correct— the Acolytes had managed to clear most of the vines away from the archway, revealing words carved above the entrance, words in the same language that had been on the slabs and beneath the portraits. But what was more, they had managed to uncover a statue that stood to the right of the tunnel, and part of its twin on the right. They were women, both, standing demurely with their hands folded before them, their heads bowed, and their eyes closed. Atop their heads, they wore the same veil and circlet of braided wood that I'd seen every day since we'd arrived at Syr'Aliem upon the brow of a silent woman whose very existence seemed designed as a torment to me.

"The Tacé," I whispered.

In order to divert the king and his sister from where I'd hidden in the crypts, Elyan had used his magic to bring down a part of the main passageway and staircase, and so we had to slip between cracked and precarious fragments of stone as we ascended back into the palace. As we neared our rooms, I heard music in the distance, and laughter; the ball, it seemed, was still well underway.

Arlo and Phyra still sat by the fire, though the game of glass was no longer between them, and they had been joined by Thaniel, whose golden hair looked as though he had raked his nervous hands through it over and over again, leaving it permanently disheveled and his hands streaked with gold paint. They all looked up as Elyan and I burst through the doors, the relief evident upon their drawn and worried faces.

"Thank the Gods!" Thaniel stood, and I noticed that he very deliberately avoided meeting my eyes as he did. "Where have you two been?"

"By the looks of you, nowhere good," said Arlo.

"Do you remember the two doors on either side of the Incuna that I told you about?" I asked.

Phyra frowned. "They are both locked."

"Tonight, the Ita Hypogaeum opened."

Then, with all eyes upon me, I settled onto one of the couches and began to recount all that had transpired. I told them that I'd not yet reached the stillroom when the blackout happened—which was a lie and Thaniel well knew it, though he did not contradict me—and that Tansy had appeared and bid me go with her at once. I told them of the crypts and the hall of portraits, of the painting of Anwar's thrice-great grandfather and the unknown woman who'd come after him. And when I'd told my tale in full, I looked to Elyan for his thoughts or his judgment or his condemnation or any words he might wish to share, but he did not stir himself from the position he'd taken in front of the window, gazing mutely at the moonlit courtyard, hands clasped behind his back. And from his silence, I realized that 'twas a momentary truce only that we'd struck in the catacombs below.

It was Arlo who spoke first:

"Anyway, we're fine, aren't we? As far as they know, no one went anywhere near their creepy tunnel tonight."

"Well, about that..."

Elyan looked at me suddenly. "What about that?"

"While I was inside the crypt, the Acolytes cleared some of the vines away from the entrance. I'm afraid King Anwar and Princess Evolet noticed."

Elyan swore spectacularly.

"They know someone cleared the vines away," Thaniel said. "They do not necessarily know it was you."

No sooner were those words spoken than there was a knock upon the door of our suite, and they opened to admit King Anwar and the Dowager Queen, flanked by two heavily armed palace guards.

"Oh Gods, they've figured you out," Arlo muttered, and I shot him a furious glare.

"My friends, I am glad to see you safe," King Anwar greeted us, arms outstretched. He was still in his costume from the ball, though he no longer wore his mask. "We have never experienced a blackout so long. Tell me all of you are well and hale."

"We are well, your highness," Elyan answered airily. "And the court?"

He fluttered his hand vaguely in the air. "Fine, of course. They ever are. But you..." And his eyes were on me as he said this.

"We are well," I rushed to say. "And we have most thoroughly enjoyed this evening."

"Enjoyed?" Anwar's eyebrows rose. "But the festivities are far from over."

"I fear they are for us, your highness."

He tried quite vigorously to persuade us otherwise, particularly Arlo, whom he thought to tempt with the promise of games and drink and other frivolities, but even the Naturalist demurred. In the end, Anwar left disappointed, though I did not believe for one moment that he would be disappointed long. Long into the night, the Court Eternal would revel, and they would forget us in a euphoric haze, only to happily make our acquaintance in the morning and we would begin anew this tiresome splendor.

Once the door was firmly closed behind the king and his entourage, Thaniel set free a tremendous sigh of relief. "If he suspects anyone here of anything untoward, he hides it with extraordinary fortitude."

"Well, if we're safe from the dungeons of Syr'Aliem for this night at the least, I'm going to bed," Arlo declared.

Thaniel and Phyra followed soon after him to their own chambers, and at last, Elyan and I were left alone, facing one another across the room. It felt as though we stood on opposite sides of a chasm, and I was its architect.

I began: "Elyan—"

He held one hand up. "I've no wish to revisit our earlier conversation. You made your thoughts on the matter perfectly clear."

I swallowed; the effort was extraordinary. Evidently, I'd *not* made my thoughts on the matter between us perfectly clear, for I could feel them wedged tightly in my throat, yearning to be spoken aloud, excruciating in their confinement.

"Rather, I wish to speak of the Dae Spira," he said.

I blinked in surprise. "What of her?"

"If she ever speaks to you again, ignore her. Do not ever return to the Incuna again. Forget everything you saw tonight, and do not speak a word of it to anyone until we are well enough away from this place. You must swear it."

"She chose me," I insisted stubbornly. "The Dae Spira, she chose me, Elyan. No one has seen her in an age, and yet she appeared, to *me*. She brought me to the Incuna, she opened the Ita Hypogaeum!"

"Briony, this is not our kingdom, and it is not our place to meddle in their affairs."

"There are lives at stake."

"It is for them to address. My only concern is finding the cave in the north and returning to Tiralaen."

"I have other concerns."

"They do not matter!" The words fairly exploded from his lips, and they held within them far more anguish than could ever have been caused by my stubborn preoccupation with Syr'Aliem's future. "Have you so soon forgotten Garundel's words? If I'd not reached you in time tonight, you might've been shut away inside that crypt forever. And what of the next time? To say nothing of Arlo and Thaniel and Phyra—you may hold your own life in little regard, but what of theirs? What of mine?"

He was right; I had forgotten.

And the shame of it consumed me.

"I'm sorry," I whispered.

"Then let us speak no more of goddesses and secrets and part from Syr'Aliem in friendship. Coleum knows we've danger enough yet ahead of us."

I could do little more than nod, my eyes fixed firmly upon the floor between us; I could not look at him.

"I want your word, Briony. Your word that you will have nothing more to do with Syr'Aliem's secrets."

It was far more than my word that he wanted, but I could not give it to him. I could not ease his heart, could not give him peace, could not be his wife.

And so I gave him what I could.

"I promise," I said at last, and the words fell from my mouth like stones.

23

For all that they were well versed in carousing, the Court Eternal must've collectively suffered quite unfortunately after the ball, for by the time Princess Evolet attended upon us, it was well after noon and she appeared slightly wilted and bleary-eyed.

In truth, I was not certain I looked any better than she, for after my second disastrous conversation with Elyan, I had crawled into my bed still clad in my ballgown and sobbed until I was spent.

I'd thought perhaps Isri had decided to take pity on me at last, for when I woke with eyes swollen and crusted with salt, she'd thrust a cold, wet cloth that smelled pleasantly of herbs into my hand and indicated that I was to hold it against my smarting flesh. On the tip of my tongue was hoarse, whispered gratitude, until she caught sight of the jeweled stars piled haphazardly on the table beside my bed. I'd forgotten them entirely until sometime late into the night when I'd rolled over and winced at a sudden, sharp pain in my scalp, and in an exhausted stupor, I'd pulled them out and groped for whatever surface was closest.

As I reclined back against my pillows with the cloth against my eyes, she produced the case they'd arrived in the night before and began to carefully replace them.

I'd nearly drifted back to sleep when I heard her sharp intake of breath, and her fingers reached out and pinched my arm none too gently.

I yelped, and the cloth slid down my face as I sat up and scowled. In Isri's outstretched hands, eleven gold and silver stars gleamed, nestled within their blanket of velvet black; one was missing.

When an exhaustive search of every nook and cranny of my chamber failed to produce the missing jewel, her temper grew even more foul. Any goodwill I might have harbored toward her for the cloth vanished.

"You'll be quite pleased with what we have planned for you today," Evolet said as she swept into our suite of rooms, immediately gesturing to a servant for a glass of Calique. Her voice was once more sweet and pleasing, her smile congenial; any trace of the woman whose voice had echoed throughout the Ita Hypogaeum the night before had vanished so completely that I feared I'd imagined her.

I glanced at the pale green liquid with an uneasy stomach. "Are you sure you want that, your highness?"

"Most sure." She downed the entire contents of her glass in one swallow. "Now, then. My brother has invited your prince to the library once more. No doubt he will be positively ecstatic."

"No doubt."

"And in the meantime, I thought perhaps we might attend court this afternoon, and then, perhaps a play and dancing afterward—"

"No."

She stared at me, a smile frozen upon her lips. "No?"

"No," I answered warily. "I am tired of court and plays and dancing."

"Then what should you like to do while your prince plays at

scholarly pursuits?" she asked, gesturing to the servant to refill her glass. "The palace is entirely at your disposal."

Arlo, who had until that moment been languishing on a nearby chair, sat upright, planting his feet upon the floor. "What about the village? Briony's been begging to see it for ages."

I'd expected her to laugh in that infuriating way of hers, bright and dismissive, and remind us that to do so required her brother's permission, which he had thus far been unwilling to give for reasons unbeknownst to even her, or so she claimed. Instead, she sighed and set her glass down on the table between us with unusual force.

"I do not understand why you persist in this scheme of yours," she said, her eyes fixed upon mine. "The village is deadly dull beyond the Praela. Why you should wish to see it when such splendor is at your fingertips is beyond me."

"Briony has never been one for convention. Trust me, however dull you think it is, she'll think it's positively marvelous." He winked at me before offering Evolet a brilliant smile.

He was trying to help me, and I loved him dearly for it, but the promise I had made to Elyan weighed heavily upon me, as did Garundel's words.

And yet, here was perhaps a chance to see the very thing I'd wanted since the Dae Spira had first appeared to me.

"Actually," Arlo continued. "I would like to go as well."

"As would I," a soft voice added.

Now *that* I had not expected. Phyra stood in the doorway of her chamber in a gown of ochre wreathed in gold that set her skin glowing.

Princess Evolet's glance flickered uneasily to the young Necromancer. "I suppose my brother would not mind if we viewed the Praela, and the Praela only," she said tentatively. "But you must stay inside the carriage at all times and obey my every command. Do you understand?"

"Most thoroughly, your highness," I answered in a rush, so grateful was I to finally glimpse life in Syr'Aliem outside the palace walls.

I'd assumed that because Phyra planned to join us, so too would Thaniel, but he was, quite unfortunately, nowhere to be found, not even in the stillroom, and after sending exasperated guards to and fro to check all of the places I thought he might be, Arlo finally insisted that we give up and go on without him.

We passed the library on our way, and I knocked as quietly as I could upon the door. Elyan opened it, and for the simple clothing he wore, a black vest and white linen shirt, sleeves rolled up to his elbows and collar loosened, he might've been a scholar only. Despite the heavy ache in my chest, I thought him the most wonderful thing I'd ever seen.

"I should accompany you," he said reluctantly when I'd told him where we were bound.

I shook my head. "You're needed here. The map must be found, and besides, Princess Evolet has already stipulated that we are not to journey far. 'Twould be a waste of your time, I fear."

"Nevertheless, I ask you to please remember our conversation last night," he said, and it was quite clear from his expression that it pained him to say it as much as it pained me to hear it.

"Before I go, there is something I wish to ask you."

I'd cried myself to sleep the night before, muffling my sobs in my pillow, and woken with swollen eyes and muddle thoughts of hands upon me, teeth scraping gently across my jaw, and fear in the eyes of a friend. The former would haunt me for the rest of my life, this I knew. But the latter... "Do you remember the morning you and I fetched Thaniel from his chambers and Phyra was within?"

His brows drew together. "I do."

"I asked you if they were together as man and wife, and you told me they were not, but perhaps I asked the wrong question. Marriage aside—" My face flamed as I said the words: "—are they... together as a man and a woman?"

"Ah," he said slowly. "This is about Kevren, isn't it?"

"Please. Just answer the question."

"No, Thaniel and Phyra's feelings toward one another are not romantic."

I frowned. If that were the case, I could think of no other reason for the fear I'd seen in his eyes when I'd discovered them. Yet another mystery I could not seem to solve.

"My answer surprises you. Why?"

I could not tell him; I'd already humiliated myself most thoroughly in his eyes. Instead, I forced a smile upon my face and bid him a fruitful search.

I would've been perfectly happy walking from the palace into the village, as my companions would've been, but Princess Evolet insisted we take a carriage, the largest and most sumptuous I'd ever seen. The beasts pulling the carriage were strange to my eyes: they'd four legs just as the horses of Tiralaen did, but wings as well, and feathers that covered them from head to toe, pure white feathers that they nibbled with beaks long and sharp.

Servants appeared bearing baskets of fruit and delicate pastries, bottles of Calique and crystal goblets, and wraps of the finest silks. These were placed about our shoulders, Princess Evolet and myself, for our gowns were hardly suited for anything more than sitting just so in one place so that others might admire us, a favorite pastime of the Court Eternal.

As we drew away from the palace, my eyes drank in the long,

paved road of white stone lined with trees with long, slender branches that bubbled up like proud fountains and spilled over, swaying gently, sweeping the ground below. At the end of the road stood a massive gate of curling gold, gleaming obscenely in the brilliant sun of the early afternoon.

I turned around in my seat and parted the pale green velvet curtains that covered the rear window so that I might behold the front entrance of the palace in all its grandeur. It was, oddly, the first time I'd laid eyes upon it, for we had been led in through a servants' tunnel and only allowed out through side doors into the various gardens and courtyards. I was struck once more by how very like the Citadel it was. The same white stone, the same towers and turrets, the same gleaming windows, the same arches and porticos and courtyards, and I thought suddenly of my idle words on the evening we'd dined with the royal family. This palace had been built upon the Incuna and prospered by its power; could not the same have been true for Iluviel and the Gate? The Gate may be the very reason the Shining City grew and flourished as it did. Perhaps I had unwittingly stumbled upon the evidence that Tiralaen's scholars had so desperately sought.

Noticing how I stared, Princess Evolet smiled and asked: "What do you think of our palace from the outside, Mistress Briony?"

"It is lovely," I answered with perfect honesty. "In fact, it's made me rather homesick for it looks very like the Citadel of Iluviel."

Her smile hardened. "Is that so?" she asked. "Well, I must defer to your expertise in this matter as I have not seen your Citadel. Oh, look! Aren't the gates splendid?"

I turned in time for a stately pair of golden gates to part, admitting us into a most pleasant drive lined with trees that led to the village beyond.

"This is the Praela," Princess Evolet announced proudly, gesturing out the window with her goblet, already nearly empty. "All who live here are members of the court."

The dwellings that made up the Praela were modest gray stone but were no less lovely for it. They were several stories high and boasted tall windows on each floor, as well as several balconies of varying sizes upon which grew charming potted gardens. Their denizens, some of whom I recognized from the pleasure gardens and the ball, stared in surprise as we passed, scrambling too late to bow, and I wondered how often Princess Evolet ventured among them, or if she ever brought visitors with her. With a smile fixed upon her face, she waved to them, magnanimous in the bestowment of her grace.

We ambled slowly down streets full of bustling shops, their wares primarily items of luxury: bolts of fine cloth, jewels, ceramics and glass, furniture, and exotic animals in cages.

My mouth watered at the scents wafting upon the air: fresh flowers, sweets, roasted meats, spices. It reminded me so much of Iluviel that a sharp ache gathered in my chest and squeezed. Gods, I had not realized how much I'd missed the Shining City until now; it had been so very long since I'd seen it.

I had hoped that we might stop for a time that I might explore, but before my lips could form the question, Princess Evolet rapped upon the roof of the carriage and called out: "That's quite enough. Take us back, if you please."

"No, wait!" I sprung out of my seat and slammed my hand upon the roof just as she had. "We've not finished yet!"

To my immense surprise, the carriage ground to an immediate halt, jolting the lot of us back in our seats. Princess Evolet and I stared at one another in astonishment, and then it became perfectly, wonderfully clear: the driver of the carriage was possessed of magic. *Our* magic.

She seemed to realize it at the very moment I did, for she raised her hand to pound on the roof again, but the driver's magic and mine were still tenuously connected, a fact certainly owed to his lack of control rather than the strength of mine, and I reached out and stayed her delicate wrist.

"I'm sorry. I'm not quite ready to remove to the palace just yet," I said. Then I called to the driver, my voice filled with magic: "We wish to remain here at present."

This was, Elyan told me later, the first in a spectacularly long list of foolish things I did that day.

"Thank the Gods," Arlo muttered as Princess Evolet wrenched her wrist from my grip with surprising strength. He threw open the door to the carriage and stepped out into the sunlight. "It's bloody stifling in here." He extended his hand, and Phyra followed him.

I moved to do the same, but the princess did not join us. Rather, she remained in her seat, wringing her hands, her lovely face twisted in worry. "You do not understand," she told me. "You do not know our people."

"After the courtesy we've known at your hands, how could they be any less than positively wonderful?" I answered brightly. This assumption was the second spectacularly foolish thing I did that day.

We'd been provided with an escort upon leaving the palace, and two of the guards now followed Phyra, Arlo, and me, leaving two behind with the princess as well as the befuddled driver, who could not seem to figure out how on earth he'd found it in him to disobey the princess's order and follow mine.

We had wandered no more than a quarter-mile from the carriage when Arlo glanced over at me as I pulled my wrap tightly about my shoulders. "Are you sure this is a good idea?"

I could be at no loss as to what he meant.

We saw now why Princess Evolet had attempted to turn the carriage about when she did. Here, the street was in a poor state indeed, the ramshackle homes and shops lining it drab and shockingly derelict compared to the Praela. A fetid stink permeated the air, air thick with grime, and I felt it settling upon my skin, coating my lungs as I breathed, choking me. Everything was gray, including the folk who dwelled there.

The faces that stared at me were pale and gaunt, undernourished and used to hard labor. Their clothing was faded, and many times repaired, far from the sumptuous fabric on my person. They seemed altogether primitive; shockingly so. That there was to be a marked difference between the gilt of the palace and the dwellings of the common folk was to be expected, just as it was in the Shining City. But this was beyond anything I might've imagined.

Syr'Aliem's citizens stared at us openly with their hollow, hungry eyes, and when they caught sight of the guards behind us, their expressions darkened with ill-concealed hatred; it was no wonder, then, that Princess Evolet had chosen to remain behind in the carriage, and at that moment, I began to wonder if it had been better of me to do the same.

Still, I could not rid myself of the feeling that there was something here I was meant to see, just as the Dae Spira had brought me to the Incuna. Was it her hand that guided me once more? I'd heard no whispers, and yet even as my heart began to race and my flesh grew warm, I felt certain it was right of me to press on.

We passed a stand selling fruits and vegetables I did not recognize, but even so, I could tell the crop was poor, for they were

limp and spotted with brown. At the next stand, there were baskets
of nuts and dried meat and fish, along with small sacks of grain,
hardly enough for one loaf of bread.

Children darted in and out of the legs of uncaring adults,
chasing one another and, I highly suspected, picking more than a
few pockets on their way, though it did not seem as though there
was much to pick amongst this sort.

The people in the street haggled, snarled, argued, and wailed,
and yet there was little give for either side to offer, for they were all
as poor as the next, unable to afford, unable to yield, and caught
always quite miserably between the two.

I turned to Arlo. "With the richness of the forest around them,
how can their crops be so wretched? Is it the soil? A lack of water?"

Arlo's oft-cheerful face had gone quite grim. He knelt beside a
patch of bedraggled weeds. Resting his palm flat upon the soil, he
closed his eyes. A frown furrowed his brow, and when he looked up
at me at last, his face was long and sharp, his eyes slightly wild. "I
hardly feel the Incuna. I feel it always in the palace, but not here."

We walked for some time until we reached what appeared to be
the village square, a bustling, busy place full of gaunt, harried
people who stare at us distrustfully. I was quite certain they rarely
saw nor suffered outsiders. More stands bearing faded, sorry wares
surrounded us, and behind them stood ramshackle tenements worse
than anything I'd seen in the poorest districts in Iluviel.

"How can these people have so little? The Incuna is meant to
enrich the land and make all things grow and prosper. Is that not
what the king is for? To channel that magic into the land?"

"Well, something isn't working," scoffed Arlo.

"Something is wrong with the Incuna," I murmured, and thought
of the withered roots along the walls of the Incuna's chamber. "The

channels of magic no longer flow to this place. They've narrowed or collapsed altogether, just as Elyan said."

It has always been thus, Lark had said.

How long had the village been starved of the power it was owed? And did the fault lie with Syr'Aliem's king, or had the Incuna, like the Dae Spira, begun to fade into obscurity?

I had very nearly made up my mind that we'd endured enough of this sullen place when a cry went up, a cry of panic and fear.

An enormously tall cart stacked too full of wooden crates had entered the square from a narrow side alley, pulled by a pair of most peculiar animals—stout, stocky things that looked a bit like enormous pigs covered in long, shaggy hair and with black horns that curled round and round. The driver had taken the turn too quickly and the axle had snapped; now the cart tipped precariously whilst he gesticulated madly for all to get out of the way.

Whatever was in the crates must've been heavy indeed, for in the end, the cart could not manage to stay upright.

"It's going over!" an aproned man shouted.

Chaos descended. Those in the shadow of the toppling cart rushed outward—or tried to, but they were pinned in by others rushing toward the wreck to watch the collapse. A lucky few were able to move out of the way before it came tumbling down onto its side, pulling its beasts of burden down with it, colliding with nearby stalls. Screams tore through the air as the cart came down, mingling with the sound of splintering wood in a mighty crash.

"Oh Gods," I breathed. "We have to help them!"

I took off toward the disaster, Arlo and Phyra fast on my heels. We pushed through the crowds, begging them to step aside, shouting at them that we had the means to help any victims now beneath the wreck.

A dreadful keening rose above the din, and I felt the hairs on my arms stand on end. "My boy! Someone save my boy!"

When at last we reached the cart, a group of men had already wedged their shoulders beneath it and were lifting it as best they could from the ground, but the hulking weight was proving impossible to move. Someone had released the animals, and they'd gone barreling down an alley, adding their dreadful bellowing to the terrified clamor of the crowd.

"We could levitate it," I suggested.

Arlo grimaced. "It's a fair size. It would take all three of us, and even then—"

The woman had not stopped wailing, her cries growing more and more frantic as the men struggled and failed to lift the cart, and I knew we had little time, if it were not already too late.

"We must try!" I shouted.

"Together," agreed Phyra, as Arlo nodded and slapped his hands together.

And so I called upon my magic. It was not a spell I had much practiced, and fear crept up my spine. Three Mages performing three different levitation spells upon a single, unbalanced, splintering object might well end in even more disaster than what already lay before us. My hands were shaking as I lifted them.

"Breathe, Briony," Phyra said. "You are capable."

I felt it then, the magic rising in Phyra and Arlo; and I felt the purpose of their magic, their command, and I found that I was able to balance my will with their own.

Horrified shouts went up as the cart began to rise from the ground, mere inches at first despite the exhaustive effort; indeed, droplets of sweat slid down my back and legs, and I suddenly felt rather lightheaded, bright spots dancing at the edges of my vision.

"Keep it steady," Phyra said, but it was almost a grunt, and I knew she was speaking to herself as much as me.

Then I heard Arlo call out to the villagers: "You there! If the boy's under there, now's the time! Come on, move!"

The child's mother was so consumed with fear that she could do nothing but huddle in a heap on the ground. It was two men nearby who reached beneath the cart and hauled out the broken body of her son, and she fell upon him immediately, her silence giving way to a high-pitched keening as she gathered him up against her.

"Bring it down slowly!" Arlo shouted, and not a moment too soon, for I could feel my command over my magic waning. The cart settled again with another crash, smaller this time, and I looked immediately to the woman and her son.

We were too late, for the boy was clearly dead.

Blood drenched his ragged clothing, and his skinny arms and legs hung broken and limp. Women had gathered around his mother as she rocked the boy back and forth, blubbering and moaning, his blood drenching the bodice of her faded yellow gown, and beside me, I heard a stifling sob.

Phyra stood with her hand pressed against her lips, anguish blooming in her eyes. I remembered her brother then.

And I realized all at once what she was planning to do.

"Phyra, no!"

I lunged for her, but it was too late.

The air around me stilled with the strange passing of time that accompanied Phyra's descent into her Deathscape, and I found myself quite unable to do more than stare at my outstretched hand, my desperate fingers.

It lasted longer this time, and when she did not open her eyes, when the thickness in the air did not dispel, I began to despair that

Phyra would never rejoin the living. Had Death's envoy denied her request? Had something worse befallen her there?

At last, Phyra's eyelids fluttered and opened, and just like in the forest when she'd bestowed new life upon the Phaelor, her eyes were completely and utterly black.

Within his mother's arms, the boy stirred, and I felt my body plummet suddenly through the air; I stumbled and caught myself before dashing my face upon the crude ground.

Around me, the villagers watched in horrified silence as the boy, soaked in blood from wounds that no longer existed, looked up into his mother's face. "Mama?" he croaked out.

She screamed then, a scream of unimaginable terror that stilled my heart, and flung him away from her, scrambling backwards on her hands and feet.

The boy sprawled into the dirt, still too weak from his ordeal to rise, but he stretched his hand out toward her, blindly searching for the warmth that had abandoned him so abruptly. Phyra looked to the woman, her ink black eyes widened in confusion. As realization slowly dawned, her face hardened and became winter stone, cold and merciless, and I was frightened of her.

"You dare abandon him?" Her deepened voice echoed in the square, and I shivered, my skin prickling with gooseflesh.

The woman's eyes bulged, and she pointed a quaking finger at the young Necromancer. "He was dead!" she hissed. "What have you done to him?"

"He has been returned to you!" Phyra raged, drawing herself from the ground to tower over the woman. "How can you cast him away?"

The boy continued to writhe upon the ground, hands grasping, reaching out to his mother, but she turned and spat upon the ground.

"Evil!" she shrieked. "Unnatural!"

Phyra reached for the boy, grasping him against her fine clothes without a thought, her arms encircling him protectively even as her lovely face twisted in hatred as she looked upon his terrified mother.

"You are a monster!" she screamed at Phyra. "You've tainted my son—you should have let him rest!"

The crowd that surrounded us evidently agreed. Harsh muttering broke out amongst them, their language crude and their gestures sharp.

"She's put a demon in him!" a bearded man shouted, and the people around him roared in horror and agreement.

"She's done no such thing," I heard Arlo say, as though from a great distance. "Can you not see that she has restored him to you? Given him life once more?"

"She's doomed him," one of the women near the boy's mother whispered. "A dead soul in a living body—it is magic most foul. An abomination!"

"Abomination!" another woman echoed, this time shouting the word for the crowd to hear.

"She whores herself to demons!" another shouted.

"She has doomed him!"

"We do not suffer demons here, whore!"

The cacophony of their voices rose, their faces twisted into vile, angry grimaces, more statues than men and women, carved by vicious hands.

"String her up!" a voice shouted, its cruelty rising above the din.

"Yes! String her up!"

"Send for the Skin Weaver!"

"The Skin Weaver!"

The crowd began to chant the words over and over again, their frenzy growing, and there was hunger written upon their gaunt faces; a hunger for blood.

"No!" I screamed as two men grasped Phyra beneath her arms and hauled her to her feet. "Leave her alone!"

"Bring her to the scaffold," the bearded man shouted.

Exhausted as he was, Arlo pushed violently through the villagers that stood between him and Phyra, but there were far too many of them, and their fear had rendered them no better than mindless beasts. "Stop it, damn you!" he bellowed.

But they did not, and Phyra was borne away, her feet scrabbling for purchase as she kicked and fought them. Flames flickered in her hands, and for a horrifying moment, I feared she meant to burn them all down and us with them, but the act of lifting the cart and bargaining with Death's envoy had left her utterly exhausted, and she could summon little more than sparks.

I gripped Arlo's sleeve. "They've gone mad!"

"We can't save her alone. You've got no ghosts here and I'm bloody worthless! Gods damn Thaniel!"

At the center of the square was a crude wooden platform that in happier times might host plays, perhaps, or traveling musicians. Now, as I watched in horror, men lifted tall wooden pillars and set them into grooves that had many times welcomed them, and I realized they also used this place for hangings. Or worse.

Two lengths of rope were produced, and after Phyra's wrists were tightly bound, they strung her between the wooden pillars, her arms spread wide.

"Gods," Arlo choked, and he ran toward the platform, shoving and pushing anyone in his way. I followed, screaming incoherent words and pleas, my voice growing hoarse and raw, and still they would not hear me.

The crowd at the foot of the platform stretched in all directions, their wild, vicious eyes fixed on Phyra as she struggled against her bonds. Her magic had utterly gone from her. Even if she'd been able to descend into her Deathscape, little good it would do her, for her body would still suffer the same, horrible fate it was clearly destined for.

This inevitability was favorably met by the crowd, for they roared in triumph at her helplessness; I could only imagine it was because they relished a slow death, and by their own hands, each man, woman, and child—for there were children among them no older than the boy who'd been killed.

A man ascended the steps of the platform, and they gazed upon him in the sort of hushed reverence reserved for those of great importance; for royals, or those possessed of the rarest and most powerful magic. He was a tall, shrewd person with a hawk's beak for a nose and piercing blue eyes, around which glistening black oil was smudged. His brown hair, beginning to gray, had grown long and wild and tangled, and yet it was not this nor the oil that rendered him terrifying; it was the cape he wore, for he was named Skin Weaver, and there could be no doubt as to why. Long and billowing, his cape was made of what appeared at first to be pieces of leather, varied in color and size, crudely stitched together in grotesque patchwork, but was instead made of human skin; a tapestry of people like Phyra whom these wretched people had murdered in their fear.

He came toward her, and his thin lips curved upward in a smile. "Well, look at this. Look at this, good people of Syr'Aliem! Look at her! We have, in our midst, evil of the very worst sort!"

They hung upon his every word, the villagers; they regarded him with the rapt adoration of those promised salvation. And with every square of flesh he added to his grotesque collection, they believed he delivered on that promise.

"She has performed magic most vile this day. She has stolen the peace of the dead." With these words, the Skin Weaver drew a long knife from the collection at his belt. "For her own good and ours, we must cleanse her of such foul, unnatural magic. We must cut it out of her!"

Oh Gods. As the crowd around me roared their hideous, twisted approval, my gorge rose.

The Skin Weaver moved close to Phyra, and he drew the flat of the knife slowly, almost reverently, down her cheek and the full length of her fragile neck. A terrified, desperate sob escaped her lips.

Arlo bellowed Phyra's name and lashed out violently, first with his fists and then with the whole of himself, until three men had no choice but to turn their naked fury upon him, beating to the ground and kicking him.

I took hold of the front of his shirt and pulled him free. The men did not pursue us, thank the Gods; instead, they turned their backs to us, eying the stage once more, unwilling to miss another moment of their victim's torment.

Though his lip was bloodied and one eye beginning to swell, I was relieved to see that Arlo was able to stand under his own strength. "It's no use trying to fight your way through the crowd," I told him. "Use your magic!"

"I don't know what to do! There's nothing growing here. This whole place is strangled and dead!"

Over his shoulder, my eyes were drawn once more to Phyra, prostrate with terror as the Skin Weaver moved behind her. The crowd held silent, ravenous, as he gripped the fabric of her fine gown and rent it violently in two, exposing the skin of her back.

"Call upon the Incuna," I urged him. "It's strangled, yes, but it's not gone altogether, and it favors your magic above all others."

"To do what?"

I cast my eyes about at the brown grass and pitiful weeds, then back to Phyra, now dangling limply between the wooden pillars.

"The scaffolding," I told Arlo fiercely. "All wood was once growing, yes?"

His eyes widened. "I don't know how to do that—I've never tried!"

"Try now!"

"I won't manage it. I know I won't!"

"You will." I took his face in my hands, refusing to let his eyes leave mine. "I know you will."

A roar went up, and we turned together to see the Skin Weaver brandishing his terrible knife in the air. He brought it down, traveling the length of Phyra's back from neck to tailbone, and her scream rent the air.

Arlo fell to his knees, his palms upturned.

"Do not be afraid," the Skin Weaver said into Phyra's ear, as if whispering but loud enough for all to hear. "For you shall be cleansed."

Blood had begun to pool at her feet, dripping from the hem of her ruined gown as she sobbed, her chest heaving. He lifted the knife again, digging the tip into her left shoulder and drawing it slowly to her right. Phyra's eyelids fluttered, the pain beckoning her into oblivion, her mouth slack.

It was a child who saw it first, a girl who should not have been there to witness such horror at all; perhaps she had wisely averted her eyes, and in seeking a distraction had seen the change in the lifeless spires.

"Look, mama, green!"

They were small at first, the tightly closed buds of new life rushing back into what had long been dead. They sprouted all along the length of the posts that held Phyra's bonds. I stared at them in wonder, then looked to Arlo, still kneeling, his eyes closed.

Whispers broke out among the crowd, and the Skin Weaver's blade hung in midair as he squinted at the buds, then drew close to one of the pillars that he might examine them further.

It was in that moment that branches, slender and pale, burst forth from the buds in a fearsome riot, growing darker as they stiffened, multiplying so rapidly that I'd scarce blinked before two magnificent trees stood where there had been only dry, dead wood. Arlo's eyes snapped open, and the air around him was wild and green.

Phyra's bonds snapped as the pillars grew into mighty trunks, and she collapsed in a heap on the platform, her gown sagging open at the back where it had been torn. She fumbled with the vestiges of the crude rope around her wrists, casting it away with a desperate, broken cry.

Then she raised her head.

I had never seen such black before; such endless, devouring black.

In that moment, I knew her not.

Branches snaked out, striking the knife from the Skin Weaver's hand; they began to twist themselves around his wrists, stealing up the length of his arms, coiling around his body until he was well and truly bound.

Then, and only then, did Phyra rise.

The Skin Weaver struggled against the branches that held him as she approached him slowly, and there was a smile upon her face.

"Monster," he hissed as she brought her hand to his temple and slid it slowly, ever so slowly, down his face.

"Yes."

The flesh beneath her hand began to shrivel as she drew the years from him, and he began to gape and gasp like a fish as the contours of his face became sunken hollows. The hair upon his head turned white and wiry, spilling over his shoulders as age bid it grow.

Summoning every spark of magic in my exhausted person, I wrapped it about my voice and called her name.

It was enough; thank the Gods, it was enough. She stopped, drew a shuddering breath, turned.

I darted forward and climbed up onto the platform.

"Phyra, no," I gasped as I took hold of her shoulders, forced her to face me, to look at me with her terrible black eyes. "This isn't you."

She tilted her head. "I am as I am."

I took her face between my hands, brought our foreheads together. "Come back to me. *Come back.*"

She blinked, once, twice; her fingertips dug into the skin of my arms and she was herself once more, save the ink in her eyes. Black seeped and swirled and polluted, stronger than in her Deathscape, and I feared this time it would not pass.

"Briony?" she whispered. "The boy—"

I shook my head, smoothing my thumbs across her cheekbones. "We must not worry about that now."

As I bent to pick up the discarded knife, the bound man's eyes met mine with such blazing hatred that I recoiled from it. Spit frothed at his twisted mouth as he shouted at me: "You will not leave this place alive."

"Watch us."

The villagers, shocked by what they had witnessed, had retreated far enough away that they presented little hindrance to our escape, at least for now—but even so, I doubted we could possibly make it all the way to the palace unassisted. Arlo had slumped to the ground, weakened and feverish, and Phyra leaned heavily upon me as we staggered from the stage and to his side.

"What do we do?" I asked.

He struggled to his feet, then keeled over again in exhaustion, his hands splayed on his knees. "I hadn't really thought that one out, to be honest."

"How long will your magic hold?" I asked.

Upon the platform, the Skin Weaver was cursing and shouting, bidding the villagers to bring their axes and set him free.

"Not long. I can feel the bonds weakening."

Indeed, several of the more fragile tendrils had snapped under the Skin Weaver's furious struggles; the rest would soon follow. And once they did, I did not think the villagers would remain at bay much longer.

Our salvation came upon thundering hooves, for a carriage suddenly plunged into the square, its opulence obscene in so crude and desolate a place, and yet how could I not rejoice to see it?

I thought to see the princess's guards within its handsome cab, come to liberate us, but I was rendered speechless by the sight of her own face leaning out the open window, white as any umbra, her eyes wide and frightened.

"Get in!" she called to us wildly. "Quickly!"

She opened the door wide, and we scrambled inside even as the crowd climbed the platform with crude axes, taking after the trees with vicious strokes. Princess Evolet pounded her fist on the roof of the carriage, and we lurched forward, away from the square.

"Thank you," I breathed, slumping back in exhaustion.

"What were you thinking?" she hissed, and her beautiful face was twisted in fury. "Look what you have done!"

"We apologize," Arlo snarled at her. "For we had no idea your people were fucking animals."

She recoiled at his rage. "How do you expect a starving people to behave? You saw how disgraceful they are, and still you provoked them!!"

"But why are they starving?" I demanded. "They are your people, your highness. Surely you bear some responsibility for their misfortune—and for their violence."

"They would have kept well enough to themselves had you not brought her among them, with her unnatural magic."

"Don't you dare cast blame on Phyra," Arlo said icily. "This place was already a tinderbox, your highness. All it required was a match."

"And a match you have provided, you fools!"

24

It wasn't difficult to remove Phyra's gown; it hung off her, little more than gossamer rags soaked through with rust.

I left it in a heap on the floor of our common room, then washed the sheet of sticky blood from her back as she lay upon the couch. Beneath it, an angry red line ran from shoulder to shoulder, and from its center, another stretched down to her waist. My gorge rose as I realized that he'd meant to divide her skin into pieces, rending them from her one by one.

"How bad is it?" Arlo asked.

"Not so very bad," I answered, and this was true. The cuts were relatively shallow, meant only to separate skin from muscle. "They will need to be cleaned, and a salve applied. We should ask Kevren for the same he used upon Thaniel's wounds when we first arrived."

I looked up at the guard that Princess Evolet had left with us—who stood now inside the door, rather than without—and realized that I knew him; he was Commander Nidaan's second, the young man with hair the color of hay who had been sent ahead to inform the king of our arrival. "Rimuel, isn't it?" I said. "We need a healer. Please send for Kevren."

He shook his head, though he looked quite reluctant to do so. "I'm afraid I cannot allow that, Mistress."

"Why not?"

"Princess Evolet expressly forbade all news of the Necromancer from leaving these rooms, Mistress."

"But how am I to treat her wounds without a healer?"

He shook his head mutely, and though I could tell well enough he suffered in some small measure, rage filled me beyond all thought of decorum, and I rose from the bed. I was about to pour out the full measure of my opinion on his cowardice and foolishness and breeding, when Phyra's soft voice met my ears:

"Let him be, Briony."

I eyed the fool of a soldier up and down to show my contempt, but said only: "Can we at least send for fresh water and clean towels?"

Rimuel meekly pointed to a fine crystal jug of water where the Calique customary sat, and beside it were several rolls of white cloth. I wondered that they should be there when we so needed them, and then my eyes fell upon the herbs. Nestled within a roughhewn stone bowl were cuttings that I did not recognize, not by sight nor smell, and beside them was a hastily scrawled note on a scrap of parchment: *Grind herbs, then use this water to form a paste. Apply liberally.*

My eyes drifted once more to the crystal jug, to the liquid within. Mere water, or so I'd thought. My inquiring hand lingered over its surface, then I dipped my fingertips in, and gasped.

Someone had ventured far below and brought water from the chamber of the Incuna.

"Who brought this here?" I asked Rimuel, but he only shrugged and shook his head.

A mystery, to be sure, but not one I had time to ponder—and besides, I did not think it possible anyone could use water from the Incuna to commit harm to another person, even to Phyra. So, I did just as the instructions suggested, then dabbed the concoction delicately upon the cut across Phyra's shoulder blades until I could no longer see the skin beneath.

By the time I did the same down the length of her spine, the paste across the top had already dried, and though I knew it would be better to leave it a while longer, I dunked my thumb in the water of the Incuna and wiped a small bit away.

There was naught but a scar underneath, thin and already growing faint. My breath escaped in a sigh of wonder, and when I looked up, I found Arlo watching from over my shoulder with awe upon his face.

"By the Gods," he whispered, running his own finger across the scar as though to reassure himself it was, in fact, quite real.

I laughed, for I could not contain the relief that swelled within me and dashed exhausted tears from my eyes.

Phyra stirred. "There is no more pain. How is it possible?"

"Briony is how it is possible," said Arlo, as if that might explain anything.

"Not me," I said as I used the last of the paste from the bottom of the bowl to reapply that which I'd wiped away. "Someone brought the water from the Incuna, and the herbs from the stillroom. It is by their grace that I stood a chance at all of healing Phyra."

"Who?"

"It must've been the Acolytes, though I can hardly see how they managed it without being seen. We've no other friend here save they."

Wishing the poultice to do its work upon Phyra's skin, I wove the rest of the cloth that had been provided around her torso to secure it. I helped her to her chambers and into bed afterward, arranging the heavy brocade coverlet around her as she settled upon her stomach, her head pillowed beneath her arms.

Arlo appeared in the doorway with a glass of water. He brought it to her bedside and held it to her lips so that she might drink. "I'll leave you to rest," he said, and placed the glass upon the table beside her bed.

"Thank you," she whispered. "For what you did today."

"It was nothing."

She reached out for him, and her fingertips seized his. "It was everything. You saved my life."

He looked down at their hands. "Had I been a better Mage with a better aptitude, this would not have happened to you at all. I am sorry it was me, and not anyone else with you today."

"It was not anyone else who brought life to dead things, and without a bargain to be made for it. It was extraordinary magic."

He flushed; I'd never seen him so disarmed.

"You find your magic insignificant, but to me it is beautiful," she continued, and though her voice was low and rough with exhaustion, there was strength in it. "Sometimes I wish it were mine."

Arlo's eyes widened. "Why so? You've power unlike anything I could imagine."

"And I could no sooner imagine you with it," she answered. "You could never dwell in darkness."

He laughed softly, humorously. "A soft green boy."

"No, not soft. Strong. *Alive.*"

He stood next to her in silence a while, gently clutching her fingertips, until her eyelids closed, and her chest rose and fell softly.

As quietly as I could, I brought another chair around to the other side of Phyra's bed and collapsed upon it, quite weary after so very much excitement. Arlo did not so much as move.

"Who called you a soft green boy with a pea shoot?" I asked at length.

His head rose, and he looked at me warily. "Briony..."

"Please," I said. "Tell me."

He looked down at Phyra once more, and I thought he meant to ignore me until I let him be, but at last he said: "My grandfather was an Alchemist, like Thaniel. And to my father, he might as well have been Coleum himself."

"And your grandfather did not approve of the Arts of the World? Or was it Naturalists in particular to which he objected?"

"I could not say what my grandfather thought, as I never met him. He died before I was born. His son, however, had very strong opinions on the topic."

"I see."

"Yes. Well. My father was bitterly disappointed not to have been born a Mage himself, but when the gift appeared in me..."

"He hoped you would be an Alchemist."

"He hoped I would be strong. A craftsman like my grandfather, or a warrior, or... I don't know. Someone to be admired, maybe even feared. A *man*."

"Aptitudes are neither strong, nor weak," I said, remembering a day not so very long ago when I'd told my teacher that I feared what my magic might be.

Arlo laughed bitterly. "Only our intent, yes. I received just such a lecture from the Mage who trained me. Unfortunately, he neglected to tell my father. When the flowers called to me during my Trial, he refused to accept it. He insisted I go through the whole bloody thing again, only to get the same result. Gods, his rage that day." He paused, and when he spoke again, his voice had shrunk so that I could scarcely hear him. "She thought it wonderful, my mother. She'd saved for weeks to make a cake, and when the truth could no longer be denied, she painted white flowers on it, while my father drank himself into a stupor."

I could say nothing, and I did not try to stave the tears that spilled down my cheeks, for I was so very tired and could no longer contain my sorrow.

"Better they had bound me the way your parents did you, for no matter what I did, no matter what spells I mastered, he thought me weak, thought my magic better suited for a woman. I think he would've beat it out of me were it not for my mother." Here, he paused again, and I noticed his eyes searching the room for the customary Calique bottle. Finding none, he continued: "The day she died was the worst of my life. My father cast me out to make my way, though he would not permit me his name, so fiercely did he hate the idea that he should be in any way associated with me."

"Bryn is not his name?"

"'Twas my mother's name," said he. "I became a blacksmith for a while. Did you know that?"

I shook my head.

"Very manly. So, of course, I was terrible at it. I quit and became a carpenter, and was shite at that, too. All the while, I could have been rich, you know? All I had to do was knock on the door of the closest manor house and get a job as gardener. What would your father have paid me for that?"

"A bona fide Naturalist? I doubt we could have afforded you."

"Just so! And I might have done it, too, but then I met Niven. Gods, I loved her, but I'll not deny that I married her in part because her father was rich and influential, and that in cleaving myself to her, I did not have to attempt to use my magic to carve a living for myself."

"She was a Mage, was she not?"

"An Illusionist," he answered. "She deserved a damned sight better than me."

"You cared enough for her to risk your life for her freedom."

"But not enough to use my magic to protect her in the first place when Keric's spies came sniffing round. She was ashamed of me, in the end, that I held my magic in so little regard when others were willing to die for it."

He'd never spoken to me of his wife before; without Thaniel, I doubted I would've ever known of her existence. When first I'd heard, I'd scarce been able to imagine Arlo as a husband, for I'd ever known him as a scoundrel, a handsome trickster with a head for drink and gambling and the company of women in ways most scandalous. But the man before me, with his shirtsleeves rolled up and his fingers combing gently through Phyra's tangled black hair, seemed another man entirely.

A true man.

"Since we've come to this place," he continued, "the Incuna has made me feel my magic acutely, whether I will it or no. But what I did today... I never imagined myself capable of such things."

Behind me, the door opened. I turned to see Rimuel.

"What is it?" I demanded.

Rimuel stiffened. "Princess Evolet will see you now."

"Me?"

"You."

She waited for me in the corridor outside our suite, her pale hands folded before her. Laughter nearly bubbled up from my lips when I saw that she'd changed since our ill-fated outing.

"Is your Necromancer all right?" she asked.

I could manage little more than a curt nod.

"I have delayed your prince and your knight these past hours, but they will suffer our company no longer and must return to your rooms shortly. You will tell them what has transpired, then you will pack all your things. I will see you have proper provisions, but you and your company must leave. Tonight."

"Tonight?" I gasped. "We were just attacked! Are you so desperate to keep the Skin Weaver a secret from your brother?"

"Oh, my brother is well aware of the Skin Weaver, Mistress Briony. If he cared at all, his cloak would not be so very long."

I shuddered in revulsion. "If not the Skin Weaver, then why? Why must we leave?"

"Because you are a fool who cannot leave well enough alone," she snapped. "I warned you not to wander, not to pry, but you did not listen. The longer you stay here, the more likely it is that he will discover what you have done."

She knew. I could not fathom how, but somehow, she knew I'd been in the Ita Hypogaeum. She swept past me, and I turned and called after her:

"If that's true and we must go, then tell me: what did I see last night?"

She did not look back, nor slow her pace. "It does not matter," she said. "Forget it and forget this place."

And then she was gone.

25

By the time Elyan and Thaniel returned, Princess Evolet had made good on her promise and provided us packs of sundries and fresh traveling clothes and boots, finer than those we'd brought with us from Asperfell.

Elyan entered the suite with an armful of books, took one look at the newly arrived travelling supplies—all bound up and ready for our departure—then turned his piercing gaze to me.

"What have you done?"

"I take great offense at the assumption that I was at fault."

"Were you?"

"It was a group effort, really."

He set the stack of books down on a nearby table with a thud. "Briony, what have you done?"

I stared determinedly at the floor. "Princess Evolet has demanded that we leave Syr'Aliem tonight."

"Tonight," Elyan echoed.

"Yes."

"No," Thaniel gasped softly.

I straightened. "Thaniel—"

"What's happened?" he demanded, then looked around rather frantically. "Where's Phyra?"

I touched his sleeve. "She's in her bed now, and she's safe. But there is something I must tell you."

It came pouring out of me then, everything that had happened since we'd left the palace with Princess Evolet, our ill-fated journey into the village and what had befallen us, the shocking state of King Anwar's people and the terrible wrongness of a land that should've, by all accounts, been positively thriving. When I came at last to the part where Phyra had been strung up, her flesh to be added to the Skin Weaver's cloak, Thaniel staggered as if he'd been struck.

"Oh Gods—where is she?"

"She is sleeping," I assured him. "She has been well cared for and is already nearly recovered."

"I wasn't there," he whispered. "I wasn't there."

"No," came a harsh voice from Phyra's doorway. "You weren't."

Arlo, who never could leave well enough alone, did not bother attempting to do so now. He strode boldly into the sitting room and thrust a finger in Thaniel's face. "If you had been there, none of this would've happened. But you were with him, weren't you?"

Thaniel's face drained of all color. "You don't know what you're talking about."

"No?" Arlo raised one eyebrow. "Come now, Thaniel, we've known one another a very long time. You don't think I recognize when you've an interest in someone? I should know, after all."

Thaniel's face was so twisted with loathing that I scarce recognized him. "As if someone like you could tempt me. You're nothing. Less than nothing. An embarrassment."

He might have been able to weather the assault had I not laid bare his wounds, forced him to confront his past, but now raw anguish was painted across his face. I threw myself between them, hands raised, lest Arlo throw the first blow—but it was to the other I spoke:

"Thaniel, stop. It was Arlo who saved her, who saved *us*."

This gave him pause, but I could feel the barely repressed fury radiating from him. within his powerful frame, the wild thumping of his heart, and knew that were it not for this, for my presence between them, that he would've gladly pummeled Arlo to within an inch of his life.

"You," Thaniel said, his tone flat with disbelief.

"Me," Arlo answered.

"He was brilliant, actually," I said. "And we're all right. But we must hurry. Princess Evolet was most insistent that we depart immediately before her brother is made aware of our transgression."

This seemed to distract him from his anger, for he finally looked down at me. "No, we can't leave," he whispered. "Not yet."

"We have no choice."

Elyan had remained curiously silent throughout this exchange, and I noticed now that he was staring at me rather intently. "It's not about Phyra, is it?" he said slowly. "It's about what you saw last night in the Ita Hypogaeum."

I wished I could have denied it, but I could not find the strength in me to attempt the lie.

"Princess Evolet knows I was there. It seems she was prepared to pretend otherwise and protect that knowledge from her brother, but after the riot in the village today, she does not trust us not to give ourselves away."

"And should she?" he asked.

If he hoped the ice in his voice would freeze my tongue, its effect was quite the opposite. "The people of Syr'Aliem are starving!

They are sick, and wretched, and ignorant, and full of hate, and that is why they lashed out at us today. And it's only going to get worse. That's what the Dae Spira has been showing me—they're dying, Elyan! And the cause of their suffering is right here in this palace. You've seen it with your own eyes! The Incuna cannot reach them. Its magic is denied to them because King Anwar and the Court Eternal are gorging themselves upon it day and night. Will you do nothing for them? Can you simply let them die?"

"Our people are dying as well, Briony! Have you forgotten that? It is *my* responsibility to protect the people of Tiralaen above all others. That is what it means to be their king. And I cannot allow myself to be distracted from that purpose, no matter how wretched the people of some other kingdom may be. It is not for me to bring justice to all people in all worlds."

He was not wrong.

But neither did I think he was right.

Whatever the truth, I knew not what else to say, so I said simply: "The Dae Spira chose me, Elyan. That has to mean something."

"Not to me," he answered. "These are not our people, Briony. Let their goddess find some other savior."

The last of my strength forsook me then, and I allowed myself to fall into the deep cushions of a velvet chair. But Elyan, it seemed, had more to say.

"We came here for help, for a way to find the cave. Not only will we not get it, but there is every possibility that King Anwar will hunt us down in the forest over the unrest you have stirred up among his people. If you had done as I said and left well enough alone, we would not be in this sorry state of affairs. These were selfish decisions made without care for why we were here in the first place and in complete disregard for the prophecy Garundel bestowed upon you. What if, by your thoughtlessness, we are now prevented from returning to Tiralaen? There are lives at stake, Briony! There was nothing to be gained by your meddling, but *everything* to lose by it."

I could scarce breathe for the swell of anger expanding in my chest. "I did not mean for any of this to happen—"

"You never do," he cut me off flatly. "Nor, it seems, are you capable of thinking of anything but your own selfish desires."

In the suffocating silence that descended, Thaniel's eyes remained firmly fixed on the floor, while Arlo had long since disappeared back into Phyra's bedchamber.

Gradually, I became aware that I was shaking. Where there had been the fire of indignation, there was only ash left now, cold and lifeless. I thought for a moment I'd forgotten how to breathe, but the rasping in my ears, hitching and uneven in its rhythm, told me very well that I had not; I'd only forgotten how to do it properly.

"I'm sorry," I whispered. "I am so very sorry."

I left them there, and listed down the hall to my chamber, my hands groping for the wall, for my legs shook terribly and black spots danced at the edges of my vision.

Elyan was right.

I had flung his decision to bring Phyra amongst Syr'Aliem's fearful citizens in his face, but in the end, 'twas me she should've feared, for I had led her to the scaffolding with my selfishness, my insatiable desire to meddle at whatever cost.

And that was hardly my only indiscretion.

I turned them all over in my mind like the pages of a book, and the story that took shape was so suffocating and shameful that I wanted desperately to slam the cover shut, but I forced myself to read the litany of my faults. What our situation had required was restraint. Restraint, diplomacy, and fine manners, and I possessed none of these things.

A great many people had tried to teach me thus throughout the years of my childhood, rendered insufferably long by my utter disinterest in such lessons. Whatever I'd envisioned for my future, I'd never imagined such traits necessary, for even if I were to pass through life as a nobleman's wife, at worst it was ridicule I would invite upon myself and upon my husband; and honestly, any man who would've married me should've been well prepared for ridicule.

I could not have imagined then how these lessons might have served me, for I'd thought them feminine. Insignificant. Unimportant. Just as I'd imagined I myself would be, once I was a woman grown.

What an utter fool I had been!

There was nothing for it now. Princess Evolet was right: we must flee before King Anwar discovered that we knew his people were dying, and why. What would he do to protect that secret? Execute us, most likely. He did not seem to have any qualms about such things. To leave us alive in the dungeon, if he had one, would be to risk the truth coming out. Then again, perhaps he'd do no more than Evolet herself planned—to send us on our way with all due haste.

I could not say. It did not matter.

Lark, Fife, Tansy, and the other Acolytes would know nothing of our flight. They would think I'd abandoned them and I supposed I was.

We would have passed the fortnight in peace had it not been for me, and though I would've found it all dreadfully dull if not grudgingly beautiful, whether or not a map lay at the end of it all, we would've departed as friends of this kingdom, and of its people. We would have been safe.

But they will not be...

Even then I could not quiet the voice that told me to defy. To confront.

To fight.

There was a soft knock at my bedchamber door, and I swiped my hands against my cheeks and stood on unsteady legs.

It was not Elyan who stood on the other side, nor Thaniel or even Arlo. Rather, it was Isri with her face of stone and an armful of fabric. She was the very last person I wished to see. I tried to close the door on her detestable face, but she stuck her foot in the gap and pushed past me, depositing her burden upon my bed.

With quick, deft movements, she began unfastening the gown I wore until it pooled at my feet, a beautiful dead thing glittering with jewels and soaked with the blood of my friend. I kicked it away. Then, still unsatisfied, I reached down, took hold of the delicate fabric, and before Isri's face, rent it in two, delighting in the way it came apart so easily in my hands. It fluttered back down to the ground, and my eyes followed it, falling upon my velvet slippers. I wrenched them off my feet and threw them across the room. One struck the wall and sank pathetically to the floor, while the other collided with a lamp by the bedside, knocking it to the floor. A pity it had not broken.

The only thing left upon my person save my chemise was my necklace, and I clawed it from my throat, thousands of gems scattering across the floor, and threw what remained after the shoes. It burst gloriously, glittering remnants showering the bed I would no longer sleep in. My hands itched, and as I looked around me at the sumptuous room, I realized it was indeed repulsive, an offense even more horrifying in the light of what I had seen that day; an offense I was suddenly maniacally eager to correct.

Grasping one of the spires, I climbed up onto the mattress and began to tear down the drapes. Their fragile anchors gave immediately, for nothing in this gilded world was strong, and before long, they were a puddle at my feet.

All the while Isri watched me, her face infuriatingly impassive no matter what destruction I caused until, at last, I grew weary of it, for although a fissure of excitement passed through me at each rip and tear, it was over far too quickly, and the dull ache at the center of me remained, a stubborn, heavy thing.

Climbing down from the bed, I snatched up the gown Isri had brought and shoved it over my head. Even if she were so inclined to dress me after what I'd done, I would not suffer her hands upon me, a sentiment I was sure she shared. No doubt she was as glad to be rid of me as I was to be rid of her, and of this place.

The gown Princess Evolet had sent for my departure was surprisingly simple, made of sturdy, deep green fabric with a modest bodice and sleeves; it was the most familiar thing I'd worn since I'd arrived in Syr'Aliem. And this time, I stood before the mirror and looked upon myself without reservation. It was an umbra's face that stared back at me, drawn and pale and wretched, my dark eyes still far too big for my features, but I recognized myself at last, for just as I'd proclaimed to my long-suffering aunt so many years ago, I was no lady.

When at last I emerged from my ruined chamber, a traveling cloak about my shoulders and a pack slung across my back, I found my friends waiting for me similarly clad. Phyra and Arlo regarded me with pity; Thaniel, less so. He looked positively wretched. Elyan would not look at me at all.

Even had I the words to properly express my shame, to tell them all how desperately sorry I was, I'd no time to say them, for at that moment Rimuel bid us follow him out of the palace; our time in Syr'Aliem had come to an end.

He led us through a series of dark, fusty tunnels that appeared as though they had been little used and long forgotten, and we came at last to a narrow set of stairs that coiled up into the night. Across a finely manicured grove of trees, we followed the guard to what I recognized as part of the thick wall that separated the palace grounds from the forest beyond. A door, unguarded, was set into the stone, and the soldier drew from his cloak a ring of keys.

"Her highness has diverted the night guards, but only temporarily," he whispered as he hurried us through, his eyes watching the path behind us lest we be discovered. "Make haste."

With that, he shut the door in our faces.

By Magefire, we traveled the passageway to the outer door, and at last, we emerged back into the forest we'd left little more than a week ago.

"We should put as much distance between us and Syr'Aliem as possible before dawn," Elyan said grimly. "We'll use their paths, but be prepared to hide should they follow us. Do not engage them—we have magic, but they have numbers, and I've no wish to see any one of us suffer another injury this day."

He did not look at me as he said this, but I knew well enough it was further chastisement of my conduct.

We walked the path in silence, huddled in our cloaks and keenly aware of every sound and every movement in the underbrush. The hours past, and the moon continued her slow progress above us, and hope began to blossom within me that Princess Evolet's plan had worked, that we'd made it safely away.

We never heard them approach.

From the trees, no less than two dozen hooded figures descended around us with astonishing grace, arrows nocked and pointed at our throats.

"Thaniel—" Elyan began, and then his hand flew to his neck. Between his fingers, I glimpsed a gleam of silver, and then he crumpled and fell to the forest floor.

I opened my mouth to scream. There was a whistle near my ear, and then a sharp pain in the soft flesh of my throat.

The clearing around me blurred, grew dark, and then there was nothing at all.

26

The Dae Spira, when she stole into my dreams, was not gentle. I was anchored helplessly to the forest floor by her grasping hands as they traveled from my throat to my face and through my hair, turning my head to the side. I tasted dirt and decay as her veils descended over my mouth and nose and eyes, her gaping mouth at my ear.

Go back! she wept and cursed and sighed. *You must go back!*

Blackened trees and the village in ruins; rotted crops and the bloated corpses of animals; the bones of Syr'Aliem's people. All of this I saw in a terrible, sickening rush, and my mouth filled with smoke and grime.

I came awake with tears upon my cheeks.

"I am so sorry," I whispered as I dashed them away.

There was light above me, filtered through layers of sheer cloth that rippled gently on a soft breeze, and as my eyes adjusted, I realized that they were curtains hanging from a bed made of dark wood, unpolished, its posts rising in twisted spires all the way to the ceiling and disappearing into it as though they were one and the same. Strange, that. I thought I'd shredded my bedcurtains.

It came back to me in an instant. This was not Syr'Aliem; we'd been sent away, and as we'd fled, we'd been set upon by men and women in cloaks, deep within the forest. I reached up and brushed my fingers against my neck where I'd been pricked; some sort of toxin, I supposed, meant to cause sleep. How long had I been here? Where exactly *was* here?

I sat up, my head somewhat muddled, and once spots ceased dancing at the corners of my eyes, I pushed the curtains aside. All of the room appeared to have been hollowed out from a single piece of wood or a great tree, for every piece of furniture was like the bed: not separate, but rather an extension of the room in which it stood. There was a small dressing table and stool, a tall cupboard, and a handsome chair, and although they were modest in their construction, particularly when compared to whence I'd come, they were so harmoniously fluid that I found them an arresting sight.

The balmy air, fresh and clean with the scent of the forest, came from a single large window, opened to the world beyond, and through it, I could hear birdsong.

Still quite lightheaded, I eased my legs gently off the bed and leaned forward with my hands upon my knees until the room around me ceased spinning. Then I approached the window and peered out.

There had been many tall buildings in the Shining City, the Citadel highest among them, its gleaming white towers and turrets stretching high into the endless sky. They were rendered small by the sight before me.

I looked out upon a circle of trees, each more massive than any structure I had ever seen, and in their center was a bustling marketplace, green and lush, full of paths marked by fountains and benches and stalls. People, ever so many, mingled in the brilliant sunlight, the happy hum of their chatter drifting up to me. So different it was from the village of Syr'Aliem, and yet we could not have been very far away.

Judging from the windows, each tree seemed to be home to many, many rooms such as mine, and most had terraces and balconies where all manner of flowers, vegetables, and fruits grew in clay pots. There were endless sets of stairs winding up the trunks, leading to doors and archways, and through the larger windows I could see halls and rooms beyond.

It was a city. A city of trees.

There was a soft knocking at the door behind me, and I turned as the door opened, admitting a woman with skin nearly as dark as Kevren's, though it did not possess the same metallic sheen that the members of the Court Eternal prized so dearly. Her black hair was long and braided, woven through with beads of stone and metal, her eyes a startling shade of green.

I was shocked to see that she wore pants as a man might do, made of soft, supple leather the same as her bodice. Her arms were bare and covered in whorls of color, patterns and symbols unfamiliar to my eyes, and she crossed them over her chest as she looked me over most thoroughly. It was evident she found me wanting.

"The Atriyen wants to see you."

"The Atriyen?"

"Come with me."

"No."

She had not expected my refusal, but rather than anger, it was amusement that lit her eyes. "No?"

I shook my head. "No. Not until you tell me where I am and what you've done with my companions."

The corner of her mouth lifted. "They are perfectly safe."

"How can I possibly trust you? Your people accosted mine in the forest—you poisoned us!"

She snorted. "It was only a sedative, and one of my brother's making, no less. Rest assured there will be no lasting harm."

"You've taken us prisoner."

"We saved you. Now, if you want to see your companions, come with me."

She left me little choice but to follow her through the door and into a corridor, high and airy, all carved from the same great tree just as my chamber had been—a truly wondrous thing indeed, though I'd little opportunity to appreciate it. My guide's walk was as brisk as her manner of speaking, her strides full of purpose, and I struggled to keep pace with her.

"Try to keep up!" she called back over her shoulder.

"You're not wearing a gown," I grumbled.

After what seemed like a journey through the entirety of the massive tree, we came to a handsome pair of doors flanked by two guards, both female, dressed in the same oil-rubbed leather as my guide, and I must've appeared quite the fool staring at them with a delighted smile upon my face.

"You're all wearing trousers!" I exclaimed. "How marvelous!"

My guide stared back at me blankly. "What are trousers?"

"Pants!" I said, gesturing to her lower half of her body. "That is, not a skirt—you see?"

I do not think a more exasperated expression could be found anywhere than that upon her face as she turned and pushed the doors open.

My breath escaped me in a rush; I'd not realized until then how little I'd believed my escort, how little I believed *anyone* in this wretched forest, for it seemed everywhere I turned were lies and illusions. Before me were the truest things in my world: my dearest friends, the man I loved.

Phyra flew into my arms and I pressed her lissome form tight against me, smoothing the dark tangle of her hair against her neck. Thaniel followed behind her, and Arlo, both sweeping me into crushing embraces. And Elyan... he'd not forgiven me, that much was clear by the detachment in his eyes, but his fingers brushed against my own and I grasped them fast, grateful for whatever part of him I might still find favor with.

"I told you—they are perfectly safe."

My guide swept past me with a wink, and my gaze followed her to an enormous incurvate table that lay at the center of the room: beautifully inlaid with patterns of wood in a multitude of shades from palest gold to deepest russet, and stones of all sizes and colors were bound together under layers of smoothest, clearest resin. No less than two dozen men and women sat around it, watching our reunion, and like the portraits of Syr'Aliem's past kings and queens in the Ita Hypogaeum, there were few similarities to be found amongst them. The oldest was gray and wizened; the youngest was my guide, who, now that I'd been thus delivered, slid deftly into the only open seat left.

High above this extraordinary sight, a single thick trunk seemed to grow downward from the center of the ceiling, its curling branches spreading like a canopy, a strange and marvelous inversion, and from them, like drops of rain, hung countless hollow crystals filled with tiny flames: green, wreathed in black. The memory of the palace plunged into darkness, overtaken by the forest wild, rose unbidden within me.

"You are Briony Tenebrae, the Orare of Asperfell?"

The woman who addressed me sat at the head of the wonderful

table in a chair larger than the rest, directly to the right of my escort. It was impossible to guess her age. She may have been fifty; she may have been ageless. I'd never seen a woman so well formed, so strong. Her bare arms, covered in the same riot of color as my escort, were well-muscled, used to work and toil, and perhaps battle, for I knew well enough now that the women of this strange place were as capable of warriors as their male counterparts. Indeed, I had no doubt that hers were hands that had grasped the hilt of a sword or drawn back the string of a long bow.

"I am," I answered slowly, taking in the sight of them. "And who are you?"

"My name is Damiane. I am the Atriyen of this kingdom."

"Kingdom?" I asked. "Surely not, when we've only just left Syr'Aliem."

They began to laugh, the men and women seated before me, but it was not unkind. Rather they seemed to be aware of something quite humorous that I'd yet to reason out.

Damiane grinned and slapped her hand upon the magnificent table. "That is no kingdom! But I will forgive you for mistaking their riches for royalty."

"I don't understand. How came we to be here?" I asked her. "How did you know to intercept us in the woods last night?"

"They were well informed," said a familiar voice.

"Kevren!" I exclaimed, for it was indeed Syr'Aliem's healer who strode into the room, bowing to the woman they called the Atriyen.

"My apologies for being late, Damiane," he said, then turned to look over my companions and me with a physician's eye. "You're well? No lingering effects of the sedative?"

"A bit dizzy," I said, then: "How did you know we'd left the palace? Surely, the princess didn't—"

He laughed. "You've got a friend in that palace, make no mistake," he said, "but I do not think it might be her highness."

Arlo snorted. "We've no friends there."

"I think you must," said Kevren, "for someone left me a note about your departure, and the path by which you were traveling."

"Someone also brought herbs that I might heal Phyra," I reminded Arlo. "And a pitcher of water from the Incuna."

"Water from the Incuna?" Damiane said, her voice slicing through the air such that our attention was at once upon her. She leaned forward, her palms braced against the table, and she regarded me with such penetrating eyes that I quailed beneath them. "How do you know it came from the Incuna?"

"Because I've been there. I've seen it. Felt it."

It was with wonder and longing, envy and curiosity that each and every man and woman at the table regarded me, palpable and thick, though some were decidedly less friendly than others.

"You?" said my escort with disbelief—and no small measure of derision. "Why should you should be permitted to see the Incuna?"

Her sudden anger made me realize something quite strange: although we were their prisoners, these words—and the accompanying snarl upon her face—were the first signs of open hostility I'd seen from any of our captors.

Damiane held up one hand. "That is enough, Samira."

"She has every right to ask," said an old man at Damiane's left. He had the same dark skin as Samira, the same high cheekbones and proud nose, though his eyes were brown like my own. A distant relation, perhaps? "What's so special about this girl?" he continued. "She is a stranger to our world. An escaped convict, no less. And yet she has seen the source of our magic and we have not?"

"Very well," said Damiane. "Briony, we must know—how? How came you to stand in the presence of the Incuna?"

Elyan spoke suddenly at my back: "Do not answer that, Briony."

Damiane's gaze flickered to him. "And why should she not, your highness? The Incuna is our magic, after all. Do you not believe we have a right to know why an outsider, a prisoner, has been allowed to see something that has been lost to us for centuries?"

"I certainly believe you do, but until we have negotiated the terms of our release, we are at liberty to withhold whatever knowledge we choose, Atriyen."

She chuckled at this. "We are not Syr'Aliem, your highness. You are free to go whenever you wish. Now will you not speak? Or have you more to demand in payment?"

"Damiane." The old man rested his hand atop hers. "We cannot trust them. You know full well what their kind is capable of."

Elyan ignored him, his eyes fixed upon the Atriyen. "Anwar, too, made promises, and in the end, they came to nothing."

"I am not Anwar."

"And we are not your enemy."

"Then tell me your price."

"There is a cave in the north," said he, "where the veil between our worlds is said to be thin. It is of paramount importance we reach it, and soon."

One of the men at the table, a pale man of middling years with long ropes of white hair tied back with a thick skein of leather, leaned forward. "A cave, you say?"

"There are writings of Jiva and Ereal that speak of such a place," said a woman with a fine-boned face, and her wide gray eyes narrowed in scholarly contemplation.

Damiane's eyes slid to me. "And you, Briony of Asperfell?

What is it you would know in exchange for your account of the Incuna?"

"The village," I said. "The one beyond the palace. Do you know what's befallen it?"

She did not expect this to be my price, for her eyes went wide at my words, but nevertheless, she nodded. "I do."

"I want to know."

"An exchange of knowledge, then." She sat back in her chair, her hands laced before her. "You tell us of the Incuna, and we tell you all we know of Syr'Aliem. Meanwhile, my scholars will search for your northern cave."

"I believe we have an accord," Elyan said. "Though one thing troubles me still."

"And this is?"

"I should dearly love to know to whom we have just pledged our cooperation."

Damiane smiled—an ancient, knowing smile. "Nymet Nata," she said. "The Forest Kingdom."

27

So different was Nymet Nata from Syr'Aliem—indeed, from any kingdom I had ever known (and I was hardly ignorant of the matter)—that I had a great deal of difficulty believing it to be the true Forest Kingdom as Damiane so claimed.

There was no grand throne room to be seen, no gilded fantasias or endless dining rooms, and certainly nothing like the pleasure gardens to be found, let alone the Thesa.

Indeed, there was not even a palace; rather, it was the great tree in which we all gathered that served as such. Known as Uuna Tree, or First Tree, it housed the council room and the families of those who served upon it, as well as the Great Hall, where meals were taken and entertainment could be had if those gathered were so inclined to sing, dance, and tell stories amongst themselves.

"But if this is a kingdom and you its ruler, should you not sit upon a throne?" I asked Damiane as she guided us through the Great Hall, where the thick, hand-hewn tables were being set for supper.

"We've not had a throne for a very long time."

"Why?"

She glanced sidelong at me. "That is a very good question, and one I will answer tonight at the gathering. Besides, I do not rule Nymet Nata, not on my own, at least."

"I must confess, I do not understand you."

"I lead a council, and though they are deferent to me in most things, there are times in which a decision is made by many rather than one."

This was such a shock to me that for a very long moment, during which Damiane must've found me quite ridiculous indeed, I could do little more than gape at her. "You mean... the men and women at the table... they may gainsay you in the governance of this place?"

She nodded. "They may, for they represent the many who dwell within my care, and it is their families who benefit or may be harmed by the decisions I make."

"Represent the many," I murmured. Then, as the truth of her words washed over me, my breath escaped me in a delighted rush. "They're common folk!"

Damiane's brow quirked. "We've no court, and thus no one is common at all."

"We've nothing at all even remotely like it in Tiralaen!"

"Ah, yes. Tiralaen. I understand from the writings of your ancestors that your kingdom is quite brutal. Oppressive."

"Not so!" I exclaimed.

At Damiane's other side, Elyan cleared his throat. "Tiralaen, particularly its capital of Iluviel, has progressed dramatically in the two hundred and fifty years since our countrymen escaped Asperfell. Indeed, under my family's rule, our kingdom and its people have flourished."

"And have they ruled a very long time?"

"Nearly eight generations."

"So many," Damiane said, and I heard in her voice the

unspoken thought that followed: *Too many.* "And what are these improvements that your family has made?"

Elyan spoke in measured tones of the cleanliness of Iluviel's streets, the health and prosperity of its citizens, their safety, and the abolishment of draconian laws, particularly those regarding imprisonment and indentured servitude. He spoke of guilds and societies, arts and invention, and there was pride in his low voice, but there was also great sadness; he'd not seen what Tiralaen had become, what the Shining City had become, for so very long.

"And what of their learning?" Damiane inquired. "You speak of tutors. Are they provided for all?"

Elyan was rarely discomfited, but a slight frown appeared upon his face. "Unfortunately, no. Men and women of learning are quite difficult to come by, and therefore—"

"Only those with wealth can afford them," she finished. "I suspected as much. And these... what did you call them... universities? Can anyone attend them?"

It cost Elyan dearly to admit it false. "Only sons of noble families."

"Only sons?"

"Yes."

"A pity, for you apply but half of the intelligent minds among your populace to obtain such progress," Damiane remarked drily. "Tell me, do women hold positions of power within your society? Have they occupation?"

If Elyan was discomfited before, he was positively unsettled now, a flush upon the sharp angles of face, his brows drawn together. "They do."

Damiane looked to me. "Is it so, Briony?"

I was certain she did not mean to cleave us, to pit us against one another, but she must've also suspected that, as a woman, and a decidedly outspoken one at that, I would not seek to conceal that which I, in truth, found terribly lacking about my home, however beloved to me her rightful ruler may be.

"'Tis so," I ventured. "And yet, 'tis not. Women with magic may hold certain positions relating to their aptitudes, but beyond that, I have ever seen women in positions of domesticity."

"Even women of means?"

"There are few women of their own means, for property and titles are primarily held by men, and bestowed upon women at their leisure."

"They do not make decisions, then, for *that* is power, and your women have none," she said. "And yet you call it the Shining City. A beacon of progress." Her voice had taken on a most peculiar quality with these words; she did not mock me, but neither was she sincere, and I found myself torn between the defense of my home and the condemnation of it.

"Come," she said. "I will show you what true power is."

The great library of Nymet Nata was the largest I'd seen outside of the Byblion in Iluviel, and though its books were not bound in leather, nor its shelves and alcoves and windows covered in gilt, and statues of scholars long dead did not stand sentinel at each corner, it quite stole my breath away.

Two stories high with a domed ceiling from which hung the same upside-down branches and the same crystals full of flame, the circular room was all but painted with shelves of books and scrolls. Those on the second floor could be accessed by a series of spiral staircases as well as ladders, and reading nooks were set into alcoves punctuated by windows through which the rich sunlight of the golden hour poured forth, dust motes dancing merrily within their beams.

But more remarkable than the architecture, more marvelous than the sheer vastness of the collection before me, were the people: dozens of them, men and women both, sat at tables, stood upon ladders, walked to and fro with books, smiled at one another. They wore neither jewels nor silks nor bore any indication of elevated rank; they were perfectly ordinary. It was the most wonderful thing I had ever seen.

I wished to go forth, but Damiane's hand stayed me, for it was Elyan whom she'd truly intended to see this place, and the people within it.

He stepped slowly down into the room, his eyes sweeping over the towering shelves until they fell upon a man studying a thick tome at a handsomely carved table, scratching notes onto a piece of parchment. Beside him sat a girl who could only be his daughter so similar were they: the same strong features, the same wild, dark hair, the same shrewd eyes. She could not have been more than five or six, and yet it was with diligence that she studied the small book before her, her tiny forehead wrinkling in consternation and her mouth moving silently with the words upon the page, her finger moving with them.

Elyan knelt down at their table, and the girl looked up from her book.

"Hello," she whispered.

"Hello," he answered. "What are you reading?"

"It's the story of a man who fell asleep in a patch of moonlilies and awoke in a world that was his own, but such a very long time ago so that those he loved had never even been born."

Elyan's brow rose. "Is that so?"

"Yes, 'tis so."

"And is he ever able to return to those he loved?"

The girl's little face twisted. "I cannot tell you that, for it would spoil the story, and it's so very lovely you mustn't do so."

The man, having only just realized his daughter was engaged in conversation, leaned over and offered Elyan an apologetic smile. "She does love to talk, my Mahia."

"That is quite all right," he answered. "I know a young woman who is much the same."

I flushed as Arlo snickered at my side.

"Who taught you to read, Mahia? Your father?"

"Of course not!" She shook her head as though this were a very funny thing for him to have said indeed. "Deda Luloa, at the school. I like her much better than Deda Tival. She's very stern."

"Mahia!" her father blanched.

"What?" The girl's head tilted and her brow furrowed. "She *is*, da."

Elyan was silent as we left the library, but I recognized well enough the furrow of his brow and the subtle clenching of his jaw that accompanied the frenetic churning of his mind, and I worried my lip near to bleeding with the urge to take him aside, speak with him alone, parse out his troubles, and try as best I could to mend them; I could not. The wounds that lay between us were still too raw.

"The evening meal will be served soon," Damiane told us. "But there is one last thing I should like you to see."

I thought perhaps she meant us to see the enormous, bustling square at the heart of Nymet Nata, but instead she led us into the forest behind Uuna Tree, where we came to a crossroad.

Damiane pointed down the path to the right, a path lined in lanterns that disappeared into a dense thicket. "Later tonight, that is where we will convene to share our stories," she said. "But, for now, this is our path."

She led us left, down a friendlier route where the trees were less wild, less tangled, and the thick honeyed light of the fading day cast our steps in warmth and amity.

We did not walk for long before we reached a grove, and the moment I laid my eyes upon it, I knew that I was meant to be there.

"You've been to the Place of Ways beneath Syr'Aliem's... palace," Damiane said, and the derision when she said this was not lost upon me. "You've seen the doors."

"Seen them," Arlo snorted. "She's been inside one of them."

Damiane stopped. "Truly?"

I nodded. "The Ita Hypogaeum."

"We shall speak further of what you saw later, at the gathering. In the meantime, do you know what lies beyond the other door? The Ita Hominaeum?"

"Not in the slightest."

Her answering grin, all gleaming white teeth, was infectious.

Two trees stood entwined within the grove, and at the base of their thick, twisted trunks was a yawning cave and a set of worn stone steps that descended into the black below.

"A little light, if you please?" Damiane asked of us, and five handfuls of flames illuminated our descent.

"Where exactly are we going?" asked Arlo. "This isn't an elaborate plan to murder us and dispose of our bodies in some underground pit, is it?"

"Gods, Arlo," Thaniel groaned.

"What? It might be."

"Yes, but you're not supposed to say so."

"Why not?"

"Because if it's not, you've insulted our hosts."

"And if it is?"

"Then you've tipped your hand and lost the element of surprise."

"Ah," Arlo mused, and I heard rather than saw the sage nod of his head. "Push *them* in the pit first. Wise, your knightliness. Very wise."

"Will you both shut up?" Elyan groaned.

In the flickering light of the Magefire, I saw the shaking of Damiane's shoulders.

We came at length to a landing, a grove below, its ground lushly carpeted with moss and toadstools and all manner of flora and fauna, tiny lights whirling about, and at the center of this strange and beautiful place was a man—or was he a tree? Perhaps he was both, for his gnarled legs disappeared into the earth below him, and his hair was a tangled canopy within which resided a plethora of creatures that blinked at us with enormous, jewel-bright eyes. Some resembled birds, while others were decidedly mammalian, and most puzzling and delightful of all were those that looked a bit as we did, with limbs and fingers and toes however small, and I was reminded so fiercely of the Morwood that my chest ached.

The man's torso—or was it his trunk?—was wrapped in a cloak of green, leaving only his face visible, and I drank in unabashedly his strange features: a long, proud nose, and hollow cheeks made of roughened bark, and a beard of lichens.

"Is he sleeping?" came Phyra's soft question.

Damiane chuckled. "The Dendor is always sleeping. Come now, old soul, and awaken! I've brought someone for you to meet!" And with playful irreverence, she slapped one strong hand against the sizeable mass of his torso beneath his shroud of growing things.

The bark of the Dendor's eyelids scrunched slightly, shifted, fluttered, and I found myself staring into deep pools of dark water rimmed in moonlight. His nose came next, nostrils wrinkling, flaring, and at last his mouth dropped open to emit a truly impressive cloud of dust.

His voice was a rumble that shook the ground beneath me as he grunted and groaned away the stiffness of sleep, and at last words that I understood poured from his mouth of wood. "By the two groves, Atriyen, that hurt."

"Old bellyacher," she laughed. "Shake off your dreams and make this remarkable young woman's acquaintance."

Her hand on the small of my back propelled me gently forward, and I blinked up into the strange, unsettling pools of the Dendor's eyes.

"This is Briony," Damiane said. "And you'll never believe where she's been."

"Oh, aye?" he grumbled, tilting his great, tangled canopy of a head down to take in the sight of me. "And where've you been, hmm?"

The resinous scent of him filled my nostrils and I struggled to find my voice. "Why, I have been many places, my lord," I said, for how could he be anything but? "A prison is my most recent home, and of late, I've been a guest of King Anwar of Syr'Aliem, though I am informed I'm mistaken in referring to such as the Forest Kingdom."

"Indeed," the Dendor growled. "And where else?"

"The Place of Ways."

The Dendor's reaction was immediate and visceral. The

creatures that resided within the canopy of his hair screeched and whirled and took flight as he stretched and grew, every inch of him simply *more* as he loomed over me, and for a moment I was afraid. Then his great mouth stretched into what I supposed could be considered a smile, and the boom of his laughter echoed throughout the stone that surrounded us.

"Ho, ho!" he bellowed, shaking off loose bits of his lichen beard. "Truly?"

"Truly."

His great, booming voice dropped suddenly to a breathless hush: "And my gift? Her Acolytes? I cannot hope they live still, and yet..."

A smile of unabashed joy nearly split my face in two. "Oh, but I know exactly who you are," I exclaimed, laughing. "Of course! You created the Acolytes for the Dae Spira."

He spluttered. "How came you by that knowledge?"

"They told me, of course. Truly, they are the most lovely company, so fierce and kind."

Another enormous, joyful shout poured from the Dendor's mouth, and then the most peculiar thing happened: his eyes crinkled, a great racking breath shook his trunk, and he began to sob in earnest.

Helplessly, I turned to Damiane. "Oh Gods, what did I do?"

"Nothing," she snorted. Bracing her hands on her hips, she fixed the Dendor with bemusement. "Sunshine through the leaves one moment, darkest soil the next, this one."

Tears streamed in rivulets down the grooves in the bark of his cheeks, and I squeaked in surprise when one landed atop my head, thoroughly soaking my hair.

"Sorry," the pitiful creature mumbled, and lifted a corner of his cloak of growing things to dab at his eyes. "Don't mind me."

My heart clenched at the sight. "How long has it been since you've seen them?"

He paused in his ministrations and blinked down at me with the midnight puddles that were his eyes. "I... I can't remember."

This was evidently the wrong thing to have asked of him, for he was assailed with a fresh bout of sobbing, and I leapt back just in time to avoid being soaked by the fat droplets of the Dendor's misery.

"Oh, don't cry," I begged him. "Please."

He sniffled and blew his nose loudly into the cloak. "Oh, my little lost souls... how I've missed them."

Damiane grimaced. "I would tell you not to mention *her* for fear he'll flood the lot of us, but I suppose he ought to know."

If news of the Acolytes had quite overwhelmed the Dendor, the fact that I had laid eyes upon the Dae Spira set him off so completely that we were all forced to retreat several steps for fear of a deluge upon our heads. We waited patiently until his sobs receded and his ramblings resembled words before we approached once more.

"Where are my manners?" With these words, the Dendor shook the great canopy of his head and six stones rose from the moss at our feet, forming a semi-circle before him. We sat politely, mindful of the damp at our feet, and listened as he regaled us once more with the tale Elyan and I already knew, of his hopeless devotion to a goddess who preferred to wander the wilds of her beloved forest rather than break the soil with her roots, and yet he loved her still.

"I will always love her," he sighed, his roots sinking deeper into the loam, and I despaired at his affection, that although he could never hope to have her such as she was, he still hungered; he still wished.

I knew a little of what he felt.

We could not stay, for the hour grew late and the Dendor's eyes were once more growing heavy with sleep despite the animation with which he had spoken of such wondrous things, and so we bid him a polite good evening and left him murmuring quietly to himself of her, his goddess, his love, and ascended weathered stone into the gathering dusk.

For our evening meal, we were invited to the Great Hall, where everyone sat where they pleased and did not always stay there if there was a conversation to be had on the other side of the room. We served ourselves from dishes shared with those around us, and the food was simple and hearty, and utterly delicious. I hadn't minded the extravagant fare of Syr'Aliem, but there had never seemed to be enough of it to sate me, or if there had been, it was made perfectly clear by the withering glances of the Court Eternal that I should eat as little as possible.

There were no such looks here, and I set about happily filling my plate with whatever was in reach: tender chunks of meat in a hearty sauce aromatic with spices, whole fish stuffed with herbs, savory vegetable pies, nuts and cheeses and fruits fanned out on wooden platters. Every morsel was delicious, and soon I found I could scarcely move, the already snug laces of my gown stretched taut.

As I ate, I learned that Samira and Kevren were, indeed, brother and sister, and their father was none other than the old man who had come to Samira's defense in the council. Zayir was his name, and Samira's temperament favored his, all fire and teeth and grit. With his steady warmth and ease of spirit, Kevren must've favored his mother, whom I'd yet to meet. She was a healer like her son, though her blood did not carry our magic as his did.

Damiane, I learned, was not sealed, nor had she ever been, but she and Kevren's mother were occasional lovers, or so 'twas said. It was so unlike anything I'd ever known before, and yet so very right; far more so than the hollow lust of Syr'Aliem or the staunch, loveless duty of my homeland.

One thing Nymet Nata and Syr'Aliem did have in common was their love of drink. There were clay pitchers of wine and a cider made of a fruit that tasted a bit like plums, but it was Walfrey's enchanted bottle of Laetha that everyone gathered around to try, though I suspected they were far more fascinated by the nature of the spell upon the bottle than what it held.

"It's very strong," I warned Zayir as he gestured to Arlo to pour him a generous measure. "Be careful."

Zayir snorted. "I am a warrior of Nymet Nata," he said, as if this perfectly explained away any concerns regarding his ability to hold his spirits. He lifted the cup and gulped down the entire contents.

We leaned forward expectantly, poised between delight and apprehension as he slammed the cup down on the table. At once, his eyes bulged and he wheezed, an enormous gust of breath reeking of alcohol. Arlo gave a shout of merriment and pounded him soundly on the back as everyone around him fairly exploded with laughter. To his credit, once he'd gained his wits, Zayir joined in, agreeing heartily that Laetha was, after all, to be enjoyed slowly and sparingly.

The smiles and laughter of the men and women around me, the abundance of food and the strains of music should've lifted my spirits immensely, but what had happened at the palace before our departure, the words that had been spoken, still weighed heavily on my mind, and I found myself unable to settle even as the two cups of cider turned my blood to warm honey in my veins.

Phyra had not joined us despite my pleas that the food and company would do her good, but Damiane took great pains to assure me that she'd sent a plate to her room, and that Kevren's mother would brew her a restorative draught sure to rejuvenate her. As for Kevren, he sat beside Thaniel farther down the table, their heads bent low together, smiles upon their faces that were for them alone.

Once darkness fell, we were to gather in the grove down the second path to hear a most fantastical tale, or so I was told, and I hoped Phyra would join us then. If she did not, I was quite determined to visit her after, even if I had to climb out of the window of my bedroom and scale the side of the Uuna Tree to do it. I'd not stopped worrying for her since we'd left Syr'Aliem, and though I did not expect nor hope for forgiveness, I was desperate that she know how terribly sorry I was. I thought perhaps I would always be sorry.

As for Elyan, he had eaten little, and left without a word to anyone.

Arlo nudged me gently. "Chin up," he said. "He'll come 'round."

"I don't think so," I told him miserably. "Not this time."

Darkness fell at last, and Damiane led us from the hall to the cleaving, and down the path to the right, away from the Dendor and his cloak of green. Lining the path were thousands and thousands of lanterns bearing green and black flames, some so large I could never have held them even with both hands, and others so small they might fit into my palm. Their light blazed and shone, beckoning us forth, comforting us upon the journey so luminous were they and so dark the path ahead.

We emerged at last into a clearing with even more lanterns, and in its center was an enormous tree with a thick tangle of curling branches from which hung hundreds of tokens, each as different as the next: a feather, a cluster of beads on a string, a rusted metal bell, the small skull of an animal tied to a faded blue ribbon. They swayed gently in the warm, indolent evening air, and I wondered how many generations had lovingly placed them upon the branches, hope in their hearts and prayers upon their lips.

Before the tree was a circle of weathered stone benches that surrounded a fire larger than any I'd ever seen, save the harvest pyres in the fields at Crenswick Castle in my youth. It was tended by a gray, wizened old man who sat cross-legged before it, a worn leather pouch in his hands.

Damiane took her place directly below the tree, and just as it had been at the council table, Samira and Zayir sat on either side of her. The rest of the council fanned out around them until only five seats remained, and these we took, completing the circle.

Drawing a deep breath, Damiane began the ceremony: "Long ago, before your prison, before this place, was the Dae Spira."

28

The old man before the fire thrust his gnarled fingers inside the pouch in his lap and withdrew a handful of what appeared to be perfectly ordinary dirt. He held it aloft, and then with great ceremony, he flung it into the flames. They roared to life, hungry and hot, and as they rose high into the night, the goddess took shape before me, made of earth and ember and smoke, familiar to me now with her billowing veils and crown of branches and fire.

"She walked alone through trees still young, feet forging paths others would one day follow, hands shaping clearings and glades, the trailing shadows of her veils bestowing mist," intoned Damiane.

The old man lifted his hands, his fingers weaving patterns in the air—and above the Dae Spira, a glowing speck grew into a sphere of firelight, her hands rising to hold it fast. I lifted my face to the glow, just as I'd done that first night I'd stood before her likeness and let her power pour over me.

"The Incuna. It was her gift to us," Damiane continued. "Our soil grew rich and our waters ran clear, and the people within her care flourished and thrived within the shelter of the forest."

In the flames below the Dae Spira, I saw the figures of people planting, ploughing, fishing, weaving. Children darted about their legs, laughing, and they sang at their looms as they wove cloth. Hands carved the wood of the great trees, and little by little, a village grew before my very eyes, and those within it lived in perfect harmony with the natural world around them, made lush and fertile by the Incuna.

"As the years passed, we found that some of us were able to wield the power of the Incuna for ourselves, and thus did we become the people of Nymet Nata."

The people within the flames now nourished the crops with their own hands, called water and vine and root, healed one another, shaped wood and stone and minerals at will.

"Their city of trees grew, and so did their minds and imaginations," said Damiane. "They began to write down their history, their stories, and knowledge became a prize sought and passed down through the generations."

Rows of children sat eagerly before teachers as they learned the symbols of their written language, how to weave them together to form words and sentences. Slate tablets gave way to scrolls of parchment, then to books, at first primitively bound like the ones in Kevren's stillroom, then in leather and dye and gilt, worthy of the knowledge possessed within their pages.

"And then came the throne."

Above the glowing sphere of the Incuna, still suspended above the flourishing kingdom, roots and tendrils appeared, woven by the old man's hands, and even as they encircled the source, binding it as fast as the Dae Spira's hands below, they crawled atop one another, stretching high into the night sky to form a throne, savage in its beauty; I recognized it at once.

I gasped and cried: "Anwar's throne!"

Damiane's eyes found me across the flames. "Not yet," she

chided softly. "Patience, Briony, and all will be revealed. We needed a leader, so great had we become; a leader blessed and beloved of the Incuna, chosen by the Dae Spira to channel the power—*her* power—to the land."

Wreathed in flame, a face appeared, and I found, much to my astonishment, that she was familiar to me.

"I know her," I said softly. "I've seen her portrait."

"Her name was Amiyet," Damiane told me. "She was the first."

Other faces followed hers, a dizzying blur of men and women, girls and boys, nothing alike between them other than the Dae Spira had chosen them as vessels through which the magic of the Incuna flowed strongest. Always upon their brow was the crown of wood and flame, and always in their hands were the keys.

"This is what you saw," said Elyan softly at my side, and I could do nothing but nod. I felt his fingers brush my own, tentatively, and a rush of breath escaping me, I grasped his hand with such force I felt surely I caused him pain, but he bore it with no evidence.

"What do you think is in that dirt, exactly?" I heard Arlo whisper to Thaniel at my other side, and a moment later: "Ow."

The faces within the flames disappeared leaving only one: a man with a strong, square jaw and merciless eyes; eyes I knew all too well.

"His name was Aliem," Damiane said. "And when dozens of men and women appeared from the south, claiming to be escaped prisoners of the tower upon the moor, he graciously offered them a home amongst his people. And in doing so, he doomed us all."

The old man looked to her, his hand poised over his bag of precious earth, and her eyes were full of sorrow as she nodded. He drew a second handful and cast the dirt into the flames.

The image of Aliem disappeared, devoured by tongues of fire, and in his place, men and women came forth, dressed much as we had been, and with fire in their hands. At the sight of them, a cold fear seized me despite the lick of flame at my face.

"Your people were welcomed here despite the misdeeds of their past, for they expressed with sincerity the desire for a fresh start," Damiane continued, though her voice was tight now, with barely repressed anger. "And we marveled at the wonders they could perform without a connection to the Incuna."

In the flames, our people bid water rise, shaped wood, plied metals, spoke to animals, and helped crops flourish. They soothed injuries and troubled dreams, and perhaps worst of all, for I knew how such magic welcomed fear into the hearts of men, they bid the dead to rise.

"The Incuna strengthened their magic, as it does yours, and they used it to help us, so grateful were they to be free. They also told us of Tiralaen, beyond the Gate, and the way of life they'd known there, so very different from our own."

The Citadel at the heart of the Shining City rose before us, earth forming its great walls and towers and turrets, the glow of the flames emanating from its many windows. The old man's hands came briefly together, drew apart; the great doors opened and we were suddenly inside traveling down halls I recognized from my childhood, however fleeting my time within them. Beside me, Elyan gasped softly and I realized he'd not seen the likeness of his birthright in thirteen years.

"As their power grew, so too did their influence," Damiane continued, and the Citadel collapsed into clouds of dirt, reforming into an incurvate table I recognized immediately. Aliem was at its head, and around him were seated men and women of the forest, but it was our kind who sat closest to the king, and he looked not at all to his own people, but only to the Mages at his right and left.

"For, you see, they fawned over Aliem as if he were a king like they had known back in Tiralaen. They flattered him and bowed to him, and this was much to his liking. And he began to lust for the power and wealth that the newcomers assured him was his due. With their magic, they said, they could remake the forest kingdom into the likeness of Tiralaen. And so, when they asked to see the Incuna, Aliem was all too willing to oblige them."

The statue of the Dae Spira appeared before us once more, the glowing sphere of the Incuna held aloft, and before her was the luminous water, and all around her were the walls of twisted roots and vines. They were aglow—all of them—in a way they'd never been before my eyes.

The old man drew his arms wide, then slapped his palms together so hard I felt a shudder pass through me. The fire roared to life, claiming the Incuna completely, devouring it in unhinged jaws of flame, and then, just as quickly, it all collapsed upon itself, leaving nothing but a bed of glowing coals.

I watched the old man carefully, for here at last was what I desired most to see: the truth that the Dae Spira so desperately wished me to know. He moved his fingers slowly at first, eyes closed and lips soundlessly whispering words in an ancient tongue. Coils of firelight began to rise, and they were black; black with a heart of green.

"Have you seen a blackout, Briony of Asperfell?" Damiane asked me, and her eyes met mine across the rising fire, throwing her strong features into sharp relief.

"I have," I whispered. "Four, now."

"And what do you believe they are?"

"I was told it was your people causing them. That you've been stealing power from the Incuna, causing the palace to be overtaken by the forest."

She laughed. "Is that what they've told you? No, the palace isn't being overtaken by the forest. It is returning to it."

Into the black and green flames, the old man tossed one last handful of dirt, and before me rose a strange place, a hallowed place; I had no memory of it, could not recall its name, and yet it was familiar to me, as though perhaps I'd seen it in dreams.

Its halls were wrought of modest stone, hand-hewn and roughly shaped, though each and every one fit together quite harmoniously. Its windows were large and airy, beckoning the outside world in—and oh, did it rush in, filling the liminal space languidly with green, curling and twining and embracing, touched with light and dappled with water.

Heads bowed before altars, wreathed and crowned, women in white sang hymns to their goddess in voices unheard in the centuries since. They carved her likeness with hands full of magic, and they tended her gardens, learned to heal, and wrote down their wisdom and their stories. In a humble refectory, they gathered together over simple food, and when the people of the towering trees sought remedies or advice or sometimes even sanctuary, they gave it, guided in all things by the Dae Spira and the Incuna at their feet.

"What is this place?" I asked.

Damiane tilted her head. "You do not recognize it? Perhaps you are used to seeing it quite differently."

The old man, it seemed, had been waiting for her acquiescence, for at her nod, his hands began to move and the image to change.

The vines slithered away, retreated from sight, and the gray stones turned white. No longer rough and uneven, they were pristine, perfect, and shot through with gold. The halls grew, the vaulting stretched, the windows with it, and panes of stained glass grew within them. The black and green flames that lit them grew fat and golden, set within sconces of gold and chandeliers dripping with crystal. Trees were replaced with statues and fountains, and the moss upon the walls made way for gilt and rich wood paneling.

A pair of doors, once lovingly carved from the wood but now smothered in gold, flew open to reveal a cavernous hall beneath a glass dome and a night full of stars. Only one thing alone remained unchanged—could not be changed, not by any magic of this world or ours—and that was the savage throne of grasping, twisted wood.

Elyan's hand gripped mine tightly as the same realization flooded through him. "By the Gods," he gasped. "It was never a palace. It was—"

"A temple," I finished. "*Her* temple."

"It was a holy place, not meant for mortals," said Damiane, her eyes closed and her voice bitter. "But Aliem claimed it as his own seat of power. And so, he uprooted the throne from its rightful home beneath the boughs of the Uuna Tree where the Dendor had made it, and he planted it anew above the Incuna itself. And there, under the guiding hands of his Mages, its roots sought ever downward toward the source of power, worming its way to the heart of our magic."

"But why?" I gasped.

"From the moment your people saw it, saw the Incuna, truly felt its power, they knew that with its amplification of their magic, they could create whatever they wanted. And what they wanted was life as they'd known it in their old world. And so, they took it."

The Incuna diminished before my eyes.

"Before the Mages of Asperfell arrived," continued Damiane,

her voice somewhat softer now, "Aliem had been considered a fair
ruler of the Forest Kingdom. He was kind, though quick to anger;
generous to a fault, though he favored those in his inner circle
above all others; and he was charming.

"His predecessor, a woman named Filieh, had not been
charming. She had been straight-faced and stern, with little to no
humor to be found within her, and Aliem had not cared for her at
all. It was thus most vexing to him when, after she died and he was
chosen to replace her, she was spoken of as one of the greatest rulers
the Incuna had ever chosen.

"Aliem's ego was frail, made frailer still by the Filieh's shadow,
and so, when two dozen strangers from another world blundered
into his kingdom, he saw an opportunity to establish himself as the
greatest of all who had come before him. Their magic would be his
triumph. They would build great things together, and his reign
would be remembered forever.

"They spoke of wonders, these Mages, of a palace at the center
of a city of prosperity and progress, of education and commerce and
fashion, of marvels he could only imagine, and he had never had
much imagination. One of them, a man who had been a confidant
of Tiralaen's king until he had a mind to betray him, was an
Illusionist—and oh, the images he conjured!

"Aliem could scarcely believe the beauty of the Citadel, the
majesty of its splendid halls and ceilings of glass and gold; Nymet
Nata could scarce compare, and he began to think it very dull,
indeed.

"Desperate to curry their favor, desperate for their respect, he
showed them the Incuna. He'd not known, of course, what effect it
might have on the otherworldly magic in their blood, but the
change it brought upon them was immediate and intoxicating.

They began to have whispered conversations amongst themselves, secret conversations at night, behind closed doors, and Aliem began to resent them most bitterly.

"That was, of course, until they revealed the reason for these clandestine meetings: they wished to bestow upon him a mighty gift, greater than the sum of all the riches of Nymet Nata; a gift that would ensure his legacy forever.

"A palace.

"It would rival even their own Citadel, they promised him, and a village would grow up around it, and his people would thrive, and they would love him.

"He agreed right away, for their conditions were perfectly agreeable: places upon his counsel, in his court. Some measure of influence upon his governance. A pittance, really, for what they offered.

"Of course, they could not conjure such a thing out of thin air, and Nymet Nata had little in the way of resources, save trees; endless trees. No, what they needed to make their palace was the Incuna itself, and the temple that enshrined it.

"Aliem hesitated at that. The temple was sacred, and he feared angering the goddess who had chosen him to rule, feared losing his sacred connection to the Incuna.

"But, in the end, the temptation proved too great. And, really, why shouldn't the temple be his palace, for the whole of the Forest Kingdom was his by her divine will and grace. The Mages assured him it was certainly so, and Aliem allowed himself to be convinced."

"I cannot imagine your people reacted well to having their temple so defiled," Thaniel spoke up. "Surely there were repercussions?"

Damiane nodded. "A war," she answered. "A very short one.

"After that, everything seemed just as the Mages had promised:

Aliem's gilded palace was magnificent beyond anything that the king of Tiralaen could ever hope to build in the old world, and the new village outside its walls grew with each passing season.

"Aliem was happy for a while, and the Mages celebrated him most lavishly. But when his son was born, a secret dread crept into the king's heart. He despaired that one day, when he was dead and his bones lay within the Ita Hypogaeum, his son would not sit upon the throne and rule the people, nor be allowed to live within the palace, nor carry on his father's legacy.

"No, the Dae Spira would choose another not of his blood, and all he had built, all he wished to build, would be stolen away from his children and given unto the hands of a stranger.

"'It wouldn't be difficult to defy her,' the Mages crooned. And they could help him! After all, were they not friends and counselors? Had they not built wondrous things for him with their magic and his own? They'd no wish to see his family cast out, nor to see his people return to their savage ways in the forest, little more than animals, bereft of all that had been bestowed upon them by King Aliem, the greatest and most accomplished of all kings, whose life should be celebrated forever.

"And this one fear above all else, even the love of his son, finally won Aliem's heart over to the Mages' sinister urging: he could not tolerate the idea that his people might ever again live as they did under Filieh's rule and not as they did now, under his.

"Aliem repeated this fear over and over to himself, and eventually to his son, like a hymn, like a song, until it became their truth.

"And when the father drew his last breath and the Incuna chose a woman named Tabras to succeed him, the son took her life with terrifying ease, a deed he'd been trained his entire life to perform.

"Sephrem was the son's name, and he declared himself chosen, never mind the fact that the Dae Spira had never before bestowed the honor upon two generations of the same family before. It was a sign, he said, that the Dae Spira was well pleased with all Aliem had done, and that they must carry on his legacy and embrace the new ways, and forget the old entirely.

"And he renamed the kingdom in his father's honor, that he might never be forgotten.

"It was easy enough to convince his court, and eventually the village accepted his words, but the people who remained in the forest—those who still lived within the great trees of Nymet Nata—saw through the lies at last.

"From that moment on, our people were forever cleaved.

"In the years that followed, the Mages who had fled Asperfell began to die off one by one, though not before mingling the treasure of their blood with that of our people. Soon, Sephrem found that, to his horror, the children of Mages, whether of half-blood or full, could little use their power, for there was no one to teach them how to do so."

I thought she would continue, but instead she looked to the old man with a solemn nod. He lowered his hands, and with them, the palace of smoke and ash and dirt collapsed into the fire. Tongues of black and green rose to devour it, bearing it down into the coals until nothing remained but smoldering embers. Then the old man snapped his fingers and the fire was as before: a merry orange blaze.

Across the flames, Damiane fixed her eyes upon me.

"Do you see now why your arrival was so fortuitous to King Anwar, and why he is so desperate for you to stay?"

They were watching me, the people of the forest, most with keen interest, others with doubt. Kevren smiled encouragingly as my gaze fell upon him; his sister decidedly less so.

"Please believe me when I say I am no one of significance," I said at last. "The Dae Spira only chose me because I am an Orare. Because I can speak to magic... and understand it."

Zayir steepled his fingers together as he observed me with thoughtful eyes. "Your magic is not our magic."

"Just as the Incuna amplified our predecessors' magic, so too is ours strengthened in its presence," Elyan reminded him.

"I cannot speak to the Incuna," I admitted. "But the Dae Spira can speak to me. And yet, I wish it were not so. Heeding her call has brought me nothing but sorrow. I have betrayed the trust of my friends and exposed them to danger of the greatest kind, so fully did I believe I was meant to help her. But you are right, Zayir, and I was wrong: I am not the one to whom your goddess should reveal herself. Do not for one moment imagine I do not bitterly regret leaving my bed the night when first she summoned me."

The dour expression upon his face did not alter, but neither did he challenge me further.

It was Samira who spoke next: "But she did reveal herself to you, worthy or not. Now, I believe it is time for you to live up to your agreement and share the story of your calling with us."

And so I began my story.

29

By the time I finished my tale, the fire was but dim ashes, and no one spoke for a very long time.

"So the village is cut off from the Incuna," Damiane said at last, and the weight in her voice, the regret, was suffocating. "Nymet Nata less so, though that day will come. In time, it will be devoured entirely by Anwar and his descendants."

"Has Anwar any connection at all to the Incuna?" asked Elyan.

Kevren shifted where he sat beside Thaniel, offering an apologetic shrug as he answered: "From what we've been able to tell, if he does, it is extremely weak. No one has ever seen him do so much as conjure a Lumen."

"It is the Court Eternal who sustain the palace and the riches within it," Damiane said. "They are chosen to join the court because of their strong connection to the Incuna, and they are rewarded with lives of wealth and decadence until their dying day, so long as they continue to maintain the spellwork."

"Rewarded?" I said. "I wonder how many would describe it thus. For all the leisure and luxury afforded the court, I cannot think of a one of them who seemed truly happy there."

"Nor I," mused Elyan. "But, boon or curse, if magic is not

reliably inherited from parent to child, where are these new members of the court found?"

"An astute question," said Damiane. "And a sad one."

"They're stolen from the village," I breathed, and I remembered a frightened little girl running through the pleasure gardens. Rosael had been her name, and she had begged me to let her go home—her *real* home.

"A connection to the Incuna manifests itself quite early in children of our kind—almost from birth," said Damiane. "Most are young enough to forget entirely their lives before."

Elyan's brows drew together. "So many crimes. So much tragedy. And all for the selfish glory of one family."

"*Not* for one family alone," said Zayir, and his fierceness of his gaze rested wholly upon Elyan. "You forget who was the power behind the throne. It is your ancestors who are the true architects of all this madness. So confident were they in their own superiority that they recklessly sought to remake our civilization in your likeness, rending our kingdom in two and despoiling all we had built for ourselves. That is the true legacy of your people in our world, your highness. And you dare to ask us for help finding your cave? So you can simply walk away from the mess your people created?"

Damiane held up one hand. "It is Samira's decision to make, Zayir. Not yours."

Zayir's jaw clenched, but he did not appear keen to contradict her further.

"When did Anwar's father die?" asked Elyan, his eyes flitting between Samira and her father.

"Nearly five years ago."

"And when he died, did the Dae Spira select a new sovereign for her people?"

"No, for Anwar's father was never the rightful king, and so his death did not necessitate a new Choosing. There was already a queen who, by rights, should have been seated on the throne—a young woman named Isabis. She was a member of the Court Eternal."

I did not need to ask what had befallen her, for it was horrifyingly evident: Anwar had disposed of her and stolen her throne. How many times had his father done the same? And his father before him, all the way back to Aliem.

Instead, I asked: "When this woman died, did the goddess choose another?"

"She did—almost one year ago. Only this time, the Dae Spira chose one of our own. And we have protected her ever since. Because she yet lives, hope yet lives."

The breath was ripped from my lungs in a rush. "What? The chosen ruler is here? Who is it?"

But I already knew.

It is Samira's decision to make, Damiane had said. Because it was Samira's throne upon which Anwar sat.

Across the flames, her eyes met mine, and there was pride in them, though her manner was reticent, as if still unused to her own power, her own position; she was, after all, still very young.

"How perfectly marvelous," I said, a wide grin spreading across my face, and slowly she smiled in return.

Elyan leaned forward. "Does Anwar know of Samira and what she is?"

"He knows another Choosing has occurred, and he has exhaustively searched the court as well as the village. We can only assume that he harbors some suspicion that the Incuna's chosen dwells among us."

"Will you attempt to unseat him?"

Silence fell upon the clearing as Samira and Zayir looked to Damiane. She, in turn, studied us all for a very long time before she rose to her feet.

"We've said much this night," she said. "I believe it best that we refrain from further questions until the morning, when our heads and hearts are clear."

It was not a request but an order, however politely given, and none amongst us seemed keen to contradict her.

The fire was nothing but a vast bed of coals now, glowing hearts smothered by cooling black, and in the dim light afforded by the lanterns that ringed the sacred grove, the members of Damiane's council stood one by one and disappeared into the darkness, following the path that would lead them back to Uuna Tree and the warmth of their hearths. The story we'd just been told was already known to them; it would not haunt them the way I knew it would me as I lay in my lonely bed that night, unable to close my eyes for fear *she* would appear.

"Briony!" a warm, rich voice called, and I turned to see Kevren striding toward me. "I wanted to tell you. Believe me, I wanted to tell you everything, but you were still guests within his walls and I could not risk it."

"It's all right," I assured him. "I understand, truly I do."

"I hope you realize now that what you did for Cylene was no small thing."

"I only wish I could help the others who will come after her," I sighed. "I've the knowledge I wanted now, and yet I've never felt more powerless."

"You certainly are not," said Damiane from behind, approaching us with quick steps. Her hand landed upon Kevren's shoulder, and she said to him: "That Alchemist of yours is looking for you. Go now, and I'll escort Briony back to the Uuna Tree."

Kevren offered me a smile before he turned and loped back down the path.

"Your heart is heavy, I think," said Damiane.

"I am glad of the weight, for now I understand."

"It is a burden," she agreed. "But it is one I believe you are capable of carrying."

It was not enough simply to carry it, but this I did not say; not yet.

When we reached the Uuna Tree, Damiane offered to escort me back to my chamber, but I could not think of sleep until I'd seen Phyra, if not to tell her everything that had transpired that night, then to assure myself that she was well and hale. Shamefaced and heartsick, I told Damiane then of all that had transpired in the village and of Phyra's torment beneath the knife of the Skin Weaver, all because of my recklessness and naivety.

"I think perhaps you judge yourself too harshly," she said when my confession was made.

"You are kind," I winced. "But from the moment the Dae Spira appeared to me, I've thought of little else. It was my blindness that brought her into danger and nearly delivered her to her own death."

When we arrived at Phyra's chamber, I was surprised to hear voices within: Arlo's, and one I did not recognize.

The Naturalist was sprawled insouciantly in a chair while a lively woman in her middle years bustled about the room, seeing to the Lumen in the grate, stoking its light and heat through her magic, her connection to the Incuna. I knew her at once to be Kallee, Samira and Kevren's mother, for her soft cheeks and easy smile were a mirror for her son's. Once the Lumen was merrily ablaze, she bent over a clay pot and poured the contents into a cup.

"There, now," she said cheerfully, and handed the cup to Phyra, who reclined against a mound of pillows upon a bed similar to the one in my own chamber. "A bit of warmth and a posset will set you to rights."

Steam rising about her face, Phyra brought the cup to her lips, drinking long and deep. Then she caught sight of me lingering in her doorway.

I fiddled with my skirts. "I don't mean to intrude."

"Nonsense," Kallee clucked. "She's been asking about you, and about the gathering! I imagine you've much to impart."

"Indeed," I agreed. My glance flickered to Arlo, still sprawled in the chair. "Might I have a word with Phyra alone?"

He made a show of righting himself, dropping his feet to the floor and heaving himself upright. "Fine. I know well enough where I'm not wanted, though I cannot imagine why anyone wouldn't want me around."

"Well, I don't mind having you around," Kallee chuckled. "I quite enjoy that singing of yours."

"Kallee, you absolute fiend, I *knew* you fancied me." He followed her to the doorway, then turned to glance back at Phyra, the devious glint in his eyes softening as he took her in. "Will you be all right?"

"Good night," she answered softly.

"We missed you tonight," I told her, once Kallee had disappeared down the hall, Arlo on her heels. "Have you been well looked after?"

"Kallee has been most kind. Though I fear you are in more need of her ministrations than I."

"Me?" I scoffed, clamoring upon her bed and drawing my knees to my chin. "I'm not the one who was nearly flayed yesterday."

She regarded me in that solemn, thoughtful way of hers, her eyes betraying nothing. "I have healed well enough."

I'd meant to take delicate care with my words so that she could be in no doubt as to my sincerity; but subtlety, it seemed, eluded me still. I clutched her hands tightly, and words poured from me, rushing faster and faster as though a dam had broken.

"Oh, Phyra, I am so, so sorry. More sorry than you can ever know. If it weren't for me, you wouldn't have had to heal at all. I was reckless and stupid and, oh Gods, *so* selfish. I never should have stopped the driver that day—we never should've gotten out of the carriage! It was my fault, all of it was my fault, and I can only hope that you will one day forgive me."

She watched in soft silence as I babbled on, my face alight and burning, my grip tight enough to shatter bone, and yet she did not pull away. When at last I could think of nothing else to say that might properly convey my thoughtlessness, my utter disregard for one so beloved to me, I slumped back, shamefaced.

"Do you remember what I told you the night I took you into my Deathscape?"

Of all the things for her to have said, this I had not expected. "You told me many things," I answered slowly.

"What a splendid reputation you have cultivated."

My mouth twisted bitterly. "For endangering those I love at the expense of my own desires, I suppose you mean."

"You do me a disservice by believing that you are the only one."

"But you are not... you do not—"

"Do not think for one moment I did not know exactly what it was that I risked when I raised the boy; not only for myself, but for you and Arlo."

I declared fiercely: "I would have had you do no less."

"Nor would I you," she answered. "For such is the nature of love. You make choices, you do what you think is right, and you must allow others the same, even if the risk is great, even if they suffer regret. To do so is their choice, and theirs alone."

"Surely you cannot regret your choice—the boy lives."

She thought to draw her hand from mine, but I held fast. And so, with a tight, sad smile, she instead laced her fingers through my own and squeezed so tightly that I winced.

"When I plead for life, I must prove that there is reason for that life to continue; that there is balance to be found," Phyra said. "'Twas not so with the boy."

"Then how were you able to raise him?"

She was silent so long I feared she'd told me all she was willing, her eyes fixed firmly on our entwined fingers. At last, she lifted her gaze, and my breath caught, for in her eyes darkness gathered.

"Death's envoy told me that, should I desire the boy's life, I must trade another for it, another life in the village."

The horror of it quite stole my breath from me, and I sat in perfect stillness, watching the tendrils of black coil into the whites of her eyes as she spoke. "I begged for him to be the one to choose, but he would not acquiesce, for he wished me to feel it; to feel the weight of the choice."

She'd agreed, of course; I'd seen the boy reborn, gasping for breath as he reached for a mother repulsed by that which she'd loved when lifeless. "Who did you choose?"

"The envoy did not demand a name right away, only a commitment to choose. I gave it, and the boy was returned to us." She closed her eyes then, and when she opened them again, no white at all was left in them. "Almost immediately, I thought the choice made for me."

"The mother," I said.

"After the way she rejected her son, yes" she answered flatly. "But I was not without pity, for her ignorance and fear were cultivated by another, and so I chose him instead. One who was truly deserving."

"The Skin Weaver," I whispered, remembering all too well the life being stolen from his face, just as Phyra'd done with the Borage blossom in the Healer's Garden at Asperfell. "I stopped you."

"I know why you did."

"You should have told me!"

"Would you have stood idly by if I had?" The black had disappeared at last; perhaps become a part of her, the way that Death was ever her constant companion.

"You are not a killer."

"Whether I am or not is my choice. You cannot make it for me, not even if you stay my hand."

"What will become of the boy?" I whispered. "Oh Gods, Phyra, tell me—"

"I did not fulfill our bargain," she said simply, and the horrible truth settled into my bones.

It had all been for naught, then, everything that she had suffered. The boy had died after all, and the Skin Weaver lived.

"I hate this," I shuddered, and my voice was far too harsh and severe for this warm, peaceful place. "I hate that you must endure such pain for the sake of your aptitude. Would that I could take it from you, make it my own. Bear the burden for you, for just a little while."

"But you cannot," she answered. "For our magic is within our blood, determined before we are born, and we must find within ourselves that which is strong enough to accept it."

Damiane had spoken of my strength, but I realized then that it paled in comparison to this woman whom I had thought fragile once, like vapor, but was of steel stronger than any Thaniel could forge.

I looked down at our hands, one brown, one pale and freckled, entwined as fiercely as my love for her, and everything I wished to tell her, everything I wished to ask her crowded my throat until I could not breathe for it all.

She squeezed my hand tightly. "Now, tell me: what did you learn at the gathering?"

And so, I recounted for her everything that had occurred in the grove in as much detail as I could remember. The Lumen shrank in the grate as we talked into the night, and we conjured Magefire in our hands to continue our conversation. When at last I came to the end, I found that, having spoken it aloud, I felt a curious sort of peace, that which came from clarity, and from reflection.

"And what shall we do now that we know the truth?" she asked, smoothing down the blankets upon her lap.

It did not escape me, her use of *we* rather than *you*, and a warmth settled deep within me that had nothing at all to do with the fire in our hands.

"In truth, I do not know. But perhaps a good night's sleep will make the path ahead a bit clearer."

I made to stand, then hesitated, for there was one last thing I would know, and no one save her that I might ask.

"The night of the ball, when I went to the stillroom to get a posset for myself... there is something I must ask, only..."

"You speak of Thaniel," she said, and when I lifted my head, I found that she was smiling. "And of Kevren."

"You knew?"

"Of course I knew."

"Forgive me, I thought for so long that you and he—that you were—"

"He is my dearest friend. And I shall always love him as such. That is all."

'Twas exactly as Elyan had said. "But then why did he look at me the way he did? As though he were afraid of me?"

She reached out and touched my cheek lightly with the tip of one finger. "Do you wish the truth, or a very lovely lie?"

I swallowed hard. "I wish I could accept the lie, but I think you know I will always choose the truth, however much it hurts."

"Very well," she said. "Thaniel knows you carry strong opinions of those whom you do not favor, and that you are free with these opinions."

I would have sworn to anyone in that moment that my heart stopped altogether. "He believes I do not find favor with him? Because of Kevren?"

"He fears that you see him as less now that you know."

"Why, that's... that's utterly... that is to say—*what*?"

Phyra chuckled. "I told him something quite similar, only with slightly more eloquence."

"But he did not believe you."

"He did not," she answered. "Love such as his and Kevren's is not well accepted in Tiralaen, and even less so among its noble families, who cling so tightly to their traditions and propriety."

"But do I not often mock such pointless propriety when it flies in the face of pragmatism and reason?"

"You do mock these things," she said slowly, "and much else besides. And Thaniel... Well, he has often been subject to mockery and gossip, even by those who had been his dear friends, once they learned the truth."

I desperately wanted to argue, to be offended at his assumptions of me. And yet, had he not seen me so very often making sport of those whose behavior I found lacking? Especially the men and their indiscretions, their illicit romances, their carnality, and the failings of their restraint and fortitude.

I longed to protest that it was for their hypocrisy, and for the inequity and pain to women, that I despised such things in men. Such was the truth, or mostly so—surely Phyra must understand that!

But how could I expect Thaniel to know it? Believing myself safe in the company of a friend, I'd hardly held my tongue, particularly when there was Laetha involved, and I had filled many long nights beneath the stars regaling my companions with stories of the prancing fools of King Gavreth's court and their personal failings and how ridiculous I found them all.

Why should he not think that with my unruly mouth, my insensitive mouth, he might become one such story, another unfortunate subject of my ridicule and judgment?

Miserably, I lowered my head. "I am the fool, not he. I have behaved most appallingly to give him cause to distrust me so."

"If so, then we are all fools, for none of us know fully the lives of others, what paths they have tread, or the fears awakened along the way. But we may learn of them by speaking together. That is your especial gift, is it not? If your rift was caused by your words, then perhaps they might also mend it."

I sighed. "It is not only Thaniel whom I have wronged."

She reached out and stroked my hair gently. "Elyan."

"He asked me to marry him," I said, tongue thick in my mouth. "And I refused."

"You love him."

"With everything that I am. But there are complications, reasons why we should not, cannot be together."

"They must be very important reasons indeed," she said mildly. "I ask you only to remember what I said about the nature of love. And of choice."

She would say no more, and indeed, even if I had wished it, the pallor of her skin and the pronounced bruises beneath her eyes were enough to deter me.

I stayed with her in silence a while, until she was half-asleep against the pillows, and then I tucked the blanket around her and took my leave.

Thaniel stood just outside Phyra's chamber, and as I emerged into the dimly lit corridor, he pushed away from the wall where he'd been leaning, waiting; I wondered how long he had been there.

"How is she?" he asked.

"I've exhausted her, I'm afraid. Best wait until morning."

He shifted on the balls of his feet. "Actually, it's you I've been waiting for. We've not had a chance to speak since that night in the stillroom," he began, rubbing the back of his head and looking everywhere but at me. "And I—"

"I am so sorry I ran from you. I should have stayed, but you looked upon me with such fear. And I'd only just left Phyra..."

"Phyra?" he said. "What does Phyra have to do with it?"

"I thought you and she intimately connected. And when I saw you and Kevren, I thought you had betrayed her."

He raked a hand through his golden hair. "Briony—"

"No," I said. "No, please let me speak. I am so sorry that I have given you cause to doubt me, and fear my judgment. I have behaved rather appallingly toward those whom I find ridiculous, and you've witnessed it all."

"Well," he acquiesced, "we've encountered many a ridiculous person."

"I will not disagree with you, but my treatment of them has led you to believe that I might judge you similarly. Is that not so?"

The guilt in his eyes answered my question more than words ever could, and although I'd already known it to be truth, the foreknowledge did little to pry loose the fingers that grasped my heart at the telling of it.

"For all your adamance to the contrary, you are a well-born woman of good family," he said. "I do not think you would ever be caught alone in a stillroom with a man who is not your husband, to say nothing of a person of your own sex. You've mocked many a fool for far less."

"I am a self-righteous fool," I admitted. "But there is something I think you should know about me. While it's true that you could not catch me in a stillroom engaged such as you were, the same is not true for all other rooms in the palace."

I was proud to see that I brought a blush to his cheek with my confession—and relieved, for my own face burned quite hotly.

"That was not easy for me to admit," I said.

"I believe you," he said, and there was a soft smile upon his face.

"I had to say it, however, because I want you to know that I do not hold myself above you, Thaniel."

"Not even for loving a man?"

I grasped both his hands in mine and looked into his sky-blue eyes. "I know your heart, Thaniel, and it is a good one. Kind and honest and valiant. And if your heart loves Kevren, I do not begrudge its choice, nor judge you for it, and I never shall. *Never.*"

He exhaled and pulled me into his arms, crushing me against him such that I let out a most undignified squeak and he laughed, though I could not discern whether I was the cause or if he could no longer contain his relief.

"Thank the Gods," he said, his chin resting upon my head. "For I could not have done without you."

He drew back, his hands heavy and warm in the most wonderful way upon my shoulders as we regarded one another. "In Tiralaen, I hid my true self, but at Asperfell, there was such glorious freedom. Perhaps I did not speak of it aloud, but neither did anyone else, and I was allowed to simply exist as I was. And it seemed to me a wonderful thing, for it did not occur to me that I might ever find a place where a love such as mine was truly free, not before—"

"Before this place," I said. "Nymet Nata."

His whisper was full: "But we cannot stay."

Here was a pain I understood all too well.

"I've never met anyone like Kevren," he said, and he held my hands as fiercely as though, should he let go, he might be borne away upon a great wave, never again to see the shore. "And I don't believe I ever shall. Gods, Briony, how am I to live without him?"

Bending low, I pressed a kiss to his knuckles and whispered as much to him as to myself: "As best you can."

30

Unaccustomed to the chill in the night air now that we were farther from the Incuna, I'd buried myself so deeply under the covers of my bed that when I finally came awake under the prompting of urgent hands, it took several attempts to untangle and present myself to what I fully expected to be the Dae Spira's veiled form by my bedside.

Illuminated by black and green flames, it was Damiane's face instead that emerged from the darkness.

"Get up, Briony. We've a visitor from Syr'Aliem who would speak with you."

I stared at her, my eyes still blurry with unshed sleep. "Who?"

But she did not answer me; she swept from the room, taking the light with her. Shivering in the thin fabric of my nightdress, I grabbed one of the blankets from the bed and, wrapping it about myself, followed her into the corridor. Elyan, Thaniel, and Arlo waited for us, and the wariness in my eyes was mirrored in their own, for behind them were no less than a dozen men and women, fully armed.

We marched down the corridor or and through the bowels of Uuna Tree until we emerged into the velvet darkness where the two forest paths met. We took the path to the left, the path to the Dendor, and at the entrance to the Dendor's cave, we found Zayir and Samira standing guard, awaiting our arrival.

"Where are we going?" Elyan asked Damiane, his voice sharp in the steeply descending stairs as we passed by the Dendor's vestibule.

"I had hoped to show you this place tomorrow, and under different circumstances," she answered. "But our visitor has made doing so impossible."

The tunnel surrounding us widened, and by the light of the flames in my hand, I managed to make out an archway of stone lying ahead at the bottom of the stairs. Two ancient lanterns stood ready on either side, and Damiane's people stepped forward to fill them with Lumens, bright and strong.

As we passed beneath the archway, we stepped into a place familiar to me, though I had never seen it. The stone floor and walls were carpeted by the same mosses and flowers and vines as the Place of Ways, but there was no Incuna here, of course, only a single door at the far end of the cavern, ancient and weathered, set into an archway carved with familiar symbols like those I'd seen etched above the Ita Hypogaeum.

The door was open wide, and within stood a solitary figure.

Clad in a cloak and hood made of pure silver and gold, I recognized her pale, flawless beauty at once, cold and serene within the shimmering folds. It was an impossibility that she should be here in this place, until I saw what was held in her delicate, white hands: a ring of ancient bronze from which hung two heavy keys.

Princess Evolet had opened the door to the Ita Hominaeum; this was where it led.

"Your highness," I stammered when at last I'd found voice enough to speak.

She held up one hand inquiringly, for the men and women behind me held their weapons aloft and ready, as if they expected Syr'Aliem's army to pour through the door at any moment and lay waste to their city.

Zayir moved past me, unsheathing a long, curved blade as he did. "How dare you set foot in this sacred place!"

Indeed, Princess Evolet was made of far sturdier mettle than I'd ever imagined, for there was no change in her impassive demeanor, even in the face of such provocation. "I've come to speak to Briony Tenebrae, and with her alone."

"You have no power here," he raged.

"You are wrong, for I wield the power of the Incuna."

"As do I," a voice rang out, and Samira pushed past Damiane to stand defiantly before the princess. "You are not welcome here."

"I wish to be here no more than you wish me here," Evolet answered. "I am quite content to turn around and go back without delivering my message to Briony, but it will be your people who suffer for it if I do."

Samira looked to me, but my gaze was fixed most firmly on the woman I'd thought so many times I'd reasoned out, only to realize once more she had eluded me. I was left once more in doubt as to how I could've ever thought myself clever.

"Stay your weapons, please," I said at last. "I will speak to the princess. Full of surprises she may be, but I do believe she means no harm."

"Her and her family have caused harm enough," Zayir spat.

"Please."

Damiane studied us quite closely, the princess and I, and I wondered what she saw, for perhaps she now doubted my intentions. But a woman of sense was she, and at last she nodded.

"I trust Briony, and if she believes the princess means us no harm, then so, too, do I."

Zayir evidently did not agree, for his narrowed eyes darted between us, his body taut and his weapon ready.

Neither, it seemed, did his daughter, and it was to her that I turned. "Samira, I know she is a stranger to you, and has done nothing to earn your trust, but please, let me hear this message."

She gave me but an acquiescent dip of her chin, but it was enough for the men and women under Damiane's command to lower their weapons.

They left one by one, Zayir last of all, save Elyan.

"She'll be perfectly safe with me, your highness," said Princess Evolet, though her voice dripped with mockery at his concern and hesitation. "But I am glad to have a final word with you as well, for I must bestow credit where it is due. No man has ever refused me as you did."

"Unfortunate, for they ought to have," he said, and with one last look at me, he disappeared through the archway and back up the stairs.

I'd never expected to see her again, but I realized in that moment I was glad to be wrong, for there was so very much more to know. Were it information she sought from me, I would demand the same in return, beginning with—

"You've held the keys to The Ways this entire time," I said, glancing down to the bronze ring clutched in her hands. "Was it you who opened the Ita Hypogaeum on the night of the ball, then, and not the Dae Spira?"

"Me?" she spat. "I cannot think of anything I should desire less than to involve myself with you and your pitiful quest on behalf of the Dae Spira. I must confess that I did not even believe Isri when she told me that she had shown herself to you. I thought their goddess long dead, and besides, what is so special about you?" She laughed then, a mirthless sound. "Your magic, I suppose. Isri certainly thought so. Have you ever wondered why she dislikes you so?"

"Not a whit."

"Indeed?" She smiled at that. "Well, I think I'll tell you anyway. It is because, for some unfathomable reason, the goddess chose you, and she did not believe you equal of the task."

I bit back my rage. "I did not ask for this."

"Neither did I! The Dae Spira should have stayed dead, for this crusade of hers is pointless. There is no going back from where we are now. What's done cannot be undone."

I shook my head. "All is not lost."

"Of course it is," she sneered. "Anwar will father a child with even less of a connection to the Incuna than he, and that child will be miraculously 'chosen' as all of the men in our family have been for generations. The village will wither and rot, and the Incuna sucked dry until there is no more magic in this land."

"You know all this, and still you help him," I said. "Why? Are the balls and the gowns and the *men* worth so much to you?"

"You know nothing."

"Or are you just like your mother? So eager to sacrifice everything for the men of your bloodline? How much of yourself are you willing to give so that he may have everything he wants?"

"However much I must."

"By the Gods, why?" I breathed, shaking at the absurdity of it all.

"Do you know how to stop a forest fire, Briony?"

"What?"

"With more fire. You clear all the land so that the blaze is contained and can burn itself out without spreading."

"I don't understand."

"What do you know of Anwar's wife?" she asked suddenly. "He must have told you about her. No doubt the story wrung tears from your eyes, as he knew it would. Did he tell you that she jumped from a parapet?"

Unease began to unfurl within me, for there was a brightness in her eyes, sharp and feral. "Yes."

"She did no such thing."

Oh Gods, it was too terrible to be true, and yet I knew it was. "He killed her."

"Yes," she said. "He should have done it at once, of course. But he hoped to avoid it altogether by marrying her instead. You see, she was the one chosen by the Incuna for the throne, not he."

"Isabis was his wife?" I gasped.

"By marrying her, he thought to avoid the long chain of assassinations in Syr'Aliem and Nymet Nata that had been necessary throughout the reign of his fathers. And, I dare say, he thought there might be an even greater benefit to marrying someone with such a strong connection to the Incuna. He might, at last, be able to rid himself of me entirely."

"You?"

"What am I but a mask and a shield? By keeping me at his side, my brother hides the fact that he has no magic of his own. That is my purpose, you see. But... if he could take the rightful queen as his wife, she could supplant me entirely, for my magic is nothing compared to hers."

"Why did she agree to this?"

"She was a fool, just like you."

Evolet fell into silence for a long moment, and the weight of it was heavy after the madly shifting current of her thoughts before. Then she said: "From the moment she was chosen, she believed she could unseat him. And once she did, she could restore the proper balance of the Incuna and heal the land. But she could not, and she should not have tried. He cannot be removed."

There was grief in her voice, and though she was far better than I could ever hope to be at concealing that which she felt most deeply, she could not conceal this: her grief was not for her kingdom, nor her brother's ruinous reign, but for Isabis herself.

"You loved her."

"Sometimes I wish I were like my mother," she said, as if I'd not spoken at all. "She was never more content than when she was miserable."

"If only your mother did not esteem sons so much more than daughters, she might have seen you installed upon the throne in place of your brother. You have the very magic he can only pretend to wield."

"You sound just like her. Like Isabis."

"Why should you not take the throne from him? Do what Isabis planned, restore the Incuna to the people of Syr'Aliem—and of Nymet Nata as well?"

Her face twisted in rage, and I knew immediately that I had miscalculated, grasped for a star too high.

"If Isabis could not, what hope might I have?" she bellowed. "No, that foolish dream died with her! There is only one way to end my family's reign over the Forest Kingdom, and that is to end the Forest Kingdom itself!"

I did not shrink back from her, I am proud to say—but neither did I know how to respond, and so I let the heavy silence fill the chamber once more as I considered the full meaning of her words.

"Why do you think Anwar wanted you to stay so very badly?"

My shock at her words—and the perfectly calm and measured way in which she spoke them—rendered me quite without sense. "What did you say?"

"Oh, Briony, come now," she tutted. "And you believe *me* the ignoramus between us. Do you think yourself so alluring that no less than two kings would throw themselves at your feet?"

"I do not know your brother's mind. Indeed, I think I understand him now less than ever."

At this, she gave a bitter smile. "He knows the village is dying, and the palace will fall with it. He has no hope to prevent it—or he had none, until you arrived. Suddenly, he has within his grasp five Mages trained in the very magic that created Syr'Aliem to begin with."

I remembered the king's insatiable curiosity about my training at Asperfell, how long it had taken me to master the simplest spellwork. "He wants us to train your people in our magic?"

"Your magic sleeps in the veins of so many of our people, and yet we know not how to awaken it, nor how to train them in their aptitudes on the rare occasions when it does present itself. That is why he needs you to stay, even if it means marrying you."

"He cannot restore the Incuna, so he wants to renew our form of magic instead."

"If he does, this nightmare will never end," she said. "And that is why I have come here. You must leave, all of you. Leave now. For all our sakes."

"And allow Anwar and his court to continue ravaging these lands until the Incuna is no more?"

"At least then it will all be over. If you stay and become his prisoner, my family's reign will never end."

"You truly believe any of us would help him?"

"Of course you would," she snorted. "Look how quickly you rushed to defend your Necromancer. You care too much, and you make little effort to hide it. The moment any one of you is in danger, the rest will give him anything he wants. Especially you."

"Does he know we are here?"

"He's already gathering his soldiers for the march. First, he'll try to bargain with Damiane for your release. She will refuse, of course, and then he will lay siege to this place and burn it to the ground."

"He cannot," I shook my head. "I've seen his soldiers matched against theirs. They do not stand a chance."

"You saw a half-dozen men against a hundred," she snapped, her eyes glittering as she beheld what was, evidently, my endlessly naiveté. "Anwar has thousands of knights and soldiers, and they are armed with finer armor and weapons than these forest dwellers could ever dream of. If you care at all for their survival, you will leave, immediately."

She must've seen my hesitation, the anguish in my face. And yet, had I not promised my father that I would see Elyan returned to Tiralaen? Had I not promised Elyan that we would leave this divided kingdom behind to shape its own fate? Evolet was asking no more of me than I already purposed to do.

And yet.

And yet.

Oh Gods, it was an impossible choice, and the death of a people lay at the end of either path left unchosen.

"You must not hesitate," she said at last. "My brother's army will march into the forest within the hour."

"So soon!" I gasped. "But Nymet Nata—they've no time to defend themselves!"

"You cannot save them," she said. "But you may yet save yourselves. To stay here is to be surrounded and captured. You must be far away by the time my brother arrives with his army. There is no other choice. Be done with it, then."

She did not wait to hear my reply, but turned and strode back through the archway that would take her back to the Place of Ways. The door was nearly closed when I spoke one last time:

"There were herbs and water from the Incuna waiting for us in our suite when we returned from the village, that I might tend to Phyra's wounds. Was it you?"

She turned back, her face nearly lost to me within the shadows of the tunnel. "Would it matter if it was?"

I nodded.

"Then it was."

A flick of her hand, and the door slammed shut.

31

By the time I passed beneath the archway and faced the long, lonely climb back to the forest above, I felt as though I'd been hollowed out and all magic had gone from me. Every step was a torment, for my feet were made of lead and my heart even heavier. I dreaded to face them, my friends and our hosts alike, for even now I could not say with certainty what I believed to be right, what I should do to make it so.

I stumbled into the Dendor's vestibule and fell to my knees, my hands sinking into the soft carpet of moss and flowers.

He was still asleep, and as I entered the grove, he grunted and stirred, pulling his cloak of green tighter about himself. I envied him, and hated myself for it, for in my weakness I thought to lay down beside him and allow myself to be swallowed slowly by growing things, to forget that which I now knew, what I now faced.

I stayed with the Dendor, safe within the peace of his grove for far too long.

When at last I did emerge, they were waiting for me, and every one of them fixed me with wide, anxious eyes.

"Well?" Samira demanded. "What did she say?"

Across the grove, my eyes sought Elyan. "You were right,"

I told him. "King Anwar did want me to stay. He wanted all of us to stay."

As quickly as I could, for time was running out, I told them everything save Evolet's past with Isabis, for it was not my story to tell.

When I'd finished, Zayir surged forward, eyes alight. "Far too long have we cowered in fear from a man who cannot do the simplest magic. I say, let them come! We should fight!"

"I fear the princess is right with regard to your ability to best their army," I said, and he snarled helplessly, for though he hated it, and despised me for it, he knew 'twas truth I spoke.

"Then help us," Samira said, her imploring gaze fixed upon me. "Join your magic with ours. With you, we might stand a chance to end all of this."

"How do you propose we do that?" Elyan said flatly, and I flinched at the words. "We are but five, and our aptitudes do not work the way you imagine they do. Your people will be slaughtered, and the people of Tiralaen also, when I fail to return and reclaim my throne."

"Your throne!" Zayir spat derisively upon the ground at his feet. "You are as selfish as your ancestors were."

"I am not responsible for the actions of men and women long dead, and I will not stay here to die for their crimes."

"Enough," Damiane growled. "Prince Elyan has made his decision, and he is free to leave."

Samira turned to me then. "And what of you, Briony? What do you want?"

"That is irrelevant," Elyan snapped.

Outrage suffused me, and I whirled upon him. "You seek to speak for me? I am the Orare, not you, and I shall speak for myself."

He loomed over me, his face full of thunder. "Then speak."

But the words would not come, for I wanted too much.

To love Elyan, to return to Tiralaen with him and my dearest friends, I wanted. To fulfill my promise to my father and protect the magic born of Tiralaen, I wanted. To see Anwar unseated from a throne he did not deserve and punished for his crimes, I wanted. To see the Incuna returned to the people of Nymet Nata and the village, I wanted. To see the grievous wrongs done by my countrymen to these people righted after so many years, I wanted.

I could not have all that I wanted; neither could I choose.

And so, I said nothing.

Across the top of my bowed head, Elyan looked to Damiane. "I am truly sorry for what has befallen your people, and I hope that when they do not discover us here, they let you be. But we must depart within the hour. All of us."

He turned then and strode from the grove into the night beyond.

No one spoke, nor could they meet my eyes; filled with pity, sorrowful of what they had witnessed, angry and desperate and afraid, they looked everywhere save at me, and I was grateful, for neither could I face them. I'd demanded to be heard, and when the moment came, could not find my voice. A sorrier excuse for an Orare could not have been found, of that I was certain.

Unable to bear the weight of their eyes any further, I fled.

Stumbling into the darkness, I ran headlong into the forest until I reached the crossroads. I could not go back to Uuna Tree, for I could not face him; I could not face anyone. And so, I took the path that led away to the clearing.

The lanterns had long since gone out, and I could scarcely see the path by the light of the moon. I tried to call Magefire to my palm, but again and again the flames flickered weakly and sputtered out, for I could not command it; I could command nothing.

I tripped more than once, blundering upon my hands and knees, careening into low-hanging branches until, at last, I entered the clearing.

The great fire had burned until it was nothing more than a vast bed of coals, but I could just make out the tree where the relics of generations of Damiane's people swayed gently upon the branches.

Sinking to my knees, I spoke to the Dae Spira, a whispered prayer to an eldritch goddess, for I had no one else.

"Tell me what I ought to do, for I cannot see the way ahead."

Naught but the wind answered as it gently ruffled the branches above me and set dancing the ephemera upon them. So many lives did they represent, lives that had been deprived of the promise of the goddess, of her gift to them.

"I thought perhaps I would find you here."

I started at the low, familiar voice, and looked up to see Damiane standing just inside the clearing, watching me with her arms crossed over her chest.

"I, too, come here to think sometimes. I cannot decide whether it is because it is quiet or because I hope that in being in the presence of the goddess, her wisdom might pass to me."

"Has it ever worked?"

She lowered herself onto the ground beside me and looked up at the tree, and the beads and metal woven into her hair tinkled softly. "I like to think so, but I suppose history will judge whether it is true."

"I'm so sorry we cannot help you," I said, my voice thick and miserable. "If it were me, and me alone, I would. I promise you I would."

"But it is not you alone."

"Zayir will never forgive us. And Samira—"

"Samira's anger burns bright, for she has felt the strength of the calling and suffers the indignity of a throne denied her. She is young and sheltered; all she knows is this forest. She cannot fathom of a kingdom as large as yours, or of war."

"It is war you now face, and it is my fault." I buried my face in my hands. "I've made a terrible mess of everything."

"You are not responsible for what has befallen us."

I choked on bitter laughter. "But we are. Or rather, Tiralaen is. And yet, Elyan denies we can be held to account for actions of our countrymen. Is that not strange? How is it that we can so fiercely claim responsibility for our kingdom's future and yet absolve ourselves of responsibility for its past?"

She shifted beside me, and I regarded her through the tears that still clung to my lashes. "You have a fierce heart, Briony Tenebrae," she said. "And with it you will do extraordinary things. But not here."

"I don't want to do extraordinary things. I just want to do the right thing."

I sought Elyan in his chamber and found him as I'd often found him these many months: standing before the night window, hands clasped behind his back as he stared out into the vast swath of stars above. He was dressed in traveling clothes, his bag packed and resting at his feet, ready to depart.

"You've come to speak," he said.

"I have."

He turned, but only slightly, and the soft light of the near-dawn moon illuminated the sharp angles of his face. "Then speak."

I drew a deep breath and held fast to my courage, and to the choice I had made. "I'm going to stay and help Damiane and her people."

For a very long time he did not answer me. When at last he turned and we regarded one another fully across the darkened room, I scarcely recognized him, for cold and beautiful and unattainable now was he, as he'd been that first night when I'd arrived at Asperfell.

"You know I cannot," he said softly.

"I know."

In the square below, Damiane's soldiers rushed about, their heavy footfalls mingling with the sounds of steel, and he turned from me, hands braced against the window ledge and eyes fixed firmly upon their progress. "So Garundel was right, then. In the end."

A shuddering sigh escaped me. "I was certain, so certain she meant death that I never imagined—"

"That any of us would choose to stay."

That you would choose to leave me.

The words hung heavy between us as if he'd spoken them aloud, and I watched as his fingers flexed and curled against the window ledge.

"I would have chosen this regardless of what was said between us that night," I whispered. "I need you to know that."

"You are who you are. No one can change that. Not even me."

"Would you want to?"

"No," he said at last, and his voice was so low I could scarcely hear him. "I would not. And our companions? Your friends?"

"I would never ask them to stay."

"Their love for you far eclipses their duty to me."

Knuckles rapped sharply against the door of Elyan's chamber, and Damiane's face appeared. "It is time. You must go."

She disappeared, and my heart seized, for here at last was the moment, and the resolve with which I had faced him only moments ago had grown so frayed that mere threads held me to the path I had chosen.

I reached out and grasped his hand, forced him to turn and face me. "I love you," I said, and though the words were sweet and new to my lips, each one was a torment. "I love you, and I promise you I will find a way back to you."

He took my face in his hands and drank my tears as he kissed me for perhaps the last time, for although my words were a promise, a seal I set upon his heart and mine, they were hope, not truth, and I feared at last my hope was failing.

32

"You are a warrior now, like us."

Damiane said the words kindly and in perfect sincerity, and I was deeply grateful for them. But I did not believe them.

Still, I did look the part, for Samira had presented me with a truly wondrous gift: a long tunic and bodice made of sturdy, forest green, the skirt split gloriously to reveal a pair of the same leggings made of leather that I'd so coveted.

Unfortunately, even thus garbed, any bravado I possessed ebbed as we drew to the border of Syr'Aliem, and I tried desperately not to imagine all the many ways I was unequal to the task for which I had sacrificed everything I loved.

"It will be slow going in the dark," Damiane said, "but you must not summon flame, or you'll be found and brought to the palace in chains."

I shook my head. "I fear by the time I reach the palace Anwar's men will already be upon you and all will be for naught."

"There is no other way than by foot."

"Yes, there is."

The voice cut through the dark ahead of us, and I could do little but stare in astonishment as Phyra appeared upon the path, naught

visible but her face under her hood. So astounded was I to see her
that at first I did not see the gaunt, black creature slinking behind
her until the surprise began to fade and suddenly it was all I saw.
It was, unmistakably, the Phaelor she'd raised from the dead, the
bones of his ribcage gleaming through his oil slick fur.

"Phyra," I breathed. "What are you doing here?"

"Helping you," she answered. "You'll never make it to the
palace in time without him."

It set in then exactly what sort of help it was that she offered,
and I blanched. "I cannot."

"You must."

Damiane said thoughtfully, "My people rode these creatures
long ago, but only if the beasts imprinted upon them at a very young
age and were thoroughly trained."

Phyra turned her fathomless eyes upon Damiane. "He will carry
her. We are bound, this creature and I, and he will carry her, for it
is my will that he do so."

I had not the time to ask how she knew this with such certainty,
but because I trusted her, because she was Phyra, I gathered my
courage and stepped forward.

"Make haste, then," Damiane said, her eyes scanning the forest
around us. "If you are certain."

Phyra took my hand, pulled me closer. "I have given him a name:
Vindar. In the old tongue, it means *avenged*. Command him thus."

I reached out and brushed my hand against his sleek fur and felt
a shudder pass through his powerful frame. "Vindar," I tested out,
and the Phaelor turned his great head toward me, watching me with
bulbous, milky eyes.

"The choice is yours, Phyra. I understand that now. But I hope
that you will honor my wishes and leave with Elyan."

Phyra reached out and grasped my hand so tightly I feared the fragile bones beneath my skin might break. "I must remain. I can raise you."

I shook my head. "No. I don't ever want you to descend to that place for me. To make that choice for me."

By what little of the moon broke through the canopy of branches and leaves above, I could see the tears sliding down her face. She drew me to her then, and I buried my face in her hood. A strangled sob escaped me, for I could bear the weight of my fear, my grief, no longer, and I clung to her, my shoulders shaking and my tears making a horrid mess of her cloak.

It was Vindar's paw, impatient upon the ground, that reminded us both what precious little time I had to reach the palace and open the Ita Hominaeum, and so I reluctantly pulled away, wiping my miserable face on my sleeve.

Phyra reached out and rested her palm against my cheek. "We will see each other again."

I did not ask her how she knew; perhaps she did not; perhaps it was only a wish. In that moment, I cared not.

She and Damiane helped boost me onto Vindar's back. Wild thing that I was in my youth, I'd ridden plenty of horses bareback, for otherwise I would've had to ask a stable hand for help with the saddle and I was usually in some sort of trouble that precluded me from being allowed to ride in the first place. But a Phaelor was not a horse, and I was terribly awkward as I scrambled up and gripped the skin of his neck to steady myself. Steam from his nose puffed into the air, and I hoped I'd not hurt him; it would not do to be thrown from my mount halfway between Nymet Nata and Syr'Aliem.

My hands and thighs gripping the fearsome beast below me as

though my life depended upon it, I chanced to look down at Damiane and Phyra.

"Are you certain he knows the way?" the first asked the latter. Phyra nodded.

"Ride hard, then. As hard as you can."

"Goodbye," I said.

Damiane answered: "Good luck."

It was entirely by the grace of the Dae Spira that I did not slide off Vindar within the first few feet, and in the end, I wrapped my arms about his neck and pressed my face against his back. The forest blurred around me, shadowed and sinister, and the moon slipped in and out of view, illuminating the shifting colors of Vindar's fur one moment and plunging us both into darkness the next.

Just as I began to despair that we'd too far to travel, I felt the familiar warmth of the Incuna begin to stir languidly beneath my skin, but unlike the first time I had drawn near the heart of Syr'Aliem, there was now an urgency in its call, and an urgency in the way my magic responded.

"Vindar," I urged. "Faster!"

He answered me with a growl that rumbled beneath my hammering heart and a mighty surge in his powerful limbs; we flew, shadows both.

When at last we reached the secret door in the palace wall that Princess Evolet had used to secure our escape, Vindar reared back, and I slid to the ground, my legs buckling beneath me after my madcap ride. "Go," I whispered to the Phaelor, not knowing if he truly under-stood me or not, nor if he would heed me. "Return to her for she may have need of you."

The Phaelor disappeared into the forest, and I studied the door before me. It took a rather embarrassingly long time to coax the lock into submission, but at last, the door creaked open and I peered into the darkness. The tunnel through the wall was, thankfully, empty, save for a few rather large nocturnal insects who regarded the interruption through the glowing spheres of their eyes.

A tendril of flame illuminated my journey through the wall, and when at last I reached the end, I cursed aloud, my voice ricocheting off the stone surrounding me, for I found the inner door locked as well.

This time, no amount of spellwork nor coaxing bent it to my will, and gasping with the exertion, I slumped against it, my heart racing.

I could not unlock the door, but perhaps I could destroy it.

Standing once again, I placed my palm upon the wood and trembled as I attempted to call forth Magefire. If I could not control it, or if it were magic that bound the door, magic far beyond me, I was not entirely sure that I could quell the blaze. But I had to try; I had to try anything and everything that I could.

Beneath my palm the wood began to blacken, smoke curling from between my fingers. The stain spread, edges curling like parchment, but no matter how desperately I channeled my magic, however I strengthened my command, I could not bid flame to rise.

'Twas magic, then, that held the door.

Whatever enchantments had been placed there fought me bitterly, struggling, resisting, and fear whispered cruelly in my ear.

No, I whispered back. I would not permit it to end like this: pitifully lost and alone in the darkness, full of power, yet full of doubt.

I'd only ever spoken aloud when commanding my aptitude,

never for magic of any other kind of spellwork, and I'd little confidence that it would make any sort of difference, but I had to try; it was not within me to yield.

"Rise," I whispered, wrapping my magic around my words. "Burn. *Consume.*"

The heat at the center of my palm grew as flames enveloped my hand, and the wood caught fire at last. I scrambled back, well away of the smoke, and watched as the door crumbled to smoldering ash.

Past the smoldering embers, I spilled out onto finely cut grass and lay upon my back, gasping as threads of light swirled beneath my skin, for I'd not had cause to use so much magic in a very long time. Exhaustion began to settle over me, and I clenched my teeth furiously against it, for the battle was not yet won.

Shaking and feverish, I pressed my hands into the thick carpet of grass and slowly pulled myself up onto my knees. Across the expanse of slender, white trees, the Lumens of the palace were aglow, and I remembered with chagrin that the Court Eternal frequently gamboled well into the night.

Dashing from tree to tree, I embraced their shadows and shrunk from the moonlight until I reached the same servants' entrance through which Commander Nidaan had led us not so very long ago, and the door gave way easily under my spell. Voices rumbled in the distance, and the metallic scrape of armor mingled with the heavy footfalls of Anwar's men.

I had very little time.

Until Princess Evolet had appeared in the Ita Hominaeum with the Keys of Ways clasped in her hands, I'd never seen them upon her person, the fear of revealing Anwar's deception too great to risk for little more than a show of power and position. I imagined this pleased her endlessly; the crude, cumbersome relics would hardly have suited the fine lines of her gowns.

She must've kept them somewhere far out of reach of the Court Eternal, under locks and keys of their own.

Once she'd spoken of gowns and jewels not yet worn, housed in her chambers. Perhaps she kept a similar treasure close at hand.

I encountered no one in the corridors, either because it was close enough to dawn that the Court Eternal had finally retreated to their beds or, more likely, because all who were still awake had gathered in some courtyard or other to watch the mustering of the army. It took me several attempts to remember the location of Evolet's rooms; I'd only been there once, and I'd paid it little mind. After encountering several dead ends and unlocking more than a few chambers that turned out not to be hers, I finally found what I sought.

The Lumen in the enormous hearth had long since gone out, and only a few of the sconces that lined the walls were lit. Her chamber was, predictably, larger than the largest receiving room, and even in the dark I knew it to be sumptuous and, unfortunately, full of places one might think to hide a priceless artifact so that none would ever discover it. I drew the heavy brocade curtains so that none outside should see me, summoned flame, and set to work.

There was an ornate writing desk just below the window and I decided to begin my search there, pulling drawers out and fumbling within, finding nothing at all but cobwebs and emptiness.

"I take it you've come to steal the Keys of Ways," a familiar voice drawled behind me. "Well, I'll save you the time. Evolet would never hide something of such importance in something so tedious as a desk. You'd be better served to check her dressing room."

I whirled around and lifted the flames in my hand.

Anwar pushed himself away from the wall where he had been waiting, cleverly shrouded in darkness, watching me. His amber eyes, which I had thought beautiful once, and warm, gleamed ferally, and the smile upon his lips was anything but charming.

"Lighting an entire door on fire is hardly subtle, my dear, but then, neither are you, so I suppose it is hardly a surprise that my guards spotted you so easily," he continued, lowering himself into one of the chairs facing the cold hearth and stretching his legs out as though there were not a war to prepare for at that very moment. "Come," he said. "Sit with me as we used to."

I longed to lunge forward and crush my blazing hand into his face, but I could not help Damiane and her people in chains, and so, though I howled with rage within at the doing of it, I snuffed out my Magefire and approached him.

"I did not expect to see you again," he said as I reluctantly perched upon the arm of the chair.

"You are mistaken," I answered tightly. "I've not come to steal anything."

"I knew the blackout could not have been the reason for the door to open," he continued as though I had not spoken. "We've had hundreds of blackouts. Thousands. And yet, the doors have remained as they have always been, save for that one night." He tilted his head, studying me with keen interest. "You were lovely, you know. A pity that you did not stay, for I had such plans for our evening."

He drew something from the depths of his robe and turned it over and over in his hand before he cast it at my feet. I looked down, and my breath caught in my throat.

It was a star, a star of gold and diamonds, the very same that Isri had woven into my red curls the night of the ball. The one I'd lost.

"I found it just outside the entrance to the Ita Hypogaeum," he told me absently, as though we might be discussing books over tea in the parlor of Orwynd. "A pity that Isri is not better skilled or you might never have lost it."

I lifted my gaze from the glint of metal and stone.

"It is well for you that you caused a riot in my village the very next day. Had you not been forced to flee, you would have been in chains by nightfall. But by then, you were already on your way into the arms of the Nymet Nata, who have, I am sure, lied to you most thoroughly."

"They've told no lies," I hissed. "You and your forebears are monsters."

"If 'tis so, then so were your ancestors."

"I do not deny it. But you had the power to rectify hundreds of years of deceit when Isabis was chosen, and you killed her instead."

He uncrossed his legs and leaned forward, bracing his elbows upon his knees. "And what if your prince discovered that his family had no true claim on the throne despite generations of custodianship? Would he abdicate? Or would he choose to remain for the good of his people?"

"There is nothing good about the way you have ruled these people."

"And who are you to decide such things? You're nothing more than an escaped criminal who came into my kingdom uninvited, begging for my aid. And when I received you graciously and made you guests in my home, you exploited my kindness and betrayed me with crimes most vile." His lips curled into a wicked, terrible smile. "And now you shall answer for them. Guards!"

The door opened, and the heavy footfalls of armored men approached my chair.

I had failed.

With rough hands beneath my elbows, they wrested me to my feet though I offered no resistance; I could not best them, weak as I was and with little more than sparks with which to defend myself. Anwar rose lazily and, reaching into his pocket, withdrew a handful of what I thought at first was mere dust, but as the grains began to slip through his fingers, glittering silver by what little light remained, I realized all at once what it was.

"Pleasant dreams, my dear," he whispered. "At least for a little while."

He smiled at me, then parted his lips and blew.

33

I scarce remember my journey from Princess Evolet's chambers to the throne room, for I drifted in and out of consciousness, necessitating the dragging of my person down the gilded hallways. At the edges of my blurred vision, I began to see figures, faces, and I realized that the Court Eternal had gathered to watch my shameful progression toward their sovereign, toward my fate.

I began to recognize them, particularly as we neared the great hall: there was the cluster of dazzling women Princess Evolet and I had sat amongst at the pleasure gardens; they'd been enthralled then by my magic. Now, it was my torment that set their eyes alight, and *oh* but they glittered!

There were Wynsel and Carlew in robes of brocade and velvet with jeweled collars and trains so long they held them slung over their arms, their faces shockingly impassive for the laughter we had shared. Beside them was Braesor, whom I'd once found pleasant and thought a friend. Our eyes met, and he averted his own, but not before I saw discomfiture upon his face.

Help me! I longed to cry out, but the words caught in my throat, my tongue too thick in my mouth for them to pass.

Their perfect, painted faces began to blur, amalgamating into an infinite sea of beautiful indifference. Of course they would not risk their place and privilege to aid me, for they knew not that they were gilded hostages in an endless deceit; they did not even know their own origins, their families. They'd never known anything at all but this.

We passed through the doors to the throne room and I was unceremoniously deposited in a heap at the foot of the dais. With extraordinary effort, I managed to turn myself onto my back. High above me, through the ceiling of glass and gold, the velvet blanket of night glittered with so many stars, and tears leaked from the corners of my eyes and spilled into my hair.

It seemed I was doomed eternally to be brought low before kings undeserving of the thrones they sat upon.

"Briony Tenebrae!" King Anwar's voice rang out from the dais at the head of the room, and I craned my neck to take him in. At his right, his mother's eyes gleamed in triumph.

Facing them was a torment.

Facing the princess herself was worse.

The loathing in her eyes was terrible and absolute. She had told me to flee, to starve Anwar's rule and let the terrible legacy of his family die along with the Incuna rather than allow such cruelty to continue in perpetuity, but I had thought myself equal to an impossible task. Now, we would all pay the price for my hubris. That I'd sent Elyan away, and my friends with him, was a bitter comfort to me now.

Behind the three thrones, no less than two dozen of Anwar's guards stood in full regalia, their armor and weapons gleaming.

Rise, a familiar voice whispered.

I tried to obey. But my limbs would not heed my command. I

pressed my palms upon the cold marble beneath me, tried to lift myself onto my elbows, and collapsed again in a quivering heap.

I cannot, I answered. *I am so tired.*

The edges of my vision blurred, and I saw a ripple of white, nearly transparent.

Rise!

Slowly, so very slowly, I pulled myself to my knees.

Anwar's grin was feral. "What a shame it had to come to this. I had such hopes for your future amongst us, Briony."

Were I close enough to spit at his feet, I would have done so; instead, all I could offer the usurper king was the hatred in my eyes. "I would never have helped you."

He dismissed my words with a wave of his hand. "Oh, but you will. Though I would have preferred you do so willingly."

"You mean in ignorance."

His eyes narrowed. "Someone in this palace took great pains to ensure you were neither. I would not have believed there to be traitors amongst my court, but it appears I am mistaken. Believe me when I say it will never happen again."

Princess Evolet's face was calm, impassive, and I might have thought her undisturbed by Anwar's denunciation, save for the way her hands gripped the arms of her throne.

"Tell me who helped you," Anwar demanded.

I lifted my chin in defiance. "The Dae Spira."

He flinched as though I'd struck him, and the smile disappeared entirely from his face.

"The Dae Spira is dead," he hissed.

"She lives."

"*Liar.* Tell me who helped you!"

But I would not speak, and at the sight of his mounting anger,

I began to smile. My fate may have been certain, but the women who had helped me, who had lost so much, and risked so much, they would be protected. They could fight on.

"Very well." Anwar sat back in his throne. "If 'twas truly the goddess who guided you, perhaps we should question her disciples."

He waved his hand, and the smile died upon my face as his guards brought forth a dozen women in robes of green and billowing white veils. Among them, I saw Isri, proud and defiant, and despite her regrettable opinion of me, despite every scowl and pinch and slap, my heart leapt into my throat.

"No," I said, and the word was a hoarse, cracked thing. *Oh, no, no, no—*

"It is said they are as old as the goddess herself, that they cannot be cleaved from the temple, nor can they be killed," Anwar mused. "Aliem tried, of course, and failed, but that was hundreds of years ago. As their goddess has faded, so too, perhaps, has their tether to the Incuna. Shall we find out?"

Anwar gestured sharply and a guard came forward, unsheathing a knife. He grasped one of the Tacé about the neck and wrenched her from her companions, forcing her to her knees.

"No!" I gasped. "Please, do not do this!"

"Then tell me who helped you!" Anwar demanded.

"I don't know! Please, don't hurt her!"

"Tell me now!"

"No one helped me!"

With unnatural calm, he lifted his hand again. The blade flashed as the guard brought it down in a slender arc, slicing the Tacé's neck from ear to ear, a ghastly red smile.

The other Tacé could not scream, could not beg; with desperate hands they clutched one another, faces stretched in silent agony as their companion's body was dropped unceremoniously upon the glittering floor of the throne room. Her hands fluttered to her throat as she gaped like a fish denied water, drowning in her own blood as it sluiced through her fingers and pooled under her head.

I gave voice to their pain, a piercing wail that echoed through the cavernous throne room.

Anwar's eyes glittered. "Tell me who helped you."

"I don't know," I sobbed. I'd not thought it possible to feel such pain and yet live. "I don't know—please!"

The Tacé was still alive, and I cursed the magic that bound her to this place, for though she suffered, she could not die.

Anwar sighed, and gestured once more.

The same guard lunged forward and grasped another Tacé, and my heart leapt into my throat because this time it was Isri. My eyes found Princess Evolet's, and they were as desperate as my own.

Isri met her would-be executioner with her chin raised in defiance.

"Speak, Orare," Anwar taunted me. "For that is what you are born to do, is it not? To speak?"

"Please," I whispered, my voice gone hoarse from screaming. "Do not do this."

"So proud of your magic, and yet where is it now? Where is your voice, Orare?"

There is power in a voice such as you cannot imagine. Do not doubt it.

But doubt I did, for even in the amplifying presence of the Incuna, I was a speaker with nothing to command, no magic to heed me.

The guard's knife was still slick with blood when he brought its edge to Isri's neck, waiting for the command.

Anwar's terrible voice echoed upon the stone that surrounded me: "Speak!"

And then another joined it.

And another.

Speak!

They skittered softly at first in the very farthest corners of my consciousness, rustling like dry leaves caught in an autumn gust, fluttering and scraping; thin as morning fog, insubstantial as shadows cowering from the golden light of the afternoon sun. My breath caught, and in the silence, I heard the words once more.

The night of the ball, I'd thought it helplessness that had bid the spells within me rise, the terrible sensation of being swallowed whole, the indignity of another's hands, another's will, the loss of myself entirely, that had bid the ancient words of magic to take shape within me. But it was not helplessness I felt as I looked up into Anwar's terrible eyes, nor was it fear.

It was power; it was justice.

I'd not strength alone to give it voice, but I was not alone. The goddess was at my back, and upon my head, I felt her brittle fingers rest; this was no dream. I welcomed the vice of her grip, and the pain, for with it came that which I needed, and her voice, deep within:

Together we are strong.

My hair lifted gently, and the wind that had rustled the leaves began to churn around me as the spells grew. And it was not only my magic that sang within my veins, rushing to the surface of my skin to suffuse me with light, but the Incuna as the goddess worked through me, bestowing upon me her strength, and her grace.

The guard who held Isri began to glance around uneasily as the wind unfurled past me, ruffling the veils of the silent women who clutched one another, though they were no longer afraid. Could they see her, I wondered? Could they feel her in the wind?

"What is this?" Anwar's voice was suddenly sharp. "What are you doing?"

Within my throat, the ancient tongue of the first spells clamored for release, and this time I did not swallow them down. I opened my mouth and gave them voice, the words pouring from me like rain as the wind churned and roiled, a storm of my making, and of hers. They surrounded me, whispers echoing in a tongue I knew and yet did not, for it was in my blood.

I opened my eyes.

Anwar was upon his feet, gesturing to me madly, but no matter how furiously his guards tried, they could not breach the storm. They were tossed mercilessly away, striking the base of the dais as the Tacé clambered away from them, clutching one another against the onslaught of my magic. I'd no wish to hurt them, but the spells were coming faster and faster now, a tempest meant to destroy.

There was a flash of silver at the edge of my vision, a swirl of golden hair, and Evolet was gathering the Tacé to her, and although I should've liked to see her upon her knees in judgment for all she had wrought, the Dowager Queen was also amongst them.

Anwar's guards moved to stop the Tacé from reaching the nearest door, but they had underestimated their princess, believed her merely decorative; believed her magic as delicate as her porcelain skin.

I had never been so fiendishly gleeful to see anyone proven wrong.

The princess raised her hands, and from the very air between them, she gathered the wondrous gift of the Incuna. But unlike the warming glow of Lumens, these were blades of light that shimmered in the air before her, taut as a bow ready to fire. Her fingers sliced through the air, and they flew free.

She did not miss.

Pierced by her magic, the guards were thrown back, impaled by light against the wall. And over the howling of the wind and my own words, I heard Anwar's distant shriek.

Evolet herded the Tacé through the door, her hands aglow, weapons at the ready, until only one remained. This last Tacé was Isri, and as our eyes met, she nodded, just once, then fled; and with a powerful gust, the door slammed shut.

Anwar was still bellowing orders as he clung tightly to his throne, but his remaining guards no longer cared what their king demanded. After what Evolet had done, they desperately sought a door, any door, through which to escape. But they were as trapped as he, and my spells were spiraling out of my control, my tenuous hold upon them fraying, a cord ready to snap.

It was with borrowed magic that I had called them forth, and now they had grown beyond me; I was a vessel; I was overgrown.

As the last of the words rushed into the howling void, I pitched forward onto my hands, but the spells did not end with my voice; they had their own life now, and they screamed with such force that I knew the room could not hope to withstand it; all within would be destroyed.

I'd no strength left to conjure a shield. All I could do now was to let it engulf me. The howling wind embraced me as a lover might, and I curled onto my side and closed my eyes as it washed over me, and I hoped that when it came, it did not hurt so very much, my passing.

From a very great distance, I heard pounding, steady and solid, drawing near even as the spells pushed everything outward, seeking freedom. Lifting my face from my arms, I looked desperately to the sound, and a joyful sob bubbled up in my throat.

Elyan was hurtling toward me, eyes wild and desperate, and there was magic in his hands; I had never seen him so undone. He slid to his knees beside me and thrust his arms into the air. A shield, shining and strong, erupted above us as the world stilled and went silent, the culmination at last upon us.

His ragged breath, and mine, were the only sounds left in the world.

The explosion was deafening.

Glass shattered, the ceiling and windows giving way, and jagged shards hurtled in every direction. The stone followed, cracking, crumbling, great chunks of it torn free from the columns and archways; and the gilt and crystal were reduced to nothing more than glittering flecks of sand.

Gods, but he was beautiful above me, his bowed head crowned with light and every inch of him held taut against the onslaught as he protected me, protected us both from what I had unleashed. Glass and gold and marble hurtled through the room, pummeling his brilliant shield again and again.

It was not until the roaring of the wind finally died away and the last of the debris settled upon the shattered floor that the shield dissipated into the air. Elyan rocked back on his heels, his chest rising and falling, veins of light unfurling beneath his pale skin. His face flushed from the expenditure of so much magic, his limbs spent and limp, but he was *there*, and a sob choked in my throat as I hurled myself into his arms, holding onto him so tightly he gasped.

"You came back," I whispered against his neck.

His mouth against my hair, he answered: "I never should have left."

I could've stayed that way forever, the world silent at last, the ancient spells receding into fleeting memory, his arms surrounded me like a bastion, warm and sure. But all was not won; there were battles left to fight.

"Anwar," I gasped, drawing back and searching for any sign of him amongst the rubble of the once magnificent throne room.

The bodies of the king's guards littered the perimeter of the room where they had been thrown, tossed like ragdolls by the force of the spells, but I did not see the man himself.

"He's gone!"

"We need to help Damiane and her people," Elyan said as he lifted me to my feet. "They don't have much time. Anwar's army has reached Nymet Nata."

I looked around me at the devastation my spells had caused, made possible only by the grace of the Dae Spira and the Incuna, her gift to Damiane's people.

Such unimaginable power.

And they'd been cut off from it, starved of its strength and magic.

"Elyan," I gasped, gripping his sleeve in my trembling fingers. "We alone cannot save Nymet Nata. But what if we could give them back the means with which to save themselves?"

His brow furrowed. "I do not understand your meaning."

"The Incuna is their birthright, and our ancestors stole it from them. It's time to give it back."

34

As we traveled the now-familiar path to the Place of Ways, I explained in a breathless rush the idea that had quietly taken root inside me.

"Siphon the Incuna," Elyan said flatly. "Have you gone mad? Siphon it into where?"

"Back into the land! The Nymet Nata will be able to draw upon it once more, and with its power, they may yet have the strength to defeat Anwar's soldiers."

"What makes you think I am even capable of such a thing?"

"Asperfell," I told him as we neared the door to the vestibule at last. "You tried to siphon magic from the prison itself. You can do the same with the Incuna."

"I suppose it is possible..." he said slowly.

"Possible is all I need."

"You *have* gone mad, then."

As we tumbled from the stairway into the vestibule, we were met by a rush of tiny limbs and wide eyes as the Acolytes swarmed around our legs.

"Briony!" Lark cried, overjoyed. "You came back!"

I knelt, and he threw himself into my arms. Tansy followed,

tears streaming down her face, and the rest followed. Even Fife, who had never trusted me, never liked me much, pressed himself to me swiftly before retreating, his cheeks pink, mumbling under his breath.

"I need your help," I told them. "I need you to find Princess Evolet. I need the Keys to the Ways, and she—"

"But she is already here!" Tansy squeaked.

I stared at her earnest face, then lifted my eyes.

From within the Place of Ways, Princess Evolet was watching my reunion with the Acolytes with an expression I could not mete out upon her face. Clutched in her hands were the Keys.

I stood, and we faced one another once more, and I wondered what facet of her I was to learn next, for it seemed I would never discover them all.

"Your highness," I began.

"Orare," she answered. "You did not heed me."

"I could not."

"Disobedience is in your nature."

"And courage is in yours."

The faintest of smiles appeared upon her lips, quickly smothered. "You know nothing."

I merely shrugged. "The Tacé?"

"They are safe. As is my mother."

"The Atriyen of Nymet Nata and a handful of her soldiers are waiting beyond that door," I said, pointing to the Ita Hominaeum. "Open it, and perhaps we can end all of this."

"What of Anwar?" she asked. "Does he yet live?"

"I don't know," I admitted. "He escaped the throne room like the coward he is."

"You must know he will not easily surrender."

Smiling grimly, I answered: "He will not be given a choice."
Then I turned and reached for Elyan. "Go. You know the way."

He kissed me swiftly, then sprinted toward the Incuna.

"Watch over him," I murmured, and I hoped that she could hear
me; I'd not felt her presence since the throne room.

"We'll go with him," Lark told me stoutly.

Fife nodded in agreement and swung his axe. "And protect him."

"No," I said, going down upon one knee. "There are men coming,
men with swords and armor and death in their hearts. You must
hide."

"Where?"

"I've unlocked the Ita Hypogaeum," Evolet answered. "The
Tacé and my mother are ensconced within. Hide yourselves there
and barricade the door."

They were quite reluctant, and only agreed once I tasked them
with the protection of the Tacé who served the goddess for whom
they were made. With rushed embraces and kisses to my face, they
disappeared through the doorway.

"I hope you know what you are doing, Orare," said Evolet, as she
fitted the bronze key into the ancient lock of the Ita Hominaeum
and turned it with both hands.

The door creaked and swung open, revealing Damiane's drawn,
harried face.

"What took you so long?" she demanded as she stepped into the
vestibule, twelve men and women in leather armor behind her. I
heard her sharp intake of breath as she beheld for the first time the
true seat of her people's power.

"Forgive me," I answered. "I was... detained."

She tore her gaze from the splendor around us and beheld me
with a raised brow. "Detained?"

"I'll tell you all about it someday."

She huffed. "All right then, Orare. Where is Anwar? The fighting has already begun, and my people cannot last long."

"I do not know," I told her. "But much has happened here in the palace, and now we have a new plan."

I told her as quickly as I could what Elyan was at that very moment attempting within the chamber of the Incuna, and what I hoped would be gained were he to succeed, and I saw hope blossom in her eyes, hope and longing.

"You do realize this is madness, don't you?" she said.

"I have been made aware of the fact."

"Still, it is possible... and I fear we've little other option. What is it you need from me?"

"Time," said I. "Guard the stairs, lest Anwar bring his soldiers to stop us."

She nodded and turned to go, but I grabbed her arm.

"But first," I said, "you should see it."

It was, after all, hers.

I led Damiane and her soldiers into the chamber, and the light seemed to me brighter, stronger than it had ever been before.

Across the water, still as glass, Elyan knelt upon the dais, one hand lifted toward the blinding, brilliant orb held in the Dae Spira's stone hands, the other stretched, fingers splayed, toward the withered threads of power upon the walls. His limbs were taut, every muscle and vein held fast in the merciless grip of his magic and the raw power that he channeled, and in that moment I feared for him.

"Go," I breathed to Damiane. "Hurry."

She reached out and clasped my arm in hers, and I returned the grip with equal fervor. Then, across the Place of Ways, I heard a distant clamor echoing down the ancient spiral stairs—and I knew it to be the steel boots of Anwar's soldiers upon the stone steps.

We'd run out of time.

"Be careful," Damiane said, then she gathered her warriors.

When they were gone, Princess Evolet stepped into the Incuna chamber and stood by my side.

"Is it working?" she asked.

"You are more likely to know the answer than I."

Evolet closed her eyes. "I think it may be. I sense the Incuna not just in front of me, but all around us."

Suddenly, we heard shouting and the distant clash of steel. I held my breath and listened, as if I might be able to discern the course of the battle from these noises, but no—'twas only chaos to my ears, and far away.

"We need to protect Elyan," I said.

"Lead the way."

We were halfway across the stepping stones to the dais when a cold voice called out from the entrance to the Incuna's chamber.

"Hello, Orare. And to you as well, *Sister*."

Together, we turned.

Flanked by two of his guards, Anwar stood in the archway.

"How?" I managed to spit out. "How did you survive?"

"Evidently your goddess is not as powerful as you believe her to be."

Princess Evolet stepped forward. "It is over, Anwar. Give up the throne and the people of the forest may let you live."

"Will they do the same for you, I wonder? Do you think this pathetic attempt at treason is enough to absolve you and save your own skin?"

"I do not seek absolution, brother," Evolet answered. "I seek to end this."

"Imagine what will become of you should you do so," he said, and although his voice was measured, friendly even, there was no mistaking the threat simmering beneath it all. "There will be no place for you amongst such creatures when our palace becomes a temple once more. No more jewels, no more gowns or pleasure gardens. Think of what you shall lose."

"I shall endeavor to survive it."

Beneath our feet, something seemed to shift, and the walls around us contracted once, twice, pulsing; 'twas as if they drew breath. Beside me, Evolet gasped. Tendrils of light began to unfurl upon the walls, reviving the old roots and threads of power, returning the magic to a land long starved.

Anwar's gaze flickered to Incuna, then down to Elyan upon the dais. "What have you done?"

I lifted my chin, and in that moment he understood.

"End them," he ordered the guards at his side.

Evolet moved past me, her eyes fixed firmly upon the two guards. "Go," she told me. "Protect him."

"Are you sure?"

"Yes, are you sure?" Anwar's mouth twisted. "As exceptional as your skills of illusion are, you are no warrior."

Something flickered deep within her eyes. "You know nothing."

"I know you."

"You do not."

And she lunged. Her fingertips reached out, gathered, *pulled* at the air, and within her hands she held a blade of such light that it blinded me.

"Go to him, Briony," she hissed. "Protect your prince."

This time, I did as she bade me and fled along the stepstone path toward Elyan. When I reached the solid footing of the dais, I turned around to find Evolet had the two soldiers on their heels, but King Anwar was not with them. The coward had abandoned the fray to pursue me across the glimmering water.

In desperation, I tried to summon my magic, to conjure a shield, but all that I could manage was a meager handful of flame, which I flung at him. He sidestepped it easily, and my heart hammered wildly in my chest.

Elyan was still upon his knees, rendered helpless by the magic of the Incuna flowing through him, nothing more than a vessel now for her magic, and fear gripped me anew, for what if it were too much for his body to bear? What if, even now, the Incuna burned him away from the inside, until he was no longer Elyan?

I could not, *would* not think of it.

My feet had scarce touched the stone of the massive dais when Anwar was upon me, and I only just managed to throw myself out of the way of his blade as he swung at me viscously and the blade whistled through the air.

My useless hands conjured a shield that held for mere seconds before it shuddered and dissolved into the air, and in desperation, I conjured another; it shivered in the air between us before it, too, disappeared.

"You've spent it all, haven't you," Anwar scoffed. "As if you had much to begin with."

"More than you," I shot back, and took a perverse sort of pleasure at the flush that crept up his neck.

"Perhaps so," he said. "But without your magic, you're helpless. I am not."

He swung again, and this time I was not fast enough. The blade bit into the skin of my arm, and I gasped and stumbled. My vision went white, blinded with pain, and in desperation I called what magic I still possessed and grasped at the only spell I could think of in that moment, the spell of banishment, which had served me well in my first encounter with the people of Nymet Nata, when I'd foolishly rushed into a battle I did not understand, upon the wrong side.

In the tunnel, I'd spoken my magic aloud and given it power, and so I thrust out my hand and roared: "Away!"

Anwar was blown backwards, stumbling over his own feet and collapsing in a heap, his blade skittering across the stone dais between us.

As one, we lunged for his lost steel—but I was weary and Anwar was faster.

He lashed out, kicking the blade from my grasping fingers, then crushing them beneath the heel of his boot. Through a haze of pain, I heard the sickening sound of snapping bone. I could not scream; could not form the words to curse him; could do nothing but bite back the wave of nausea that threatened to overwhelm me as Anwar stepped away to retrieve his blade.

"Get out of the way, and I won't hurt you again," Anwar commanded, and my gorge rose as he pointed his sword at me once more, beads of my own blood sliding down the blade and dripping onto the stone at his feet.

"You will not touch him."

"Get out of the way!"

"*No.*"

With a bellow of anger, he lunged forward and drove the point of his sword into the soft flesh below my shoulder, twisting, dragging the blade through sinew and bone and I screamed. It was pain beyond anything I had ever known; my vision went white.

"Anwar, stop!"

I turned to see Evolet making her way across the stones, a purloined blade in her hand, slick with gore, her gown covered in it.

"Oh, hello, *sister*," Anwar said, as though he did not at that very moment have his sword buried in my body. He twisted the blade one last horrible time, then withdrew it that he might face a more formidable opponent than myself. I collapsed with a guttural cry.

As Evolet stepped onto the dais, I cradled my ruined hand to my chest and dragged myself to where Elyan knelt. I could not touch him for he burned, far hotter than ever he had been when siphoning before.

"Briony," he rasped—and then he fell, the last vestiges of the Incuna fading from his ravaged body, and all around us the threads of power glowed so brightly that I shielded my eyes against it.

There was a great rushing—a howling, joyful wind—and I fell upon Elyan and pressed my bleeding body to his.

"It's done," I told him, my voice a hoarse whisper and spent. But Elyan did not stir.

Behind me, Evolet raised her blade. "You've lost, brother. The Incuna's magic released unto the people for whom the gift was intended. Surrender, and perhaps the Dae Spira's chosen will show you mercy."

"The Dae Spira has no right to choose our rulers," he growled. "The throne is mine."

He lunged forward, sword raised, and I bent myself over Elyan as the sound of metal upon metal rang out through the chamber and brother met sister upon this most sacred field of battle.

And then the wind began to rise in the underground chamber, and a voice rang out—a voice that sounded like many; hundreds; thousands, a guttural, otherworldly sound.

"USURPER!"

I lifted my head; Anwar's grip upon his blade slackened, and he turned.

Upon the dais at the feet of her likeness stood the Dae Spira herself, arms outstretched as she called her power to her. It rushed to heed her, enveloping her, filling her. Her veils stirred and rippled, and the flames in her crown flared and blazed. She shone, and I had never seen anything so magnificent.

Anwar did not move as she approached him; perhaps he could not. The sword in his hand fell, clattering uselessly upon the stone, and then she was upon him.

With her long, brittle fingers, she seized him by the throat and lifted him slowly until his feet dangled pathetically in the air, scrambling for purchase. He clawed helplessly at the fingers that grasped him, eyes bulging as they tightened.

"*Look upon me, usurper. Look into my eyes and know from whom you have stolen so much!*"

He whined, a high, terrified squeal, and then it was swallowed by the cacophonous roar of whispers and wind as the veil that hid the goddess's true face rose and billowed behind her.

I gasped and turned away. And before me, I saw Evolet, her eyes wide and lips parted in wonder. "Evolet!" I called. "Do not look! Do not look upon her."

She rushed to me and threw herself upon the stone ground. Our hands fumbled, our fingers laced together, and we bowed our heads over Elyan, holding one another fast as the howling reached a crescendo, a thousand voices screaming in triumph; in joy.

We dared not lift our heads until silence had fallen.

In the Dae Spira's grip, Anwar had gone slack, his limbs hanging uselessly, a grotesque puppet, as her veil once more descended upon her face, concealing her true visage. She let him go then, and with a sigh I heard in the very marrow of my bones, and a ripple of white, she vanished.

Anwar began to stagger toward us like a mad man, eyes wide and rolling in his head, gibberish spilling from his lips. Beside me, Evolet's hand tightened on the hilt of her stolen sword. But she had no need for it.

Anwar stopped, gasped; went taut.

A hand tightened in his hair, jerking his head back to expose the long, bronze column of his throat. His eyes bulged, his mouth opening and closing rhythmically, a plea, a prayer—and then came the blade. His amber skin opened and blood poured forth, drenching his front, dripping onto the stones below.

He jerked once, twice; his feet scrabbled uselessly, and at last he went slack. The hand that had held him aloft released its hold upon him, and his body crumpled to the ground.

Standing behind him, holding the knife that had opened his throat, was Isri.

"It was a kindness," she said, her voice little more than a hoarse whisper after hundreds of years of silence. "One he did not deserve."

"You can speak!" I breathed.

"We have always been able to speak," she answered. "It was their spells that prevented us."

Beside me, Evolet stared at the inert body of her brother, her tormentor, watching the pool of his blood spread and seep into the stones. "What do you mean it was a kindness?"

"No mortal man who gazes upon the face of the goddess may do so and yet live. It would have driven him insane."

"Would the same have happened to us?" I asked. "Had we not looked away?"

"Of course not," she answered, and a smile tugged at the corners of her mouth, the first I'd ever seen upon her face. "For we are women."

35

Elyan lay in a sleep like death for five days. On the morning of the sixth day, as sunlight spilled into the stillroom where I had slept at his side, he stirred and his extraordinary eyes fluttered and opened at last.

He turned his head, and seeing me, a slow, exhausted smile spread across his face.

I promptly burst into tears. His strength allowed him to do little more than rest his hand upon my head as I sobbed, thoroughly wetting the simple tunic he wore, and although I should have been the one to assure him that he was safe and hale, that everything was well, he murmured to me in a low, rasping voice, his fingers threading through my hair, and my heart broke and mended itself again and again.

"How long?" he asked when at last I lifted my head. When I told him, he sank back against the pillows in disbelief. "The last thing I remember was the siphoning. After that, it is light; only light. And burning."

I shook my head miserably. "I should never have asked it of you. You could have died."

"So could you have, in the throne room."

"You came back for me."

"Thankfully, I realized my mistake before I'd gotten too far."

"How?" I breathed. "You were meant to have gone, to have taken them with you to the cave. Why did you come back?"

He reached up and brushed a lock of hair away from my face with fingers so achingly gentle. "A good king cares for his people," he answered, "but a good man cares for *all* people. To be a good king, I rather think I must first be a good man."

"But you are a good man!"

"No, I am not. At least, I am not half so good a man on my own as I am with you. If I were, I would've offered my help to Nymet Nata the moment we learned the truth. You saw it right away; I did not."

"Elyan—"

"You may have gone about it in a way that was, unsurprisingly, entirely regrettable—ouch—" He rubbed his arm where I'd poked him soundly. "—but you were right, and I should have trusted you."

"I understand why you felt you must leave."

A laugh escaped him, soft and low and rasping, and my blood sang with it. "You are my lodestar," he said, and reaching up, he took my face gently in both his hands and lowered my forehead gently to his. "How could I have ever thought it possible to leave you?"

With little thought to either of our condition, I swooped down and captured his lips with my own, laughing and crying in equal measure, and I poured into that kiss all the pain and fear and joy of what we had endured and survived together, and also the promise of what might be; what I hoped would be.

He gasped, falling back against the pillows, and I pulled away guiltily. "Kevren told me not to exhaust you."

"Did he now?" Elyan murmured. Then, as I settled him more comfortably, he said, "Tell me what happened. After."

This I could not do without crying anew, for as much as we had gained, as much as we had won, we had also lost.

Damiane was dead.

She had fallen at the threshold of the Place of Ways, stabbed in the back while pursuing Anwar down the stairs. She was alive, though barely, when I found her lying in a pool of her own blood and surrounded by the bodies of fallen soldiers bearing the sigil of Syr'Aliem.

I had grasped her hand tightly in my own and shouted to Evolet: "Get a healer!"

"It is too late for that now, Briony Tenebrae," she whispered.

"Then I'll find Phyra."

"No!" she said. "No. Do not raise me if I fall. I will not have another pay for my life."

"Damiane..."

She reached out and gripped the front of my tunic, pulling me down so that our faces were mere inches apart. "Thank you," she whispered. "Thank you."

It was many hours later when I learned the news of what had happened beyond the palace walls, where the forest warriors defended their homes from soldiers with steel armor and ornately decorated helms. Once Elyan had released the magic of the Incuna to the land, Syr'Aliem's soldiers had buckled under the sheer majesty of a people suffused at last with the power rightfully theirs, and Nymet Nata's forces had easily overwhelmed their attempted invasion.

'Twas Thaniel, Arlo, and Phyra who had brought the news.

I was, by then, in the stillroom under the care of the Tacé. Their primitive magic was not so elegant as Kevren's and would leave many ugly scars, but they assured me that I would survive, and this was enough.

The moment I saw my friends, I gathered them to me so fiercely I thought I might steal the breath from them, only they were not quite ready to forgive me for leaving them, and I was duly chastised for not informing them of my foolish plan to steal the Keys and inviting them to join my hopeless expedition.

I had known love in Tiralaen, the love of a family I knew to be true and enduring, even though I had little seen them since I was a child.

But this... this was love I chose, love I had been chosen to receive, and it was truly wondrous indeed.

Kevren had arrived with Thaniel, of course, and it was he who kept watch over Elyan, doing all he could with his magic and his elixirs to bring down the fever in Elyan's flesh while he lay unmoving upon the stillroom cot for day after day. All the while, the steady rise and fall of his chest was the only indication he yet lived.

"There is nothing further I can do for him," Kevren had told me, and there was such sorrow within his voice that I could not breathe. "Either he will wake, or he won't."

"How long will that be?" I had whispered.

"I don't know. It could be days... it could be years."

It could be never, were the words he did not say out loud, but I heard them nonetheless.

What Elyan had done below in the Place of Ways was magic strange and wonderful, magic no one had dreamed of let alone performed, and the treatment of his condition was as much a mystery as how he had managed it.

"I suppose I should be thankful, then, that it was only six days and not six years," Elyan said, then looked to me, suddenly alert. "You were hurt?"

I loosened the ties of the simple white gown I wore with my good hand, and gently pulled the fabric down that he might see the mess Anwar's blade had made of the pale skin of my shoulder. This wound, at least, was but a scar now, thanks to the Tacé's magic and Kevren's herbs.

The other, where the blade had slipped between my ribs, was more stubborn, and it continued to sting me with sharp pain when I took too deep a breath. That wound, I did not show him.

I felt the tips of Elyan's fingers ghosting gently across my skin, then his lips, chaste and trembling, pressed against my ruined shoulder, and I shivered.

He lifted his head. "I am so sorry."

"I'm not. I'll wear this scar proudly for the rest of my life."

We spent the next few days in the stillroom together, watching vines lazily twine and coil around the windows and cover the walls.

Each night, I thought perhaps the Dae Spira would appear to me; I both hoped for it and feared it in equal measure. But I did not hear a single whisper, nor see veils of white, and I was allowed to sleep soundly. In time, I decided it was best; the secrets of the divine were, perhaps, not mine to know.

Anwar was laid to rest quietly, and with no one in attendance save the Dowager Queen, Princess Evolet, and myself. His bones would not reside in the Ita Hypogaeum like the true kings and queens of Nymet Nata, but in the forest, his grave marked with only a simple stone.

It was, I thought, more than he deserved.

The Dowager Queen had since been imprisoned in her chamber, and though Zayir insisted that she be guarded at all times, I knew there was little point. The shell that had once been Urenna had, with the death of her son, lost any purpose she might've still had. If once a fire had burned in her burnished eyes, even the embers had at last gone out. She did little but sit in silence with Raolin's effigy on her lap, her arms fast around it as though it were the only thing that remained in the world. Perhaps, to her, it was.

Despite how fervently and passionately I spoke of Evolet's character, of what she had done, of how we could not have hoped to succeed without her, Damiane's people were still quite understandably wary of Syr'Aliem's princess.

They had confined her to her chambers as well, though it had less to do with trust and more to do with the fact that they simply did not know what to do with her. She answered their every question and withheld nothing. Her tone was somber and reticent, her manner withdrawn. She asked for nothing but that her maid be allowed to attend her. No one seemed to need convincing that she was truly grateful for the fall of her family, or that she had done all she could in the final battle to bring it about—but I persisted in telling them all so at every opportunity, nonetheless.

Samira had not yet claimed the throne. She planned first to hold a summit to begin the reconciliation process between the village and Nymet Nata, as well as to decide what to do with Court Eternal.

"I would point out that you are far too weak to even dream of attending," I told Elyan, "but I know my words will fall on deaf ears."

"I'm sorry, did you say something?"

He grinned weakly as I dug my elbow gently in his side.

Two days later, Princess Evolet and I sat facing one another in her chambers, a Lumen glowing merrily in her hearth and glasses of Calique sparkling with borrowed radiance. Pleasantries were exchanged regarding my injuries and the state of Elyan's health, and she assured me she had been well looked after.

"Samira in particular has been kind to me," she said. My face must have revealed my complete bewilderment, for she added: "Yes, it was the last thing I expected as well. But she has a good head on her shoulders, it seems, and some instinct for diplomacy. She wants my help to bring the Court Eternal into her schemes for a renewed kingdom."

"They will not be imprisoned, then?"

"Amnesty is being offered, believe it or not, but only if they agree to bear the full cost of reconstruction, plus reparations for the people of the village. 'Twas Samira's idea, and it's far more generous than any of those fools deserve. Even so, it will cost them everything, and many say they'd prefer to rot defiantly in prison than acknowledge any fault with the lives they have lived until now."

"Do you think you can convince them?"

"Not truly, no. But I will try, and perhaps I can persuade a majority of them to see the wisdom of acknowledging the reality of their situation, if not their crimes. Regardless, they will never thank me for it."

"I suppose in the end *I* must thank you," I said, sipping my Calique politely. "Had you not warned me that night in the Ita Hominaeum, none of this would've been possible."

"Perhaps, though I rather think you would have found a way regardless."

"Did you just compliment me?"

"You may choose to see it as you will."

We spoke of trivial things then, mostly gardening, and I was surprised to discover Evolet knew much about the various flowers in her courtyards and their cultivation. I thought she might now need such knowledge just to maintain her own chambers, which were green and lush with thin vines that traced intricate patterns on the walls where there had before been gold filigree.

"The reclaiming of the palace continues apace," I said.

"I suppose you think it an improvement?"

"Yes," I said, "and no. In truth, it makes me homesick all the more to watch this reflection of Tiralaen slowly fade away. You do not know what joy was awakened in me when first I laid eyes upon Syr'Aliem."

This kingdom had been so like my own, and yet only an impostor. Underneath, they had so little in common, nothing at all, really—save an unfathomable source of concentrated magic at their hearts.

I thought then of my revelation that Syr'Aliem was proof that our Gate must have existed before Iluviel, and that the Shining City must have been built upon it and because of it.

And I knew, with crushing urgency, that I needed to share this knowledge with Elyan immediately.

I'd gathered all my companions together in Isabis's favorite garden that I might share my newfound revelation with them, and the utter blankness in their eyes now that I'd finished my explanation told me how thoroughly I'd failed at the task.

"'Tis fine enough reasoning," said Elyan at last. "Worthy of a treatise, at the least, should you ever find yourself at leisure to write one."

"No, no, no, no," I told him. "This isn't some academic curiosity, Elyan. This is about the cave!"

"What?" he said, and his bemusement was reflected in the faces of my friends, who had not, until that moment, been fully absorbed by what I was trying to tell them.

"It is the concentration of magic that matters. The veil between worlds is thinnest where the presence of magic is the greatest."

Elyan furrowed his brow in contemplation. "Then you think there will be a city built upon this northern cave?"

"I think there most definitely is. Only, it isn't in the north—I mean, it *is* north, but north of Asperfell, not north of Syr'Aliem."

"Briony." This from Arlo.

"Yes?"

"Get on with it, will you?"

"Right. My point is, the cave has been right underneath us all this time."

Elyan blinked. "Excuse me?"

"When first we entered the chamber of the Incuna, you said it felt like Tiralaen. What if Tiralaen is exactly what you felt?"

I expected him to curse quite spectacularly at the terrible, terrible irony of it. Instead, he threw back his head and laughed.

"Well, that's it then," Arlo said. "You've broken him."

"You're saying the cave and the Incuna's chamber are one," said Thaniel. "Is this a jest? Is that why Elyan is laughing like a madman?"

"The first prisoners to come here would not have known there was a cave they should be seeking at all," I continued. "They knew of only one Gate, and thus no one ever attempted to open another here in the temple of the Incuna, much less in its very chamber."

"Well, that's fucking brilliant," Arlo declared. "I was not looking forward to sleeping on the ground again." And he joined in Elyan's laughter, though he was a touch less maniacal.

Thaniel, however, was uncharacteristically reserved, his smile tight. Beside him, Kevren covered his hand and laced their fingers tightly together.

36

The day of Samira's coronation dawned clear and bright, with such promise in the air that no one could deny that the Dae Spira's blessing lay upon the forest and all within.

'Twas not at the palace we gathered, but at Uuna tree—Nymet Nata, Syr'Aliem, and we prisoners of Asperfell together. The courtyard beneath the towering city was full to bursting with those eager to celebrate at last the end of division and oppression, and the return of magic. Tables groaned with food, drink flowed freely, and the sounds of raucous laughter and music filled the air.

Rather than silk and jewels, we wore simple garments and crowns fashioned of branches and flowers and vines as we watch Samira ascend the petal-strewn steps of Uuna Tree and kneel before those who had helped to bring about this joyous day, and who would help her through all the days to come.

It was Isri who crowned Samira the new queen of both Nymet Nata and Syr'Aliem, placing upon her head a tall crown of spires fashioned after those who had come before; at her waist hung two heavy bronze keys.

The princess who had once been their keeper stood tall and somber beside the Tacé, a respectful distance away from the still distrustful Zayir and the rest of Damiane's counsel, now Samira's. A long road lay ahead with regard to those she'd wronged, and I hoped that she proved worthy of it.

When Samira stood, beaming, I cheered and grinned so wide my face ached with it, my cries joining those around me in a joyful cacophony. We embraced one another, my companions and I, mindful of my injuries. Though he still exhausted easily, Elyan had grown stronger with each passing day, and when he gathered me against him and kissed my temple, I wound my arms tight around him.

Watching the coronation and us with equal amusement were Garundel and Tarseth.

At my request, Samira had sent her fastest riders to their meadow, bearing an invitation and an escort, and mere days later, she had arrived with the boy in tow and a delighted laugh rumbling in her chest.

"I saw that you would be important, but who could've imagined that the sorry bunch I rescued that day in the forest would've ended up changing our world?" she cackled. "And in such a way!"

That night was to be our last in the Forest Kingdom; we were set to depart at first light, and so we made the most of our time, reveling in the infectious jubilation that Samira's ascension brought to all. We caroused long into the night, the others gradually retiring until, at last, only Elyan and I remained, my head drowsing against his shoulder as I watched with a wonderful sort of peace the silhouettes of dancers against the flames.

He lifted my hand, pressed a kiss upon my palm, and whispered soft and deep against my skin: "Come with me."

He led me away to a quiet grove of pines far beyond the circle of great trees that was the city proper.

There were no words spoken between us now, only his lips upon mine, his teeth against my jaw, my neck; his fingers in my hair and mine in his, my gasps swallowed by his greedy mouth; his answering laugh a low rumble in his chest.

He did not ask; I did not answer; perhaps we should've done, but a certainty had settled between us that neither of us were inclined to disturb, regardless of what awaited us on the other side of the veil, the enormity of our task, the terrible consequences should we fail.

And so, we spoke of other things, and despite the magic in my blood, we did so without words.

With somewhat muddled heads, my companions and I rose the following morning and dressed in the new clothes and boots that Samira had provided for our journey, as well as packs full to bursting with sundries and foodstuff, for even though we'd only a little way to travel in this world, we knew not what lay before us on the other side of the veil.

"You'll leave us better than you found us," she said, teeth gleaming white as she grinned. "It is the least we can do."

I threw my arms around her, heedless of propriety, and she gripped me so fiercely that when we drew apart, she had to straighten her crown.

Hers were far from the only gifts presented to us.

Yveme, who had wished so desperately to paint something new, had done so at last, and presented me proudly with sheafs of parchment tied with a ribbon: they were sketches of the village, of the forest, and of the temple.

"So that you will have a way to remember this place," he explained. "And to thank you."

After Samira had finally seen the Ita Hypogaeum and the portraits of her forebears, I suggested that Yveme be the one to paint her likeness. He'd fainted when I told him she'd agreed.

From Isri and the Tacé, we were given packets of healing herbs and a stoppered bottle of water that I knew the moment my fingers brushed against it was from the Incuna.

"For any dangers you may encounter upon your journey," Isri explained. "For if we know anything at all of you, it is that you do not hesitate to help those in need."

And from Evolet, spoils of the Thesa: a chest bearing gold and silver and gems, their value incalculable.

"I doubt it is enough to retake a kingdom, but you'll have nothing with you when you return save that which you carry with you today. Perhaps this will ease your burden somewhat." The princess turned to me, and I saw that she held one last gift within her slender, white hands. "And this, Briony Tenebrae, is for you."

I took the thin lacquered box from her and lifted the lid. Within, nested delicately amongst velvet black as night, twelve jeweled stars glittered up at me.

"I hope that you will wear them on your wedding day," she said, and glanced knowingly at Elyan. A flush rose to my cheeks, and I thanked her, sliding the precious gift into my pack.

Side by side they faced me, princess and Tacé, extraordinary women both, and I remembered Elyan's words to me our first day in the palace: *Nothing here is as it seems.* Oh, how right he had been.

I embraced Evolet first, and although she stiffened at first, surprised and, perhaps, unused to such affection, slowly her arms came up around me, and I smiled into her golden hair.

I looked to Isri next, and although her face was set into its familiar scowl, she sighed and jerked her chin toward me; an invitation. She held her arms stubbornly at her sides but allowed me to embrace her nonetheless, and when I withdrew, she met my eyes and dipped her chin, the barest of nods.

It was Garundel whom I spoke to last. She took my hands in her gnarled ones and tugged me down to brush a kiss against my cheek. "Safe travels, Briony. My blessing goes with you, such as it is."

"I suppose after all your prediction was wrong," I answered. "And I cannot say I am sorry for it."

Her head tilted, and she regarded me with her strange green eyes. "Was it?"

Her words quite preoccupied my thoughts as we marched from Nymet Nata to Syr'Aliem.

We emerged from the long, winding stairway into the Place of Ways, and reverently we stepped across the threshold where Damiane had laid down her life for her people.

Lark, Tansy, Fife, and the rest of the Acolytes met us with Lumens in their hands to light our way, their smiles nearly as blinding, and I fell to my knees and gathered them to me, laughing and crying in equal measure.

Kevren was quite astonished to see that my outlandish description of the diminutive caretakers of the Place of Ways was not at all embellished, or that they had not been a fiction I'd invented altogether. He was the only representative of Nymet Nata or Syr'Aliem to accompany us down into this most sacred place, and it was only by special permission of the Tacé and his sister, the queen, that he had been allowed to make the descent.

The most remarkable member of our company, however, was the Phaelor.

We had come across Vindar in the forest almost as soon as we left Nymet Nata, and it was clear at once that Phyra was not surprised to find him waiting for us.

"We've a bond, he and I," she'd explained. "He must come with us to Tiralaen."

Arlo had never heard a jest so outrageous and nearly doubled over in riotous laughter. Thaniel, however, had seen the sincerity in Phyra's dark eyes.

"He will evoke fear in our world, and that will endanger both him and you," Elyan had told her gently.

"I cannot leave him," she'd said simply.

To the bewilderment of us all—even Phyra—it had been the Tacé guiding us back to Syr'Aliem who spoke in Phyra's defense. "Your Necromancer is correct. This creature is no longer of our world, and it cannot remain here when she is gone. At best, it will go mad and cast itself from some great height to end its suffering. More likely, it will become a terror that haunts the forest in a tormented rage, killing and devouring all it sees. You must either kill it now or take it with you; all other choices are evil."

What argument could be made after such a declaration? And so, the Phaelor had become a shadow at Phyra's side, as it was even now.

When we explained to the Acolytes our plan to pass between worlds through spellcraft, they were distraught that we purposed to leave them forever. Even so, they were quite determined to help, and begged me to instruct them how.

"I do not rightly know," I confessed.

When I'd first proposed we open a Gate here beneath the temple, I'd imagined we need only to stand in front of the statue of the Dae Spira, beneath its upstretched hands, where the Incuna had rested for a hundred generations or more, and cast the appropriate spells. But it was not so, and discovering the right place to pry open a Gate between worlds proved to be an arduous task indeed.

The Acolytes did their best to give assistance, revealing to us many caves and tunnels hidden beneath the vines upon the walls, and for several long, frustrating hours we searched them, reaching out for the familiar thrum of our magic and meeting one dead end after another.

It was Arlo who found it at last by virtue of his magic; he recognized at once the green of our world and the pull of its growing things.

And when we gathered together in that place and held aloft our hands full of Magefire, we prisoners of Asperfell, we Mages of Tiralaen, could see clearly what lay beyond: trees where there should have been stone; another world.

Home.

Elyan's breath had escaped him in a rush, and he moved forward, hand outstretched, and brushed his fingers tentatively against the shimmer in the air, what little remained of the veil. "By the Gods," he said, a shudder passing through him. "I can feel it."

Arlo shook his head. "I'll be damned. For once I am thrilled to have been proven wrong."

A moment later, Elyan and Thaniel began to draw the same gleaming lines in the air that I'd last seen upon a scaffolding more than half a year ago, then they pulled at the delicate vestiges of the veil until it was ripped asunder and the forest was clear and sharp before us.

They made this new Gate large enough that we might all fit through at once, for we did not entirely trust that it would not collapse upon itself and strand one or more of us here. Then, with shaking hands and racing hearts, we gathered our packs and cloaks. Phyra called forth Vindar, and suddenly we were ready, and my heart leapt into my throat, for although I'd been dreaming of this moment, fighting for this moment since I'd tumbled through the Gate, I could never have imagined what I would be leaving behind.

It was not until I stood gripping Elyan's hand, Arlo beside me and Phyra sitting astride Vindar, that I realized that Thaniel was not with us.

Turning, I beheld him standing beside Kevren, their hands clasped tightly, tears streaming down his cheeks as they faced us.

"I am so sorry," he said, and in that moment, I knew.

Phyra slid down from Vindar's back, her dark eyes wide and full of anguish as she approached them.

"I'm sorry," he repeated, and though he spoke to us all, he looked only at her. "I cannot go with you."

She shook her head. "No, no. You cannot stay."

Thaniel let go of Kevren's hand to take both of hers, holding them fast against his chest, against his heart. "I love him, Phyra. I love who I am with him; who I am here, in this place, where my magic can heal, not just harm. We can make a difference here, Kevren and I."

"You *cannot* stay. You cannot leave me!"

He shook his head, his tears flowing freely now. "Do not ask me, Phyra," he begged, and his voice broke with it. "Do not ask me to choose."

A sob tore free from her throat. "But I need you. I cannot do without you!"

"You can."

"I am nothing without you!" she cried, and the agony in her voice, the raw, terrible pain, set free my own tears.

He framed her face with his hands, his strong, calloused hands; the hands of a warrior. "Listen to me, Phyra. You are so, *so* strong. Stronger than anyone I have ever known. And you need no one."

They collided, her arms tight about his neck and his hand tangled in her hair, and her sobs echoed throughout the cavern. And when at last her sobs subsided and she shuddered within his steady arms, it was Arlo who laid a strong and steady hand upon her back.

"It's time, Phyra," he murmured. "Let him go."

As she drew back, her body quaking with unspent sobs and hitching breaths, the eyes of Alchemist and Naturalist met over her dark head.

"She does not need anyone to take care of her," Thaniel said, "but I hope that you will remain by her side all the same."

Arlo nodded. "I give you my word."

"You know, you turned out all right, in the end."

"Did I?" Arlo arched his brow. "You know, that might be the nicest thing you've ever said about me."

"It's the nicest thing anyone has ever said about you."

A grin split Arlo's face. "Believe it or not, your knightliness, I will miss you."

"I won't miss you at all," Thaniel replied, but what passed between them was something sweet and deep; it was respect; it was forgiveness.

Phyra grasped Arlo's hand and he led her gently back to Vindar's side, as Elyan stepped forward and he and Thaniel came together in a fierce embrace.

"I wish I could have seen you crowned, your highness," Thaniel whispered. "My king."

"If I do, it will be because of your courage, my friend."

"You will."

And then, it was my turn.

"I will miss you so," I whispered. "But I am so happy for you I fear I may burst."

His warm laughter fell upon me. "Without you, without your courage, none of this would've been possible. How can I ever thank you?"

"You can thank me by helping them," I answered, smiling through my tears.

"I will," he promised. "I will."

I drew back and Kevren pulled him close, pressing a kiss to his temple.

Elyan laced his fingers with mine, but my eyes remained fixed on Thaniel, and on Kevren—of them together and perfected by one another—and I drank in the sight of them until the very last, until Arlo was by my side and Vindar towered over us all, Phyra astride his back. And then we turned to face that for which we had given our full measure. Glimmering beyond the stone were the forests of my homeland, of my people. Home.

At my side, Elyan murmured: "Are you ready?"

"For anything," I answered, and we took our next step together.

THE SHINING CITY

Book Three of the Asperfell Trilogy

Coming in 2022

ABOUT THE AUTHOR

A certified Language Arts teacher and classically trained opera singer, Thomas lives in Wenatchee, Washington, with her husband, daughter, two enormous dogs, and two mischievous cats. She aims to smash the patriarchy one novel at a time, creating characters and worlds that inspire, empower, and elevate women.